A DARKNESS
AT THE END

RUTH FRANCES LONG is a lifelong fan of fantasy and romance. She studied English Literature, History of Religions, and Celtic Civilisation in college and now works in a specialised library of rare and unusual books. But they don't talk to her that often.

Ruth's first two books about Izzy, Jinx and Dubh Linn, *A Crack in Everything* and *A Hollow in the Hills,* are published by The O'Brien Press. Ruth is also the author of *The Treachery of Beautiful Things*.

A DARKNESS
AT THE END

The shadows know your name.

RUTH FRANCES LONG

THE O'BRIEN PRESS
DUBLIN

First published 2016 by The O'Brien Press Ltd,
12 Terenure Road East, Rathgar, Dublin 6, Ireland, D06 HD27.
Tel: +353 1 4923333; Fax: +353 1 4922777
E-mail: books@obrien.ie
Website: www.obrien.ie

ISBN: 978-1-84717-863-3

10 9 8 7 6 5 4 3 2 1
19 18 17 16

Printed and bound by CPI Group (UK) Ltd, Croydon, CR0 4YY.
The paper in this book is produced using pulp from managed forests.

Published in

DUBLIN
UNESCO
City of Literature

Dedication
To Pat, Diarmuid and Emily.

Acknowledgements
It's strange to reach the end of a trilogy. So many people have made all this possible and I'm sure I will forget someone (because my brain is a sieve). If you have had anything to do with this book and its predecessors, thank you so much!

To my wonderful agent Sallyanne Sweeney, so many thanks for your continuing support and belief. I'd also like to thank my editor, Helen, and all at The O'Brien Press, especially Emma for her magnificent cover designs.

My YA bookclub people, the Irish SFF community (Dublin2019!) and wonderfully shiny writer friends – you all regularly keep me sane (well sane-ish). And the other people who have to put up with me and my writer-brain, my lovely family. Yes, I am still dragging you around random places, but you love it really. And I expect you to keep telling me that.

Dublin is such a wonderful location for a fantasy trilogy so thanks to all the locations and sites, businesses and cultural institutions I've shamelessly used. A special thanks to all at the wonderful National Leprechaun Museum who just 'got' what the Dubh Linn books were about and have been amazingly supportive.

I'm so so sorry, guys …

For this is the truth: all things must come into balance.
Order and disorder, light and dark, truth and treachery.
If the seed is sown, the harvest must be gathered in.
As the night falls so the dawn will come.
Where the flower blooms so too will lurk the thorn.

From heaven above to hell beneath,
to the left and right hand sides of the path,
balance is all.
The Grigori stands between them,
keeping that balance.
Once balance is lost,
all is lost.
And chaos reigns.

The Grand Compact,
Volume 13, Chapter 47, verses 12-13

Cross a fae before a Matriarch
Cross a Matriarch before a demon
Cross a demon before an angel
Never cross a Keeper

Fae proverb

Chapter One

Dark Wings

The black birds arrived with the dawn. On every branch of every tree, perched on the rooftops and chimneys, picking through the bins and scrabbling in the dirt of the pristine lawns, crows of every shape and size gathered. Ravens came too, aloof and judgemental, perching on the pillars marking the driveways of otherwise perfectly normal suburban homes, on electrical boxes and gas meters. They alone stood silent, watching over the raucous morning chorus.

That was how Izzy woke up now, to the cacophony of a host of corvids waiting for her. All kinds, except for magpies. They didn't come. Just their cousins; the crows and the ravens, rooks and hooded crows, jackdaws, even the occasional choughs with the bright flash of red beak straying far from their coastal homes in the west and the south. All of them black as night, or cowled in grey.

All of them birds of death.

Mum ran out with a broom the first few times which caused the birds to take off in a flurry of wings and indignation. But they just flew around out of her reach and then settled down again.

Izzy knew to expect them now. Every morning, they waited for her. They left presents, little shining trinkets, pretty stones, tin foil and buttons. Forgotten, broken things. Lost things. They left them on the doorsteps and windowsills, spread out like offerings. Gifts.

Izzy didn't know how to stop them. She was sure she would, if she could figure out how.

This morning, on her windowsill, on top of the layer of gleaming frost, there lay a polished stone, two buttons and a single silver loop earring. It wasn't big, and it was tarnished and discoloured as if lost some time ago and left to brave the elements. But it was the first thing her hand gravitated towards. Or at least, she started to reach for it but then she froze, her muscles cramping, tendons like wires. Breath caught in her throat and pain like white acid burned through her chest.

She saw him again, in her mind's eye. The boy with black hair – like crow feathers – skin as white as the snow on the hills, marked with swirling indigo tattoos, his eyes silver, like the piercings he wore. Just like the silver earring.

With a sudden jerk, she pushed the gifts off the sill. The birds took flight, crying their outrage to the heavens and Izzy slammed the window shut, turning around and sinking on to the ground. She huddled there, holding herself in a tight ball, trying to force the terror away, the unknown grief and pain, the holes in her mind and that familiar sense of devastation, always old and always new, a never closing wound. All the maelstrom of emotions she always felt when she saw something that stirred a broken memory of him.

'Jinx,' she whispered at last.

There were only fragments of him left in her mind. He was gone, she knew that. Dad said he was dead – *everyone* said he was dead – but that didn't feel right. She was missing something. The problem was she had no idea what.

Mum opened the door. She still looked frail though the bruises from her captivity had faded. Something lingered in her eyes, in the sharp lines under her features. 'Izzy, love?'

Her arms didn't look strong, but they wrapped her daughter in an impenetrable barrier.

'I'm sorry,' said Izzy. 'Mum, I'm sorry. I'm so sorry.' Once it started she couldn't stop that litany. Time and again, she said it, over and over, but it didn't make a difference. It never did.

Mum rocked her, murmured soothing words, and whispered her name until Izzy quietened again. Nothing made sense but until the storm of grief passed there was nothing that could actually be said.

You've had a breakdown, Izzy told herself, her voice distant and removed, watching herself from far away. It helped to do this, to tell herself the things she had been told were true when she felt this way, when it all started to crumble around her. *You saw your boyfriend die. You killed him.*

But she couldn't remember it. They'd had to tell her. No one really managed to make eye contact when they said that.

She couldn't remember him. Not really. Just in fragments and moments. Nightmares and impossible horrors drifted up through her sleep, sometimes when she was awake too. But they made no sense. Nothing did.

'It's going to be all right, Izzy,' said Mum. 'We're going to make it right, I promise. Dad's going to fix it.'

Fix it? Dad thought he could fix *this*? He could barely keep the peace talks between the angels and the demons going, let alone make them include the Sídhe. Mum had more faith in him than Izzy did. How would he even find time to attempt to fix this? And how could it be fixed?

No, it wasn't this he needed to fix. It was *her*. She was broken and she didn't know how or why.

School was intermittent. Most of the time she just couldn't handle it. They couldn't exactly go to a regular doctor about her memory loss and depression, not when the cause was magical. Not when there was no way to fix it by normal means. And what did normal even mean anymore? Her whole life was so far from normal. The only friends she had left were Dylan, Clodagh and Ash. And they tried to help, they really did, but they had lives of their own.

And they didn't understand. They didn't know about the empty places inside her.

Eventually the tears stopped. She stared at the wall over Mum's shoulder, wishing it would just vanish, or that, better yet, she could just vanish. Gran knocked on the door and gave Mum one of those meaningful looks.

Austere and elegant, Izzy's grandmother had moved in with them, to help out during their 'troubles'. They didn't talk, not really. Generally Izzy just got the impression that she was a dreadful disappointment to Isolde Gregory, who had married one Grigori, and served as his right hand while raising the next one. Duty, knowledge, honour… these were the things that mattered to her grandmother. Not a hysterical, depressed, broken child.

Mum wrapped the throw from Izzy's bed around her shoulders. It was soft and comforting and smelled of home and sleep. Then she followed Gran outside. They didn't quite close the door behind them, so their voices, though soft, were still audible.

'David phoned. They're going today. Now.' Gran didn't sound happy about it. Whatever 'it' was. Obviously they weren't planning to tell Izzy. She didn't warrant explanations like that.

'I should be there too.'

'You're needed here. With the girl. She's too fragile now.'

'Does he really think this will work?'

Gran sighed heavily 'It's our last hope. Even her mother couldn't—'

'*I'm* her mother.' Mum's voice came out sharp as a blade.

'Of course you are. You know what I mean.'

'She didn't even try.'

'Yes she did. Rachel, you know she did. She cares for Isabel, as much as any of them can care for one of us. You didn't give her enough time. You need to send the girl back to her.'

'No!' The ferocity in Mum's voice made Izzy start. 'No,' she said again, a little more calmly. 'Not yet. We'll find a way. We have to. Since Jinx died …'

Jinx … the name was like a barb inside Izzy's chest. Jinx was dead, that was what everyone said. But it didn't feel true. It didn't feel right. And in the space between what she was told and what she felt – in that place where all the memories were a pile of broken glass – well, that was where she was being torn apart.

'It's an unadulterated mess,' said Isolde, disgust colouring her tone as she marched down the stairs. 'What was she thinking? Any Grigori who would risk their *mind* by taking the Story-teller's book and reading it, to find a *boyfriend* – and a hound at that! – shouldn't be surprised to have holes in their recollection. Even if there was something in that mess of stolen memories from all down the ages that might possibly have helped, she should have known so much magic all at once would overwhelm her and backfire. Of all the stupid, childish behaviour – I've never seen the like. But this endless moping …'

Her voice faded, but no doubt the tirade continued.

Endless moping. That was what her grandmother thought of her. Probably her father too. An idiot, a fool, who had read the Storyteller's magical book – the source of her power which stole the memories of countless others – and expected somehow to get away with it. And all for someone she could no longer remember, someone who was nothing more than a gaping chasm in her mind. Because that was what the book did. And she had known that when she took it up. How had she expected to survive unscathed? It seemed idiotic even to her now.

Izzy turned back to the window. The crows were still there, watching her. They were always there. On every tree, every roof, every wall, waiting.

But for what, she didn't know.

She closed her eyes and wished them gone, but when she looked they were still there. Izzy backed away. Her bag – now a battered, mud- and grass-stained wreck – lay in a heap on the floor by her bed. She never let it out of her sight. She couldn't.

She sat down again, rolled up her sleeve and took out the knife she had taken from Pie. More correctly, the iron knife she had pulled out of … of a body where Pie had left it. Whose body though? That was the question. The holes in her memory couldn't tell her that, but she remembered the feel of it in her hand. Cold iron, old iron, with a handle of bone. She'd used it to kill. She knew that. Not who or why. She remembered fire and the hulking shadow of a ruin, of tears scalding her face, of pushing her knife into a living, breathing body and letting the life inside drain out. And this knife. This piece of iron.

Vibrations rippled up its length when she touched it and the fire in her blood answered. The Blade that Cuts swirled through her veins. Not an actual blade, not like the one in her hands. It was magic, powerful and terrible.

She had destroyed Eochaid, King of the Fear with it. She hadn't meant to but it slipped from her grasp, or maybe she had released it to do its own will. And afterwards – after yet another blank space in her memory she couldn't fill – she had gone back into the Realm of the Dead. She'd tried to give it back to Donn but he was already dead and it had bonded to her, flowed back inside her. Now it filled her in a way she couldn't control. Well, almost. Her iron knife could quell the fire of the Blade. At least she had that. Her hand shook, though whether from fear or anticipation, she didn't know.

She didn't want to know.

She slid the knife along her skin, cutting through it effortlessly until the thin line of blood came and the sting of pain reached a crescendo. Gasping, she let herself breathe through it, let herself feel it as she hadn't felt anything in days. Not since the last time she had done this. Clarity settled over her, clear and cold as ice, and she watched the glossy blood on her pale skin, adding a new line to those that decorated her arms, some still bright and red, some pale ghostly scars.

Her memories were broken, she was broken, but she knew what she had to do.

Chapter Two

Cheating

Dylan shuffled his feet and turned up the collar of his coat again. Thick wool just wasn't cutting it in this temperature. He was already wishing for something thermal. And sunglasses just made him look like a git, like some kind of wannabe.

Clodagh elbowed him. 'Come on.'

They stepped closer to the door in the slowest moving queue in history.

'We should have pre-booked online,' he said.

And behind him he heard the now inevitable voices.

'It *is* him.'

'Well, ask then.'

'No, *you* ask him. I'm not asking him.'

'Are you *sure* sure? Like, what if it isn't?'

Clodagh stiffened and clenched her teeth.

'Don't,' Dylan murmured.

'I can tell someone to bog off and mind their own business if I want.'

'You can, but it confirms what that person is thinking. And it'll be all over the internet in seconds.'

Then he heard the sound of photos being taken and a wave of poorly suppressed giggles.

'Hate to tell you this, Dylan but it's all over the internet already,' said Clodagh dryly.

Of course it was. It always was. It was only a short step from that to the next thing.

'Hey mister,' sad the most brash of those eager voices. 'Mister, it's you, isn't it?'

The others hissed and recoiled in embarrassment, but they didn't back off. They made a show of it but didn't actually do it. The sin was breaking that wall between someone in the public eye and everyone else. Not being there to see it happen and benefitting.

What if I said no, he thought. What if I just pretended I wasn't me for once?

It wouldn't work. Then he'd be 'stuck up' and 'full of himself'.

Swallowing down a sigh so they'd never see it, Dylan turned around and treated it in exactly the way Silver had taught hm.

Love them, she said. No matter what. No matter if you're feeling shit, or impatient, or fed up, they don't need to know that. As far as they're concerned you're awesome. So be it.

Give them what they want. They'll love you for it.

Dylan slid the sunglasses down his nose a little so he could peer over them in a shy but sensitive way. And he smiled his most brilliant smile, before lifting a finger to his lips.

The girls, none of whom were over fifteen, grew round-eyed and even more giggly.

'I'm supposed to be incognito, ladies,' he teased.

'Incog-*wha*?' said the nearest while her friends laughed and whispered.

'Undercover,' he said and the poor thing turned scarlet.

Her words came out in a rush of breathless excitement. 'Can we get a selfie with you, Dylan?'

Dylan quirked his lips into his most professional smile. 'Course you can,' he said. 'But we need to be quick. I've got to go in.' He nodded towards the door and the impatient Clodagh waiting there, tapping her foot.

They all had their phones in hand in microseconds.

Clodagh watched all this with a blank expression, though he could tell her patience was at its thinnest. He signed autographs on scraps of papers and they were off again.

Grim held the door open for him.

'You should come in,' said the bodach. 'It's looking dangerous out there.'

Dylan wasn't entirely sure he was joking.

As they stepped inside the Storyteller's domain, Dylan felt the shiver in the air which told him they were passing from Dublin and his world, to Dubh Linn and theirs. Or maybe this was his world now. With so much of Silver's power in his body it was hard to tell. But he couldn't let that bother him now. He had a job to do.

Grim led them straight through the outer halls, where elements of Dublin's Leprechaun Museum blended with a place older and more primal by far. Echoes of the Giant's Causeway lined the passage, stone bleeding into wood and back again. Bronzed walls and ceilings reflected other times, so many lost stories. He reached out and felt Clodagh's hand slip into his, her fingers very cold and thin, like brittle twigs. He could sense her fear. He just hoped no one else would. Being human made her a target down here all by itself. Being a frightened human would be like setting off a beacon. Mentally, he projected a shield around them both and felt some of the tension in her bleed away. Silver's lessons were really starting to pay off. Since the magic seemed determined to seep out of him one way or another, she'd told him, it was better that it do so on his own terms. Use it, rather than let it use him. Or God forbid, let someone else use it.

That still didn't mean he had full control of it though. But who did?

The Storyteller waited for them in the dark forest at the heart of her Hollow. Sometimes, he knew, it looked like cut-outs of trees and Christmas lights, like the set of a school play. But not today. There was no doubting the reality of these trees, the way they swayed and creaked in a breeze he couldn't smell or feel, the way they crowded in close as if to steal away the unwary. They were the dark woods in every fairy tale, in every nightmare, where you'd get lost never to find the way home, where monsters lurked in the shadows, where the stories were born. Lights hung between the branches, tangled in the roots, lights that moved and danced and led you so far off the path, the path became a dream of what was. Sheeries, Silver had called them, or will o' the wisps, drawn to magic, and never to be trusted. Ignore them, she'd said. It was easier said than done. They caught the eye, entrancing, glittering little things.

The chamber thronged with them, blinking in and out of the darkness, like countless glowing eyes. Clodagh moved closer to Dylan and he struggled to keep his face from showing his own nerves.

'Come closer, Dylan O'Neill,' said the musical voice of the Storyteller. She sat by her glowing well, hooded and hunched over, her hands folded in her lap. 'We've been expecting you. Although—' she paused, turning her head slightly towards Clodagh, '—not your little friend.' Dylan was glad he couldn't see Clodagh's expression.

'Clodagh's with me,' he replied firmly.

'So I see. Well, come then, you and *Clodagh*.' She said the name as if tasting a fine wine and it sent chills skittering along his spine. Never underestimate her, Silver had said. And he'd just told her Clodagh's name. 'Sit down and we'll talk. That *is* why Lady Silver sent you, isn't it? To talk?'

Ah well, that was the problem. Dylan didn't move.

'Silver didn't send me.' Silver didn't even know he was here because if she did, Silver would flip out completely. But he couldn't afford to let the Storyteller know that. 'We're here on behalf of a friend.'

'A friend? Really?' She purred as she spoke, delighted with the intrigue, as he'd hope she would be. 'And what friend would that be?'

'Isabel Gregory.'

Instantly all the sheeries vanished, blinking out in a heartbeat. The only light remaining, the blue glow from the depths of the well, cast the chamber in a dark and terrible light.

'She is not welcome here. She will *never* be welcome here again. She'll enter this Hollow over my dead body!' The Storyteller surged to her feet, her long cloak and gown billowing out around her.

In the silence that followed, Clodagh opened her bag and took out a box. It was hand painted, pink, with little white flowers.

The Storyteller stared at it, her eyes narrowing with suspicion.

'We have a gift,' said Clodagh, without even a quiver in her voice. 'But we need to see the book.'

'No,' the Storyteller snarled, though she didn't move or call for her attendants. All her attention was fixed on the box. Slowly, as if she was teasing a great reveal in a play, Clodagh opened it.

Tinkling music filled the chamber and inside the box a tiny ballerina began to turn in a delicate pirouette. Clodagh said nothing, but smiled.

'What is it?' the Matriarch said at last.

'It's a music box. And it will be yours if we can just see the book.'

The old Sídhe twitched, clearly torn between her desire for the box and her need to protect her book.

'Just see it,' she breathed at last.

'Yes,' said Clodagh. 'See it, perhaps hold it and—'

'You'll not read it. You'll not even open it. And *he'll* not even touch it.' She pointed an abnormally long finger at Dylan. 'I know about you, about the power inside you. I know what you're capable of, boy.'

Did she? That was news to Dylan, who wasn't even sure himself what the power inside him could do, let alone how to fully harness it.

'This is Clodagh's show,' he said calmly, although his heart was hammering in his chest with fear. Clodagh's show, her idea, her disaster if it all went wrong. No, a disaster for all of them.

'Izzy's memory is broken,' the girl said. 'We're looking for a way to help her.'

'True,' said the Storyteller smugly. 'Because she broke faith with me. She read the book, too much of it, took it by force and—'

'She made a terrible mistake for which she is sorely sorry,' Dylan interrupted. 'We're trying to find a way to make things right.'

'With my book? Never. She'll never come into my domain while I live.'

'But if we could just—' Clodagh began. The Sídhe Matriarch cut her off.

'See it? Touch it? Why not, but you shall not open it. It will be of no use to you. But why not let you see how close you are?'

'Do I have your word?' Clodagh asked.

'For that pretty box? Yes, my word. But if you would read the book I'll need more. Much more.'

Clodagh blinked at her, like a rabbit in headlights. 'Like what?'

The Storyteller pushed back her hood, revealing her face. Her dark skin contrasted with the glowing gold of her eyes. She smiled and her teeth were sharp and so very white. 'Your eyes, perhaps? I could steal your sight and leave you permanently in the darkness. The box is yours, is it not? It's old. A childhood treasure. Did you dream of dancing? I could keep you here to dance for me along with your music box.'

'Let us see it first.'

This was skirting too close to danger. He couldn't let her risk this. 'Clodagh, no!' Dylan said, but she waved him aside and advanced on the Matriarch. She seemed strangely fearless, as if she didn't get how dangerous this was. Or she didn't care.

'Do we have a deal?' Clodagh asked.

'Yes,' said the Storyteller, her eyes gleaming with greed. 'Fetch the book,' she snarled to her waiting servants. 'Now!'

Clodagh said nothing, waiting now, her expression betraying nothing. She knew not to show fear at least.

'Clo,' Dylan said. 'This is a really bad idea.'

Her lips moved briefly to a smile, one which melted away almost instantly. What was she doing? This wasn't the plan. She was supposed to leave all this to him. He would do the talking, the convincing. Even if they both knew it would never work.

Before he could say more, the leps arrived in a flurry of activity. The book was pale and threatening, the way the Storyteller ran her hands over the binding deeply disturbing and Dylan felt his own skin crawl with alarm.

Clodagh held out her hands. 'You promised.'

'So did you. When you open it—'

The girl took it from her, folding her arms around it and her smile came back, bright and terrible.

'Oh, I shan't be opening it.'

'Him?' Her gaze zeroed in on Dylan again and the light of greed blazed twice as bright. Oh, she wanted at Dylan all right. All the Aes Sídhe did. They knew the power locked away inside him and they wanted it, the great and the lowly that would be great. It sickened him to the core.

'Not him either.'

Clodagh raised her eyes to the ceiling, lifted her voice and said five words which shook the entire building. 'Ash? I'm ready. Come in.'

A hurricane burst through the chamber. The Storyteller shrieked in shock and rage as a figure appeared behind

Clodagh and Dylan, bright as an after-image on closed eye-lids, her black wings spread wide. The primary feathers, long as his arm, curved around the two humans. With the briefest movement, Ash gripped Dylan's shoulder with one hand and Clodagh's with the other and, in the blink of an eye, and a disorienting twist of reality which left his stomach contorting and retching, the Hollow around them was gone.

Dylan stumbled from her grip and crashed against the metal rail. Below him the dark river water swirled and bub-bled as it passed. They were on the banks of the Liffey, on the boardwalk just above the Ha'penny Bridge. He pushed him-self back, trying to see how far from the Leprechaun Museum they were. Ormond Quay. Not far enough. As he turned he saw the angel sink to her knees on the wooden boards, the wings invisible now. Colour drained from her face and her hands trembled when they hit the ground. Her arms struggled to keep her from falling further. She looked as if she'd throw up, pass out, or possibly both.

'What did you just do?' Dylan yelled, outraged, appalled. They'd broken every rule there was, possibly even the Grand Compact itself. They'd broken everything!

'Got the book,' said Clodagh, and she had never looked so pleased with herself in all her life.

Chapter Three

Lost at World's End

There were moments when it was so quiet Jinx could hear nothing but his own breath and the rush of his blood as it surged around his body. His heart beat a strong, implacable rhythm and he hated it for that. It ought to be still. It ought to be dead and him with it. He couldn't will it to stop. He couldn't even take matters into his own hands. They saw to that. Silver and iron manacles bound him, metal which burned his skin and a collar which choked him. He had gone hoarse from shouting and screaming.

He didn't know how long he had been there. All his life, it seemed. Or perhaps that was what every slave felt. He remembered a time before, a brief shining moment of hope, of love. Of a time with Izzy. All gone now. Swallowed up in pain and darkness. From the moment Holly brought him back from the shadows of death, dragging him down here, ignoring his protestations and pleas.

He had been dead. He had been at peace. Just for a moment. And then Holly had pulled him back into the light, back into her thrall, and made him her captive once more.

At least in the dark he was relatively safe. They brought light. And when Holly came the light was brightest of all.

And more terrible than anything else.

The key in the lock made him start, hackles raised, body twisting in a thwarted effort to shift to hound form. The shackles and collar stopped that. He shrank back, horribly aware of his vulnerability. The lock ground open and the door creaked. It seemed to move in slow motion as he tried to will it not to. But that never worked.

Osprey filled the space where the door had been, a fearsome silhouette. His feathered cloak whispered around him and though Jinx couldn't see his chief tormentor's face, he knew the assassin was grinning. Malice coloured his voice.

'She asked for you.'

Jinx found the words escaping before he could stop them. 'Osprey, please …'

'*Please*?' The word dripped mockery. 'What kind of fae warrior are you? Get up boy, or I'll drag you there.'

He wanted to be defiant, but his body moved against his will. Osprey was right. He had no choice. He struggled to his feet, his movements hampered by his chains. Osprey didn't make a move to help him which was for the best really – Osprey's help wasn't kind.

'Hurry up, you pathetic cur. She's too lenient by far with you.'

The blow caught the side of his face and sent him down in a heap, his ears ringing and vision blurred.

'You can't do this. I'm Silver's emissary!'

'You're a dead traitor. Get a move on.'

They had been through this a hundred times. Probably more. Jinx knew what would happen but he couldn't help himself. What did it matter anymore?

'I am still Silver's emissary.'

Stubborn to the last. He'd learned from the best. He didn't know how to be anything else. He didn't know how to stop fighting. It would be easier if he did …

The kick to the stomach drove him back against the wall, winding him and leaving him spasming in pain. It wouldn't be the worst, he knew that, but if they wanted to drag him before Holly again, they'd *have* to drag him.

It would infuriate her … if she bothered to notice. Sometimes she seemed elsewhere as if, while her body was present, her mind wandered some far distant paths.

Away with the fairies.

It would be funny except for every way in which it was not.

Time passed in hammer blows and gasps. Osprey tired of Jinx as his personal punching bag and called in two of the Aes Sídhe attendants to hold him up. Coal, who was a vindictive little bastard with dead eyes newly come to Holly's service, having murdered Reaper for her, once Reaper had done her dirty work. The other one, the laughingly named Hope, liked to watch more than anything else. Jinx knew them well. And in the back of his mind he kept their names on a list.

It was a long list, getting longer all the time.

Punches and kicks rained down on him. Even if he'd had the liberty to fight back he couldn't have. Finally, all resistance beaten out of him, they dragged him along the corridors of Holly's new domain.

The debris strewn, dusty floorboards still showed up the trail of his blood, and the many stains of others' bodily fluids. Who knew how many? Who cared? She had taken over an abandoned mansion, a monster of a place forgotten in the boom, now filled with true monsters. He could hear traffic outside, a siren, shouting voices – all far off but still there. They were in the human world then. The house squatted in the old heart of the city – a mostly forgotten place called variously Nighttown, the Monto, and the World's End. The building was bleak and unwelcoming, a harsh place, swallowed by ivy on three sides, with a modern extension perched like a parasite on the other. There had been talk of redevelopment, of humans buying it and bringing it back to life, but since she had moved in, no one would dare, whether they knew why or not. Disasters happened, strange accidents, financial misfortunes – they dogged anyone who tried to meddle with what belonged to her. And Holly reigned supreme in this broken palace with crumbling edges. She did what she wanted here. Whatever she wanted.

The room would have been a ballroom in another time. But now it was hers. It was mostly empty. No one liked to linger here if they could avoid it. Those she had chosen to serve her, those she really wanted to punish, waited nearby, trying to press themselves into the walls, to be as invisible as possible.

Blood smeared across the floor, hastily wiped up, and there were burn marks everywhere, ashes and scorches where people might have stood. Once. Large sash windows dominated the far wall, the light streaming through the grubby glass blinding him. Dust motes glittered and danced lazily, strips of wallpaper hung in wan loops from the walls and cracks had appeared in the plasterwork. He tried to look anywhere but straight ahead. But there was no ignoring the silhouette he faced.

His captors stopped in front of her throne. None of the other Matriarchs had a throne. Holly had always said they didn't need one. Like any other paraphernalia of royalty. If a Matriarch needed such props to hold onto power, she wasn't a Matriarch.

She'd changed her mind. So much had changed.

Holly had whatever she wanted now. Anything.

'Osprey?' Her voice, still beautiful, had taken on a dreamy, half-there note, and it reverberated through his chest in a way it never had before. Jinx kept his head bowed because it didn't do to look her in the face. It never had of course, she'd seen it as a challenge, and she needed to put down anyone who would challenge her. Or at least she had, in the past.

It was different now. Everything was different.

Now it was much worse.

'Lady, I have brought him.' Even Osprey was more deferential than before. Because he had to be. All their lives balanced on the razor edge of her fluctuating will.

Those carrying Jinx dropped him and he fell to the floor. Pain lanced through him, every inch of him feeling everything. He let out a sob. He couldn't help himself.

And everything went so very quiet. He heard her rise, the rustle of her clothes, the tap of her heels on the bare boards. The sound stopped in front of him. There was nothing else, as if everyone present held their breath. He squeezed his eyes even more tightly closed.

Holly crouched down and touched his head, his face. Her questioning fingertips tingled against his skin, warm, with a charge like static electricity.

'Poor hound,' she purred, her voice still vibrating with unearthly music. 'Look at me. The pain will end.'

But he couldn't. He just couldn't. 'I'm Silver's emissary.' He managed to force the words out, just about. They didn't want to come. 'I'm protected by the Compact.'

A small laugh rang around the huge room. Holly's laugh. Or rather the ringing laugh of the thing that had once been Holly. He didn't know what she was.

'The Compact is broken, Cú Sídhe. It lies in ashes, like those who came to bid me obey it. It means nothing to me. Its Keeper has no power over me. All posturing aside, their weakness has been demonstrated.' She hooked her hand under his chin, lifted his face. He could feel her warmth against his skin again, see the dance of light through his eyelids. 'Look at me, Jinx by Jasper. I can take away your pain. Come now, do as I tell you.'

He couldn't help himself. When that voice spoke, he had to obey. In her presence, when she touched him, he was lost.

Jinx opened his eyes to gaze on her glory. And it was glorious. The Shining One in Holly's form smiled and it was true. All the pain fell away. Wounds knit themselves back together. The echoes of torture faded to ghosts. Muscles, tense and aching with terror, relaxed with unexpected relief.

'Mistress,' he murmured, entranced. He hated that word. He knew he hated it. But he needed to use it. For her. After so many years, when even death didn't release him, he had lost all hope of release. It was better to placate her, to do as she wanted. Because otherwise …

'There, see? You belong with me. You always have. In the darkness,' she told him tenderly. 'Heal and be mine once more.'

But he couldn't do that either. His abject compliance snagged on a half-remembered memory. That was impossible. He needed to get away from her. Back to Izzy. He had to find Izzy.

Sensing the resistance in him, Holly's grip tightened, fingers digging into his jaw like steel.

'Jinx …' That warning tone was never good. 'Do I need to punish you again?'

'No,' he whispered. Fear stole his voice. Fear of her, of what she could do. 'Please.'

But it was already too late. She released him, a move so sudden and shocking that he cried out. All the pain came flooding back at once, slamming into him. Wave upon wave of agony, everything he had been able to suppress or endure, everything meted out to him over the months of his captivity, over the course of his miserable life. All of it, at once.

Izzy's knife sank into his chest once more, the cold iron burning inside him. Jinx threw back his head and howled. Tears streamed down his face. His own bile choked him.

Holly watched, her glowing eyes never leaving him as his howls went on and on. Finally, when his voice broke to a strangled sob and he collapsed, his body heaving on the floor, she smiled.

'We'll try again,' she said when agonized silence claimed him. 'Maybe the hound can be more readily trained, what do you think? We'll get there eventually. Together, Jinx. And your pain will go. The fire will burn it out of you. You'll see. You'll serve me as once you did. Better. And with joy.'

She stretched out her hand and stroked his bowed head. 'Change for me, Jinx.'

He couldn't help it. His body acted against him and her magic flooded through him. His body shifted, tearing itself apart to obey, to become the beast in spite of all the spells and silver piercings that made it agony to do so. Or perhaps because of them, because they were her spells. Everything about him was hers and he was just a creature, her creature, with nothing like free will left to him.

Chapter Four

Consulting the Oracle

Izzy waited until dark to sneak out of the house. That wasn't long to wait in December. As twilight fell, a strange calmness swept over her and she knew what to do. Time was, she would never have left without permission, or without at least checking with her parents. Everything was different now. Since the angel. Since she'd found out all about her secret life. And it was hardly the first time she'd absconded, since October. She opened the bedroom window and escaped into the darkness.

It wasn't even late, but this close to Christmas, night came by early afternoon. Cars with their lights on, streetlights glowing yellow and orange, and various houses covered in fairy lights and decorations – it all lit up the winter's darkness with a garish defiance.

The crows were waiting at the end of the road, clustered

on telephone wires, and the walls between the houses. Black, beadlike eyes watched her approach. When she gave a curt bow, they bobbed their heads in response.

'What do you want?' she asked carefully. But the birds, as ever, didn't answer. They cawed, the sound an admonishment. She ought to know what they wanted, they seemed to say. But she didn't. Whether it was because of the holes in her memory or that she had never known to begin with – that was anyone's guess.

Izzy shrugged and turned away from them, walking through the night, beneath the Christmas lights which gleamed and glittered, the bare trees spangled with stars instead of leaves. She found the magpie at the bottom of the hill, on a low wall. It bobbed its head at her as the others did, and she bowed in response.

'Good evening Mister Magpie,' she said softly, the rhyme reeling around her mind. *One for sorrow, two for joy.* 'I need them.'

The black and white bird took flight and she followed its path, the crows following her, all the way down to the coast, but when she turned down the narrow one-way street leading to the rocky shore at Sandycove, they stayed back. Two figures waited at the other end. Dressed in immaculate black and white, they watched her approach with identically cruel eyes.

'Heard you wanted us,' said Pie, grinning that nasty grin. He was playing with the long, bone-handled knife, identical to the one she carried, tucked into the bag on her shoulder, a familiar weight.

'Yeah, little bird told us,' his brother Mags went on. 'What are you up to now, little Grigori?'

'I need information.'

'Sure, what do we know?' Pie laughed. 'And what'll you pay for it?' His grin turned into a leer. Izzy scowled.

What indeed? She didn't want to imagine. She kept the icy cold calm wrapped around her and met their gazes levelly, not willing to give anything away.

'I'm not asking you.'

'What are we then? Moral support?' Pie cackled at his joke, but Mags didn't even crack a smile. He was the clever one of the pair, the one with the really terrible imagination.

'There's nothing moral about the two of you,' she replied. 'Amadán's offer still stands, doesn't it?'

'Of course. Until it suits him otherwise,' Mags said. 'Still, why are we here?'

'I need some answers. And the support isn't so much moral as brute force.'

'Same old, same old,' said Mags.

The sea rushed in on the rocks, huge boulders and shallow pools as she made her way unerringly to the biggest rock, the furthest out. The gate to Dubh Linn was fixed here. Anyone who wanted to consult the Oracle had the chance, if they were brave enough, if they had the price.

Izzy wasn't paying in tears this time. When she had been here before, the merrows had almost dragged her under the waves – *them*, she corrected herself. Murderous, carnivorous mermaids had almost killed *them*. Although she couldn't remember Jinx, there was a gap. Always a gap. A Jinx-shaped hole in her memories. She could almost piece it together. She had given up her silver salmon of knowledge – another gap in her memory from an earlier time at the Storyteller's book – to drive off the merrows, and she had cried for the Oracle. It had hurt so badly, whatever it was that had made her cry. She thought she knew, or could guess.

There were no tears now. She held out the silver bangle over the water and summoned the Oracle, exactly the way Dad's books said it should be done. She hadn't been idle, but had tried to find out anything and everything that could help her get her memories back.

To get *him* back.

It was a whispered admission, one she was too afraid to voice aloud. So she studied, she read, and she filled the blank places with new information.

She ought to be studying for her Leaving Cert. Not memorising summoning spells and supernatural lore. Life wasn't fair. She hated her life more than anything she could imagine. But it was better to have a life to live. The alternatives presented to her weren't appealing.

All the time she spoke, she felt the Magpies watching her, judging her. They'd report everything back to Amadán of course, but she needed muscle that wouldn't ask too many questions if things went wrong. Who better?

She felt cold inside, as if she had broken to pieces and been repaired with steel. She had to use that. She focused on it and said the final words, letting the fire in her blood rush outwards.

The water rose ominously around the rock, cutting her off from the land, and a seal popped his head out, dark brown eyes glistening. It was young, far too young to be the one she was looking for. After a moment it vanished and another took its place, up and down again.

A man's head appeared the third time, his eyes very dark and his hair gleaming wet against his scalp. She remembered him. That was a relief. She had feared he could have been one of the many memories that had leeched away into the book. And clearly, from the frown, he remembered her too.

'Isabel Gregory,' said the Oracle. 'Why are you here?'

'To ask questions. Will you answer?'

He eyed the bangle warily and then held out his hand for it. She let it go and he caught it deftly, examining it with a prac- tised gaze before throwing it out to sea. Izzy watched it spar- kle in the moonlight and just before it hit the waves, a small figure leaped up and snatched it from the air. A child. The selkie whose seal form she had already seen she supposed. She watched as two other young seals appeared from the water a little way off and then vanished just as quickly. Laughter rip- pled through the water.

The Oracle had a family then. She turned her attention back to him. He was watching the Magpies.

'You still keep poor company.'

'Needs must,' she murmured. 'I need to find Jinx by Jasper.'

The Oracle sighed. 'What has he done now?'

Izzy almost groaned. He had that tone of voice. Such a parent.

'He died.'

'Ah, then you would need to seek him in Donn's Hollow.'

She shook her head. 'Been there. Someone took him and killed Donn. So where is he?'

The Oracle frowned. 'Donn is dead?'

No one had told him. And he didn't know. *Oracle of the sea, my arse*, she thought and ice stabbed through her. The words sounded horribly familiar but she didn't know why.

She shook the sensation away, letting the cold centre itself in the tattoo on the back of her neck, letting it burrow into her the way the knife did, making her mind clear and hard.

'Very dead,' she replied. 'Shouldn't you know all this?'

'It does not work like that. I do not see all, or have constant access to those things to come. I reach out to the future, to see the things I will see. If you would have me do so ... '

She tried not to glare at him. Why else would she be there? 'Please,' she said curtly.

He closed his eyes, the water moving around him in hypnotic ripples. She couldn't take her eyes off them. It wasn't natural, the way the water moved. Nor was the sound of his voice. Distant, echoing, as if he stood in a vast cavern instead of the open air.

'Death lingers in the halls of the dead. Tread carefully. There are plans within plans.'

Oh good, she thought, riddles. She straightened her back, glaring at him. 'Jinx by Jasper,' she repeated. 'Where is he?'

'He'll come to you.'

'That doesn't help.'

'It's all the help I can give you. You've changed, Grigori.'

'More than you can imagine. Where is he?' She took the iron and bone knife from its hiding place and fixed him with a meaningful glare. 'I don't want to ask again.'

He swam back from her, wary now. 'You can make threats but I have seen my fate. Yes, even I could not resist knowing that. Jinx by Jasper will come for you … *is* coming for you. Don't go to the island, Isabel Gregory. You must not set foot on the island.'

'What island?'

He shook his head, like he was trying to clear a headache. 'I see you there. And you … you will burn the world.'

'I need to find him.' More than that, she needed to find herself, to get her memories back. And he was the first step to doing that. She knew it. Or at least she thought she did. What else could she do? Burn the world? She hardened her thoughts, took hold of her fears. She meant what she said. Some dark part of herself would do whatever it took. She knew that now. The same darkness that had driven her to invade the Storyteller's Hollow and read the book.

'And would you know him if you saw him? We will see, Grigori. You should leave now. I can tell you no more.'

'Yes, you bloody well can,' she snarled at him. 'Where's this island? Is he there already? Being held captive? You're meant to know everything. Tell me—'

'Izzy!' Pie yelled from the rocky shore. 'Company.'

She twisted around to see what he meant and saw he hadn't lied. A company of Sídhe were approaching down the other road, passing in front of the Martello Tower and the chic seafront villas. At the forefront walked a figure she couldn't fail to recognise.

Golden and beautiful, aglow with power – Holly.

What hole had she crawled out of? And what did she want? Okay, the last part Izzy could guess and it wasn't anything pleasant.

'Shit,' she muttered and concentrated on scrambling back across the rocks to the Magpies, leaping the last bit over open water. 'We need to get out of here,' she told them.

'Damn right we do,' Mags said and then stopped, staring intently at the group like a predator about to strike. 'Jaysus, do you see that?'

'What?' she asked, backing away towards the slip.

Holly had stopped, her eyes burning into them. Osprey stood behind her, his feathered cloak gleaming as it billowed out behind him. But the Magpies were not staring at him. At Holly's feet, an enormous striped dog crouched, lifting its muzzle to sniff the air. It looked lethal, all hard muscle and wiry speed. A silver collar surrounded its neck and points of silver pierced its long, lynx-like ears and body. It looked like a

Cú Sídhe, muscled and sleek, the fur striped green and black, but the eyes gleamed gold. No, not Cú Sídhe, not like one she could ever remember seeing. This was something else, though it appeared close enough. Everything about it screamed danger. Inside her, the Grigori instincts she relied on for survival went into full meltdown.

'What is it?' she asked, her mouth dry, her heart beating hard in her throat.

'You don't know?' Pie sounded freaked.

Shit. It was bad then. Whatever it was. Really bad. 'Just answer me.'

'It's dangerous, that's what. It's a feckin' Púca. And they're always bad news. We need to get the hell out of Dodge, girl.'

They backed up and she matched them, never taking their eyes off the host ahead. The Aes Sídhe following were pointing, laughing, taking delight in their retreat. Banshees watched them too, but without the mirth. They were fighters. They didn't appreciate a rout.

'Going so soon?' Holly called. She sounded amused, which was never good. 'But I wanted to introduce you to my pet. He only wants to play.' She laughed out loud, a note of hysteria in her voice making her sound unhinged. Before Izzy knew what was happening the beast was off the leash and pounding across the grass, straight at her. It snarled as it slid down the slope to the rocks, claws striking sparks. The creature was huge, powerfully built and fast, too bloody fast. Muscles bunched together as it leaped at her and she ducked, rolling aside on the concrete of the slip.

The Púca landed heavily in a spray of shingle and turned on her, even as she brought up the knife. Cold iron, old iron. Reliable. She had that at least. As cold as the screaming ice that marked her tattoo on the back of her neck. Then the fire of the Blade filled her, blotting out any thoughts but survival and combat. The creature watched her, turned and paced back and forth, examining her with a keen intelligence. Looking for an opening.

'Come on then,' she growled at it.

'Grigori,' Mags whispered, his voice carefully pitched so as not to antagonise the beast. 'Don't. Leave it. We need to get out of here.'

She ignored him. Something rose in her, something deep and primal. She needed to kill the thing. She knew that the same way she knew she was Grigori, a watcher, a guardian of the places between men and Sídhe, between heaven and hell. And this thing had no place in her world. It was awash with wild magic. Holly's power swirled around it, through it, controlling it and goading it on, but still – she could sense the strange nature of the thing. Chaotic. Every heightened sense she had come to rely upon told her to kill it.

'Come on, you monster,' she crooned at it, feeling the weight of the knife in her hand like an extension of the Blade's magic. 'Try it.'

The hound drove itself at her, full force, and for a moment she thought she'd made a fatal error in judgement. It snapped, its jaws missing her and her knife scraped along its flank. The creature screamed as the iron met fae flesh.

'No!' Holly bawled, genuine horror draining the colour from her face. She didn't want to lose this creature, which just made Izzy want to kill it all the more. 'Back here, now!'

The beast recoiled as if struck a second time at the sound of her voice. It snarled, pain and anger making it wild, but it still turned on its feet and bounded back to her. It quivered as it dropped down beside her, bleeding from the wound. Its chest moved fitfully, breathing hard.

How had it missed her? It should have taken her throat out. She knew that.

But it had missed. If she didn't know better she'd say that was deliberate.

Strong arms seized her, one Magpie on either side of her, and they lifted her off her feet, running hard in the opposite direction, back up the road and away. She screamed at them to let her go, but they didn't. They didn't even hesitate, just carried her off.

'Jesus, didn't think you'd actually take the bugger on,' panted Mags as he finally slowed. They were up past the ornate gates of the private school, halfway back home before they slowed.

Izzy struggled free of them, shaking all over with rage.

'What the hell – ?' she ranted at them. 'I had it. I could have killed it.'

A lie … probably. It hadn't wanted to kill her. She was sure. It had missed. Why had it missed? And why had she felt such a need to kill? That wasn't like her at all.

'I know. We saw you,' said Pie. 'But that's—'

'*That's Holly's.*' Mags interrupted. 'And you aren't ready to piss her off by killing her favourite pet. Not another one.'

She rounded on him. 'What do you mean?'

His face froze and he scrambled for words.

'She had … plans for Jinx, didn't she? But you stopped that.'

It was like being doused in icy water. She took a step back and shoved the knife in the bag.

'She sent it to kill me, that …that … what did you call it?'

'A Púca,' said Pie, slowly. Then he repeated it, drawing the word out. '*Pooh-kah.* A shapeshifter, like a Cú Sídhe, but worse. Much worse.' He grinned like it was all a colossal joke she wasn't getting. The word was familiar. Wasn't a Púca some kind of ghost? She shivered again and her stomach twisted in knots. A memory she had lost, perhaps? Or something else. It was like her body knew something she didn't, something she was missing. A Grigori thing, Dad said. She hated the feeling.

'Right. Fine. A Púca. And the Oracle was useless.'

'Not entirely useless,' said Pie, but Mags dug his elbow into his ribs. They both howled with laughter.

Brilliant. A near death experience with a monster and Holly, and no new information at all. And here she was stuck with the chuckle brothers. She hated them, but Amadán had promised to help.

Some help they were.

'Jesus, just go away,' she told them, and stalked off up the road, heading for the little bridge over the railway line and the narrow lanes known as the Metals which led right up to the quarry on the hill. From there, it was a short walk to Brí's Hollow.

'Where are you off to?' Mags called.

'Never you mind.'

'Secrets, is it?' Pie jeered. 'I know secrets too.'

'Shut up you eejit,' Mags told him but Pie called after her until she turned off the road. His singsong jibe and howls of laughter echoed after her.

'Hey, Grigori! I know something you don't know!'

Chapter Five

Reckless

Dylan walked in angry silence. Ash followed, saying nothing, just staring at the city at night as if she had found wonderland, all the Christmas lights and partying people. Clodagh cradled the book against her. He'd never been so furious with anyone in his whole life. Not even Mari.

It was meant to be a negotiation. Not a theft.

But Clodagh and Ash had made plans of their own. They hadn't thought to fill him in on it, oh no. They knew exactly what he'd have said. What Silver would have said. So they just cut him out altogether. Angry didn't come close to describing what he was feeling.

David Gregory waited by the Four Courts, his coat wrapped around him. Where he had been working – or indeed which job he had been doing – Dylan didn't know. He didn't much feel like asking either. He made straight for Clodagh as they approached and took the book, wrapped in her cardigan, from her.

'What on earth were you thinking?'

'We had to get it, didn't we? Izzy needs it.'

'I would have got it. You were only meant to talk to her, to persuade her to let me in.'

Ashira narrowed her eyes. 'With all due respect, Grigori, the Seanchaí made it perfectly clear she wanted neither you nor Isabel in her Hollow again. This way—'

He lunged forward at her, his voice uncharacteristically loud, '—put two *children* in terrible danger.'

The children part hurt. Dylan wasn't a child. He was almost nineteen. He had a recording contract and a host of gigs lined up. The single was everywhere. He was probably already making more money than David Gregory ever would.

But then the job of Grigori probably didn't pay very well. And he didn't have much time for any more regular employment these days.

Ash recoiled, momentarily and Clodagh bristled, stepping up to her side. The angel glanced at her, just for a second, and a smile ghosted on her lips. Dylan was sure of it. She looked stronger, heartened once more.

'They were never in any danger,' said the angel, calm as anything. 'They were with me.'

David turned the full force of his disgust on Dylan. 'I thought *you* would have known better.'

'Which is why we didn't tell him,' Clodagh interrupted

curtly, clearly as put out by the children crack as he was. David's face turned white with rage.

This was getting them nowhere. They needed to be logical now. What was done was done.

'It was the quickest way,' said Dylan. Anger didn't matter so he pushed it aside. It would only escalate the situation, make everything worse. He might not like being called a child, but that didn't mean he had to act like one. Clodagh was proving how successful that tack would be. 'And it's done now. It doesn't matter. She's getting worse, Mr Gregory. And you know it.'

'You broke the Compact.'

Ash shook her head. 'I was invited by Clodagh.'

'Who has no authority at all.'

Clodagh cleared her throat loudly. 'And she didn't need it anyway. The Compact is in tatters. If it wasn't, you wouldn't be so busy, would you? Trying to keep them all from tearing each other's throats out. The angels broke the bloody thing to pieces in October. *They* don't care.' Ash cleared her throat, and Clodagh rolled her eyes to the stars overhead. '*Most of them* don't care then. Everyone who has tried to get Izzy's memories back has failed. They're in that book somewhere. We have to try.'

'Anything could have happened to you, Clodagh,' he tried again, less convincingly than before.

'Sometimes you have to take risks. You do it all the time. All on your own. I had Dylan and Ash. I've obeyed the rules. She said I could touch it. Holding it is touching it. So is leaving with it. She said I couldn't read it and I didn't.'

'Are you planning on becoming a lawyer or something?' Izzy's father asked, biting out the words. But he didn't sound so enraged now. More resigned. That had to be good. Or at least better than before.

Clodagh grinned. Dylan knew that grin. She'd learned it from Mari and it was irrepressible. 'There's a whole new world of jobs opening up for me.'

He shook his head, exasperated and clearly at his wits' end with the girl. 'Let's get this thing to safety.'

Dylan only half blamed him. Clodagh's growing reckless-ness was terrifying. But it didn't come from nowhere. She'd always had a streak of it. Just like his sister. Being around Izzy and Ash just made it worse.

And probably being with him as well.

'Where?' he asked.

'Silver, if she'll have us. After this stunt ...' He took in a heavy breath. 'I wouldn't be surprised if the fae never let us darken their doors again.'

The city was crowded. In spite of the threat of snow, Dublin was swallowed up in all the excesses of the party season. Christmas markets and garish lights festooned the streets broad and narrow. The pubs and restaurants were so packed that the clientele spilled out on to the streets, even early in the evening. Music blared out of doors and windows. He even heard his own song on more than one occasion, which was deeply weird. He supposed he'd get used to it at some point. Other people did.

They made their way slowly towards Smithfield, Dylan fully aware that Mr Gregory was still fuming at them and peering down every street and laneway as if expecting an attack. Clodagh and Ash followed behind them, huddled together.

David Gregory led them over the Luas tracks and up by Saint Michan's Church and they had reached the end of May Lane at the Jameson distillery when he stopped, turning on his heel as if he had forgotten something.

'There's a shade.' He said it so calmly, so normally that he might have been referring to a poster or a pub, nodding over his shoulder towards the huge redbrick building to their right. There was a kind of balcony over the entrance, an imposing grey stone contrasting with the blue door and elaborate fanlight. The shadow hung there like a bat, watching them.

The angel twitched, irritated, but stayed silent. She hated them, of course. Couldn't help it. David made eye contact with her, nodded, and handed the book back to Clodagh. 'When I give the word, you're gone, right? Both of you. You know where to go. Don't look back.'

And he turned to the building, gazing up at it, hands folded in front of him.

'I don't like this,' said Dylan.

'It's moving.' Clodagh didn't point. She didn't have to. They edged around behind David, watching it and him with frightened eyes. The shadow slid down one of the pillars, towards their friend's father. He just stood there, waiting, but when it got within an arm's reach, he took a step back. Another figure appeared in the doorway, taking the steps two at a time as he descended, like a child.

'Azazel,' whispered Dylan.

'I see him,' said Ash. 'Oh Lord, this is bad.'

They were almost past David, but the demon was more powerful than the shades and they didn't dare draw attention to themselves. Not with the book in their hands.

Izzy's dad spread his arms wide as if in greeting. 'Azazel, are you following me?'

'I'm concerned is all, David. I'd be a sorry excuse for an uncle if I wasn't.'

'You aren't my uncle.'

The demon laughed. 'Godfather, then. I like that. How is Izzy?'

The wrong thing to say to Mr Gregory, Dylan thought. Very wrong. 'Leave her alone,' said David. 'You've done enough.'

'Come now. Just showing concern. It was unfortunate, last October. But no damage done. I gave Rachel back unscathed. I made amends, did all she demanded. No harm, no foul.'

Even worse to mention Izzy's mum. Azazel had kidnapped her. David Gregory was never going to forgive that.

'I'm warning you—'

'Of course you are, David. We know each other of old. Be reasonable, boy …'

'I'm not under any obligation to you.'

'If it wasn't for me you wouldn't have that idyllic little life you guard so closely. We can help you get it back. Get Izzy back to the way she was before. That's what you want, isn't it? Give me the book.'

'Shit,' said Dylan and grabbed Clodagh's arm, even as David Gregory turned towards them and yelled. 'Now!'

Shadows rose from the gutters and the rooftops, poured up out of the drains, shadows that spilled across the cobbled ground like tar.

'Run!' Dylan yelled and Clodagh leaped forward with him. But Ash didn't. She stopped and light burst from her.

'No!' Clodagh screamed, trying to stop with her. 'Don't Ash!'

But Dylan was stronger than she was, dragging her with him, putting all the distance he could between them and the demon's servants.

They skidded around the next corner, where a little terrace of redbrick houses began, and tore down the narrow one-way street, past graffiti and parked cars and into the wide plaza at Smithfield. The odd quiet that always hung around the centre closed over them, eerie and unnerving. The entrance to the Market shimmered, half there and half not, as they plunged inside.

Clodagh rounded on him the moment he stopped running, shoving his chest with both hands which sent him reeling back a step.

'What's that for?'

'You left her! You just *left* her!'

'I had to!'

'We have to go back.'

'Clodagh!' He grabbed her again before she could take off out through the gate and back to Dublin. 'Clodagh, she'll be okay. She's an angel.'

'Facing a demon.'

'She's with the Grigori and besides,' he looked pointedly at the book she was still holding, pressed against her chest. 'That's what they wanted. If anything they'll leave Ash and Mr Gregory and follow us.'

She slumped against the bronze wall and stared up at the gate, willing it to open and show her the angel, for Ash to follow. But nothing happened. 'Can they follow us here?'

'No. Not in here.' At least he hoped not. He remembered the Liberty though. Angels had torn their way through its protections with demons hot on their trail. And he wasn't so sure anymore.

'Ok then.' Her voice shook. 'But I need to know she's okay.' There was something desperate in her voice. Tears filled her eyes.

'She will be. She'll let us know. They both will.' He held out his hand to her, feeling a surge of relief when she finally took it. 'I'm sorry. Let's find Silver. Stay with me now, the Market is dangerous too.'

Izzy headed up towards the hill which stood silent and wreathed in the blissful relief of darkness. It wasn't Christmas up here. There was nothing festive to be seen once she got out of sight of the houses.

Everything was perfectly dark, calm and cool.

She could breathe again. Finally.

Izzy cut off the main path and onto a dirt track, silence closing over her. Peace. Relief. The world fell away. She could almost hear the soft whisper of bird wings which told her that the crows had followed her again, all that host of dark feathers.

But no magpies, thank God.

The air was sharp with the cold, the taste of frost and snow not far off. Overhead, through bare branch tangles, she could see stars, an array of them in the perfectly clear sky. Normally the sky was stained with the lights of the city, its orange glow polluting what she could see. Not anymore. She knew she ought to mention that to her parents, but there never seemed to be time. And she never saw it as clearly as she did in the night, in the darkness. It was going to snow. She was sure of that. Not just the light dusting of snow that was little more than frost, or that turned to slush minutes later. This would be the type of snow the country hardly ever saw, the type that locked up the roads and stopped public transport, that left everyone sick of it after only a couple of days. The TV and the radio kept raving about a white Christmas, predicting traffic chaos and other disasters. But this was the first time she had really felt it coming.

Her breath misted in front of her face, like the mist from which the Fear had appeared. A shiver ran through her at the unwelcome memory. Eochaid, King of the Fear, had wanted to drain her life in order to be free. They had killed indiscriminately and only the Blade that Cuts had stopped him. Every time she saw mist, she thought of them. She couldn't help it. And every time it terrified her, even though she knew they were gone. A fleet shadow slipped through the trees to her left and Izzy paused, waiting. With a rustle one of the crows came to settle on the branch over her head. A huge thing, bigger than usual. Not a crow, a raven, she realised. It let out a harsh cry and then fell still. Izzy looked back to the trees and a woman stood in front of her.

'Hello Isabel Gregory,' she said, bowing her head formally. Her long black hair spilled around her, covering the pale skin of her naked body. Izzy could only just make out the tell-tale patterning on her skin, faintly iridescent in this light. Her eyes glinted like polished metal.

'Blythe,' Izzy said, only half sure she had the right name but when Blythe gave a tight smile, she knew it was. 'How are you?'

'Healing.' She turned slightly, showing Izzy her side where an ugly red gash was almost healed, though the skin was puckered and stretched, not quite right. Cú Sídhe healed faster than any other fae creature – something to do with the shapeshifting abilities – and they could take punishment that would kill a human and shrug it off. That it had taken Blythe so long to heal, and the results were so imperfect, showed just how serious her wounds had been. Holly's kith had almost killed her and her brother when they had tried to help Izzy and Jinx. That either of them had survived was a miracle.

'How's your brother?' Izzy asked, cursing silently when his name wouldn't come to mind. So many holes, so many gaps in her memory.

Blythe's mouth tightened in a hard line. 'My Lady Brí does what she can for him.' That didn't sound good. Izzy frowned and opened her mouth to apologise, but Blythe waved a hand to silence her. 'Blight would not have been anywhere else, Grigori. He sleeps mostly. It is for the best.'

'Still?'

'I hope there will come a day when he wakes. May I ask why you are here? It is late and the night is dark and cold. It is dangerous.'

She didn't add 'for a human' but she might as well have. It wasn't dangerous for a Cú Sídhe, definitely not for a warrior like Blythe. She'd been out too, albeit in hound form. Izzy was sure no one was going to mess with her.

'I needed to see Lady Brí, if she will see me?'

Blythe smiled then. Always brief and to the point, never indulging in the expression for more than a moment. That was Blythe all over. She got on with things, eternally pragmatic.

'My Lady will always make time to see you, Isabel. You are her daughter, after all. Come, I will accompany you.' She glanced up. 'The birds, however, may not come. Our Hollow is not a place for them, do you understand?'

Not really. There was so much she didn't understand but she wasn't going to let on to that now, was she?

'They're just birds.'

'They're following you. You should tell them to wait here.'

She glanced up at the raven and that was when she realised it wasn't alone. There were hundreds of them, like black leaves on the bare trees. They covered every branch, watching her and Blythe.

It should have been threatening. She'd seen the Hitchcock movie. It should have been terrifying. So she had to ask herself why it didn't bother her in the least. Blythe didn't look happy though and Izzy would have bet that nothing would upset Blythe before this moment.

'Wait here,' she said, her voice so soft she was sure it wouldn't carry, but the breeze took it on the cold air and when she stepped forward to join Blythe, the birds didn't move.

The temperature had dropped again and as they walked through the trees and out into the open space on top of the hill, snow began to fall. Izzy glanced back towards the other hill above the quarry, topped by the signal tower and the swathe of gorse in between. Beneath it, the beach and the black sea spread out and the dark clouds gathered over the island.

'Isabel?' called Blythe. 'Come, it will be warmer inside.'

Of course it would be. Brí commanded fire. It threaded

through everything about her. Her powers, her temper, her red hair … Izzy had to have got that from somewhere. Strange how she could remember Brí but not Mum's birthday, or all of primary school. Or Jinx's face. His voice.

She swallowed hard on her suddenly tight throat. It was just a name. It shouldn't make her feel like her insides were being ripped out with dull gardening tools.

Pushing the thoughts of him down, she focused on Blythe as well, standing there in the falling snow.

'Does it bother you when you're naked when you change?' Izzy asked.

'Why should it bother me?'

'Well, you know. It's cold. People stare.'

'Do they?' Blythe smiled, not the brief unamused smile but something altogether new.

'Yes.'

'Who stares?'

'People. Men.'

'Like your friend Dylan?'

'Yes – no – I mean, well, men.' And not just men. Anyone would stare at a woman as beautiful as Blythe, naked or not.

'Men stare at me, and women too. Grigori, it isn't my doing, is it? If there is a problem, I rather think it is theirs instead of mine.'

'You don't care?'

'Not really. If others do they should examine themselves.' She stopped at the stones beneath the Obelisk, where the entrance to Brí's Hollow opened at her touch. 'After you, Grigori.'

Chapter Six

From the flames

Every fire in Brí's cavernous hall was blazing. The light bounced off the polished bronze ceiling and reflected in the wide shallow pool. In one corner a harpist was playing, the music spritely and a little wild. Elsewhere the low hum of conversation dropped to silence when Izzy entered. They all knew who she was – Brí's daughter. The pack of Cú Sídhe rose to their feet, most in hound form but one or two looking more human, meeting her gaze in a mark of respect and acceptance for which she felt unexpected gratitude. But other gazes were less than kind. She expected that.

'Lady Brí,' said Blythe, 'your daughter is here.'

'My daughter?' Brí's voice rang around the now silent chamber. 'Is that who she is today? I've heard she doesn't know herself anymore. And precious little about anything else.'

Izzy lifted her chin but didn't reply. She wasn't here to talk to disembodied voices. If Brí wanted to bitch and moan, well, they could both do that face to face.

'The silent treatment, is it?'

The flames roared higher, turning white in their fury, and one rose higher than the rest, hovering over the pool of water. It moved forwards, a Biblical pillar of flames, until it reached the edge. Izzy watched as the fire took the shape of a woman, as beautiful and terrible as the flames themselves. Her long red hair tumbled around her face and shoulders, flowed down her back. She wore an amber pendant at her throat, aglow with fiery light, and her eyes were bright and knowing, as keen as Izzy's own. She didn't look old, not at first. Like a supermodel in her early twenties – almost human, almost perfect. It was when Izzy looked into her eyes more deeply that she could see just how ancient she really was. Many things were afraid of Brí, terrible things, which made Izzy wonder what they knew that she didn't.

Fire seemed to flow through her skin, the veins alight – the way Izzy often felt after Donn's Blade that Cuts ran wild through her body – but after a moment it faded, and Brí stepped out onto the cold stone floor. Just a woman. Or so it seemed.

'After what you did, child, you're lucky to be allowed in anyone's Hollow at all.'

She could apologise. Izzy knew that. She could claim she had no memory of what happened. Or that she hadn't realised what she'd been doing or thinking.

Who knew? Brí might even believe her, though Izzy doubted that. Or at least she might be prepared to pretend she believed her.

After what Izzy had done … That was an understatement. She had forced her way into the Storyteller's Hollow and read the book, the whole book. It had been stupid because whatever she learned, whatever secrets she had discovered, she had lost them all the next second and along with that most of her memories, all her broken and jumbled thoughts.

There was no time for any of that now. She faced Brí, defiantly. 'My grandmother believes you can help me.'

'Does she now? Isolde Gregory believes something so it must be true, is that it?'

'My mother doesn't,' Izzy added, half out of spite.

Brí's mouth hardened. 'Rachel doesn't know what she believes anymore. Not since Azazel got inside her head. Oh the things I could tell you about her. And about the things demons like to do when they carry people off. And we're the ones with the bad reputation.'

It was Izzy's turn to stiffen as the barb struck home. The demon had held Mum hostage for days. No one knew what the repercussions of that might be.

'Haven't you wondered, Isabel?' asked Brí, smiling a cruel smile. 'Haven't you thought of all the wondrously deviant things he could have done while he had her?'

'Shut up!' She couldn't help herself. She needed help, not a taunting. It was just that most of her interactions with Brí ended up in a slagging match and neither of them knew how to break that pattern. 'This isn't about me. It's about Jinx.'

The malicious glee faded from her birth mother's eyes. She wilted just a little and the glow from her amber touchstone faded.

'Jinx by Jasper is dead. You killed him yourself.'

That was true. Izzy knew it, but after that — after — there was more. She knew that too. Well, not knew it. It was one of the things that was gone, wiped clean. But she felt it.

'I need to remember. The book showed me. I know that much. I went for a reason. I know there had to be a reason to read the book.'

'You told everyone he wasn't dead, Isabel, but we all saw him. We saw his corpse.'

'And then it vanished. Please, Brí …'

Izzy screwed up her eyes tightly to stop the tears that already threatened to spill out. She was rubbish at this, even when she thought she had herself together.

Brí's hands wrapped around hers, long gentle fingers which stroked and soothed her knotted fists.

'I'll try. I can promise no more than that, but I will try.'

'I'll do whatever it takes.'

'Will you indeed? Even step into the fire with me, daughter?'

Izzy stared at the dancing flames behind Brí, willing herself to do it, to take that step. But she couldn't. She didn't know why. Just …

She saw the fire wreathing her hands, knew it wouldn't hurt her – not this fire, the fire within her mother and the same fire within her – but at the same time, her body went rigid. Other hands reached into the fire for her, hands which only wanted to help but ended up scorched and blistered, burning for her, the skin blackening where the flames licked at it. Izzy pulled back, her breath tight and desperate with panic. It was a memory – one of those teasing snatches of memory that haunted her, tormented her.

'I can't. I just can't.'

If Brí was disappointed she didn't show it. Given the Matriarch's reputation Izzy expected a raging tantrum. But the Aes Sídhe just sighed, her eyes narrowing ever so slightly in speculation.

'Very well. We'll have to try something else. Someone fetch me some wine. Tell me what you want.'

'I went to see the Oracle. He said … he said Jinx was coming. But Holly came instead.'

'Holly?' Brí peered at her. 'What did Holly want? What was she doing?'

There were other questions she should have asked. Why was Holly so close to her Hollow unchallenged for one? What was Holly doing in the back garden of the Grigori and the Cú Sídhe without anyone stopping her?

So many questions about Holly had gone unanswered. She had escaped from the hilltop at Halloween and had obviously set up a new Hollow somewhere but no one knew where.

Dad had tried to find out, of course. Izzy had heard him discussing it with Mum, but they knew no more than she did. Perhaps less now. At least Izzy had seen her. And the thing with her, the thing that had almost killed her. But somehow hadn't.

'She set her new pet on me. A Púca.'

Brí stared at her for a moment, and then buried her face in her hands. 'A Púca? Did you kill it?' Her words came in a rushed whisper.

'No. Almost. Why?'

'Oh Isabel,' she sighed, and looked up, furious. 'There's so much to explain I don't know where to begin. Where's my bloody wine?'

A girl ran from a passage to the left, carrying the tray holding Brí's wine. Small and lithe, like a sapling, her long hair reminded Izzy of ivy. She stopped at the foot of Brí's dais and curtseyed, though she eyed Izzy warily. Stories were spreading then. Well, good. Maybe it would mean fewer crazy monsters attacking her and more answers. Right now, Brí wasn't saying anything.

She reached out, beckoning. The girl took a step up.

And froze. Something shook the whole chamber, a ripple of light and rage that Izzy hadn't felt since the angels violated the Compact and invaded the Liberty. The girl staggered to one side and both bottle and glass shattered like a gunshot, the red liquid pooling like blood around her feet.

'What is it?' Izzy gasped, but Brí was already on her feet and the Cú Sídhe began to howl in agony.

The Market this quiet, Dylan decided, was even more terrifying than he had ever seen it. And it was quiet. It had lost that buzz of excitement, the terror and thrill combined that he had come to expect. It was a vast, echoing mausoleum. Few fae came here because travel wasn't as safe as once it was, not with demons and angels roaming the city. As they passed, Dylan heard snatches of conversation from those who remained, and probably never left. None of it was good.

They gathered around the abandoned stalls, some still packing their belongings, others just loitering because perhaps they didn't know where to go. Dylan glanced at them, at the girl with green skin and a patterning like scrolling flowers, at the old man built like a rough hewn block of granite, one so tall he towered over everyone else like a pine tree, another short and squat, his hair like tinsel. They vibrated with panic, with fear, embracing each other, whispering and shuffling, and trying to get a move on when they had nowhere to go.

'They've taken the old Clery's building. Demons and shades everywhere. And they've some sort of hive down in Temple Bar. Azazel himself, I heard. Drawing in humans, fae … anyone he can get his hands on. And they don't come back.'

'And that house, the old one falling down, up beyond the Five Lamps … there's all sorts moved in there. Rogues and exiles. Fae vanish, turning up dead. Summer said it was Holly. He said it for sure.'

'Where's Summer now?'

'Dead. They found him in the canal.'

'I saw angels up by Wormwood gate. A whole host of them.'

'I'm leaving, that's it. I'm getting out of the city.'

'And go where?'

'I dunno. Somewhere. Somewhere far away from here.'

He passed by unnoticed with Clodagh, that's how caught up in fear they were, not giving anyone a second glance. Not wanting to draw attention. But the atmosphere was wrong. And what was worse, though they were all talking about leaving, they were all still here. They didn't dare go.

They'd almost reached Silver's sanctum in the heart of the Market when an unlooked-for figure joined them.

'Dylan, you have to help me,' said Meridian and he recoiled as her musical voice jarred against his ears. Holly's daughter, Silver's sister, she was Leanán Sídhe, beautiful and strange and so dangerous he didn't have words for it. She was also Holly's to the core, her servant and her right hand.

'What are you doing here?'

She appeared to be alone, but he didn't trust that for one minute. He looked around, trying to find the many guards she might have brought with her, but there was no one. Just her.

'I can come to the Market. It is open to all, is it not?' She laughed, but it was an empty sound. 'I am here to see my sister. You have to get me an audience.'

'With the sister you sided against? I'm sure she'll be delighted.'

'You are her touchstone. Surely you'll speak for me.'

She reached out towards him, but Dylan shied back, the magic kindling inside him ready to defend himself and Clodagh at all costs.

But Clodagh remembered Meridian well from that night at the Hellfire Club, when they'd lost Jinx and almost lost everything.

'No one is speaking for you,' she said. 'Except maybe Holly. And she wouldn't like you being here, I guess, would she?'

Meridian's smile was cold. 'You'd be amazed what people will say for me.' She peered at the book in Clodagh's hands. 'What have you got there?'

Clodagh gripped it tighter, instantly and obviously defensive. 'Nothing.'

'Didn't think you could hold *nothing* quite as close as that.' Her voice took on a velvet ripple that Dylan remembered too well. 'Show me.'

Clodagh's' fingers began to uncurl, just for a moment. Then they turned to iron, gripping the book even harder. 'No.'

'It's rude to play with someone else's toys,' Meridian purred, taking another step towards them, too intimate by far. She brushed a strand of Clodagh's blonde hair back from her face, so tender a gesture, and Clodagh shook from head to toe. Her eyes lost focus and her mouth opened on a breath. The magic of the Leanán Sídhe slithered around her and she was helpless.

'Enough,' said Dylan and felt the music in him turn hard. It bled through his voice until it resonated with threat. 'Leave her alone.' Meridian faltered, her face snapping around to his, her façade crumbling. He could see fear there. And not just fear of him. She was in Silver's territory, proposing to betray Holly. His magic was probably the least of her fears.

'Quite the magician you have become, Dylan.' She tried bravado but it failed. 'She's been teaching you at last? It only makes sense. Otherwise you're a liability.'

He balled his fists, felt ozone crisp the air and energy run over his skin like electricity.

'Am I now?'

'Please, talk to Silver for me. I need to see Silver. I have … I have information.'

But she couldn't tear her longing gaze from the book. Even if she didn't know what it was, she could sense the power in it.

'What information?' Silver asked. Dylan hadn't heard her approach, but he wasn't surprised. He knew she wasn't far, that she would sense the magic he was weaving and come. Their connection held true, stronger now than ever.

Meridian bowed hurriedly, more deferent to her sister than on previous occasions. But then, so much had changed, not least Silver. No one doubted that she was the Matriarch of the Market now.

She still looked the same, unchanging, timeless beauty in every movement, slim and elegant as a dancer. Her long, white-blonde hair framed delicate features and piercing grey eyes which seemed harder in moments like this – and there were far too many moments like this these days, Dylan thought. She wore a black trouser suit and a dark grey blouse, all fitted closely like armour. And in a way, it was armour. It shielded her, made her appear the way she needed to appear – confident, assured, in command. Like the Silver her Market needed.

Meridian's sly eyes grew wide with shock. 'About Holly, about … about … what she's become, what she's done, what she's planning. She has prisoners, Silver …'

Silver nodded to her guards. 'Get someone to interrogate her and then get her out of my Market. I don't want to see her again. Dylan, the Grigori is on his way. We haven't much time.'

'He's okay?' Clodagh blurted out in relief. 'What about Ash?'

'Clodagh,' said Silver, not unkindly but firmly. 'It will take more than demons to stop David when he wants something done. Do you have it?'

Clodagh nodded, but didn't release the book. Just as well. Silver glanced at it as if it was poisoned.

'We follow the plan then,' said Silver. 'Get this done as quickly as possible and get it back.'

'About that …' Dylan began and Silver frowned. It wasn't worth explaining. From that look he realised David had already told her what they had done. He'd hear about it later, he had no doubt. So they would follow the plan. Even if the plan was terrible. 'Where's Izzy?'

'At home, I suppose. Are you ready? This could be difficult

and it could take more magic than either of us would care to channel.'

He nodded and held out his hand. Silver took it and pulled him forward until she could fit herself into his arms. She rested against him, her head in the curve of his neck and sighed. 'It's going to be okay,' he assured her and kissed her head.

Silver smiled against his skin. 'I wish I was as sure as you are, my love.'

Chapter Seven

Prophecy and Mercy

Holly had killed another angel to feed upon. He knew it from the screams, of course, knew that something powerful had died in that evening. They'd echoed down to his cellar room, the old iron radiators and the pipes running through the walls reverberating with the cries and sobs, the tortured voice. But seeing the remains felt different.

There wasn't that much to see of course – a ghostly after-image on the wall of the entrance hall, like old paint and chalk splattered on the peeling paint. She had crucified this one. The nails still jutted from the wall. They bore an eerie glow. Someone would pry them out eventually and ferret them away safely because things that killed angels were powerful indeed.

'She's waiting,' said Osprey and Jinx stiffened, expecting another blow, another kick. Nothing came this time. At least they hadn't bothered to chain him up again. His wrists and neck were still raw, but healing. And somehow the thought that they didn't feel the need now made him even more wary.

Nothing compared to the raw emptiness inside him.

Izzy had seen him. Izzy had tried to kill him. The look on her face, the blind hatred … he hadn't been expecting that. He'd thought –

He didn't know what he had been thinking.

The floorboards groaned and creaked beneath each step. The air was dusty and clammy, the whole place falling apart around them. She didn't bother with how the rooms looked, not unless she was actually in one. Then its former glory bled in around her, chandeliers gleaming overhead, the colours vibrant and fresh. Sometimes. If she felt like it. Other times she didn't. He could never be sure which mood would take her.

The first time he'd seen Izzy had been because of the after-image of an angel. Something inside him trembled in a way it never should. He locked it deep inside, piled all his rage and disdain on top of it to keep it down. Survival was all that mattered now. Even if he didn't want to survive.

She hadn't known him.

What had Holly made of him that even Izzy didn't know him anymore?

At first he had hoped for death, invited it, even though he knew that she'd only bring him back again. But the pain was easier. She could take that away, she could bring it all back. She governed everything about his life and there was nothing he could do about it. Fight and that would just continue. Serve her and survive? He might have lost his soul but he hadn't lost his mind. What choice did he really have?

The room Holly had chosen this time was beautiful, unlike the rest of the house. The air shimmered as he stepped inside. Light streamed in the windows, spilling over lush carpet, and overhead crystal chandeliers glimmered like an enchantment. Perhaps it was magic, or an illusion, or perhaps they were in a pocket of Dubh Linn. Was this all she could manage now? She was weakening, he was sure of it, the Shining One burning through her stolen power so quickly that she needed to replenish it almost daily. Holly was weakening. Or so he hoped. He wanted to think that, but he didn't dare. What if she could look inside his mind? What would she do then?

Holly was never alone but this time there was another prisoner as well as her attendants. Jinx stared, unashamed of his interest, at the figure slumped on the floor. They didn't need chains for this one either. Naked and pathetic, lost. A selkie without his skin, out of the water, made for a sorry sight. He looked up at Jinx as he approached, huge brown eyes widening with recognition.

And Jinx knew him too. The Oracle. He had watched as they dragged him out of the water at Sandycove. Not just him either. He had a family.

Holly held the skin, a soft brown and grey seal skin. She ran her elegant fingers over it again and again. A pile of skins lay before her but there could be no doubt from the avaricious way she looked at the selkie kneeling beneath her throne that this was his skin. And that she had him just where she wanted him. The other skins were smaller.

'Good, you're here, Jinx,' she said. 'He's been reticent. Even when I showed him my other treasures.'

'My ... my family,' the selkie said, or tried to say. His voice was a whisper of despair. What had she done to his family to break him so? Not kill them. Not yet. Jinx felt for him but could allow nothing to show. The selkie had never been a friend to him. He kept his mask in place, cold and heartless, unmoved. But there were three or four other skins. Some of them were very small indeed.

He tried not to think of it. He tried to make his mind empty.

Blood smeared the floor, as it always did, and most of it was fresh this time. How much was the Oracle's? How much had Jinx left here after his last visit? How much more would spill? He didn't know.

'Do you remember him?' asked Holly, a teasing tone in her voice.

'I remember him,' Jinx replied. He'd tried to get help from the Oracle once and it had almost cost him his life. And Izzy's too. And all he'd got from the Oracle was abuse. 'He almost let the merrows have me. Called me cruel. And a bastard, I believe. Son of a turncoat.'

Holly smiled gleefully, light gleaming from her eyes. 'How right he was. Probably not a comfort now. He wanted to see you, said the prophecy was for you.'

Jinx bowed his head. Better not to accept that. She might get jealous that anything might be for anyone other than her. Holly was more dangerous than ever with the Shining One inside her. Who else would dare kidnap an Oracle and his family? She was insane.

'Well?' she went on. 'Tell him.'

'She'll open the gate. The woman with two shadows. One is darkness and the other one burns. The Great Queen will come.'

His heart gave an unpleasant jolt. This was true prophecy then. And it had found him. 'The woman?' He looked up at Holly, who smile nastily until he looked away again. The selkie's brown gaze pleaded with him.

'You must stop her, Jinx by Jasper. She'll enslave you. You'll kneel before her and call her Mistress. And everything will burn.'

He narrowed his eyes, watching the desperate selkie, and then steeled himself to meet Holly's gaze again. 'Mistress?' he tried, tentatively.

She spread her hands, the sealskin dangling like a scarf. 'I know nothing more than his mangled words. Although apparently you should no longer call me that. I was hoping he'd share with you.'

'The Thorn Gate, the first on the rock, with Grigori blood and all the Shining Ones. A grail. The Queen,' the Oracle screamed. 'The Sídheways fail and everything burns. I know what you'll do. She must not go to the island. She'll enslave you and walk where we cannot walk. Please, please don't. Please let them go.'

And Holly smiled. Jinx knew that smile. It haunted his nightmares.

'Shall I, Jinx?'

'Mistress.' There was no point in giving an opinion. He knew that now. She would do what she wanted to do. He bowed his head again, but not fast enough. Holly smiled her most horrible smile and the light spilled from her eyes. The light of a seraph, a Shining One. She'd planned to do this to him, and had woven all kinds of spells on him to control him but the whole thing had backfired when Izzy killed him.

At the thought of her name he felt the freezing line that had pierced his chest, that had killed him. All down his side, his skin still ached from her latest attack. Why had she attacked? Why didn't she know him? It hurt all over again. Everything about Izzy hurt. He sucked in a breath and tried to calm his lurching heart.

'It's her!' screamed the Oracle. 'It's always her. You can't escape it. But if you obey her, she'll burn the world. You must not call her Mistress. *You must not obey her!* Please, Lady Holly, don't hurt them. Let them go back to the sea. Keep me if you must but let them go. Please don't do this.'

The seal skins at her feet burst into flames. Green and purple fire danced for a moment and then blazed to an incandescent white.

The Oracle's eyes went wide and his mouth opened in an endless scream, so high, so desperate that it barely made a sound at all. He threw himself forward, plunging his hands into the flames, trying to put them out. But magic couldn't be smothered as easily as fire. They went on burning.

From somewhere far in the bowels of the house turned Hollow he heard shrieking – a female voice, children. Terrible cries of agony, of death. The voices screeched, dragged out to desperate and agonised torture, moving through unnatural octaves and discords. Finally, after what seemed an age, they fell silent.

The only sound that remained was that of the Oracle sobbing, his words incoherent now, his mind and will broken. A selkie couldn't live without his pod, his family. She'd taken everything.

'Jinx,' said Holly, her voice a caress. 'Come here.'

He walked forward without hesitation. Hesitation would bring punishment and he couldn't take her punishments any more. Worse, it would bring subjugation, as she would wind the will of the Shining One about him and he'd lose himself in her light once again. He couldn't let that happen because if it did he'd end up facing Izzy again. He needed his own mind, alert and free.

He had to do what she wanted. No matter what. He had to survive.

The Oracle looked up, eyes like shattered glass, his heart and reason to live gone. Holly wouldn't stop torturing him.

She'd never stop. The Oracle knew it too. Holly would never stop torturing either of them. They stared at each other, recognising their shared plight.

'He bores me,' she whispered. 'What should we do with him next?'

What should they do? He knew what she wanted. She was in a playful mood. She wanted to drag out this pain, to make him suffer for the defiance he'd shown by not giving her his answer directly. She wanted to see him reduced to a babbling wreck. It wouldn't take much more. Not now. She could snap him like a dry old twig, but she'd keep him alive for weeks, months even, to teach him and others that she got what she wanted. Jinx knew her too well. He knew all her predilections.

'Mistress?' he said, desperately trying to stall. He would always call her Mistress now, even though he loathed the word. It placated her. Why did the Oracle's prophecy think this was a big deal?

'If you take off the seal skin you find an Aes Sídhe, or something that looks like one, anyway. What happens if you take off that skin? Is there more seal skin underneath? Or something else?' Glee filled her face. 'Bring me a hunting knife. We can find out. What do you think, Jinx? What will we do?'

Staring in the selkie's eyes, Jinx saw something new. So this was why the creature had always hated him. Because Oracles saw the future and he had seen this moment. How long ago? How long had he known? Certainly by the time they'd faced each other on the rock with Izzy, when the Oracle had called him cruel. He must have known then that they would be here like this.

Jinx reached out and held the selkie's head in his hands. Strong, sure hands.

'I was wrong,' the Oracle whispered so softly that no one else could hear. 'Not cruel. I see that now.'

Jinx closed his eyes and snapped the Oracle's neck before he could take another breath.

The body slumped to the ground with a sigh and a terrible silence settled over the room. Holly's nails rapped on the arm of her chair like machine gun fire.

Osprey cleared his throat. 'Well, 'tis efficient,' he said, not what Jinx wanted to hear but at least it wasn't condemnation.

Holly however looked far from impressed. She'd wanted to torment the selkie longer, to make it last. With a huff, she flung his skin at one of her attendants. 'Make me something from that. Gloves perhaps. And you can wipe that smirk off your face,' she told Osprey, who was beaming like a proud father. 'We have business to attend to. Where's Meridian?'

'You sent her away, my Lady.'

'Why would I do that?'

'She was looking at you too much.'

'I should have taken her eyes out. Find her. I want her back.' For a moment no one moved, no one dared breathe. She gripped the arms of her throne. 'Now!'

He could only imagine what she'd do if her daughter

couldn't be found.

That was probably what Meridian was afraid of. Not so much sent away as packed up and made a run for it, Jinx suspected. He'd do it himself if he thought he'd make it but for now he had to bide his time. Obey her. Serve her. And wait.

And pray he wasn't already too late.

Izzy hadn't known him. What had Holly made of him since she captured him? What sort of monster was he now? One who could kill in a heartbeat, without feeling remorse. He bowed his head, gazed blankly at the floor and prayed for help. But no help was forthcoming.

A rush of activity at the door heralded Meridian's arrival. Holly had summoned her and she didn't have much of a choice. Not if she wanted to live. She might find a hole to hide in, a place to shelter for a little while. But eventually, Holly would find her. Because when annoyed, Holly would tear apart anything to have her way.

'Where have you been?'

'Gathering information, my Lady.' Meridian bowed low and kept her eyes averted. All the same, she glanced at the Oracle's corpse and Jinx felt her gaze trail over him as well. He could smell her fear. 'I see you have been busy.'

'What information?' Holly said, ignoring her comment. She surged to her feet and towered over her daughter. 'I smell the Market on you. *My* Market. Have you been with Silver?'

'I saw her. I was ejected.'

Holly bent down and cupped Meridian's chin, lifting her

face. At the same time light rippled through her skin and eyes, illuminating the Leanán Sídhe's face and waiting for adoration to fill her. It didn't take long. Meridian's mouth opened and she breathed her next words.

'I saw him. I *almost* had him.'

Holly smiled. 'No,' she said, as if condescending to a child. 'No, you didn't. You fool.'

'I have information. I heard them. I know – '

Holly grabbed her throat and Meridian convulsed, gasping for air. For a moment he was sure Holly was going to crush the life out of her.

'The Seanchaí … the book … they took …'

Holly dropped her. Meridian hit the floor hard, heaving in breath after breath, her hands like claws as she tried to push herself back up.

'They took her book,' Holly breathed, and smiled. That broad-mouthed, teeth-filled, terrible smile that meant blood would flow, death would follow.

Too late, Jinx realised Holly's attention was on him again. She got to her feet, stepping delicately around the smouldering ashes and the corpse, heading straight for him.

'I have a new game,' she told him as she laid her hand on his chest, splaying her fingers and dragging them across his skin as she circled him. Jinx held himself perfectly still, too afraid to breathe. Her games were played in blood and pain. 'I had all these plans for you, Jinx, but you and your Grigori had to ruin them. Not that she's so keen on you now. How's the gash healing up?' She ran her other hand down his side, over the still-raw skin and smiled as he winced. 'But I have other plans, my sweet boy. I always do. And you can still be of use. Great use. Perhaps in this more than anything else. An old enemy has shown herself to be weak, vulnerable. She has power for the taking. But then the Storyteller always was arrogant and stupid beyond compare.' She grabbed his face in both hands, delighted with herself. 'Shall we call for the Wild Hunt?'

There hadn't been a Wild Hunt in a hundred years or more, and for good reason. All the fae could lose themselves in a Wild Hunt. It seized their will, made them insane, frenzied. The Cú Sídhe most of all. Jinx knew that much from his patchy history. But what did Holly care? She wanted a Hunt. And she would have one.

All around him horns were suddenly blown and drums beaten but he couldn't move. Holly's hands on his body held him in place. The former Matriarch glowed with stolen power and wild magic of the Shining One inside her. She blazed with it. The drums were like a heartbeat, driving blood higher and higher. They hammered their way through his body, making him shudder.

What was she doing to him? What was she pouring into him? The beast inside him was snarling, frantic, and his skin burned with a fever.

Time slipped sideways, speeding up around him as the fires burned higher and the drums thundered on. Holly's fae gathered around him, writhing against each other, drinking lilac wine, a feverish look in their eyes.

What did he know about the Wild Hunt? He had to remember. He had to hold on to himself but he was fast slipping away. It needed Cú Sídhe. It needed a Cú Sídhe at its heart. But that role didn't belong to the Cú Sídhe, not originally.

'There won't have been a Hunt like this in thousands of years,' Holly murmured in his ear, her breath tickling his hot skin. 'Not a true Wild Hunt. Not with a Púca leading it.'

'I'm not …' he tried to say, but she covered his mouth with her hand hard smothering his voice. She giggled. He'd never heard such a noise from her. She sounded insane. And more frightening than ever before.

'I know what you are, boy. I know what bred you. I know everything about you, remember? I know what Isabel Gregory saw today, what she tried to kill. Final proof, if it was needed.' What did she mean? Izzy had tried to kill him, even as he had fought to avoid hurting her. Though he was maddened by pain, he couldn't do that. But Izzy … she hadn't known him. And he knew the look of hatred in another's eyes. The need to murder … Holly grinned at him, a far too knowing grin. Her hand spread out, her fingers wide, covering his face, digging into his skin. 'You're mine. I made you. You'll be *whatever I tell you to be.*'

The light burned through him and his head spun sickeningly. Or maybe it was the room around him. He couldn't tell anymore. Holly's power flooded his veins and the pathways of his mind. She pushed back his head so his mouth was open, and poured something inside. It filled him, choking him, spilling out of the edges of his mouth and he had to swallow. He had no choice.

But he knew that taste. Knew it and wanted to spit it out. But he couldn't. He swallowed down the warm fresh blood. And hated himself for it.

Whose blood? His mind whirled. Did it matter? But it did. It mattered to him. And it didn't. She had easy access to blood of any kind. But he needed to know whose blood.

He dropped to his knees before her, his face raised in adulation. She stood over him, aglow and golden. She could do anything to him right now – kill him or take him to her bed, torture him, use him – and he would welcome it. He'd hate himself but he'd welcome it. Anything. She was all he could see – Mistress, Shining One, Goddess.

She pressed her fingers to his forehead and he could taste the blood again. It was all he could taste, all he could think of. He stared up at her in adoration, shocked by this blessing. Terrified.

'Be my huntsman, Jinx. Go forth and bring chaos. Do my will and my will alone. Hunt, my hound.'

'Where do I go?' His words were slurred, breathless with the need to obey her. His mind whirled. 'What would you have me do?'

'An old enemy is weakened. Let's bring her down. Together.'

Holly snapped her fingers and Jinx transformed. It didn't

hurt. Not anymore. Not when she commanded it. He flowed from Aes Sídhe to hound like music, more fluidly than he had ever done in all his life. Muscles primed and ready, knowing their purpose, his blood surging in time with the horns and drums, wild music that drove him. His mind felt wild with the need to hunt and kill, to run his prey to ground. He snarled and Holly sank her fingers into his fur, into the skin beneath.

And the Wild Hunt raced towards Dublin at her command.

Chapter Eight

The Wild Hunt

The Cú Sídhe felt it first. Blythe and her pack shuddered all at once and stiffened, as if scenting prey.
Izzy turned around as the air trembled and she felt the earth
beneath her twist.

'She wouldn't dare,' said Brí, so softly it was no more than
a whisper.

No need to ask who. Not even for Izzy. Holly was all they
spoke of and Holly was one of the few things that remained
clear and terrifyingly bright in Izzy's patchy memories.

She would. Izzy didn't know what but she knew Holly
totally would. What did she have to lose?

'What's happening?' she asked but Brí didn't answer. She
slapped her hands together and flames erupted from them, so
much stronger than anything Izzy could manage. Or maybe
Brí was just angrier.

'Fight it, Blythe,' she said. 'You can't let it take you and your pack. Fight it!'

The Cú Sídhe, already back in hound form, whined piteously. All over the Hollow, howls went up, desperate with longing. Tortured. Blythe stood firm where the others collapsed but Izzy could see she was trembling all over, barely keeping her ground. For a terrible moment it looked like she'd break and run, or attack anyone who came too close, but after that moment passed, the dreadful drumbeat in Izzy's ears faded and Blythe sank down to the ground, panting, her tongue lolling from her gaping mouth.

'There,' said Brí softly, approaching the Cú Sídhe with all due care, her hand outstretched but the fingers curled in. The fire dwindled and died as she got within reach. 'There, it's okay. It's gone. Can you change back? Can you talk to me?'

Izzy took a step forward and Blythe's head came up, snapping around to stare at her. All violence, all aggression, no recognition at all. She snarled, poised to attack, and Brí cried out.

'Stay where you are, Isabel. Don't move and don't make eye contact. Look down.'

The growling got louder even as Izzy obeyed. The sense of being prey was too great. She wanted to run and knew that would be suicide.

You didn't run from the Cú Sídhe. They'd catch you. And Blythe wasn't alone. Her pack was circling.

'That's it,' Brí continued to croon. 'Take a breath, Blythe. Calm yourself. That's my girl. Look at me. Just at me.'

It took an agonisingly long time, or perhaps it just seemed that way to Izzy. Perhaps it only took minutes but they were minutes dragged out to millennia by terror. Blythe whined again but gradually she changed back, inch by inch. Izzy almost wished she hadn't. Her eyes hollow with tears, her limbs shaking and her skin pale and bloodless, she looked like she was going cold turkey.

'She called the Hunt,' she whispered finally, her voice hoarse and grating.

'I know.' Brí wrapped arms around her Cú Sídhe and helped her from the ground. 'Someone fetch a blanket and water. Where are they heading?'

'The city. Oh Brí … I needed to go. I needed to run and to kill. She must have blood of my blood to affect me so. She must have kin.'

'The pack is all accounted for.'

'I don't understand,' Blythe dashed her tears from her sunken cheeks. At the same time, anger blazed in her eyes.

Brí shook her head. 'Don't.'

'Izzy says she has a Púca – My Lady, we have to follow, to find out …'

The same word the Magpies had used. The thing Holly had brought with her.

'Can you track it?'

'Yes.'

'Safely?'

Blythe looked away, unable to lie to her Matriarch.

'Lady Brí! Blythe!' A courtier ran in as quickly as he dared, dropping to his knees on the cold stone floor. 'Your brother, Blight, he's awake.'

Blythe only hesitated for the moment it took to sink in, glanced at Brí, and then bolted from the chamber, heading for the tunnels which led deep underground.

Brí watched her go, her face unreadable.

'What does it mean?' Izzy asked.

'Holly is playing with very old magic indeed. She has called forth the Wild Hunt which needs at least one Cú Sídhe at its head. It affects them all, beating them into a frenzy. It takes a strong pack leader to resist it. She saved them all, you know?' The pride in her voice was unmistakable.

'Would they all have gone?'

'If it wasn't for Blythe, they couldn't have helped themselves. Other packs will fall beneath the spell. Who knows how many? The Wild Hunt can run until even the hunters die of exhaustion and they'll kill everything in their path. Not just the one they are sent after. Fae, human, even angels and demons. Anything. If they're strong enough. And that was stronger than I have seen for thousands of years.'

'That's not good, is it? What's a Púca? What did Blythe mean?'

She could tell in that moment that Brí would lie. She wasn't sure how she knew but it was written clearly on her face and Izzy could see it at once. 'They were things of wild magic, shifters like the Cú Sídhe. Once upon a time, they were the heart and soul of the Wild Hunt, not just its head. But they are all dead. Wiped out by angels and demons and Sídhe alike. By the Grigori.'

Of course. It had to be something like that. She remembered the way she'd felt, the need to kill the creature. Though she hated it, she couldn't deny it. 'But—'

'Shall we find out what Holly is doing?' And that was that. Brí glared at her and Izzy knew the argument was over. She held out her hand. 'I warn you, it may not be a pretty sight.'

'*May* not?' Izzy stared at the hand she wasn't quite ready to take.

'I was trying to make it easier on you, child. It won't be pretty. It won't be pretty at all.'

They swept out into the night. The Cú Sídhe led the way, Blythe rejoining them with a look of grim determination in her eyes. There was no sign of her brother but then again, Izzy wouldn't have recognised him. It made her feel dreadful, but it was just another missing memory and she had so many of them. Her favourite food – no idea. Her grandfathers' faces – gone. Jinx – a mystery, a word, a name tag hanging in a void the thought of which brought only pain.

Each stolen memory took a piece of her with it. And that was what she needed to retrieve, herself.

The Sídheways were more ragged than ever, a broken jumble of places all threaded together by a madman. Izzy followed Brí, mainly because she didn't know what else to do and this Wild Hunt felt like something a Grigori should be investigating. She didn't know where her dad was. Belatedly, she realised, she should have phoned him. She glanced up and saw the black birds, flying overhead. Following her, no doubt. No one else seemed to notice them so she said nothing and hoped for the best. She still didn't know what the crows wanted. Part of her didn't want to know. Birds of death since time began.

Even as Blythe and her pack led them to their final destination, Izzy felt a chill of certainty settle over her. It was a horrible feeling, that sense of being right before she knew she was right, of having every suspicion confirmed even before she really knew what those suspicions were.

They stepped out into the cold night. Every star was visible overhead and thick frost lay on the ground, even though they were in the centre of the city. On one side Jervis Street Shopping Centre towered over her, on the other lay Wolfe Tone Park. It used to be a graveyard and in front of her the gravestones were piled up against the wall. She knew that wall, knew what dwelt on the other side. She took one involuntary step back. She knew but she didn't know. She knew it was wrong, bad, that she shouldn't be here. She couldn't go inside that place, not again. Even if she could bring herself to cross the threshold, she wasn't allowed.

Over my dead body, the Seanchaí had said.

The door at the side of the building hung off its hinges. Izzy shuddered as the Cú Sídhe entered and then Brí followed, but many of her attendants lingered behind, too afraid.

Izzy knew she would have done the same if she could, probably should have. But she couldn't. She swallowed down her terror and stepped inside, into the darkness.

It was black inside and she could smell nothing but death. She'd waited too long. There was no sign of anyone else. But then again, the Storyteller had told her the first time she'd come here that there were many rooms in her Hollow. How did she remember that? How could she remember that and so little else? But Izzy knew more about this Hollow than she had ever dreamed she'd know. The Sídheways were twisted and contorted inside this place, one second in Dublin and the next in Dubh Linn. She conjured a flame to light her way. That was when she found her first body, small and hunched on the ground. Her stomach twisted. It was a child. Oh God, there had been children here ... but then she saw it was a leprechaun. Just a lep, she tried to tell herself, but that didn't make it much better.

He looked like he had been hurled against something hard. His body twisted in unnatural ways, every bone broken. His eyes stared up past her, at something far away, so far away she couldn't hope to see it. And she didn't want to. There was no hope there. Only terror. Even now when he was dead.

She moved on, stepping over more bodies. Leps, one of the bodachs and a few who looked disturbingly human. Visitors to the museum? Tourists caught in the crossfire? She didn't want to think about that. The implications were just too huge.

Some of them had to have escaped. Some of them. A good

number of people worked here, didn't they?

Where the Wild Hunt went, death followed. Nothing stood between them and their quarry and anything that got in their way was simply collateral damage.

She drew in a shaky breath. It was one thing to read about this, or hear Brí speak of them, and another to see the devastation they left behind.

All the decorations had been torn down, everything breakable broken. Glass scattered across the floors of the corridors, glinting like stars in the light of her flames.

The Blade that Cuts uncoiled itself inside her, singing as it wound its way through her veins. It sensed danger as well then, or reacted to her growing fear. She could feel it, sucking away at her free will, dizzying her. She wasn't sure how the Blade worked and didn't really want to know. She just wanted it to be quiet and leave her alone.

She'd tried to give it back to Donn, but it had been too late. He'd died right in front of her.

Izzy turned a blind corner and stopped as she realised the door ahead hung off its hinges.

Beyond it, light flickered and glowed, light filtered through water, light that lived and breathed. Light in the form of a woman, ageless, beautiful and terrible.

Holly. It was Holly. Again.

Why couldn't she have forgotten her? But then again, the idea of being unaware of the danger the former Matriarch presented wasn't a thought Izzy relished. Golden haired, slim and deadly as a sword, Holly held a limp body with one hand like a ragdoll. She smiled like a lunatic and a dreadful light spilled out all around her.

The Storyteller gasped for breath, eyes bulging, face turning almost black as Holly, being Holly, slowly squeezed the life from her, drinking down the pain and suffering, the last remaining power of the Aes Sídhe as she did so. She smiled, her eyes wild with power and madness. Izzy's lungs ached. She owed the Storyteller nothing and the old Aes Sídhe was as good as dead. Anyone could see that. The woman had been nothing but a bitch to her, taunting, tricking, cursing … Her book had stolen Izzy's memories when she'd hoped it would help her.

But Izzy couldn't help herself.

The Blade that Cuts blazed to life and Holly turned, a scowl ripping the glee from her features. With a brief, dismissive gesture she crushed the Storyteller's windpipe and dropped her. The old Sídhe fell like a puddle of clothes and didn't move. Holly stepped over her, that enemy forgotten now. Light flooded through her body, incredible, iridescent light which came from every pore and made Izzy's fire pitiful. She had always been beautiful, but now she was mesmerizing.

Izzy faltered and Holly's smile – radiant and dazzling – returned.

'Isabel Gregory.' Her voice was a song, music in every syllable 'I have been so looking forward to this moment. Put the Blade away, that's a good girl. Kneel to me.'

The Blade shrank back – not the whole way perhaps but enough. Izzy trembled, part of her longing to obey, the rest of her screaming that this was a suicidal idea. Horror and adulation warred inside her.

Holly was almost within reach now. Just another step or two. Light imbued each strand of hair like the sun had come to earth and had been poured into the woman who stood before her. Or perhaps she was the sun itself. Her eyes shone and all Izzy could think was that this was a goddess in human form. How had she ever dreamed she could stand against her? Holly had killed angels, and archangels. And she was nothing in contrast – just a girl, just a shadow.

She managed a cry, a small murmur of dismay, one last plea for help.

Somewhere in the shadows, darkness answered.

Holly reached for her, a black knife in her blood-stained hand. A knife? Where had she even got a knife? But then again, Holly was never far from a weapon. And knives were her favourite. Sensing a threat, the Blade spluttered back into life and instinct made Izzy twist aside. Awkward and off balance, she felt her feet slipping and Holly laughed, the noise echoing around them, reverberating inside Izzy's cranium.

A shape detached from the shadows, a hound so much bigger than anything natural. He leaped forward, snarling as he landed between the two of them. His eyes were bright and golden. Points of silver pierced him, from the tips of his long ears to his snarling muzzle, and elsewhere, points that blazed in the reflected light. The silken fur was patterned with whorls and spirals in blue and green. He swept around in a circle, driving them back from one another. She could see him more clearly now, see him, study him. She remembered him from the shore. She ought to know him. She knew that.

But his eyes were wrong. All wrong.

Holly's confident demeanour slipped with growing outrage but Izzy couldn't tear her eyes off the hound. So familiar, so other. She should have known him. Should have …

He changed, shifting to something else entirely and just as alien.

'No!' Holly said, her voice a thin hiss of rage. 'No, I forbid this.'

But that didn't seem to matter anymore.

A man, pale and handsome, stood before her, long black hair tumbling over his face and shoulders, matted with God knew what. Tattoos marked his skin, the Celtic and tribal patterns so much clearer now, dark indigo against his pale flesh. They highlighted the planes and angles of his body, the curve of his muscles. He looked at her, lost and desperate. She knew him. She had to know him. But his eyes should be the colour of steel instead of that infernal gold. He spread his arms wide before her, like a crucifix, and then when he spoke, her throat tightened to agony.

'Izzy,' he said, in a voice that haunted her darkest, unremembered nightmares, the voice which brought her screaming to wakefulness. 'Izzy, please …'

Panic seized her, panic like nothing that had gone before. This was primal, instinct alone driving her. He wasn't – he couldn't be – and her mind refused to fill in the rest of the thought, shying back from it and into terror.

Rational thought broke apart like a sheet of glass and she threw herself into her attack.

The Hunt swallowed Jinx whole, and he was lost in it, running, his blood racing faster than ever before, his mind reeling. He couldn't follow the events, the sequence of things, and it didn't matter. He was free, possibly for the first time in his life. He was free to be as wild as he had always dreamed of being, as his nature had always told him to be. It didn't matter anymore. Nothing mattered but the Hunt, the chase.

They tore through the city, broke into the Storyteller's Hollow, and he was the heart of the Hunt. Where he went, it followed, where he ran, it ran. Death came with them. He knew that in some distant part of his mind. All around him the Sídhe killed, maimed and slaughtered. Blood and screams, the scents of terror and death swamped his senses and he was lost in it. What did he care? The Hunt was all that mattered, the wild magic devouring him, and using him.

And behind it all came Holly, aglow with power. She seized the Storyteller, their prey, and when she throttled the old hag he howled with the rest of them. Prey was taken, run to ground.

And then … and then … something changed. A light, brighter than even Holly. The banished part of him, the part that knew sanity and pity, perhaps even a distant memory of kindness, rose up. He saw the girl, like living fire with her shadow so very dark behind her. Her hair was bright as the flames in her hands. She stepped from the darkness and for a moment he couldn't believe what he was seeing.

How was she here?

The spell around him crumbled and the realisation of where he was and what had happened – *what he had done* – slammed into him like a wrecking ball.

Izzy. His Izzy. He had seen her at the beach, when Holly made him become a hound and almost drove him mad with pain. He knew her, like he knew his heart, his missing soul. Which was to say only in parts and at times, in between the madness and the bloodlust, but he knew her nonetheless.

Holly dropped the dead Storyteller and approached the girl, the monster inside her flaring bright and terrible. *New prey*, something whispered at the base of Jinx's brain. Izzy just stood there, lost and helpless. The Sídhe blood in her couldn't withstand a Shining One. None of them could.

Holly reached out for her. Grigori or not, Izzy stared open-mouthed at her enemy. Holly spoke, but Jinx didn't hear her words, drowned out by the roaring in his mind. He didn't need to. The tone did it all – the Blade that Cuts died in Izzy's hand. Her one defence, gone.

Once you were sworn to protect her, the treacherous voice in his mind murmured. *Once you said you loved her.*

He couldn't let this happen. He had to stop Holly.

Freedom tasted harsh and bitter, but it was freedom. Real freedom. It was harrowing and aching, terrifying. It left him hanging over an endless hole, all certainty gone forever. Holly had no power over him. He didn't know how or why, but at least for once he knew it was true. Knew it with all his heart.

Izzy twisted aside as he leaped forward, landing between them and trying to drive them apart. His hound shape fell away and the Blade rose up like a pillar of fire between them. He saw her face, her gaze, her complete lack of recognition.

'Izzy,' he said. She had to listen to him. She had to get away from Holly. She had to know him. 'Izzy please ...'

Her eyes didn't know him. She saw only monsters. And standing here, changing form, covered in blood and sweat and the gods alone knew what else, he was a monster. Her eyes showed disgust with everything before her. Hatred. He knew in that moment what she saw. He was Holly's now. He was lost and she was lost to him. His way had been chosen for him but what did that matter? It was done.

Devastation crashed down on him. Death followed him and he had brought it here.

She knew what he was. She recognised that much, even if he could not.

Or perhaps he did. Deep down. He was what he had always been.

Holly's dog. Her creature.

She had crafted every element of his life. How could he be anything else? How could he have dreamed he was free?

Izzy slashed towards him, the Blade that Cuts in one hand, blazing through the darkness, and the iron knife in the other. Her knife. The one she had used to kill him. He ducked aside, quick as a prayer, aware that Holly was gone, that the rest of the Hunt was coming to and fleeing, that it was all breaking apart and the sick realisation of what had happened, of what they'd done was sweeping over them all. Those who would care.

Monsters. All of them. And he was the worst.

Holly had escaped. Damn him, he had saved her again and she'd fled when faced with attack.

'Isabel, no!' A new voice burst into the room and another Cú Sídhe rushed to block the conflict. Blythe. It was Blythe. There was no one else it could be. He knew her instantly and she knew him. He saw by the way she staggered back, unsure for a moment when faced with this impossible thing. Behind her, trying to get a grip on Izzy, he saw Brí, saw the shock in her face as she recognised him as well. Only Izzy didn't. She didn't know him at all.

Enough. He couldn't stay here, couldn't face them. Not now, not after this and everything else. Izzy screamed at him, a threat, a promise, incoherent with rage and doubled over in Brí's arms, still trying to reach him. Jinx dived through the broken door, rolled along the glass-strewn corridor, oblivious to the stabbing pain of the glass. That was just physical, nothing to his internal agony. He transformed as he ran, leaving the emotions and feelings of the Aes Sídhe behind and plunging deep into the mind of the hound. Safer that way, he thought, one last thought. His claws tore groves in the wooden floor as he turned the corner and made it through the final door.

The night opened up to him and he fled. Welcoming the darkness, he threw himself into it and into one single thought with all his will – to run.

Chapter Nine

Touchstones

Dad's voice, that was what she recognised as she came around. Dad's voice calmly handing out orders. She couldn't see him but she could hear him, somewhere off down a corridor or around a corner. She clung to that, to the one recognisable thing, and opened her eyes.

'Izzy?' Dylan looked down at her. She lay on the floor with some sort of rolled-up material under her head. 'Are you okay? Hey, she's awake.'

Another gaping chasm in her memory. The last thing she recalled was chaos and death, the Storyteller's corpse and Holly. And that creature. That shapeshifting thing who knew her name.

'What happened?' she asked carefully.

'It's okay. Just take it easy. Don't – don't get too excited.'

He was choosing his words so carefully. That really wasn't

a good sign. Izzy knew that much now. She sat up, slowing down as her head swam, and she hoped he didn't notice. No such luck. He took her hands, guiding and steadying her.

'Blythe and Brí stopped me ...' she said, trying to piece together what she could recall. 'Holly ... Holly got away. And that – that *creature* of hers ...'

'Creature?' His face fell in dismay. 'Oh, Izzy, no.'

'What was it?'

'At home,' said Dad, striding into the room and glaring down at them. He looked furious. 'We'll talk about it at home. She's had a shock.'

No I haven't, she wanted to say, but she knew there was no point in arguing with him when he had that look on his face. She gave it to him right back anyway.

'We will talk about it at home,' he repeated, firmly, daring her to argue. 'The Storyteller is dead and so are many of her people. We should leave this place.'

'We should burn it to the ground,' said Silver, joining them. She looked miserable and just as cranky as Dad.

To Izzy's surprise, her father just shrugged. 'If that's what you want. Wasteful though. Someone else can use it.'

Mr Recycling strikes again, thought Izzy and something hard and jagged inside her melted a bit. He was still Dad.

'They won't,' Silver replied. 'Not one of our people, anyway.'

'People have jobs here, Silver,' he told her. She frowned, as if he was speaking in riddles. 'Human people. You know?'

'Dad?' Izzy whispered. 'I want to go home.'

He gathered her in his arms and she wilted against him. 'Then let's go home, love.'

Home should have been comforting. It should have been safe but when it held a large contingent of the Sídhe, including some of their most powerful leaders, Silver and Brí, that wasn't the case. Mum stared at Brí as if looks could kill and didn't say a word. Even worse was the coldly formal way Gran greeted the Matriarch. Brí herself didn't appear in any way upset, which was probably just as well, but kept staring at Izzy as if she could see far more than Izzy was comfortable with her seeing.

Dad made tea, a huge steaming pot which he set down on the kitchen table. Izzy watched him pour it, focusing on the stream of amber liquid and not on the others. Just on her dad. He handed her a mug, poured in milk and squeezed her shoulders as she blew on the hot liquid. When she looked up, she caught sight of Mum glaring at them both.

'What happened?' Mum asked.

'Holly called up the Wild Hunt and killed the Storyteller,' Dad replied.

The corner of Mum's eye twitched and her mouth tightened. 'But she's a Matriarch, isn't she?'

'She was. She's dead now,' said Brí. 'Someone took her touchstone.' She cast a deliberate glare at Clodagh who shrank back, her arms curled around a large bundle.

'We didn't know,' Izzy's friend breathed. Dad steered her to a chair on the far side of the table from Brí and poured her tea as well. Dylan joined them, bringing with him a packet of biscuits, and Silver trailed after him, clearly finding this somewhat uncomfortable. But all the same she sat down as well. Just a group of people, sitting around a kitchen table trying to work out a problem with an age-old Irish method. Tea.

To Izzy's surprise, Brí just shook her head and the threat drained from her. She sank into a chair and took a mug of her own. 'She had it coming. Heartless bitch. Preying on other's lives, on memories. Disgusting. I'm more concerned with the Hunt. Give that to me, girl.'

She held out a hand, but Clodagh didn't release the bundle. Instead, she looked at Izzy's dad for a sign of what to do.

'Fewer orders in my house,' he said, his voice full of dire warnings.

Brí glanced at him. 'Yes, Grigori,' she said, not sounding for a millisecond as if she meant it to be respectful. 'But if I'm here to help our daughter regain her memories, I'll need the thing which took them.'

Mum scowled at her and wrapped her arms around Izzy, squeezing tight.

'You don't have to do this, love,' she whispered.

Oh, but she did. Izzy squirmed and closed her eyes. His face reared up in her mind, pale as snow beneath the splattering of blood and indigo tattoo. His crow-black hair was matted with the stuff and his eyes glowed gold.

They were never gold. They were like polished steel.

The unbidden memory burst like a firework in her mind and she recoiled, staggering back out of her chair and almost knocking Mum off her feet.

'What is it?' asked Dad, suddenly concerned.

'Who was he?' She gasped, fighting through a wave of pain and grief. 'That … that man – that thing – defending Holly …'

Dad's face fell, but he didn't answer.

'Just having the book near her is starting the process,' Brí interrupted. 'Let me finish it.'

'But—' said Mum.

'Enough!' Exasperation coloured Gran's voice. She had no time for any of them, not joining them at the table or taking part in this impromptu debate. She treated everyone with the same disdain whether they were Matriarchs or granddaughters. How did she get away with that? 'She needs her memories back. All of them. Some of them are going to hurt, Isabel. Be prepared for that. Endure it.'

'Heartless to the last, Isolde,' Brí murmured, almost singing the words as she twisted the knife. 'You never change. I thought that was supposed to be our trait.'

'From whom did I learn it, Lady Brí? My husband and my son have been burned by association with you. I suppose it's time for my granddaughter to have the same treatment. Are you going to get on with it or talk more nonsense?'

'Mother, please!' said Dad, who looked like he would rather

be anywhere but here. Isolde threw up her hands and turned away, marching back towards the kitchen counter where – from the sounds of thumping and crashing – she was making an extremely angry pot of tea of her own. Izzy didn't look, already making for the door to the hall.

'Dylan, Silver.' Brí smiled, delighted to be firmly in control again. 'I'll need your help. The rest of you, stay here.'

What happened to fewer orders in Dad's house? Izzy saw him flinch and Mum took his arm, holding him back. Izzy locked eyes with Clodagh and nodded upstairs. If she could get her and Ash to her room then maybe she could get some answers. They moved as one.

'Not you, Isabel,' Brí barked. 'Come with me.'

Dylan wasn't sure what Brí was planning as she ushered Izzy into the sitting room, and he definitely wasn't sure that he would like it once it got underway, whatever it was. Her expression was cold and calculating. Silver didn't look much happier. As Izzy sat down in the armchair, more frightened rabbit than he ever recalled her being before in all their lives together, he took a place behind her, reached over and took her hands, holding them against her shoulders.

'Do you know what you're doing?' asked Silver critically, her gaze never wavering from Brí. She wasn't deferential to the other Matriarch these days. All they had been through had knocked that out of her.

'In a way.'

'*In a way*? Have you told David Gregory? I don't think he would take kindly to us tinkering around with his daughter's mind based on *in a way*.'

'Oh, *whisht*,' said Brí and handed the book to Izzy who took it with hesitant hands. 'No one knows how this might work. There is always an element of experimentation when it comes to touchstones, as you and Dylan here proved so dramatically. Open it, Izzy, but don't look down. Not yet. Put one hand flat on the page and Dylan, keep a tight hold of the other one.'

'Explain it to me first,' said Silver. 'I won't have you put him at risk.'

Of course she wouldn't.

She'd no more risk him than he would risk her. The power they shared was nothing next to the way he loved her.

'He isn't at risk.' He tried not to hear the implied 'much' she didn't say.

'It's okay, Silver,' he assured her. 'I'm willing to take a risk to help Izzy.'

A brief smile flickered over Izzy's face as she looked up at him and she squeezed the hand he still held. Silver, however, scowled at them both. But she didn't argue. She might not like it, but it was his decision, not hers, and she knew it as well as she did.

'Here,' said Brí and she unfastened the enormous amber

necklace around her neck. She slipped it around Izzy's neck and the stone began to emit a soft light as soon as it touched her skin. 'Oh yes, it likes you. Naturally. Blood of my blood, you see?' Pride made her beam at Silver, but it was like trying to get a response out of a stone.

'This is dangerous. Is it safe here?'

'The Grigori's house? Are you even listening to yourself? Of course it's safe. Safest place there is.'

'But this … *Three* touchstones, Brí …'

'To overpower the book. And it's *four*, not three – Izzy has the Blade that Cuts, remember? That was Donn's. The Story-teller was never as strong as any of us individually and given that she's dead, it shouldn't be too much of a struggle. It's an old spell. And something of a nasty trick if I'm honest but I'll use whatever means necessary. Now, we need to concentrate. You most of all, Silver. Your touchstone is most likely to have ideas of his own. Whatever happens, Dylan, you must not let go, understand?'

He tightened his grip on Izzy's hand again while her free hand, the one that wielded the Blade that Cuts, splayed out on the page. He could feel Silver in the back of his mind now, a familiar intimacy, a sense of belonging. He met her unsettled gaze and smiled, longing in that instant to kiss her. She read his thought and the heat in her eyes intensified.

Light from the pendant filled the room – Brí's doing, he supposed.

'Now, stay with me,' she murmured. 'Follow me. Izzy, call

up the Blade and at the same time, look down on the page.'

For a moment nothing happened and then a hurricane burst into life in the middle of the room. Dylan was almost flung off his feet. The book bucked in Izzy's lap, the pages under her hand rustling violently as if trying to escape her. He could feel both Silver and Brí now, like two sheepdogs corralling a herd, keeping the undirected magic in check. It raced through him, power upon power, singing and screaming in his blood. He drew in a shaking breath and Izzy gave a violent, wrenching sob.

'I remember. Oh God, I remember!'

She tried to pull away from him, but he hung on grimly. He didn't know what would happen if he let go now but Brí had been very clear. He'd never encountered fae magic like this. Glancing down he saw words spilling across the pages, words and languages he didn't know, all glowing like a fiery light as they seared their way onto the parchment. So many words.

'It's too much,' Izzy cried out. 'Please, stop. It's too much.'

The pages shook like an enraged animal and her fingers sank into the pages, nails digging grooves in them. And the words kept coming, but they weren't just on the words now. They dragged themselves up her skin and winding around her hands. They tangled about her wrists and slid up her arms, flaming words, twisting lines of fire and amber. He could hear the songs they sang, the lyrical melody of each phrase, the rushing, breathless sighs.

Remember, his brain told him, curiously detached all of a

sudden. *Capture this for later. You can recreate this.*

The rush of energy quickened, the wind howling around them, the curtains billowing in as if the wild storm raged outside, as if the maelstrom with Izzy at the centre sucked all the air into it. Silver staggered where she stood, colour draining from her face. Her eyes met his and he saw panic in them. Real fear now.

'Hold on,' said Brí, her voice shaking. She wasn't faring much better than Silver.

'I can't,' Izzy replied. 'There's too much. I can't ... I just ... Brí!'

But the Matriarch didn't reply. She stiffened and then convulsed, her body jerking like something else had control of her. Her eyes snapped open, bright and terrible, light spilling from them.

Izzy screamed, the piercing sound shattering the spell. She flung the book away from her and it burst into flames as it hit the carpet, ghastly green fire dancing over it and devouring it. Brí shuddered one last time, throwing her head back, her spine arching. She let out a long, desperate groan and then collapsed.

The wind stopped, like someone had shut off a machine. Silver dropped to her knees and, breathless, Dylan started forwards in case she fell as well. But he still held on to Izzy. He couldn't seem to let go.

In the silence, only their laboured breathing could be heard. David Gregory flung open the door. 'What the hell – ?'

he began, but stopped as he saw the devastation, Brí's body and the now blazing book busily burning a hole in his sitting room carpet. The stench of burnt flesh filled the air, sickening and rank. 'Izzy?'

She let go of Dylan's hand, leaving a red mark behind her and reached out. 'Dad?' she whispered. 'Dad, I remember.'

And then she fell too, like a stone, tumbling off the chair and onto the floor.

Chapter Ten

Dreams and Nightmares

Izzy knew from the start that this wasn't real. It couldn't be. She was standing beside a mound of rotting flowers, the aroma sickeningly sweet, beneath a glass ceiling with rainbow hues running in ripples over the gleaming surface, like oil reflecting light. The walls were the same and the floors, scattered with slips of paper, scraps of cards. She didn't like to think of the dizzying view down if she looked too closely. Beyond the walls of the glass tower she could see only darkness, and specks of light, like endless stars. It was a clear winter's night, the air crisp and cold, but she didn't feel that. She didn't feel anything and that was the most frightening thing of all.

Full of fire and fury, she stepped forwards and saw him. He dropped to his knees, a shape like a tangle of bandages standing behind him, gnarled hands digging into his shoulders. Like a nightmare from childhood holding him, controlling him. He looked up at her, his golden eyes blazing with need and desire.

'Mistress,' he said, and the word made the world around her shake.

The world rippled and changed, reformed in a wave of darkness. Wind tore at her body, but she still didn't feel the cold. This time she was surrounded by sea, black and wild, a raging storm which lashed the coast. Thorns burst from the shallow, rocky earth beneath her, thorns which reared up like a living creature and wrapped themselves around her, winding around her arms and legs, the tips pricking into her skin.

But even that pain was nothing. She was used to pain, used to the feeling of her own blood. Thorns tore into her.

And he still knelt before her again. He lifted his eyes to meet hers and she saw it again – desire, worship, adulation. Golden, glowing eyes that weren't human, weren't fae, weren't … weren't his.

'Mistress!' he said.

'No, Jinx. Please. Don't … don't let me get lost again.'

But another voice answered. A voice not his, not real, a voice that haunted her dreams. A chorus of voices, all of his kind blended together in terrible harmony. A black shape circled him, a dog one moment, a goat the next, a man for a moment and then a horse, a huge black stallion, larger than anything she had ever seen.

'He cannot help you, Grigori,' it said. *'He cannot help himself.'*

'Izzy?' It wasn't his voice this time. It came from somewhere else and the tower started to shake. 'Izzy, wake up. Talk to me.'

Mum? It sounded like Mum, but how was she here?

And then the world dissolved. Izzy was back in the sitting room which reeked of smoke and burning paper, and worse, the skin in which the book had been bound, human skin. Mum called her name again.

'Jinx,' Izzy said and hiccoughed on a sob.

'I know, sweetheart, but just take it easy. I think …' She looked up at the others. 'I think it worked. David, did it work?'

'Jinx,' said Izzy again.

Silver crouched down in front of her and reached out a hand to stroke her face. 'Yes. It was Jinx, though Holly has changed him. Take a breath Izzy. You need to breathe.' The Matriarch shivered and retreated, going back to the sofa where she curled in against Dylan. He watched her anxiously. A flow of energy passed between them. Izzy could feel it from here, rippling through the air.

On the other side of the room, Brí lay on the other sofa, her eyes closed, her chest barely moving. Her skin was as pale as a corpse.

'Is Brí okay?' Izzy asked, finally able to form words other than his name. It felt like normality returning. But then again, what was normal about any of this?

'She'll be fine,' said Dad but he didn't sound so sure.

Suddenly Izzy remembered Brí's touchstone, still around her neck, and she took it off. Her hands shook and the bloody thing started glowing again.

Move, she ordered herself and levered herself out of the chair, ignoring Mum's protests. She managed to cross the expanse of the carpet, and dropped to her knees beside Brí. Carefully, she placed the necklace back around the woman's neck, and knelt there, unable to find the strength to get up again.

Jinx. She had dreamed of Jinx. But worse, she had seen him too, on the shore and in the Hollow. She'd called him a monster and she had tried to kill him.

Jinx. Jinx was alive.

Her stomach heaved and her mouth filled with cloying sweetness. Clamping her hand over her mouth she fled from the room and up the stairs to the ensuite in her bedroom. She collapsed on the cold tiles and vomited into the loo, her hands clawing at the plastic seat until she thought she'd rip it off. She didn't know what there was to throw up but it kept coming until she was dry-heaving and bringing up only burning bile.

Sweat beaded on her skin and she was too hot and too cold all at once.

Jinx. She could remember Jinx. The first time they met, his long slender hands holding the pieces of her phone, the way he moved as he walked her to Wicklow Street. The time she had tried to kiss him and the time he'd kissed her on the rock, delirious with the merrows' song. When he'd vanished. When he'd returned. Jinx saying he loved her. And when she killed him.

Every instant of that.

The way the knife slid in so smoothly, just as he told her to. The light fading in his eyes, that terrible burning light. His body so cold in her arms.

Dead. He had been dead.

And though she had run to Donn's Hollow to demand the Lord of the Dead give him back she was too late. Donn was already dying and Jinx was already gone.

And tonight, she knew why. Holly had him. He was Holly's creature once more. Body and soul. She'd changed him, made him a monster.

Izzy scrambled to her feet, wiping her mouth. Long red hair fell over her face. She hated it, the way she suddenly hated everything. With mounting hysteria, she turned out her bag until she found the iron knife she'd used to kill him. Izzy grabbed a fistful of her hair and sliced through it. The action brought out a sob of grief and loss, a release. She did it again and again, her sobs coming thick and fast as she cut it off. But it did no good. She couldn't stop all the feelings, all the memories sweeping back over her. So much information, so many sensations and emotions, all coming back, all revolving around Jinx.

He's lost, so lost. More than ever. I've lost him.

Her hair shorn off now, she turned the knife on her arm. A long, fluid stroke, deeper than she had meant to cut. The slight-est pressure and her blood started to flow, splattering down onto the waves of hair. Stinging pain followed and that at last focused her. Just for a moment, before her panic resurged and she had to do it again. Cut over cut, each one steadying her for a moment, bringing her the one clear understanding. She deserved agony.

'Izzy? Jesus, Izzy. No!' Clodagh grabbed the knife from her and flung it away. 'What are you doing? Oh God, you're bleeding.'

It was worse than she had thought. There was blood and hair everywhere and her arms looked like she'd been at them with a cheese grater. But there wasn't enough pain. She was drowning in memories again. Not all of them her own. She saw a ragged woman, dressed in scraps of materials, wailing in the night. *'I want to forget him. Don't you see? I have to. I can't live with the memory.'* Someone screamed over and over again, incoherent words in a language long forgotten. There was a song, a nursery rhyme. And a series of curses which made her cringe inside. Izzy sank into her friend's arms while Clodagh shouted for help, and then slid from her grip, folding in on herself, trying to make the flood of memories stop.

Suddenly everyone was there, everyone was shouting. It was all her fault. Everything. And she couldn't find a moment's quiet. She'd lost him and Holly had him and she had attacked him because she hadn't known him. And more, because she had needed to kill him, driven by something far beyond her understanding, something deep and primal. Something Grigori.

'Izzy,' said Dad in a calm, soft voice. She opened her eyes and saw his face through the haze of pain. His eyes glittered with magic and the sharp edges of her world softened a little. 'You need to stop. Please, Izzy. Just breathe. Nothing else. Breathe.'

'What …' she found her own voice at last, twisted and mangled though it was. 'What did I do? What did I do to Jinx?'

He didn't answer at first. His hand stroked her cheek, wiping away blood and tears and the bits of her hair which had stuck to them. 'It wasn't your fault. You couldn't help it. It was a Púca, that's all. They're meant to be dead, so you … your instincts …' He trailed off guiltily, or perhaps he wasn't sure how to say what needed to be said. 'You need to sleep,' he finished and she felt the soft pulse of magic which came from his fingertips. Dad could do magic. Who knew?

And he was always gentle with her. She should have remembered that. Even his lies were meant in a kindly way. Warmth suffused her skin, enveloped her mind. So gentle. Almost like music, like a lullaby.

Her body sagged, asleep before she could register another thought.

The first thing he knew was sunlight on his face. Weak winter sunlight. That and the cold. He lay in deep snow, his body covered with the stuff, shivering and pathetic. There were crows watching him from the bare branches of a tree nearby, very black against a pale, featureless sky. Snow below. Snow clouds above.

Jinx struggled to sit up, his body stiff and unresponsive, shivering too much, wrung out with exhaustion. Everything hurt. Everything. Everywhere. Even breathing.

'I wondered if you was dead, lying there,' said a voice, too familiar and most unwelcome.

'Yeah, I owe him a pint now,' said another, almost identical. 'That's not healthy, Jinxy-boy, lying around in the snow all naked like. You'll catch your death.'

Jinx almost slumped back down to allow the snow to finish the job. Magpies. Why did it have to be the Magpies? Why of all the creature of all the planes, *them*? True, it could have been worse. But not much.

He'd been firmly under Holly's thumb, her creature, her monster, until … until he wasn't. Until something snapped inside him and he was … free? Was this what it was to be free?

In spite of his prayers, the Magpies hadn't gone anywhere. They just sat there, making snide comments.

'What do you want?' His voice sounded rough, wretched, but it felt good to speak, to actually acknowledge the fact that he was indeed alive and more, that he had control over himself again.

Then he thought of what he'd done, of Izzy's look of horror. And he wished he wasn't.

'We were just passing, bud. Just passing and there you were in the snow. You stand out, like, you know? Big, naked, Cú Sídhe all covered with lines and silver, lying in the snow in the middle of feckin' nowhere. And I says to Mags, what's he doing there? And Mags says dunno, but it's brass monkeys. And there's the fact that no one's seen you for months until the other day, and that wee girl of yours was going mental looking for you a while back. And then she tried to kill you and all. So we thought we ought to have a gander. So here we are.'

They peered at him, all beady eyes as they sat on a pile of rocks passing a hand-rolled cigarette between them. Pristine as always in their black and white. Always together. Always where they were least wanted.

Why couldn't he just be dead?

'Where you been, Jinx?' asked Mags. 'Because you look like you've been on a nine-week bender in one of the nastier corners of hell. And indeed, we did hear you was dead, that the little Gregory girl shived you. But then she came and got us to act the heavy for her and said she was trying to find you. And then, well, there you were on the beach and she tried to kill you. So you can understand our confusion, like.'

Izzy. Oh god and all the ancestors, Izzy... He drew in another shaky breath and wrapped his arms around himself. His body, finally aware that not only was it alive but probably in the process of freezing to death, wouldn't stop shivering now.

'Something like that,' he said through chattering teeth.

The Magpies exchanged a glance in unison and got to their feet. To Jinx's surprise, Pie took off his long black coat and threw it around Jinx's shoulders. It was thick wool, lined with satin the colour of night and it was blissfully warm. Meanwhile, Mags stubbed out the cigarette on the rock and rummaged in his pockets until he pulled out a little bottle. He unscrewed the stop and handed it to Jinx, who eyed it warily.

'What's this? Lilac wine?'

Pie snorted. 'Nah mate, we don't touch that shit. This is poitín. Get it in you. That'll warm you up.'

Jinx took too big a swig of it and something akin to rocket fuel flooded his mouth and burned its way down his throat. Coughing and spluttering, with a gastro-intestinal system suddenly trying to decide whether to throw up, swallow, or simply give up and run away, he tried to catch his breath but found he could only wheeze. The Magpies howled with laughter. They each grabbed an arm and hauled him to his feet.

'Come on lad, let's be off.' Mags took the bottle and had a mouthful before handing it to Pie who did the same. Then they grabbed his jaw in implacable hands.

They tipped the rest down Jinx's throat before he could protest. This time it wasn't as bad. Potatoes, humans made this stuff from. Their ingenuity knew no bounds when it came to creating alcohol. But even they couldn't fix the taste.

'People to do, things to see,' Pie told him, grinning like a skull. His face swam in and out of focus dizzyingly.

Jinx didn't care, not now. A warm numbness spread through him and that was a relief. He'd never drunk anything this strong. It left him reeling.

'Let's get you something to wear,' said Mags. 'The boss is

very interested in where you've been.'

Jinx had no idea how long it took. He must have slept. There was definitely more of that burning alcohol the Magpies knocked back like water. His head swam and he shivered, hot and cold. His whole body felt weird, twisting and contorting. He must have slid to his hound form more than once. At one point he was running, faster than he had ever run in his life, unfettered. Free. Free of Holly. Free of everything. There was definitely some screaming and he was pretty sure he had torn his way through a clothes shop, though as a man or a hound, he wasn't sure.

The Magpies' laughter followed him everywhere, even now as he lay on the thickest, softest carpet he'd ever known. He stared at the bronze ceiling where he could just about make out a distorted version of himself, smoky and distant, wearing black jeans, a black t-shirt and one boot. The vision oozed and crawled, trying to slide down the sides of his eye sockets. Closing his eyes didn't help either because then he could feel the whole world spinning way too fast. He had to hold on to the floor so it wouldn't fling him off into the void.

'I said unharmed,' the Amadán growled.

'Ah now, boss, he isn't harmed. He'll be right as rain once he's slept it off.'

At least Mags had the good grace to sound tipsy. Jinx giggled at the thought.

'Do you think Holly or Silver ever let him have more than a shandy before?' asked Pie, slurring his words. 'Because I thought Cú Sídhe were able to hold their drink.'

This brought a howl of laughter from both of them, but Amadán didn't join in.

'Never mind,' he interrupted, ignoring the now poorly stifled giggles coming from the pair. 'Rothman, brew up one of your hair of the dog concoctions, if you will pardon the pun, and you two, bring him through here. We need to secure him. And *don't* let him throw up on the carpet!'

They moved him, not gently but not with any deliberate design to hurt him. They lay him in the darkness, on something cold and hard. It felt like a tomb and Jinx began to shiver again. Someone forced his mouth open again and poured a foul and pungent mixture down his throat after the poitín. Thankfully, after that, he passed out.

When Jinx came to, his body ached and there were bruises everywhere. But all the traces of the night before were gone. And the day before that. He breathed slowly, trying to steady his own heartbeat as he put back together what little he could remember.

He was in Amadán's Hollow and from the little he could see through the stygian darkness, he had been laid out on the slab in the morgue beyond the Old Man's study, the same room where Amadán had once shown him the body of a fae girl murdered by the Fear.

Lying on the same slab.

He tried to sit up sharply, horrified by the thought, and his insides lurched. Not a good idea. But after a moment he forced himself onwards. He felt ... strange. Not himself. As if he was floating just beyond his body, waiting to be let back in. He could see the room in a stark black and white, far better than should have been possible in this dark place. Even with the eyesight of the Cú Sídhe. No, this was something more.

He didn't like it.

His feet swung down to meet the floor. Bare. There were clothes folded on the end of the slab, waiting for him, no doubt, but he ignored them for now. Instead he closed his eyes, focusing on his other senses instead.

He could hear his own breath, and the rush of blood in his veins. Further off, muffled by the door and walls, he could hear music playing and the distant sound of another being, moving, breathing. Amadán, he suspected.

Beyond the reek of his own body, the sweat and vomit odours that clung to him, he could smell the old stone, the chill crispness of the air, the trace of Amadán's cigar smoke drifting through the crack beneath the door and the stale remains of the dreadful cheap tobacco the Magpies favoured. No one else. Maybe Rothman didn't have a scent anymore.

Cold brushed against his skin, the hair rising in mute

defence against it. Somewhere far off, someone was preparing raw meat, chopping through it with a cleaver. It was bloody and fresh. His mouth started to water, filling with a sweetness that left him unnerved.

He could still taste the blood. His mouth had been full of blood.

What had happened to him? What had Holly done? He couldn't deny the changes. He'd felt alive for the first time ever on the Hunt, yes and free too.

Seeing Izzy, seeing the horror on her face, just confirmed what he'd guessed. Holly had made him into a monster after all.

But here he was, free of her. He'd run and kept on running, running from Holly and what she would continue to make of him. And from Izzy and how she saw him. Until he had collapsed, unable to run anymore.

The door clicked and Jinx threw himself down behind the slab, instincts kicking in. He could ambush whoever it was, fight his way out. He could—

'Out you come, Jinx by Jasper,' said the Amadán in slow and measured tones. He spoke carefully, as one might to a berserk dog. 'I won't hurt you.'

Even Jinx could hear the lie in that. He uncoiled, rising to his feet in what he hoped was a nonchalant way, as if he hadn't just been planning an attack at all. The candlelight Amadán brought with him seemed too bright and he blinked, trying to shield his eyes.

'Well now,' Amadán said and this time a hint of wariness entered his voice. 'You've looked better. There are clothes there, you know? And we can provide some food too. You must be hungry.' Jinx's stomach did that dreadful twist and lurch. It must have shown on his face because Amadán's features looked pained. 'Or maybe not.' He didn't move any closer or set down the candelabra he held, just studied his prisoner with a calculating gaze. Finally he shook his head. 'You *are* still Jinx by Jasper, aren't you? Or is he gone?'

Jinx flinched back, unable to stop himself. Gone? No, not quite, but he half wished he was, that if what he feared was happening to him really was happening, he knew nothing of it.

'I'm Jinx,' he said, in that grating, alien voice.

'You don't look it, son.'

'I don't feel it either,' he admitted reluctantly. 'So what am I?'

'A Púca, if I'm any judge. And we have a problem.'

So many problems. Where to begin?

'Another one?' he asked.

'They're all dead. The angels ordered their destruction. It was something of a personal vendetta.'

'My father was a Púca.'

'Yes. I'm afraid he was. And I'm not sure how he survived as long as he did. Masquerading as Cú Sídhe maybe. Or a Cú Sídhe transformed to a Púca.'

'Do you know how?'

'No.' It was so final, so complete, that Jinx knew he was lying. That he didn't want to answer at all.

Chapter Eleven

Old Deals, New Debts

Izzy awoke from a dreamless sleep to pain and terrible memories. She curled in on herself, balling into a foetal position under the duvet and tried to make it not be real. The aches from her arms told her otherwise. Someone had bandaged them, an efficient and masterful job. Her gran or her dad, no doubt.

The door opened and someone came in, closing it behind them. She lay very still, keeping her breath slow and even, pretending to be asleep. The bed shifted under the weight of her visitor sitting on the edge.

'I know you're awake, Isabel,' said her grandmother.

Of course she did. Izzy pushed back the duvet and glared at her.

'Leave me alone.'

'To wallow in misery? I think not. You have to get up. You're needed.'

'Because I'm a Grigori. Right. I get it.' Venom threaded every word but Gran wasn't impressed.

'Do you? I don't think so. Do you know what that means now?'

Izzy shoved herself up on her wrists and instantly regretted it as pain lanced up the length of them, but with the pain came a fierce clarity and she sucked in a breath.

'You certainly did a job on yourself,' Gran went on, as critically as ever. Never a moment of caring, or concern. Never anything she would consider weakness. 'No sense of moderation. That's the problem with your generation. It's all or nothing, isn't it?'

'I *killed* him, Gran.'

'Yes, you did. You had to.'

'And then when I went to get him, he was already gone. Holly killed Donn. And the Storyteller too.'

Gran stroked her hair, an intimacy Izzy had never expected from Isolde Gregory. It shocked her into stillness.

'That isn't your fault, child,' she whispered. 'None of this is your fault. It is duty. You are Grigori. It cannot be helped. You have to be stronger, Isabel. We thought, with Brí as a mother, you would be the strongest of all the Grigori.'

'You didn't see him. You didn't see what she's turned him into. A killer. A monster. You didn't see him.'

'But I did,' said Brí, from the doorway.

Gran glared at her with fury radiating from every inch of her.

'Get out of here. You aren't welcome.'

Brí, being Brí, ignored her, which Izzy thought took some doing. 'Don't be a fool, Isolde. And an old fool at that. We made a deal, remember?'

'You cheated me.'

'Cheated you?' Brí laughed. She didn't have to sound like she was mocking. That would just rile Gran up even more. 'No. I gave you exactly what you asked for. You just can't see it. You were like Izzy once. A girl in love, just like her. You said you would do anything for David's father. For his legacy. And look what you did. You never had faith in David, so much so that you engineered a stronger heir for him. One you rejected when she was born a girl. You can't even see her worth. And the fae have the reputation of being cold-hearted. You put us all to shame.'

'I did what I had to,' Gran replied, suddenly stiff and formal. 'She is my grandchild, Brí.'

'Then afford her the same respect you demand. Tell her, Isolde.'

More secrets? More stupid, age-old secrets? That was all Izzy needed.

'Tell her what? That we made a mistake? That she didn't turn out as we hoped.'

'As *you* hoped,' Brí corrected her coldly.

Isolde Gregory narrowed her eyes and colour drained from her face in rage. For a moment Izzy thought she would fling herself at Brí, scratch her eyes out.

But Gran got to her feet, all tenderness forgotten, and left the room with her head held high.

And what did it matter? Izzy didn't care whatever deal Brí and Isolde had done, or why Brí and her father had ended up – she recoiled from that thought. It didn't matter now. None of that mattered. It was old history and she really didn't care anymore. It didn't help in any way and it made her too angry to think straight. She thought of that look in her grandmother's eyes. Maybe her temper didn't all come from Brí.

'Well,' said Brí. 'There we go then. That's us told.' And she slumped, catching herself against the doorframe. 'That all took more out of me than I'd thought. But it worked, didn't it?'

Did she mean the spell or facing down Gran? Izzy didn't know. But Brí didn't look too good either way.

Izzy nodded to the chair by the bed and reached out to push the laundry off it so Brí could sit down. The two of them sat in silence for some time. Outside she could hear a car on the road and the crows calling out to each other.

Calling out to her.

'What happened to Jinx?' Izzy asked at last.

Brí tried to smile, but it didn't seem to work. Her lips moved up for a moment but it was more than half a grimace.

'You killed him.'

'Yes, but when I went back to Donn's Hollow he was gone. Donn was dying.' She shuddered, remembering his papery skin, the wheeze of his last breath. 'Holly had taken Jinx, he said that she had power …'

'Oh she does. More than one of the Aes Sídhe knows how to deal with. She absorbed a Shining One, the one she had intended for Jinx. It is part of her now. Or she is part of it. Though I imagine that's the last thing she wanted. She's barely in control as it is. Now? Well, who knows. How would you know if you were controlling it or it controlling you? And it needs feeding.'

'Feeding?' That didn't sound good.

'Yes. Angels, demons, Sídhe … probably humans too though she won't get much from them. She doesn't have a touchstone so she has nothing else to sustain her. Power needs power, Izzy. Power from any source. She's probably ravenous all the time. No wonder she's psychotic.'

'Which explains what happened to her, but not to Jinx. He'd changed, Brí. He was different. And I wanted …' She couldn't say it.

'You wanted to kill him. You called him a monster, a creature. Other things.'

'Did he hear?' The guilt crushed her but she forced herself to look Brí in the eyes.

'Yes. He heard you, and saw himself with your eyes. He knows what you felt. I think he was trying to talk to you when you attacked him.'

Izzy buried her face in her hands and groaned. Oh God, poor Jinx. After all that, after being abandoned, enslaved …

'What did she do to him? His eyes—'

'It wasn't Holly, or at least not directly. His death, his rebirth

… He's a Púca. A creature of wild magic. You reacted to that. You couldn't help yourself.'

'I thought he was Cú Sídhe. And why couldn't I help it?'

'He was … before he died. But Púca are creatures reborn rather than born. Like his father. They have to die to become what they are meant to be. Like a butterfly in a chrysalis. That's all death is to them, you see? A transformation, a metamorphosis. They don't belong in this world or the next. They have no part in the Compact, no place in either heaven or hell. They are wild, beyond control. Heaven denounced them and they were wiped from the face of the earth. They are the first wanderers. The kings of the wanderers. They can slip into dreams, did you know that? Has he managed it yet?'

Dreams. She'd been having weird dreams.

'Except for Jasper.'

'So it seems. It's like a little circuit inside them, waiting to be switched on. And walking the halls of Donn's Hollow is the thing that does it.'

'But Jinx was there twice.'

'Which may just make him twice as bad. A wild Púca is a danger to us all. But you know that, Izzy. Deep down inside.'

She did and she didn't like that unexpected knowledge. It felt alien and wrong, like something else was pushing ideas and opinions into her brain. She gritted her teeth.

'Why?'

Brí smiled. 'Because you're Grigori. Who do you think the angels sent to destroy them? Who else?'

'I'm not going to – '

'Kill him? But you've done it twice already. Third time's the charm, isn't that what humans say?'

'And what would you do with him?'

'Capture him, contain him. Study him, if I can. Failing that …' her voice trailed off and for the first time since Izzy had met her, she wore her endless years, in her eyes if not on her face.

'You'll kill him.'

'Only if I have to. If I can. I care for that boy, Izzy. I cared for his father. But ultimately … yes. Any of the Aes Sídhe would do the same. The danger – the danger to all of us – is just too great.'

'Do they know what's happened to him? The others? The angels?'

'News like this has a way of spreading. Holly had control of him which I thought was impossible. I don't know how. Maybe just the years of abuse and control made him think she did. Brainwashing perhaps? How's he to know better? But when he encountered you … I think he broke free. Even someone as powerful as Holly can't fully control truly wild magic …'

'But that's good, isn't it? If he's free …'

'Good and bad. Good he is away from her, of course, and no longer part of the Hunt. You saw what *they* did and with a Púca among them, at the heart of them, all the lower fae and all the wanderers got snared in with them. They can't do that again, at least. But now he's alone, no pack, no Hunt. He will become the hunted.'

'Poor Jinx.'

'Poor Jinx nothing,' she scoffed. 'That's when he'll be most dangerous. Ugh, I named that boy well.'

'Where did he go? We have to find him, help him.'

But Brí shook her head. 'That I don't know.'

A discreet knock on the door interrupted them. Silver stood there, pushing it open. How much had she overheard, Izzy wondered, but just one look at her expression answered that. Enough.

'I may have found something. To answer that. Or rather, Clodagh has.'

Clodagh? Izzy frowned as her friend appeared at the top of the stairs, clutching her phone.

'It just came up on my feed,' she said, falling over the words. 'Reports of a huge dog loose in the city centre.'

'A dog?'

'Huge. With weird colouring. There's even some video. You couldn't miss him, Izzy. But get this, there were two guys with him, dressed all in black and white.'

When Jinx was very young, he'd listened to stories. Fae stories. Cú Sídhe stories. Mostly they involved a hero – male or female because Cú Sídhe were egalitarian when it came to heroics – who saved their pack from a great danger, often sacrificing themselves for the greater good. The more tragic the better because hounds loved to howl. But there was always a reason, always a group, always a sense of belonging to something bigger. Even when he was Holly's dog, he knew his place within the hierarchy. He was part of a collective with her at the head and him somewhere under her designer heels. Such sharp and unforgiving heels.

He had never felt as alone as he did right now. Sitting in the darkness of the morgue in Amadán's Hollow. Locked inside. He knew he was locked in because he'd tried the door when Amadán had been called away. He'd forgotten how many times but that didn't stop him trying one more time, just in case. In case of what he didn't know.

The last time he had been here, he had been an honoured guest. Amadán had wanted something from him then.

He had no doubts as to what he was this time. A prisoner.

And clearly Amadán wanted something from him this time as well, but Jinx didn't want to contemplate what that might be.

What am I? he thought desperately. *What have I become?*

And a voice seemed to drift out of nowhere, a voice familiar and the last thing he wanted to hear.

You know the answer to that, boy. You are what you always were meant to be.

That voice had guided him in Donn's realm and when he had been lost in his nightmares beforehand. It was Jasper, his father. It was the voice of all his bad dreams, the voice of the Púca.

'I don't know what *you* think I am,' he said out loud, and then felt like an idiot for venting his defiance on thin air.

Problem was, the voice wasn't talking entirely without truth. He could sense that. And it wasn't the only one to think he was a Púca now.

A creature, Izzy had called him. His mouth had been full of blood. He could still taste it. And all the time his own blood had been screaming with the need to kill. The Wild Hunt had embraced him as its leader and he had stepped seamlessly into the role.

As if it had been created for him.

Because it had. The leader of the Wild Hunt was meant to be a Púca.

Stories of the Púca always ended badly for everyone concerned. Especially for the Púca.

The lock turned and Jinx scrambled back to the darkest corner he could find. But the door only opened a crack.

'Listen,' Amadán whispered in harsh and hurried tones, 'don't say a thing. Don't make a noise. Not if you value your life.' The door closed silently and Jinx edged towards it.

Another voice joined Amadán and made Jinx's blood turn to ice. He leaned against the door, ear pressed to it, listening intently now and hoping to block it if the need arose.

'Property is property, Lord Amadán.' Osprey closed the door to the library behind him with a very theatrical slam.

'Of course,' Amadán replied, pouring himself a drink. 'Very true. But one would have to be in possession of said property in order to return it. Whiskey? It's really very good.'

'My Lord,' he said through gritted teeth. 'Your servants were seen with him. It was all very hard to miss, I believe.'

'"Servants" is an overstatement of our arrangement. I have no knowledge of where the Magpies have got to or what they may have picked up along the way. They come and go as they please. You know their reputations as well as I. Tell your Mistress—'

There was a flurry of movements, a thud and the sound of breaking glass as Osprey hurled the glass decanter against the wall beside the door. Jinx could smell the expensive liquid as it pooled in Amadán's priceless carpet and the glass shards tinkled as they fell beside it. Amadán leaped back and the door from the corridor was flung open.

'My Lord,' said Rothman, in a smooth, fluid voice. 'Perhaps your guest will find the Thompson machine gun of interest. A remarkable weapon, sir, as you can see. This model is loaded with special silver ammunition of my own devising so I should stand clear if I were you.'

The door to the morgue creaked open a little and Jinx pushed back, afraid that he had just given himself away, but Osprey, like any predator facing a hunter, couldn't take his eyes off the threat. And Rothman was indeed a threat. You could see that in his eyes. Jinx stared through the thin gap, unable to believe what he was seeing.

Osprey scowled at the butler and Jinx flinched. He knew that look too well. This wasn't over and Osprey wouldn't forget.

'Very well,' he said at last. 'But I will be back soon. And if you should find our little stray skulking about in a dark corner around here, you had best hand him back.'

Rothman saw him out, the machine gun never wavering. Amadán sank into the wing-backed armchair and drained the glass he still held in a slightly shaking hand.

'You'd better come out, boy. We need to talk.'

Jinx pushed the door open and stepped into the warmer room. The fire in the fireplace crackled and called him closer. It made him think of Izzy.

'I have to leave,' he said.

'And go where?'

'I don't know. Away from here. Osprey isn't lying. They'll be back for me. He knew I was here "skulking".'

Amadán just sighed and held out his now empty glass.

'The good stuff is in the back of the cabinet. Get it for me, there's a good lad.'

'That wasn't your good stuff he smashed? You said – '

Amadán laughed, although it wasn't as big and booming as it had been in the past. 'Not nearly. Got it from one of those German supermarkets. He'd never know the difference. Although, it wasn't half bad. Not half good either. Grand, you know? Fetch the other one.'

Jinx did as he was asked, pulling out a bottle older than he was and handing it the Aes Sídhe.

'I've always liked you, Jinx,' said Amadán. 'Liked your father too. Before he died — the first time, I mean. There wasn't another Cú Sídhe like him. And when he came back, well ... he was a walking wonder. Then he met your mother. Lovely girl, but ruled by her heart. Leanán Sídhe often are. Silver too.'

'How did he die? In the end I mean.'

Amadán finished his second glass and held it out for Jinx to refill it again. 'Holly cornered him and when he wouldn't join her ... well ... she's vicious when she doesn't get her way, as you know. Oh, but he loved that Belladonna. It cost him everything, but he still loved her. When he lost her ... he lost all hope. He went to his death himself.'

Not really an answer, was it? But it might be the best he'd get. No one wanted to talk about it. 'What should I do?' Jinx asked.

'Damned if I know, boy. Run seems the best bet. I could hand you over, but Holly's too powerful already. Rest tonight. Rothman will find you a room and I'll see what I can find in the library. There may be something. But Jinx, the other Púca before Jasper ...'

'They're dead. You said the angels wiped them out.'

'Well, yes, the angels ordered it. But they didn't do it. They didn't want to get their hands dirty on that little crusade. The Grigori were given that task, a holy diktat, no less. And it lingers on. Your little girlfriend and her family have a patho-logical hatred of your kind. They can't help themselves. It's hardwired.'

He'd seen it first-hand, although he didn't tell Amadán that. He didn't really want to admit it. 'Why?'

'Wild magic. It's beyond the laws of heaven and man. It's dangerous. And you, my dear boy, more or less embody it.'

'So what do I do? Just give up, lie down and wait to die?'

'Of course not. Heaven forbid, not in your nature, is it? I'd run, until I could run no more and go to ground. Somewhere safe, the older the better.'

Puck's castle Jinx thought, the name coming to him unbidden. That was where Art said all the wanderers were going. Before – before Holly got him. That was where he'd been going.

'I know where to go,' he whispered.

'Go then, but don't stop there too long. And don't tell me where. She'll be coming.'

'Lord Amadán, I am in your – '

He had been about to say debt, a formal and binding declaration and statement, and the only way he could offer thanks, but Amadán cut him off.

'Holly is too powerful. I don't want to be tied to you any more than I want you here when she comes back. You did me a service investigating what happened to Jay and dealing with the matter of the Fear, but we're even now, Jinx by Jasper. You can't come back here. And I'll be telling the Magpies to run you off should you try.'

Jinx nodded solemnly. It was more than enough. And he

knew better than anyone the power now at Holly's command. If he could sever ties with himself, he'd probably do it too.

'I'll go at once.'

'Ahhh,' Amadán sighed. 'Have a meal at least. Wait until dark. I'll send one of them with you to see you clear.'

It wasn't generosity. Jinx knew that. Amadán didn't want anyone to see him leaving. And he wanted the Magpies to make sure he was gone.

Chapter Twelve

Angelus

The Sídheways shivered and twisted in a disconcerting way. Silver reached out to the edges, running her hand against the divide. It clung like cobwebs on her fingers for just a moment before falling away to glimmers of light and moments captured by the corner of the eye. She frowned.

'What is it?' Dylan asked.

'They're damaged. I've noticed it for some time now. But it's getting worse. Spreading.'

'I thought … They're like paths.'

'Paths can be corroded.'

'But they've been here forever.'

She smiled. 'Not quite. A long time. I remember Amergin making them.' Of course she did. It was easy to forget how old Silver really was.

'Amergin?' He didn't like the way she said the name, softly, fondly.

'Oh hush.' She linked her arm with hims 'He was a magician. A bard. Like you. And he died thousands of years ago. *And* I wouldn't call us friends. Enemies in an uneasy truce, maybe. He tricked us all. We've never forgotten that.'

'What do you mean?'

Silver laughed at him and opened the way out. 'He made the Sídheways, split the world, having got us to agree to share the island. Silver-tongued devil, he was, but he could work magic like no one else. I never thought it would decay. I suppose nothing is forever though. I've seen Sídheways lost before, broken or torn. Just not so many and not so – '

They stepped into Dublin, into a pub carpark in the mountains, only halfway to Amadán's Hollow and suddenly found themselves surrounded. Any thoughts of the Sídheways and ancient dead magicians fled. There were angels everywhere. All of them were beautiful and grim, dressed in sombre greys and cream, like supermodels playing at being office workers.

'Lady Silver,' said one, its long auburn curls framing a face which could have been male or female and either way would have made a pre-Raphaelite painter weep with joy and despair. 'May we have a word with you?'

Silver moved subtly, placing Dylan behind her while at the same time reaching for his hand. He knew why. Even he was still feeling shaky with the after-effects of the spell this morning. Silver had shadows under her eyes and a grim cast to her mouth.

'Jophiel,' said Silver in carefully measured tones. 'It has been a long time since you trod this plane.'

Jophiel smiled, the face shining with beauty that made Dylan yearn for something. The music in him responded to the angel like no one but Silver. Him, Dylan decided. It was probably a him. But then an angel could present to the world however it wanted, couldn't it? He was so used to Ash hanging around with Clodagh and Izzy that she made it all seem very normal. Angels were far from normal, and this one was watching him with far too appraising an eye.

'Is this your touchstone? I've heard much about him. His music reaches to the heavenly court already. Most beautiful.'

Silver tightened her grip just a little, a warning and a slight show of possession perhaps, but it registered with him at the deepest level. He was in danger here. Maybe they both were.

'He is talented and dedicated,' she replied carefully.

'And successful. A *God-given* talent rewarded, one might say.' The emphasis on 'God-given' wasn't idly made, Dylan realised. It was laced with threat somehow and he didn't like it.

'One might,' Silver said. 'If one thought the Creator concerned himself with such things.' She smiled but the expression didn't quite reach her eyes. 'What brings you here, Jophiel? Not to discuss Dylan, I am sure.'

Jophiel glanced at the other angels. Dylan didn't recognise any of them and for that he was grateful. His experience with angels had not been good. Sorath had almost killed him. Zadkiel had almost gotten them all killed. Mostly, when they showed up, everything went bad rapidly. Only Ash seemed different, and even then, he wasn't sure. Maybe guardian angels were different, changed by spending time around humans. He wasn't certain if that made them lesser, as the so-called higher angels seemed to think. He was starting to suspect otherwise. Ash seemed more solid, somehow, more real, complete.

Jophiel stretched out elegant hands like spreading wings. 'Why? To discuss the *situation* of course. The situation in Dubh Linn. The balance of power is shifting rapidly. The Grand Compact is failing and the Grigori failing with it.'

'The Grigori?' Silver asked sharply. 'How is he failing?'

'He is no longer neutral. Surely you have noticed.'

'I've noticed that angels and demons keep trying to force his hand in all things, if that is what you mean. I've noticed him steering a fair path through an extremely biased river.'

The angel was put out by the reply, Dylan could tell. It didn't show on his face. But his apparent openness vanished. A veneer was stripped away, leaving something cold and impenetrable. 'We need you to accompany us,' he said. The tone was not a request. It was a cop voice, a cop face, not to be argued with, determined.

Silver didn't budge. 'Where?'

'To discuss terms. To decide on a new alliance.'

'And if I refuse?'

'There is no refusal, Silver.'

She stiffened. 'I think you'll find there is. If I decide so. Think carefully. What if I decide not to go?'

A group of people stumbled out of the pub behind them, laughing and joking about the weather. Loud and a bit pissed and in high spirits. They weren't even paying attention to the stand-off in the car park. Why should they? It wasn't part of their world. Most of them probably didn't even see it.

But suddenly the stand-off in the car park was paying very close attention to them.

They stopped, unsure, able to see far too much now. But not able to move.

Jophiel opened his mouth and a keen, high note came out. One by one all the other angels joined in, each one almost hitting the same note but not quite, each one more off key than the last. The sound built, discord upon discord. Silver clamped her hand on Dylan's and he felt her power rise, his reserves of it joining in, building a shell of protection around them both. They were stronger together and worked on that unity.

But they couldn't protect the group of human bystanders stumbling on to the scene. One of them managed a whimper of pain as she fell, as they all fell, bodies twitching, blood pouring from noses, ears and tear ducts. They arched in agony, twisting and clawing at the ground.

'Stop it,' Silver yelled, furious, but the angels didn't obey her. The sound intensified, the song flowing further afield and screams began inside the building. Shrieks and crashes followed, the sound of people hemmed in, trying to escape, unable to do so. The windows shattered, spraying glass into the interior.

And suddenly everything was still – the sound, the bodies, the air around them. They were dead inside as well as outside, all of them, everything human except him.

'Stop it,' Silver said again, but quieter now. Not defeated perhaps, but resigned. 'We'll talk. But I promise nothing.'

Jophiel smiled. Triumph didn't suit him. He looked like a smug child and Dylan loathed him even more.

'Good news,' he cried, jubilant and Dylan clenched a fist, ready to punch him if the opportunity arose. 'See? That wasn't so difficult, Silver. We have our first agreement.'

She raised her lip in disgust and glanced towards the devastated pub.

'Tell that to them.'

'They're just *humans*, Silver. It's not like they really feel anything. Not for long, anyway. Now, shall we go?'

Mum came in with a wickedly sharp pair of scissors and a gleam in her eye that said Izzy had better sit still or it'd be more than her life was worth. Clodagh carefully gathered up all the long strands of Izzy's hair and binned them, trying to make as little noise as possible. No one mentioned the cuts on her arms and all the other scars. She'd managed to keep them hidden until now. Not anymore.

But no one said a word. As if they didn't know what to say.

'Well, it's not too bad,' Mum said at long last, carefully putting the scissors out of sight. For a minute Izzy could only stare at her. But then Mum tousled her newly cropped hair. 'Although what they'll say at the hairdressers, I don't know. It actually suits you with the tattoo. I suppose it doesn't matter about hiding it anymore. They all know who you are anyway.'

Izzy reached up tentatively to her head. She felt strangely lightheaded, almost dizzy. Mum turned her ever so gently towards the mirror and some other girl stared back at her. A girl too thin for her frame, whose haunted eyes had dark hollows beneath them. The elfin haircut made her look too vulnerable, fragile. Not like herself at all. Izzy swallowed hard, aware of the way her throat worked as she did it. Her ears and the back of her neck felt so cold.

'It looks really good,' Clodagh said, loyal to the last. 'Ash, doesn't it? You'll see, Izzy. A bit of makeup, a bit of gel or something – '

Izzy ran her hand a little more confidently through her new short hair. She even tried a smile and that wasn't hideous.

'Rachel?' Dad called from the hall. 'The coffee machine is making a weird noise!'

Mum rolled her eyes to heaven. 'What's he done now? I'll just be downstairs. And Clodagh and Ash are here. Okay?'

'Okay.' Izzy tried that smile again and Mum seemed convinced because she left.

Izzy looked up at her anxious friends, the way they watched her, waiting. It was too much and she burst into tears again.

Jesus, this was crazy, she thought, furious with herself. She had to stop crying and wailing. She had to get up and get on with things. Find Jinx.

But he'd loved her hair. He used to thread his fingers through it, all the way down its length, like it was made of strands of gold or silk.

'It really does too look okay,' Clodagh assured her. Ash had joined them again and the two of them were holding hands covertly. Or rather failing to be covert about it. But that very fact told Izzy how worried they were. They'd make abysmal spies. Except, of course, that Ash had made a very fine spy indeed in the run up to Halloween, until Dad recognised her.

When she was with Clodagh, there was something different about the angel. Something almost more human, more real, as if she was suddenly grounded and stronger with the friend-ship they shared. Maybe she just felt accepted. Izzy knew how important that could be. Now more than ever.

Izzy pushed the thoughts away and tried to focus on eve-rything else. Grigori matters for one thing, like angels and demons. And Sídhe. Her friends' relationships, and her hair, didn't matter.

'Silver and Dylan should have checked in by now,' Ash said. 'There's something wrong. I can feel it. Something in the air.'

'Angels?' asked Clodagh, a flicker of concern making her step a bit closer.

'Yes. There are factions, some who believe it is time for change. Not a popular view for my kind. We don't do change.

It has led to dark places before. And yet, there are many who believe Zadkiel was right.'

'Zadkiel was nuts,' Izzy said.

'He's convincing,' said Ash. 'And not finished yet I fear. No matter how hard I've tried. He survives. He has supporters. He hates anything less than the highest of angels. Even guardians.'

But she would say no more than that, no matter how hard or subtly Clodagh pushed. She left them, saying she needed to talk to Izzy's dad.

'I have to go too,' said Izzy when the two of them were alone. 'I have to find Jinx.'

'Izzy,' warned Clodagh, 'the last time that didn't work out too well.'

'I was … angry. I didn't … think.'

'Shocking. And you're still angry. Plus a bit …' She stopped as if she had said too much.

'A bit what?'

'Nothing.'

'Were you going to say crazy?'

'I've known you since we were five. Crazy isn't the word for it.'

Izzy groaned and sank back on the bed. 'What do I do, Clo? I almost killed him. Again. I tried to. I *wanted* to.'

'Really?'

'Yes, really.' And she had. She'd looked into those golden eyes and she'd known to the core of her being that he needed to die, that this was her duty and nothing could stop her from doing it. She just … she hadn't known it was Jinx. Or hadn't recognised who Jinx was.

She was still terrified of what she might have done.

'Have you talked to anyone about it? Your dad? Brí?'

'Would you?'

'I don't know who else I'd ask. Someone I trust, anyway.'

'Like Ash?' It was, admittedly, more than a little sly but she couldn't help herself there either. 'Maybe.' Clodagh may have known Izzy since she was five but it worked both ways and Izzy had known Clodagh just as long.

'And you two – you know?'

'Izzy!'

Oh God, too much information in one exclamation.

'Seeing each other. I mean seeing each other. Nothing else. Just – I don't know!'

'Maybe. I think. I don't know either.'

'But you like her.'

'Yes, but – look, I just – She gets me'

And who was Izzy to argue or debate this? Given her obsession with a shape-shifting fae hound?

'Okay then,' she said and Clodagh seemed to relax, just a little. 'Okay, but what do I do, Clodagh? I need to find him. I need to know that he's okay. But Brí said … Grigori and Púca …' She shook her head. 'She says I'm hardwired to kill them.'

'Well, technically, you've already done that twice. Haven't you?'

Chapter Thirteen

Prey

They came with nightfall. Jinx, who had spent the afternoon and evening sleeping, woke up sharply, sweat standing out on his skin, his breath catching in his throat. And he knew. He knew more clearly than he'd ever known anything in his life.

They were coming for him.

Panic struck him first. He was locked in a room in Amadán's Hollow. He was trapped and they were coming.

He needed a way out.

Listening at the door yielded nothing. He tried the handle again, rattled it hard until, to his surprise, he heard footsteps outside. Someone cleared their throat.

'If you would be so good as to step back from the door, sir,' said Rothman in clipped tones. 'I have no wish to be set upon and I am here to release you.'

Jinx swallowed hard. He had no reason to attack the butler, especially if what he said was true. But trust came hard. He bared his teeth, ready to change in a heartbeat.

'Okay,' he said, not bothering to keep the wariness from his voice.

The key turned in the lock, the clanking echoing strangely down here, and Rothman opened the door. But he didn't come inside.

'See?' said Mags from beside the butler. 'Told you he'd be ready for anything.' The Magpie was holding a particularly shiny hunting knife. Ready for anything indeed.

'You *do* wish to leave, sir, is that not so?'

Keeping his gaze fixed on Mags, Jinx stepped out into the hall. Rothman held a sack of some kind out to him.

'Some provisions. And there are some warm clothes as well. Should you need them.'

'We'll have a rare old time,' said Mags with that horrid grin.

'Indeed,' Rothman replied, his face betraying nothing.

He was either a master of sarcasm and understatement or the whole thing slipped past him entirely. Jinx couldn't tell. But the sense of panic was rising so he said nothing.

'Where is Amadán?' asked Jinx. 'I need to talk to him. To warn him.'

'He's gone, man,' said Mags. 'And we should be gone too.'

Jinx glared at him. 'What's this "we" you keep going on about?'

Mags grinned dangerously. 'Oh, I'm coming with you. Keep

you out of trouble, you know? The boss said so.'

'Listen, they're coming. Holly and her hunt. Do you two understand what that means? What they'll do? I know there are other people here, his servants, allies or whatever. Do you realise what they'll do to everyone here when they – '

'Less than they'll do if they find you here, sir,' said Rothman abruptly. 'Forgive my impatience. His Lordship feels he can negotiate and indeed prevaricate if he has the chance, so long as you are not under his roof, as it were. You must go. Mags will guide you.'

Of course, if Jinx wasn't here, Holly and Osprey had no reason to attack. They would gain nothing. Amadán was right. Or at least Jinx hoped he was. But travel with a Magpie? He didn't like the sound of that.

'I know you think you're a hard man, Jinxy boy,' Mags told him, in that familiar, lazy drawl. 'I get that. But we don't have time for any aggro now. We've got to scatter, yeah? They're a bunch of head the balls, you know? The Old Man'll deal with it. Let's hustle.'

Though he hated to agree with a Magpie, Jinx knew he didn't have much of a case here. Mags was right. Rothman led them to a small side entrance and opened the narrow door out into the night.

'Good luck, sir,' said Rothman, as Jinx stepped out of the warmth of the Hollow onto the bitterly cold mountain-top. Mags unfolded through the door, his long coat flapping about him.

'See you, man,' he said grudgingly to Rothman. 'Ready?'

Jinx nodded and settled the backpack on his body. Mags brought nothing with him so either he didn't need anything or Jinx was doing all the heavy lifting. They set off through the snow together, heads down and silent. The coat and the boots were good, insulating him against the worst of the cold. Changing might make him faster and surer on his feet but not for long. It was cold, even for a Cú Sídhe, who if truth be told far preferred warm summers and cosy dens to running through a winter's night. No, he was better in Aes Sídhe form with Mags, looking for all the world like just another pair of hikers. One of whom looked like he was dressed for a riot rather than hiking. In the snow, in the night.

A really, really stupid pair of hikers to be out in this terrain on a night like this, but that couldn't be helped.

They hadn't got far when he heard it. Mags stopped beside him and said nothing as Jinx listened, his body stiff with alarm. A great host approached, racing through the night. It was the noise of a rushing wind, made up of howls and shrieks, of rage and spite. It echoed through the night and Jinx dropped to the ground, crawling to the cover of a rocky outcrop. Mags followed, silently and fleetly, never even raising a question. Maybe he heard it too. Jinx didn't know if Suibhne hearing was as good as that of the hounds and now wasn't the time to ask.

Monsters swarmed up the side of the mountain. They snuffed out lights as they passed, the feeble yellow streetlamps,

the lights of farmhouses and barns, even the far-off traffic
lights. The world turned primal and dark.

But there was one light. One terrible light.

In their midst, Holly walked, all aglow with power, her
golden hair like rays of sunlight. Where she passed, the show
sizzled and evaporated, leaving burnt earth in her wake.

All around her the darkest creatures of the fae cavorted.
Many more of them now. Giant figures that lurched and
roared, like walking trees and rock formations. Wisps and
sheeries bright like demented fireflies. Grey men walked,
making the world even colder as they went, freezing the air
and raising the wind to wintry storms. There were Aes Sídhe
too, led by Osprey in his fluttering feather cloak, beautiful
and terrible, their faces alight with the fire of zealots. They
gazed at Holly in adoration, but with terror too. They wanted
to look at her but were afraid she would look back. He didn't
blame them for that.

Worst of all were the Cú Sídhe, the young outcasts, ensnared
by the Wild Hunt, the feral and the wild, the rabid ones that
had no pack because no pack would have them.

Like him. Because what pack would welcome him now?
He was a monster, not Cú Sídhe anymore. Something to be
destroyed. The only person who wanted him was Holly and
he couldn't give himself up to that again.

He could see the madness in their eyes. It called to him,
the Hunt, and even now he had to fight the need to run to
them, to take his place once more at its heart, to become

its heart. For a moment he would have. He couldn't have stopped himself.

Mags hissed and Jinx glanced at him, at the giant black disks of his eyes, at his bared teeth and at the knife he held, ready to attack should Jinx make a move. He was shaking, fighting the same driving need that Jinx was and Jinx saw himself reflected in Mags' crazy eyes. He looked just as bad.

Trembling, Jinx lifted a finger to his lips and Mags nodded, lowering the knife. They were okay. As far as they could be okay.

Holly stopped at the doorway to Amadán's Hollow, her Hunt roiling around her like a stormy sea. The immense black stones loomed out of the snow. She reached out one hand, laying it flat on the space between the stones. The pulse of magic made the air reverberate.

'Come out, come out, wherever you are,' she intoned and laughed, a dark ancient laugh which sounded nothing like her at all. Holly had always been so controlled. This … this was insane, the voice of someone to whom it didn't matter what anyone thought and who found it amusing that anyone might care.

She pushed again, a second strange pulse of magic which he felt like a punch to the guts. It twisted inside him, turning into knives.

'I won't ask twice,' she said.

Jinx shrank back amid the rocks. 'They're gone, aren't they? There's no one in there,' he whispered. Mags shook his head, his mouth a hard line. 'What?'

'Some of them can't leave.'

The door opened, a shimmering line in the air between the rocks, and Rothman stood there. Only Rothman. With a jolt, Jinx realised what Mags meant. Rothman probably wasn't alone in there, but he was the only one facing Holly, a single human, over a hundred years old, with an obviously misplaced sense of loyalty.

'Lord Amadán is currently unavailable, Madam.' His tone didn't waver. He was as he always was, the consummate professional, even when faced with all the horrors the fae had to offer before him.

'Unavailable?' Holly smiled and Jinx knew that expression. Nothing good came of it. 'And after we've come all this way? Come here, little man. Let me see you in the moonlight.'

'No,' Mags hissed. 'He can't. She wouldn't ...'

But she would. Jinx knew she would. Rothman shuddered and his hand came up, gripping the stones to try to stop himself. But the need to obey her was too strong. The Shining One in Holly just laughed and the colour drained from Rothman's face.

'My Lady, please ...' He groaned, struggling to keep his demeanour now. 'I cannot set foot beyond the door.'

'We have to help him,' Jinx whispered. Maybe they could create a diversion, a distraction, anything. But even as he tried to rise, Mags clamped his hand onto his arm in a vicelike grip and forced him down.

'Brave man to speak to me so,' Holly taunted. 'Do you think I care what geis is upon you? I've given you an order and that is what you do, isn't it? Obey orders?' Her glow became even brighter, more intense and terrible.

'Madam,' his voice shook, his perfect deportment crumbling. 'Please—'

'Obey me,' she snapped, her short patience at an end. 'Outside. Now!'

Stuttering a cry of dismay, the butler stepped out of the Hollow which had sustained and shielded him for so long. Years beyond counting, he had served Amadán and remained as he once was, unchanging, like a fly in amber. But now, as his foot sank into the slushy remains of the snow, and the moonlight illuminated him, the protection fell away. He stiffened, taking a deep breath of the night air, and he raised his face to the light. His body convulsed just once and froze. Holly reached out, her hand aglow, and brushed the side of his face in an almost gentle gesture. Like paper that burnt so hot the image remains behind until disturbed, Rothman crumbled to ashes. The breeze blew his remains away across the snow.

Jinx covered his mouth to keep in any sound that might escape. What had he been thinking to face her? Only his duty, the role he played. Hadn't it occurred to him what she might do?

Mags' hand went limp and fell away from Jinx's arm. He swore, wrapping his arms around himself.

The door to the Hollow stood open and unattended. Holly

turned to her followers.

'Find Jinx. Find Amadán. Kill everyone else.'

'We have to get out of here,' Jinx said to Mags who nodded grimly. A shadow fell across them, a shadow which made Jinx freeze, his heart lurching up as if it could still escape. Osprey's cloak fluttered around his body as he perched on the rock above them. He looked down with eyes that gleamed gold and copper, made even brighter by the band of black on his face. Light swirled beneath his skin and a line of tattoos marked his neck.

'Not going so soon, are you?' said Osprey, his voice a ripple of malice.

Chapter Fourteen

Negotiations

Dylan paced the length of the floor while Silver sat very still on one of the polished benches. He knew she was fuming but could do nothing about the situation just yet. But she would. The National Gallery was deserted so late in the night but that didn't bother the angels who had just walked in and made themselves at home. Jophiel was studying a picture of hell, a huge, lurid affair filled with fire and naked bodies in torment. The expression on the angel's face spoke of confusion and when he turned towards Dylan it left him transfixed.

Angels were dangerous. He knew that better than anyone. Sorath had almost killed him, and for no real reason other than that he was close to Izzy and possibly convenient. Not because he was someone, or because he had value himself. And now he was here, surrounded, because he was with Silver.

'Humans really think it is like this?' asked Jophiel and waited expectantly for an answer.

'No,' said Dylan. 'Well, not now. Maybe when this was painted. Why? Is it?'

'It's much worse. Strange though … why portray it this way when you do not believe it to be so?'

'Symbolism.' The angel gave him a blank, uncomprehending look. 'It represents other things – loss, despair, hopelessness.'

'They don't understand abstracts,' said Silver, flatly. 'The concepts are too much for them. The less time they spend with us, with humans, on our plane, the more difficult it is for them to comprehend. Or indeed, explain anything. There's no point, Dylan.' She stood up, smoothing down her suit. 'Why are we here, Jophiel?'

'We are waiting, Lady Silver.'

'No, we *have been* waiting but now the waiting is over. I've had enough. I want some answers or we are leaving.'

'I have answers,' said Jophiel, still calm and unruffled. 'But I am expecting company. Please do not mistake my respect for weakness, Lady Silver.'

She scowled at him, unwilling to stand down, furious at being held here. 'And what company are you expecting?'

'Me, I think,' said a familiar voice. Azazel walked through the arched doorway, though he had not been visible on the other side until that moment. Shadows clustered around him, flowing like oil along the floor and walls, his shades, his constant companions. 'Though the invitation was not exactly polite, cousin.'

Jophiel shook back long red–gold curls with an air of defiance. Didn't like being called cousin, Dylan could tell that much. 'I informed you that you must come to discuss a new Compact.'

'A new Compact? What's wrong with the old one? I wrote more than half of that. And where is the Grigori?'

'I am tasked to propose a new Compact without the Grigori. As *you* know he is compromised on all sides.'

'Tasked by whom?' Azazel muttered. 'I don't deal with underlings.'

'And who is to represent mankind in this without him?' asked Silver warily.

'Your touchstone can take that role,' Jophiel replied with a dismissive wave. 'There is little to it. Now, shall we discuss terms?'

'Terms?' Silver glanced at Azazel, who just glared at the angel as if he would rather wring Jophiel's neck.

'Your terms of surrender, of course.'

'To whom? To you?'

'If we are to face the greater threat your dam now represents it is imperative that you surrender to the will of Heaven in all matters immediately – both fae and demon.'

It all revolved back to Holly, didn't it? Silver and her mother might be enemies now, Dylan thought as he tried to push down his anger, but she'd never shake off those ties. Not in the eyes of heaven. The angels just expected everyone to fall into line. Everyone. Even Silver. Even him.

'Come now, let us agree. Then we can—'

Fuming, Dylan cleared his throat loudly. 'What if I refuse?'

All three of them looked at him, startled as if he had grown an extra head.

'What?' said Jophiel, completely bewildered.

'You say if they surrender – demons and fae! You don't mention humans. What if I refuse? There are a lot of us. We don't surrender easily. David and Izzy won't obey you. Well, here's the thing. Neither will I.'

The anger simmering beneath the angel's exterior boiled forth. He reached out a hand and suddenly there were others with him, all singing, incanting that terrible tune. The air around Dylan grew thick and syrupy. He couldn't move. Worse, he couldn't breathe. Spots of light flickered in front of his eyes and he tried to find Silver through the gathering dark.

Magic blazed up in his chest, dangerous and unfocused. He didn't know if she called it or he did, and frankly he didn't care. He seized it and flung it in the direction of Jophiel's last position. It broke on the angel like a wave, driving him back only a step or two but it was enough. The spell smothering Dylan fractured and more magic flooded in to take its place. He gripped it more firmly and took a step forward.

'Lady Silver, control your pet,' shrieked the angel.

She laughed. That pure, bright, bell-like sound he loved.

'My "pet"? Dear me, Jophiel. Better pay attention to your

own words. You named him a full party to this debate. I can't control him anymore, it seems, than you can. Besides, he's my partner, rather than my pet. Don't you understand them by now? They aren't apes any more. They have free will and reasoning minds.'

The power in his grip felt warmer, as her pride in him filled him and he smiled at her. Yes, partners. That was right. Together, they couldn't fail, he knew that.

'And what say you, demon?' asked Jophiel, his voice shaking as he looked, of all places, to the demon for support.

Azazel examined his fingernails for a moment or two. 'The thing is,' he said at last, as if weighing every word. 'The thing is, I rather like the Grigori we have, having put rather at lot of work into their line over the years.' He grinned and his teeth were sharp and bright. There were too many of them in his mouth. 'So I will be saying no as well.'

The angel gaped at them, taken aback. 'But you cannot refuse. This is the will of heaven.'

'Is it, though?' asked the demon. 'We only have your word for that. The rest of us are cut off, as it were. You're no Metatron, or Gabriel. You certainly aren't a Michael, though God alone knows where he's got to. No, you may stand high-*ish* but not *that* high. I don't know if it's God's will, a collective angelic decision or just some whim of yours, or more likely whoever is your puppetmaster. So I'll stick with the Compact we have, even if it is held together with string and glue.'

'I don't – I don't understand,' stammered Jophiel.

'He said no,' Silver told him flatly. 'We all did.'

The angel closed his eyes. His lips moved for a moment. Dylan wondered if he was counting to ten to keep from losing his temper, but then he stopped and opened his eyes again. They were fixed on Silver and they blazed with hatred.

'I tried, General,' said Jophiel.

'Of course you did,' came a too familiar voice.

Silver grabbed Dylan's arm, half, he feared, for reassurance, half to keep him in check.

'Zadkiel?' Azazel gave a mocking laugh. 'Have they not seen sense and cast you out yet? You're slippier than a greased eel, my friend.'

'No friend of yours, Azazel.' Zadkiel appeared in a shimmer of light, as arrogant and terrible as Dylan remembered him. He wasn't dressed in white this time but in a pale grey tailor-made suit. In his hand he carried a spear, as tall as he was, the point gleaming with an unnatural light.

The other angels bowed and Silver frowned, although she said nothing. Not yet.

'Got an upgrade, I see,' said Azazel, his voice heavy with loathing. 'How did you swing that? Bribery? Blackmail?'

Zadkiel thrust the spear towards him and the demon took an uncharacteristic step back. 'My brethren chose me. I hold the spear that commands the hosts of heaven, foul demon. And with it thou shalt be crushed.'

'You don't crush people with a spear,' Azazel scowled as he spoke, his bored tone belied by the tension that riddled his body. 'They're more stabby, impaley, you know?' He shook his head. 'Why are you doing this particular little show, Zadkiel? You broke the compact to begin with. Why draw up a new one?'

'The Grigori have failed. To be honest the whole experiment with the Sídhe and the humans has failed. Eventually all heaven will see the truth. And if you won't cooperate we'll just have to take more direct measures.'

'What do you mean?' asked Silver.

'Show her, Jophiel.' He folded his arms, watching smugly as Jophiel rubbed his hands together, clapped them sharply and then spread his arms wide.

A shimmering net of lines appeared, each one glowing a different colour. It looked like one of those night time photos from the space station or a map of electrons in the brain. Some points glowed bright as new stars. Others glimmered, threads of gossamer on the air. They stretched in every direction, some changing colours on the way. At the edges they were weaker and worn, frayed threads, and in places it looked like holes had been torn through them. Many strands hung loose, broken.

'What is it?' asked Dylan, fascinated. It seemed to him as if the whole thing sang, tiny vibrations on vibrations making it hum with life. He leaned closer, listening. It was delicate but beautiful, this music, like the songs of distant worlds and pulsing stars.

'Silver can tell you,' said the archangel.

'The Sídheways?' she said, not sounding so sure. 'It sounds like that – but ... but how are you doing this?' She reached out one elegant hand as if to touch it.

'Ah-ah,' said Zadkiel. 'You might break something. For example, if I was to do this ...'

He grabbed one flailing strand and pulled hard, yanking it away.

Silver cried out as the strand turned to motes of dust in his hand, and three other strands snapped free, hanging limp and useless in the web.

'Stop!' she cried. 'You'll break them all. You'll destroy Dubh Linn.'

He leaned in close and deliberately wiped the dust on her sleeve. 'Yes, I will. The humans will see you as you truly are and what will they do, Silver?'

'They'll kill us. If we're lucky. Is that ... is that what you want?'

'What I want...' He smiled, a cruel and terrible expression. 'It isn't a case of what I want. But what heaven demands.'

'What?'

'You can't give me it. But Azazel can. A peace offering. Sorath's spark. Not much to ask, is it?'

She looked to the demon, hopelessly, her eyes pleading. But he was unmoved.

'If I was to hand that back to heaven, it wouldn't be to you. She was one of the most powerful angels to sit in the Holy Court, the strongest to fall since Lucifer. Her spark would raise you far too high. What's the plan? Become God? Dangerous idea that, as your unlamented brother discovered.'

Zadkiel ignored him and drew a sword. It was golden, the hilt ornate and beautiful, but the blade looked very sharp indeed. He swished it through the air experimentally.

'Please,' Silver whispered. 'Please don't. You can't do this. The Sídheways, the Compact ... everything we've built here ... everything!'

'It's up to the three of you. I want my sister's spark.'

She looked at the demon again. 'Azazel, please. What do you want? What can I offer you?'

His gaze turned cunning, nasty. He looked at Dylan, so much deliberate meaning in his eyes.

'One pure soul, perhaps?' He laughed.

'Me?' Dylan asked.

'You? Fancy yourself, don't you? No. Not you. I'll decide who. You're not pure, not anymore. Not with so much of this one's magic in you. But you could be of great use to me. Yes, you'd be a start. And someone will need to go and retrieve the thing. I'm not going.'

'You don't have it?' asked Silver.

'Not as such. I crossed someone I should not have crossed and the Keeper ... well, there was bargaining. It was a payment, recompense. You'd call it *Eineclan*.'

An honour price, a debt to repay some terrible slight against another. It was something the Aes Sídhe lived by. What had he done and who had he owed to pay such a valuable price?

'The Keeper?' Dylan asked. 'Who's the Keeper?'

Azazel grinned, all his teeth on display. 'Wouldn't you like to know?'

'Stop it, you two,' said Silver, trying to put herself between Zadkiel and the network of Sídheways, her eyes never leaving the sword. 'We'll work something out. But we need time. And we'll need to consult the Grigori, David Gregory ...'

'No,' said Zadkiel. 'If neither of you have what I want this is pointless. You're of no use to me, Silver and neither are your people. Jophiel, now.'

They turned to see Jophiel on the far side of the glowing network. He pulled a long knife, purely functional this one, and wickedly sharp. He moved faster than Dylan could follow, slicing through the lines of light.

Silver lunged forwards, grabbing the strands before they could fall, trying to pull them back together. With a word that sounded like a curse, Jophiel punched the knife right at her and Dylan didn't think. He just acted.

Lightning burst from his hands. It struck the angel full on, driving him backwards as if he had been hit by a bus. The knife fell with a clatter and Jophiel thudded against the far wall. For a moment he stared at Dylan in shock and then he burst into motes of light too, so bright the others staggered back. They hung in the air for a moment and then blinked out, leaving only an after-image of his form and horrified face on the green paint.

It looked like graffiti, a painted angel on the gallery wall.

'Dylan,' Silver gasped and there was pain in her voice. She stood, tangled in the threads. They wound about her and through her, burrowing under her skin, making her part of them.

'Oh God,' Dylan said, and reached for her.

'No! Stay back. I have … I have to hold them together. Otherwise we're all lost. The Market, the fae, everyone. All the ones who can't hide. You have to find Sorath's spark, understand? Not them. You've got to.'

As she spoke the Sídheways flared and glowed and she gasped, throwing back her head in pain. They tightened their grip on her, feeding off her like some parasitic creature.

Zadkiel drew himself up again, a look of murder in his eyes. 'You have until the solstice dawn, until midwinter and no more. If I don't have what I want, your Matriarch will die and the Sídheways will fall, leaving the fae to the tender mercies of humankind. Understand? That's only if she doesn't fail before that.'

He raised his hands and the glowing web, Silver, and all the angels were gone.

Dylan sucked in a breath, surrounded by shades and the demon who commanded them in the abandoned gallery.

'Well then,' said Azazel. 'What'll we do with you?'

'Do with me?'

He nodded to the image left by Jophiel, his features still clearly visible, his mouth open in a scream. 'You did just kill an angel, boy. I'd rather say that makes you one of ours.'

The house was quiet as Izzy slipped downstairs and out the door, closing it behind her silently. She didn't mean to sneak out, but they weren't going to let her go, not now, not after yesterday, and she knew where she needed to be now, what she had to do. Not logically, perhaps, but instinctively. Which was even more frightening. She felt like some kind of homing beacon had been turned on in her head. She couldn't fight it.

What she hadn't counted on was company. Clodagh was waiting for her at the end of the road, muffled up in overcoat, scarf, hat and gloves. She still looked like she was freezing, her breath misting in front of her.

'Have you been using your angel to spy on me?'

Clodagh tried to look innocent. 'I'm just out for a walk. That's not a crime, is it?'

'You? In this temperature?'

'Well,' she replied, her cheeks turning a little redder. 'We knew you'd do something stupid. You always do. And someone has to keep an eye on you. You've got too sneaky by far.'

'You might want to make yourself useful then. Where's Ash? I need to go somewhere.'

'She's not a taxi service, you know? Where are we going?'

She emphasised the 'we' and Izzy frowned at her. 'You won't like it.'

'When do I ever?'

The hilltop was covered in snow, far deeper and more treacherous than in the low-lying populated suburbs. Up here, the wind felt bitterly cold. The ruined cairn was invisible, covered in a thick white blanket, but the grey bulk of the Hellfire Club stood out against it like an insult. There was little sign of life around them, barely any animal tracks or sounds, but it was the heart of winter and why would there be? But it was eerie. Trudging through the knee-deep snow felt almost sacrilegious.

'Bloody *hate* this place,' Clodagh muttered for the umpteenth time, clapping her gloved hands together and blowing on them in a vain attempt to keep them warm.

'I know,' Izzy replied. 'But I need some answers.' She squinted at the entrance to the ruin. 'You can wait out here if you want.'

'Not feckin' likely.'

'Clodagh,' said Ash, also bundled up against the cold like any other, regular, girl. She even had a hand-knitted bobble-hat in bright red, but Izzy didn't think some doting grandmother had made it for her. Maybe she willed it into existence. She could hardly imagine angels sitting around with knitting needles clacking away. 'Clodagh, I can take you home and return for Izzy.'

So Ash didn't like the idea of going back in there anymore than Izzy did and she certainly didn't want her girlfriend going. But Clodagh had that fixed, stubborn look that Izzy was starting to dread.

'I'm not letting her go in there alone. And you *know* she would. No, we go in together.'

She held out her gloved hands, almost childlike, and waited. Reluctantly, because they couldn't deny her, both Izzy and Ash each took a hand and together they walked into the darkness.

Who else would do this with her? Izzy wondered. Only Dylan and Dylan was nowhere to be found, or so Dad said. To the others, not her. Everyone was being so bloody careful around her that it was becoming impossible to do anything. But she wasn't an idiot. And she could hear their whispers. Their fears. She didn't like to think what was giving her the ability to do that.

They'd been here before. When Donn had tested each of them and had given Izzy his fiery sword, they'd each seen key moments, temptations and nightmares. What Clodagh and Ash had seen, Izzy had never found out and she had never managed to get up the nerve to ask. Izzy herself had seen the moment when she realised Jinx couldn't be trusted. And the moment when she realised that he loved her.

The shiver of passing through the veil from one world to another ran through her body, right to the depths of her. It rippled through the chambers of her heart. Scorching air washed over her – so unexpectedly hot that it stole her breath for a moment. She gasped aloud in surprise and looked around, expecting fires, furnaces or lava. But there was nothing. The chamber was as bleak and empty as when she'd last been here.

She'd been alone then. The broken throne still spilled across the flood but the corpse of Donn had been removed for burial. If he had followers, other than the treacherous Reaper, they too had dispersed.

The dead were nowhere to be seen.

'What happens to the fae when their Lord or Lady dies?' she asked Ash.

But Ash just shrugged. 'They find another to follow, I guess. Or become wanderers. With no allegiance, like they used to be before the Compact. A lot of them just die.'

'Doesn't seem fair,' said Clodagh.

The angel looked deeply uncomfortable. She hated it here. 'Life isn't. Or so I'm told.'

'And what happens to the dead? He was their lord, wasn't he?'

'The dead keep dying, Clodagh. He isn't Death itself but he gained his energy from the moment of their passing. Now … now I don't know. Why are we here, Izzy?'

But Izzy couldn't answer that. She picked her way carefully through the rubble, leaving them behind her. She wasn't sure what she was searching for, but only that she needed to find something.

'Donn was the first one Holly killed,' Izzy said at last, when she was standing where he fell. 'After he gave me the Blade. And then she went after the Storyteller.'

'Not right away,' Clodagh protested. 'Months later.'

Izzy fixed her with a glare. 'Right after you took her book.'

'Oh God,' Ash whispered, staring at Izzy in horror. 'Are you saying it was our fault?'

'Mine and yours. And hers. Definitely hers.'

'What was?' Clodagh snapped irritably. She'd unbuttoned her coat and yanked off her hat and gloves, shoving them into the pockets. Her skin glistened with sweat. 'Damn, it's hot in here. Why is it so hot?'

Izzy ignored her. 'We took the touchstones. It weakened them, I think. So she killed them and took their magic.'

'Better than her raising more Shining Ones.'

'We don't even know if she's given up on that plan yet,' Ash said. 'Angels and demons are still going missing.'

'Yes, but she doesn't have any more Grigori blood to seal the deal.'

The shadows pressed closer. Izzy didn't like it but she couldn't move. It wasn't demons or shades, the darkness around her. But it wasn't entirely natural either.

'She still has a plan,' Izzy said quietly. 'Plans within plans. That's what Jinx used to say. She used him to raise a Shining One, Crom Cruach, and she used him again to kill the Story-teller. She's changed him. Why?'

The air around her thickened still further. She could feel it against her skin like syrup. This was where Donn had died, on his throne, blind but all seeing, cold as the stone on which he sat. She called out the Blade, fire in her hands.

'*To call him back as a Púca,*' came the breathy whisper. Izzy stiffened and saw Clodagh nearly jump out of her skin in fright. She spun around, but only the three of them were visible. *'When she couldn't use him for a Shining One, she went back to her original plan for him, the plan she had for his father …'*

Donn's voice, like silk around them, sank to silence and then surged up again, louder this time.

'She wants a Púca, as the Lord of the Wild Hunt, wants him bound to her will. She wants his chaos. What power that would be. If it could be harnessed.'

'What do you know of the Púca?' Izzy asked, unable to stop her voice shaking.

'They are wild and free. They are powerful. The Grigori must kill them. All of them.'

She remembered that feeling, that wild and illogical need to kill him. She hadn't even known who or what he was. She just knew he had to die. 'Why?'

'It is in the nature of you both, written on your DNA. It is so. Grigori are about balance, peace, equilibrium and order. Púca are chaos in physical form. The hated other …'

'I don't hate him.'

Donn laughed, the mockery in it setting her teeth on edge.

'Then what are you? Shall I tell you, little Grigori? Because you are not as you were.'

'Be careful Izzy,' Ash warned. 'Don't let him define you. You are not what he decrees. He is dead.'

'The Lord of the Dead is dead.' He laughed again. *'And what becomes of his realm now? Who is his successor? Who wields his blade?'*

Clodagh's eyes widened and, even as Izzy couldn't quite grasp the meaning, she saw understanding in her friends' eyes.

'Ah, shit, Izzy!'

The Blade blazed to incandescent fire. Izzy staggered back, trying to bring it under control. The shadows danced and writhed all around her, seething darkness which flapped and ripped apart as it tore itself free. Birds took flight, birds everywhere, black with feathers sheened in iridescence. Black and wild and dangerous, with beaks designed to tear carrion and claws to attack the still living, crows and ravens and everything in between. They took to the air in a great flock, whirling around the chamber so Clodagh and Ash had to drop to the floor and cover their heads. They spiralled towards Izzy but though she flinched back, they didn't hit her. Feathers rained down on her like a cloak and when the avian whirlwind subsided she stood there, clad in black, the Blade still burning in her hand.

Ash recovered first, pulling Clodagh up with her. Izzy watched them dispassionately, unable to respond, to speak, unable to feel a thing. It should have frightened her more.

'Izzy?' Clodagh said, as if she wasn't sure. And neither was Izzy.

'*Ah yes,*' Donn's voice purred in her ear, and then inside her ear, in her mind. '*She said you were the perfect vessel. She said you were just waiting for a purpose, that you would come back with the Blade and it would make you ready. And here you are. Never more ready.*'

No, not again. Never again. Izzy clung grimly to the last shred of control she could grasp. She felt him push against her defences, moving like smoke, like the Fear, one moment intangible and the next a vile, aggressive force.

'*A queen of ghosts and shadows,*' he whispered, burrowing into her head, into her mind. '*Dark and terrible, Lady of the Dead, armed with the Blade and empowered by your Grigori blood. Holly will never hurt us again.*'

Chapter Fifteen

Queen of Ghosts

Mags came up like an explosion, the knife in his hand flashing moonlight and his eyes the same colour. Osprey reeled back, taken off guard just for a moment and Jinx kicked out, slamming his foot into the back of his tormentor's knees, sending him to the ground. Mags was on him again, vicious and unrelenting.

But Osprey moved like a shadow, fleet and terrible. He slammed into Mags, sending him staggering back and turned on Jinx.

'This is the best protection you could get? You'd better run, kiddo. Run fast. Because I'm going to rip you a new one in a minute. And that's nothing to what she's going to do to you when she gets her hands on you.'

Mags dragged himself back to his feet. 'Com'ere, ye bog-monster,' he snarled. 'I'll show you what ripping a new one means.'

'Oh for the love of—' Osprey turned on him. 'Feck away off. The boy's mine and Amadán's already legged it.'

'So? Got a job, I have. And I'm going to do it.'

'Are you?' He punched Mags square in the face, and he staggered back but didn't fall. It just seemed to enrage him further. Instead of running or going down, he threw himself forwards again and this time his knife caught the side of Osprey's arm as he blocked him. With a twist that Jinx could barely follow, he slammed the Magpie against the rocks where he struggled to get up, but was too dazed this time.

Osprey turned on Jinx, his eyes glowing with an unnatural fire.

'What has she done to you?' Jinx asked, but he knew — oh yes, he knew better than anyone else in the world except maybe Holly herself.

Osprey grinned, that terrible insane grin, and touched the tattoos on his neck with his lethal, elegant hands.

'There are three Shining Ones, Jinx. And there will be three again. Three gods walking the earth. She promised. And we'll have chaos then. More than the world can bear.'

He took a step forward but staggered and folded as Mags tackled him. They went down in an ugly tangle of legs and fists.

'Get out of here, Jinx,' Mags screeched. 'Get the fuck out of here now.'

They rolled through the snow and Jinx circled, trying to

find an opening, a way to help. Mags swore, a litany of curses and words only Dubliners would know, some of them the same thing. Osprey grunted and then with a deft spin, flung the Magpie away again. His arm lashed out, faster than sight, and he had Mags by the throat. He hoisted him up, until his feet were kicking above the ground. Still Mags tried to lash out, twisting and writhing in Osprey's grip, his face turning the colour of a bruise, his eyes bulging.

'Let him go!' Jinx yelled.

'Or what? You'll do something? Not a pathetic beaten cur like you. She's going to make us great, Jinx. We're the chosen ones, you and me. She's going to make us gods.'

'She's going to make you dead, a suit of flesh for some crazy old angel to put on and wear. If she hasn't done it already. Let him go.'

Osprey smiled. It was the worst expression, Jinx knew that. It was Osprey at his most vicious.

In a moment too quick for the eye, he snatched the knife from Mags' flailing hand. He turned it this way and that, examining it with a practised eye.

'Oh, the things I could do with this,' he told them. 'The hours I could make it last. If only we had the time.'

And he slammed the knife up to the hilt in Mag's stomach and dropped him in the snow. Blood spread quickly, far too quickly.

Osprey stepped over the body, Mags forgotten.

'Now Jinx, you're coming home. Holly wants you and

that's that. She'll soon make you see sense again. She's good like that.'

Good? There was nothing good left to Holly. If there had ever been anything to begin with.

Movement caught Jinx's gaze as Mags wrenched the knife from his own body and flung himself at Osprey, using his feather cloak to drag himself up onto his enemy's back, stabbing, again and again. Osprey whirled around, trying to dislodge him as cut after cut rained down on him.

'Jinx,' Mags snarled, through blood and clenched teeth. 'Get the fuck out of here! Leg it, you stupid bastard.'

Something snapped inside Jinx, some sort of spell Osprey had over him, and the Cú Sídhe lurched forward, sprinting for the snowy wilderness beyond them. He ran so fast he didn't even think to shift, just kept running, scrambling on all fours when he fell, when he thought he couldn't run any further. He ran with the sounds of death and battle echoing in his head.

And he didn't look back.

There was nothing he could do. It was only later, when he collapsed in the frozen darkness miles away, that he realised he could have changed. He could have helped.

Disgusted, broken, he tried to drag himself upright again but ended up back on his knees, throwing up into a ditch.

A crow settled on Izzy's shoulder, cawed and preened at its feathers and then bent to pull at those she wore. Yes, Holly would never touch them again. Not her, not Donn.

Me, thought Izzy. Not him. Me. She can't touch him. He's already dead.

A queen of ghosts, the Lady of Death. There was a name for that, for a woman attended by crows who brought only death and whom death obeyed.

The Morrígan.

But she wasn't just death. Izzy knew enough about the Morrígan to know that. She was a goddess of battle, of wars and strife, where everything was lived to the utmost, on the edge. She revelled in every kind of life, every moment lived to the full, life at its most extreme.

She was alive.

Something boiled inside Izzy's chest, something which caught Donn and ensnared him. He was just a spirit, stripped of his power and his body, and she held his Blade, not him. The source of his power. He had given it to her freely. Oh he'd tried to be clever and trick her but it was a bluff. She knew it was.

He was just a ghost and he'd named her queen of ghosts.

And names could be powerful.

'I need an answer,' she told him, letting the fire rage inside her while outside the temperature plummeted. 'I saw a glass tower and an island. He was there, but I can't leave it to then. Whenever then is. Where do I find him now?'

Donn's spirit squirmed, and started to pull back but she was faster, her walls more determined. He wouldn't escape her. There was no escape. She wrapped her will around him, crushing him mercilessly. And why not? What mercy would he have shown her? Darkness swirled up in her mind, the same darkness that she remembered descending on her when she was last here, when Holly took Jinx. It was born in rage and fuelled by it. And she could feel Donn more distinctly now, like slime she couldn't brush off her hands properly.

'He's a Púca now. He'll need a wild place, a lost place, to finish becoming what he will be. You can't stop it, Grigori.'

'I can try. And Holly – what's she doing? Why kill you and the Storyteller? What is she doing?'

'Holly?' He almost laughed, but couldn't quite seem to manage it. 'Gathering power to feed the thing inside her, all the power she can muster. She's a Shining One and they want only one thing, to take back what was lost.'

'And what's that?'

Still he squirmed, trying to slip by her. He'd overpower her in a moment if he could, she knew that. But she wasn't letting him go, not yet. She held him like a fly under a pin.

'She wants the key. To the Thorn Gate. She's looking for the key.'

'Izzy?' Clodagh's voice sounded far off, afraid. 'Izzy, what's happening?'

She felt so cold, but she wasn't shivering. She wasn't moving. It was the cold of stone, of marble. It was like when she first recovered from the loss of Jinx and went half wild with the need to find him. The same distant coldness which separated her from the world, cut her adrift in a vacuum. That same unfeeling state that she had felt in her dreams.

Pain was the only thing that kept her tethered to her life. Because pain was all she knew. It led her to Jinx.

'Let me go,' Donn pleaded. 'I meant no harm. I didn't understand, Grigori. I just thought … I thought …'

'You didn't think,' she spat at him. 'You just wanted. As you always do. Greed and hunger and thoughtlessness. Monsters, that's what you are.'

'And what, then, are you?' he hissed, each word a poisoned barb.

She ignored him. It didn't matter. 'Who will she attack next?' she pressed and Donn writhed beneath her will.

'Izzy?' It was Clodagh's voice again, scared and bewildered. 'Izzy, can you hear me? Snap out of it.'

'Tell me,' she insisted.

'She's already done it. Amadán's Hollow has fallen. After that – take your pick. Íde, Brí or Silver. Who would you go after first? If you needed power but weren't entirely sure of your strength yet? Or you'd got the power but not the treasures you needed, who would you attack Isabelle Gregory? Because sooner or later you'll be asking the same questions. You have power, both mine and the Seanchaí's. Beware of such power. It will change you. I warned you.'

He wanted her to think like Holly, or like whatever the

combination of Holly and Crom Cruach had become. Asking her to think with her enemy's thoughts … it felt wrong, it felt dangerous. But she didn't have a lot of choice. Besides, she already knew the answer.

Íde. Only a fool would go after Brí or Silver. And Holly was no fool. But what did Íde have that Holly wanted?

'I can tell you,' said Donn, his voice turning wheedling, cajoling. 'I can tell you everything. If you let me – '

Let him stay? Let him become part of her. No. Never.

'Get out!' The voice, her voice, roared from her like a hurricane, driving Donn back, cowering. She was the mistress of ghosts and he was just the stubborn memory of a life refusing to move on. He had to obey. 'Go to whatever oblivion awaits you. You have no place here.'

There was a gust of wind, the sound of a desperate cry which swirled around the chamber. All around her the torches flared into light. Izzy threw up her hands and the crows took flight. The cloak fell from her shoulders and disintegrated into shadows.

'Clodagh, Ash, we're leaving.'

Light shimmered around the ends of her fingers but died as she closed them into fists.

'Are you …' Clodagh stared at her but didn't move. 'Are you okay?'

'I'm …' Was there even an answer to that? She wasn't sure. 'I'm still me.' Just about anyway. But something was different. Magic simmered in her veins, more than ever. She'd embraced

Donn's powers to drive him off. Lady of the Dead? The Mor-rígan? It sounded dangerous and very final. And what had he meant about power, about it corrupting her?

'Did you find out what you needed?'

'Not yet. But I have a start. Something to help, I think.'

'And what's that when it's at home?'

But Izzy just smiled. 'I need to talk to Dad. Let's get out of here.'

Dad, however, was less than impressed when Izzy phoned him. She left out most of the details, mainly because he was too busy yelling at her for running out on them again. And of course, she could just imagine the reaction if she told him Donn had tried to possess her but it was okay because she had taken his powers over the dead now. She'd be locked up for the rest of her life.

'We have to warn Íde. She's cut off from the others. She's vulnerable.'

'She's anything but. And there's a reason she's cut off. We have to regroup. There's a conclave … a meeting. The truce is failing. Silver and Dylan are missing.'

'Still?' That didn't sound good. Silver was powerful in her own right. With Dylan as her touchstone she was nigh on untouchable. 'Where are they? They went to see Amadán, didn't they?' And Donn had told her that Holly had attacked his Hollow, that it had fallen. Oh, this was bad. It was more than bad.

'Izzy?' His voice was a warning in just a single word.

'I'll be careful, Dad, I promise.' And she hung up. Her hand shook the moment after she did it and she stared at the screen, hardly able to believe that she'd done it. A second later, it started to ring again; even as she looked at it Dad's name flashed angrily at her.

He was going to kill her.

Rejecting the call, she glanced at Ash and Clodagh who had never looked so lost. Ice crept up the back of her neck, shivering across her tattoo.

'I need to check out Amadán's Hollow. Something has gone horribly wrong, can't you feel it?'

'Feel what?' asked Clodagh.

'Death. Everywhere.'

'We can't, Izzy,' said Ash. 'It's too dangerous. What if they are still there? What if it is a trap?'

She didn't have time for this. Why did no one understand that? Anger flared like a migraine behind her eyes.

'I know you have wings, but I didn't take you for a chicken.' The words slipped out before she could stop herself. Damn it, this was serious. Ash stared at her, open-mouthed, but Clodagh's face had gone white with rage.

'Don't you dare talk to her like that.'

But once again, that bitter, angry rage took hold and she spoke before she could stop herself. 'Or what? She's my guardian, you know. Not your girlfriend.'

Clodagh swung a half-formed fist at her, a wild and erratic blow with no real skill. Izzy sidestepped it, her body primed to retaliate, but before she could, Ash was there, holding the arm that would have hit Clodagh in an implacable grip.

'Izzy, you aren't yourself. Something has happened to you. Don't you see it?'

All she saw was everyone trying to slow her down and stop her helping Jinx, Dylan and Silver. Anything could have happened to the three of them. If Holly had them …

The Blade that Cuts reared up inside her again, snaking its way from the pit of her stomach to the crown of her head, blazing with her anger. Meek and helpful Izzy was burned away and she wasn't wanted back. She remembered how she'd gone for the book in the first place, and why. That was what she needed to be now – determined, dangerous, not to be messed with. She'd get Jinx back no matter what the cost.

The thought consumed her. Not herself? Good. She didn't want to be. Not anymore.

'I'm going,' she said and reached out, the power of the Blade coiled about her. She could feel the Sídheways, and a memory reared up. Not her own memory, not quite. It slid like a chunk of ice through her mind. Sorath had torn open the Sídheways and bent them to her will. All it took was power, and with the Blade, Izzy had that power now. And Sorath's knowledge, somehow. She didn't want to question how because she feared she wouldn't like the answer.

The Sídheway tore open in front of her, screaming and writhing around them as she redirected it to her will and stepped inside, heading for a new destination. It was a ragged and pitiful thing. Izzy walked quickly, trying not to think about the damage she was doing, or about the damage that had already been done. Whispers followed her, the sound beyond distorted and twisted. Something was wrong with the Sídheways, that was certain. She had never seen them like this.

She should know what was wrong. Jinx would have known.

A chill rippled over her, the sense of being watched, of just having missed someone calling her name. Someone who needed her. Someone she knew.

Izzy shivered and broke into a run, unable to help herself. She had a bad feeling about all of this, about the Sídheways most of all. By the time she stepped out again, the path was fraying even as she closed it. She doubted anyone could use it again unless someone knew how to fix them. She shook off the sensation like cobwebs. Amadán's Hollow wasn't hard to find. The wards on it were gone and the spells hung limp and broken. Besides, the reek of blood, viscera and ashes carried on the cold winter's air. She entered by the main gate and she knew she was already too late. Anything left here was dead.

Alone, she picked her way past broken furniture and a section of half-collapsed roof. Some of the fires were still burning, or smouldering at least. She found Amadán's study almost by accident and gazed for a long time at the remains of his books, some shredded, fluttering pages, the rest ashes. It was as if someone had walked through here with a flame thrower.

The bodies were mostly in the morgue, piled together. Holly had enjoyed herself here. They had been burned too, eventually. But they had been tortured first.

That was all she could gather from the gabble of voices, the sobs and cries, the incoherent pleas.

Their cries had fallen on uncaring ears. Even if they could have answered her questions before, now they were half mad with suffering. As she had with Donn, Izzy reached out and felt the darkness crawl up around her, through her. She could help them in this. This one way.

But she needed information.

The dead scrabbled to give it. She didn't know anyone there. They were just servants – neither the Magpies nor the Amadán were among them.

We told them we didn't know where they went, one female voice sobbed desperately. *But she didn't care. Just asked about the boy, over and over. As if we'd been allowed near him. Cú Sídhe or whatever he was …*

'Where was he?'

Gone, already gone. With Mags. Sent away. Please, Lady. Please …

And then she heard another voice, one she knew.

Let them go, Izzy Gregory. Send them onwards and I'll help you.

'Mags?' She knew his voice instantly. In her hand the Blade that Cuts burned higher as she sent the other spirits off into the darkness beyond. And then she used its light to find him, tracking her way back to the entrance and outside into the frozen night. It wasn't hard. He'd probably crawled towards the Hollow after the fight. There was a trail of blood in the snow and his remains hadn't been burned. He'd reached it when Holly was long gone or she'd have made the torment last. He'd bled out, his face even paler than usual and a wide red stain soaked his shirt, centred on his stomach. There were other wounds. God, it must have hurt.

The others got away, he said, though his voice didn't move. *Your Jinx included. I made sure, stopped Osprey taking him. My brother …* A stab of pain, of grief, ran from him and through her. She stepped back, as if avoiding a knife, but there was no escaping it. Mags couldn't feel anything anymore so she felt it for him. Was this what it had been like for Donn? Every day, throughout all those years. No wonder he'd been so cold and detached. How else could he have survived? She forced herself to breathe again. *My brother doesn't know, Lady. Will you tell him? Make sure he knows there was nothing he or anyone else could have done. That it wasn't Jinx's fault either. He's a bit thick, mind. Might take some convincing.*

'Where did they go?'

The Old Man'll make for sanctuary, holy ground, you know? And Pie's with him.

'And Jinx?'

If he's a Púca – really a Púca, like the Old Man thinks – he'll make for one of their places. Old places, old magic, you know? Nearly all broken now though.

'Like where? Please, Mags …'

He gave a laugh, brief and bitter, and that flood of pain swelled through her again. She wanted to cry but her eyes were too dry. *Since you ask nice-like … Puck's Castle, maybe? Can't say anything for sure. Jaysus, I'm knackered here, love. It's a wonder I can tell you anything at all.*

He sounded so tired she felt sorry for him, but she wasn't finished. Not quite yet.

'Silver and Dylan were coming here.'

Never got here. But there's a parcel of dead humans down the way in the pub. Other direction than Holly came. He sighed, a sound world weary with despair. Even though he had no breath in him left to sigh with. Izzy's chest ached. *If you've taken Donn's gig, love, does that mean you have all his skills?*

'I don't know. Didn't even know I had his … his *gig* until today.'

She sensed Mags' smile. *Just make me a bird, Lady,* he whispered, the plaintive sound of a last request. *Make me a bird for real next time.*

She nodded, closed her eyes and drew on Donn's powers. For a moment there was nothing, and then a flood of images filled her brain. For a moment she was in his place, fighting for his life, screaming at Jinx to run. And Osprey looked at him with the golden eyes of a Shining One in the making. And then everything went still and silent. She wished for a bird, for a magpie, tried to grant his last request, not sure if it worked or not. Silence spilled over the landscape, the deep dark, the silence of a winter night. She sat down outside the broken Hollow and stared at the moonlit landscape.

Something moved, where it shouldn't, wings in the night.

A single magpie perched on a twisted black thorn tree just beyond the gateway stones. It gave a harsh broken cry before it took off.

'One for sorrow,' said Izzy automatically, and she felt it, truly felt it. Endless sorrow filled her chest until her tears spilled from her eyes.

The strength seemed to flow from her body and she sank back against the rocks, shivering with the cold. On the road below she saw the lights of a car rear up over the hill and turn up the dirt track. It stopped at the gate, lights still on, cutting through the darkness, illuminating the snow where it was still clean and unblemished and up to the point in front of her where it was churned up and bloody. Dad walked through the night with a torch in his hand, not that he seemed to need it. He made for her as unerringly as an arrow from a bow heads for its target.

He was bundled up against the cold, the cold that she barely felt. In truth she was too hot, almost feverish.

The torch light flicked over Mags' broken body and away.

'Izzy? What happened?'

'He's gone.'

'I see that.'

'No,' she said, looking up at him and trying to gather the strength to move. 'Jinx. He was here. But he's gone.'

'Did he do this?'

She shook her head, disgusted that Dad could think such a thing. But then she remembered the scene in the Leprechaun Museum and decided not to argue. Jinx *could* do something like this. They all knew it. She was the only one who seemed intent on lying about it. 'Mags tried to save him from Holly. Bought Jinx time to run. Osprey killed him for it. He showed me ... Holly is making Osprey like her, putting a Shining One in him too.'

'So there's be three of them. All the Shining Ones free.' He held out his hand to pull her up. He was as strong as she remembered him when she was little. Or maybe she just hadn't let him help her in some time. Or maybe she had no strength left herself. It didn't matter which. He pulled her to her feet as if he was pulling up a pile of laundry.

'No,' she said. 'Not three. Jinx isn't ... she changed him all right but not into one of them. He's a Púca.'

Dad hissed, drawing back his lips and showing his teeth. They gleamed white as bone in the moonlight. She saw the disgust, the hatred, and she loathed it. Because part of her felt it too. Even if she didn't know what that meant. Ingrained, bone deep. Loathing. 'Then we can't help him,' Dad said.

'You can't, maybe. Or won't. I will. I'll find a way. I owe him that much.'

'You owe him nothing, Izzy.'

'He let me kill him. I was meant to save him and I couldn't even do that. Don't tell me what I owe others, Dad. Don't tell me what to do. Not anymore. I have to help him, somehow.'

'If he'll let you. The Púca are dangerous.'

'You don't know that. Brí said they were all dead, years ago. The angels made the Grigori kill them. When did you ever – ' and the thought stuttered to a halt. Of course he'd known one. She could see it written all over his face. He'd told her so himself, ages ago. Jasper. He'd known Jasper and hated Jinx from the moment he found out whose son he was. And there was more. So much more because she could read him like a book now, see his thoughts and regrets unfurling in his eyes. She saw more deeply with Donn's power inside her and the memories the Storyteller's book gave her. Other people's memories, sure, but people who were part of that world, part of Dubh Linn and knew. Maybe just scraps and fragments, maybe just rumours, whispers, implications.

'Izzy ...' he began warily, realising. He wasn't a fool, her father. Or rather, he was, but not such a fool as to try to lie to her now.

'You killed Jasper?'

'It wasn't like that, I promise you.'

'Spare me your promises, Dad.'

'He begged me. Just like Jinx begged you. After all Holly had put him through, after he changed, became that thing, lost Bella ... He begged me, Izzy.'

'I don't believe you. What? Did Holly ring you up and say we've a problem that needs dealing with? Get in here and bring your sharpest knife.'

'No.' He shook his head, defeated. 'It was Brí.'

For a frozen moment, she didn't know what to say. She stared at him and then lifted her head up to look down the long line of the valley. The lights picked out the road and the houses, the sprawl of the city beyond like a nest of fireflies. And after that, the sea, darkness. Nothing.

'You disgust me,' she said quietly. 'All of you. Everything you've done to him ... '

'It can't be helped now. It's in the past. And we have to safeguard the future. We're meeting in town in the morning. You need to come. I need you by my side. You're my daughter and my heir and they all need to see that we stand together. Otherwise the Grand Compact is broken for good and nothing will stop Holly. Do you understand? Personal feelings aside, Izzy. This is Grigori business. It's our duty.'

'Of course it is. Fine. Let's go. I'll stand by you and keep the balance. I'll do my duty. But don't ... just don't ever expect me to forgive you.'

Chapter Sixteen

Puck's Castle

J inx fled through the night and into the morning, running until he could run no more. He slept – or rather collapsed exhausted – in a bleak pine forest. At least there was shelter from the snow, if not from the cold, but the clothes he wore offered little protection.

Lucky to be alive didn't come into it. When he woke in the cold light of dawn, it was the first time he had felt lucky in his whole life.

Except for Izzy.

But he had to forget her now. Grigori hated Púca. It was ingrained in them, part of their being, carried in their blood. If anyone could beat it, he would normally lay money on Izzy, but he had seen her face, the way she had looked at him. She didn't know him and all she had wanted to do was kill him.

He knew that look. Hell, he had worn that look, felt that

feeling. Only her presence had stopped him in the museum, brought him back to himself. And now she was gone, lost to him forever through blood, through duty.

How he had made it down off the mountain, he didn't know. He didn't dare use the Sídheways. He couldn't be sure that Holly didn't have them watched, just waiting for him to make that mistake. So he stuck to the human world and did what he could to avoid the roads.

Dublin and the bay spread out beneath him, drained of colour and almost at a standstill thanks to the weather. By the time he reached Kilternan, the light was growing. The long trek down to Ballycorus took the last of his strength. By the time Puck's Castle was in view the feeble sun was high in the sky, but the clouds had swallowed it. Heavy snow clouds crowded overhead, grey as slate and threatening. He had to find shelter and soon. But now he knew where he was going. Or at least, he hoped so.

It didn't look much like a castle, more like the ruins of a huge house. Not the most welcoming house, with its thick grey walls and narrow windows. Ivy and other plants had claimed the exterior on one side and on the other the entrance looked like a giant had punched holes in the stone-work. A fortified tower house was the term, he thought. Art had told him about it – poor dead Art, used by Holly to betray Izzy, dead at her feet on Bray Head even though Jinx refused to kill him. Osprey had snapped his neck like breaking a twig. Art had hoped to find safety here, in this place where the

Wanderers used to gather.

Jinx climbed the gate, ignoring the 'No trespassing' sign which had seen better days. The castle looked like a square block of conquest planted in the middle of a field of snow. It was probably full of cows in better weather. But now, untouched for days, the snow was up to his calves. He struggled through it, determined.

Because if he didn't find what he was looking for he was as good as dead. He had to keep going.

Everything in him wanted to give up, to lie down and let himself die, right here and now. What was he doing anyway? What was the point? He ought to be dead. He was a freak of nature, a creature of chaos, unloved in this world. He ought to just put himself out of his misery. It would be a blessing. Better for everyone concerned. He was –

Jinx stopped, breathing hard so that his breath plumed around him like smoke. He wasn't going in a straight line anymore, but rather around in a circle. And though he often agreed with many of those thoughts, they weren't his either. They came from elsewhere and when he focused, he could follow their scent. It hung on the air, rank and horrible as old rotten fish. It made him gag.

But it was a scent nonetheless. And one he could follow. It led straight towards the ruin.

Darkness barred the broken entrance like a physical door. It didn't budge when he pushed, reinforced with magic. Jinx waited, mulling over his options and shivering. He could sense eyes on him, that someone was watching him. Several some-ones in fact. Some were hostile, others just afraid. That wasn't promising.

Winding his will to iron, because if he stayed outside in this cold he was in deep trouble, he drew in a breath.

'Hello?' he called. 'Is there anybody here? I'm looking to claim sanctuary.' What was the bloody phrase anyway? Sanctuary was for churches, wasn't it? This wasn't a church. What church would have him anyway? 'Hello? Please. I need … hospitality … or something. I need help. Let me in.'

He sagged, leaning on the stone with one arm. He knew there was someone in here and that by rights, ancient rights, they couldn't refuse hospitality to a traveller in need. But there were forms and rituals and he couldn't remember it all, even if he had once known them. There was a word, a half-remembered word.

'*Féile*,' he said. Was that it? There was no reaction. '*Coire féile. Aíocht don deoraí.* I need *oigidecht* …or … *nemed* … or … or … *tearmann* …' There were too many words for what he needed now, too many variations all with one meaning. It was so important, so much a part of his world that no one could just say it out straight. That wasn't the fae way. 'Sanctuary, hospitality, *please*.'

The wind whispered through the old stones and the ivy. It seemed to laugh at him.

'Are you lost?' asked a voice behind him. He turned sharply, and saw a girl standing there. Her clothes were old-fashioned, but beautifully made. So was the girl within them, pale and blonde with huge blue eyes, exactly the sort of human to attract many wild fae. Because she was human and there was no doubt in his mind that she was fae-touched. She smiled at him. 'I came looking for flowers but the weather turned. Strange for June, isn't it?'

June? He swallowed, nerves getting the better of him. 'Bit cold too, isn't it?'

She smiled again. 'Well, you'd better come in and talk to them.' She brushed by him, almost dancing with her dainty steps, and slipped through the darkness filling the door. She vanished from his view, but her voice drifted after her. 'Come inside. You're welcome here. All the lost are welcome.'

Then he heard it, distant music, so sweet and tragic that it tangled within his thoughts and the next moment it had drawn him across the threshold effortlessly.

It wasn't a ruin on the other side. Far from it.

Jinx stopped, staring around him in wonder at the bronze domed ceiling which shone with reflected light and life. Candles burned everywhere, great thick pillar candles the size of his arm, tiny tea lights tucked into crevices in the dry stone wall. A fiddler and a piper were hard at work in the middle of the room, making that bewitching music, and other figures danced around them, leaping and cavorting in joy. He'd never seen anything quite like it, not even in the Market. They were all shapes and sizes, these fae. Some leps, and little green-faced tree things. Some were wrinkled as old rags, their faces

scrunched with age and long-lived lives. Not one of them was
Aes Sídhe. They were indeed the little people, the wanderers,
the lowest of the fae. There was a thorn bush growing behind
the musicians, a hawthorn, black and spiny in its winter state.
To make up for that someone had strung it with Christmas
lights. They twinkled and laughter rang out over the music.

'I brought a guest,' said the girl. 'A wanderer, like us.' And
then she joined the dance, whirled in among them, her laughter melding with the song.

'Thank you, Jane, my lovely,' said a reedy voice from Jinx's
elbow. 'Well now, Jinx by Jasper, if I'm not mistaken. We've
been waiting for you.'

The voice belonged to the oldest and most wizened creature Jinx had ever seen in his life. He was propped up beneath
the tree and it took a moment for Jinx to realise that his bark-
like skin and spiny hair marked him as linked to the tree. His
eyes were bright and keen, but his smile was toothless.

'I was just seeking shelter,' Jinx said carefully.

'And sure where else would you come for that?'

The rush of fear and relief combined almost brought him
to his knees. Many tiny hands came up to help and steady
him. Many more took the backpack off before it over-bal-
anced him. He stared at the little man in the centre, hardly
daring to take his eyes off him, and was met with another
toothless smile. 'I'm the *Briugu* here. The host, as it were. Been
a long time though since we had a real Púca in Puck's Castle.'

Jane whirled by, paying him no heed at all now, her long

hair swirling behind her.

'That girl …' he said. 'She's human …'

'Yes. She got lost here and came to us for shelter like you. But she couldn't leave. It wasn't safe for her. It's been too long now. Look at you, you're almost spent, poor lad. Rest, regain your strength. You're safe here.'

'Where am I?' he asked, and a wave of exhaustion broke over him again. He knew it wasn't entirely natural but instead was amplified by the creature before him. The others crooned lullabies and smiled as they would at an exhausted infant fighting sleep. His eyes grew heavier and heavier.

'Don't you know, lad? We've been calling for you since we came back. You're home.'

Someone helped him to a chair and he sank into it gratefully. It wasn't just a chair, he knew that, somewhere in the back of his mind. It was a throne. What was he doing in a throne?

The Púca within him stirred and woke. He felt his body make those shivery little changes which made him half-fae half-beast, but this time his mind cleared. There was no Hunt to lose himself in, no blood in his mouth, no death on his hands. There was peace and warmth, the smell of a peat fire and music.

He hadn't thought of music in so long it hurt when the need for it stirred within his heart. He'd once told Izzy he hadn't played since he left her the first time and that was true.

But now he needed it. Sitting here, with music swirling around him, he wanted to play again, needed to play an instrument and capture that music for himself. The way Dylan did, without sense or reason, without conscious thought. The need echoed through him. The one thing that had been his freedom through all his youth, the only thing Holly had not been able to take away.

He only wished he had an instrument and one arrived, carried in reverent hands, passed from one to another. A harp, one of the old bardic ones, and it was old indeed, its surface smooth and dark from the touch of many loving hands. The strings stretched out like threads of gold and gold chased through the wood as well, as if each time a flaw had begun to show it had been fixed with that precious metal. Or maybe the gold was in the grain of the wood itself.

'Take it,' whispered the thorny little man, Briugu, over the noise of the other musicians and the murmuring, wondering crowd. 'It was meant for you. Take it and play. Think of what you want most and play. You honour us.'

What he wanted most?

He took the harp in his own adoring hands, cradled it and let his fingers drift over the strings. He had learned once, the first instrument he had learned to play, before he'd discovered the guitar. And he had once joked to Silver that the guitar was just a more elaborate harp anyway.

The harp sang for him, sweet and light, but with an undertone that stirred his heart and filled it with longing. He poured that, in turn, back into the music and played for his heart's desire.

He played for Izzy.

Dangerous thing, music. It was just a step away from magic, chaotic and ordered at the same time, both an art and a science intertwined, like Celtic knotwork. And here he was, at the heart of chaos. Or perhaps he *was* the heart of chaos. He couldn't tell anymore.

He thought of Izzy, in spite of the fact he was now a Púca and she was always Grigori, in spite of the fact she had already killed him twice, in spite of everything he knew. The ache was too strong, the want cut too deep. She was all he needed.

He called for her, pleaded with her, and looked up to see every eye upon him, all other instruments still, tears flowing openly down faces of all shapes, ages and colours. They weren't actually that many, the people of Puck's Castle, when they stood still. And they were small and scrawny. All hiding here.

And in the magic of this place, the wild magic swelling inside him took flight, reaching out across the snowy world beyond, looking for her, as, exhausted, Jinx slipped away to sleep.

Wherever he was, a heavy bass rhythm boomed through the floor. He could hear it only faintly, as if it was several levels below him, but that didn't matter. He could feel it – through the floor, through the bed on which he lay, through the air around him.

Dylan opened his eyes. The room looked like something between an apartment and a hotel room, one of those expensive catered places that couldn't ever really feel like a home, no matter how hard they tried to pretend that they could. It definitely wasn't his apartment in Smithfield, the one he and Silver rented because he needed an address and she needed an escape.

The world lurched around him as he tried to push himself up. It felt like the mother of all hangovers, which was beyond unfair. Kidnapped by angels, losing his girlfriend to fae magic and being carried off by demons did not equal a night of partying. He forced himself to keep going anyway, stopping once he was sitting, his feet planted firmly on the carpet and his head resting in his shaking hands. Even his fingertips ached.

He looked down at his hands, the fingers wrapped in plasters, dried blood on them. His blood.

He remembered music. He remembered playing. There had been a crowd and a horde of girls. It was a blur. He hadn't been drinking though. There certainly hadn't been drugs because he wouldn't, not ever.

But it was late now. No. Early morning although the daylight was hours off yet.

And his head and stomach told a different story.

His phone buzzed and he fumbled in his pocket, trying to get it out. There were dozens of messages and emails.

Steve from the band left a long and rambling voicemail that made no sense at all. 'You could have told us, if you were going solo. We were counting on you, man.' Going solo? He had no intention of going solo.

There were a couple from the record company, but Silver had been dealing with them. They wanted to move the dates up, release immediately. Worldwide and multi-platform. They were setting up appearances as they spoke and would confirm today. Was he dropping the band, they asked, because that wouldn't be a problem. Something cold and horrible slithered beneath his skin and he wanted to throw up. What was going on?

Silver. He needed to find her. He needed to get her back.

A discreet knock on the door brought him to his feet. A moment later he fought not to throw up.

Anyone else would wait until someone answered to walk in, but not Azazel. He wasn't alone either. There was a guy in a suit which screamed lawyer, carrying bundles of papers.

'Recovering somewhat, are you?' asked the demon. 'An incredible performance last night. Incredible. People will be talking about it for decades. All on the internet, you know?'

'What is?' Dylan asked, warily. He didn't like the sound of this. There was that horrible fear he'd just made a colossal fool of himself and couldn't remember.

'Take a look online. You'll see.'

It didn't take long. All those messages, followed by a quick search, and social media told him he'd played a guerrilla solo gig in a club called Forsaken and blown everyone's mind. More people were claiming to have been there than was physically possible, because there was no venue that size in Temple Bar. He was being compared to guitar heroes and legendary singers, being called all manner of ridiculous things, and he couldn't remember a moment of it. His fingers ached and it was only then he realised that the plasters had come loose and they were bleeding on the screen of his phone.

'Tsk,' said Azazel, taking it from him and wiping it clean with a handkerchief. Then he took Dylan's hands and began to clean them in careful, delicate strokes. 'Precious things these. You need to take care of them. Don't you see? You're a living legend now.'

The lawyer flicked around the screen on his tablet and pressed play. Music filled the air, such music. It brought tears to Dylan's eyes just to hear it and the muscles in his shoulders tensed. He knew it. It was his, but it had never sounded like that before.

Wild. Out of control. Terrifying. But at the same time, arresting, compelling.

His music without Silver.

'What do you want?' Dylan asked, trying to block out the sound.

Azazel smiled, his teeth filling his mouth. He was reading tweets from his own phone. '*Never heard anything like it. Hashtag Mind Blown.*' '*What a gig, what a night.*' '*Legend.*' Oh, and this young lady has some very interesting suggestions about what she would like to do with you. Her friends agree. In fact they want to help.'

'Jesus, will you shut up and tell me what you want?'

The lawyer sucked in a shocked breath and Dylan felt that frisson of danger charge the air. Azazel went on tapping at his phone with a look of delight. When he finally looked up, he was still grinning, but the humour didn't reach his piercing eyes.

'What I want is a signature. On a contract. What I want is you signed on with me.'

Dylan shook his head. 'I'm with Silver.'

'In case you haven't noticed, she's gone. You're a free agent. Your soul is up for grabs and I'm the one who's going to have it. You offered, didn't you? I distinctly remember that. When Silver needed something from me, you offered. Well, I accept. You saw how it was last night, didn't you?'

'I can't remember that.'

'Well, that much magic, that many people lapping it up, perhaps it's only to be expected. Probably feel rough, don't you? You'd rather sleep it off? And you can. You can have everything you want, Dylan.'

'I want Silver back.'

Azazel laughed. 'Not within my power. The angels have her tied up with the Sídheways. They want the spark to let her go. Power, you see. But give it to Zadkiel and he'll take over heaven. Not good for any of us. Accept things as they are.'

'Where is the spark?'

'Gone. I gave it away. I owed a debt. You know how it is. Now, go through the contracts if you want. Read every line. But you will sign them, eventually. You don't have a choice. And what a time we'll have of it then, you and I.'

'What do you mean?'

He leaned in close, the smell of sulphur on his breath making Dylan gag. 'You'll play. You'll play like a dream and people will do anything to hear you. Pay anything. You'll bring more souls through my door than anyone has for a hundred years.' He was almost salivating at the thought. Dylan's stomach twisted in revulsion. Azazel wanted him as a lure. Music did things, he knew that. It was magic. And to use it in this way … it felt like blasphemy.

'No.'

'No? You don't have a choice, boy. What else is there for you? Soul after soul. You benefited from last night just as much as I did. Magic needs feeding, even magic like yours. You'll carry on doing it. You need an audience. Your magic needs ears. And you'll live well, the full rock and roll life-style, I promise. In absolute luxury. You'll live far longer than you would with Silver, that's for sure. Think about it. We've a meeting to attend in a couple of hours. You'll like it, part of that whole balance of power thing, and you should be there, given poor old Jophiel's fate. He named you a representative of the human race. Let everyone know where you stand now. Who you are. Shower and change and we'll send up breakfast, that's a good lad.'

He swept out of the room, followed by the lawyer. Dylan stared at the pile of papers they'd left on the table in dismay. It was almost a foot high.

No. No way. He wasn't doing this. Never.

He grabbed his jacket and headed for the door. It was locked. Of course it was locked. He rattled the handle and tried to force it, just in case. No luck. He was stuck. And the room was too high up for climbing out of a window to be an option.

Panic rattled through him, leaving his chest tight and his sickened stomach even worse. Sweat stood out on his forehead, cold and clammy. What was he going to do?

And then he heard a voice. 'Dylan O'Neill?'

It was an old voice, gravelly and worn, the type of voice that would give him the fright of his life if it came out of a dark alley. At the same time, it sounded fragile and scared. It came from the other side of the door, as if someone crouched there, speaking through the gap at the bottom.

'Who are you?'

'Someone who can help. I can't get you out but I can help. When the time comes. I can find the angel's spark.'

He pressed himself up to the door, all sickness forgotten. He needed to get out of here. He needed to find Silver, rescue her, which meant getting Sorath's spark. Whether he'd give it to Zadkiel or not – no, that wouldn't be wise. He didn't need Azazel to tell him that. No one needed a megalomaniac in charge of heaven. And Silver would kill him if he did. But first… first, he needed to get Silver back. Somehow. Which involved getting that spark. It was a spiral he couldn't break out of. And he had to do something.

'Who is this? Where is it?'

'When you get out … and you *will* get out, you have to or he'll win, he'll win everything … come and find me in the club. Azazel's club. I'll help you.'

'Help me get out.'

The voice laughed, a frightened, desperate sound. 'I can't. I can't. They'll tear me apart. I'm only still here because I don't make trouble.'

'Who are you? What's your name?'

'Mistle,' he whispered, like it was a terrible confession. 'My name is Mistle.'

Chapter Seventeen

Holy and Undivided Trinity

I zzy had been to Trinity before, of course. If nothing else it was a handy shortcut from Pearse Street Dart Station up to Grafton Street or Dame Street. Once upon a time she had dreamed about studying here when she left school, spending her days in 'The College of the Holy and Undivided Trinity of Queen Elizabeth near Dublin' which had stood in the same spot since 1592. It had been a monastery before that, outside the city walls, and still held itself apart, an island of tranquillity in the centre, if you didn't count nights like the Trinity Ball.

But all those things, all those dreams, didn't matter anymore. They couldn't matter. She knew she was never going to be a student, not really. Oh, she might play at it for a while, pretend she had a future. Dad had trained as an architect, after all, and sometimes he still earned his living that way. But Izzy wasn't under any illusions any more. Being a Grigori was going to entwine itself around her life and rob her of any other aspirations. What did it matter if she studied here? What would she do with it anyway? Was there a course in fighting supernatural monsters? Perhaps with an option in prehistoric languages and angelic lore?

Dad had managed to study architecture. Or so he claimed. Who knew? And when had he last worked? As in really worked on a project? Maybe that was all lies as well.

At least they'd gone home first. She'd even managed to catch a few hours' sleep and a blissful shower. She doubted Dad had managed the same. He looked shattered.

As they walked past the students hurrying through the frigid morning air, she couldn't help but wallow in a jealous misery that wasn't fair on them. It wasn't fair on her either so what did it matter? She might as well feel what she felt. It was hard not to get caught up in the romance of the place – summers by the Pav, rooms in Botany Bay or Goldsmith's Hall, sitting by the cricket fields, or under the cherry trees. It was all lost to her.

She remembered the school tour which had brought them here, primarily to see the Book of Kells. The Long Room in the Old Library, which housed it, had filled her with awe at the time – a temple of ancient books and high learning. She had wished she could have stayed there, looking at the white busts of ancient scholars, the alcoves filled with leatherbound books and the gold shelf marks gleaming on the dark brown wood. It was so peaceful. It was perfection.

There were already tourists queuing outside even though it wasn't open. They stamped their feet and rubbed their gloved hands together, complaining about the cold. Who in their right minds came to Dublin in December anyway, she wondered, as Dad led her past them to the back door and knocked officially. After a brief conversation with the security guard on the door, they were allowed into the gift shop – floor to ceiling in trinkets and memorabilia, bound notebooks, quill pens, DVDs and university hoodies. From there they climbed the staircase to the Long Room. A backwards tour, she thought. What else?

It opened above them like a cathedral. She couldn't help herself, gazing up in wonder. Even though she knew what to expect, she never *really* expected it. Light streamed in from high windows, catching dust motes which circled lazily. Her first thought was that this was what heaven ought to look like. Her second was that they were not alone.

Brí was already there, resplendent in a gown of orange, gold and red, her hair falling down her back like waves of fire. Blythe and some of the Cú Sídhe stalked nearby, only a few of them in hound form, the rest, like their Matriarch, in their finest clothes.

Amadán looked less impressive, rumpled and exhausted if she was honest. Beside him the other Magpie stood very still and quiet. Izzy wondered if he already knew that his brother was dead. She also wondered if she should tell him, as Mags had asked, and how he might react when she did. But she didn't want to. The look in his eyes told her enough. He wouldn't take the news kindly.

To her surprise, she saw Meridian, a few other Aes Sídhe with her and a contingent of Banshee too, clothed in black leather and eyeing the others like prey. Holly's daughter had a furtive, hunted look and when she saw Izzy she sank back a little.

'What's she doing here?'

'We need to talk to her. And the others. It's what we do. It's good to talk to people, Izzy.'

Izzy eyed him dubiously. 'Depends on the people.'

Azazel laughed, a huge booming laugh which echoed up through the vaulted ceiling and rolled around them. At what, Izzy didn't know, but something had amused the demon who called himself her uncle. That wasn't a good sign. He was deep in conversation with someone, but she couldn't see who because the shades clustered too close.

There were angels too, Ash among them. She looked grey with exhaustion as she stood to the left of a group of shining, beautiful beings. They ignored her of course. Ash was Izzy's guardian angel which was already a black mark against her. But this looked like more. Maybe forcing her to help had been a bad idea. She felt sorry for the girl. All she had been doing was helping a friend. It was her bad luck that it was Izzy, who had failed horrifically at friendship since the summer.

'Why are we here?' she asked, when the silence stretched on too long.

'To try to stop a war. One which seems to be speeding on ahead without us. Look at them. They hate each other.'

'Of course they do. They always have. Angels, demons and Sídhe – the ones who fought and the ones who wouldn't fight – it's as old as creation, isn't it?'

'Not quite, but I see your point.'

'So what's to stop them just tearing into each other here and now?'

'This place is special, sacred,' he said. 'The Keeper would go mad if anything happened here.'

'The Keeper of the library?' she asked, surprised. What did librarians have to do with any of this?

'No. Wrong Keeper. I'll need to explain that later.' He grinned, squeezed her hand. 'And there's me, of course.'

He stepped forward, holding up his hands for silence as all eyes turned to him. As he spoke, thanking them for coming, flattering each of them in turn and trying to get them to listen to him, Izzy backed up towards an alcove.

Dad talked. He argued, he cajoled. He was amazing, if she was honest, if she took a step back and looked at him objectively. How he kept his cool, she didn't know. Her gaze snagged on the black stone eyes of Pie and she winced inwardly. He bared his teeth but did nothing else.

'We can't keep attacking each other,' said her father. 'This is exactly what Holly and the Shining Ones want. They thrive on chaos. We can't just give it to them.'

'What do you know about chaos?' asked one of the angels. Izzy didn't know her, but she knew the haughtiness, the sublime self-regard, from her golden curls to the ballet pumps she wore on her dainty feet. Just like Zadkiel and Haniel. One of *those* ones. Just like every angel she'd ever encountered except for Ash. And poor Ash spent most of her time disguised as a human until they all treated her like something unpleasant had rubbed off. Guardians were considered the lowest of the low. Most stayed with their charges, watching silently, guiding, a nudge here and there, a friendly hand. The higher angels didn't see any value in that. They always were arrogant beyond belief.

'His daughter knows enough to cause her fair share,' one of the demons said and then burst out laughing.

Morons, thought Izzy. How did heaven and hell function with so many of them milling around? Her temper snapped.

'And I'll cause more if I have to,' she said loudly, her voice shockingly loud in the hall. 'You're all in this, and you can change it or embrace it. I don't really care anymore. I do have a question though – where are Silver and Dylan? Where are my friends?'

'Izzy, this isn't the time,' said Dad.

'Perfect time. They're all here.'

Wind roared around the windows and doors, wind that came out of nowhere, wild and dangerous as her anger.

Did I do that? she wondered. She didn't mean to, but the way she was feeling …

'What are you doing?' the angel shouted in alarm, backing away.

'Izzy, stop this,' Dad warned.

But she couldn't. She wasn't even sure how she was doing it, or if she was. She was angry now, and she wanted answers. She picked out Azazel, stalked towards him, and he just smiled in response. Hiding something. Always hiding something. Always playing games and he thought he was so much cleverer than anyone else. There were shadows clustered around him. Too many.

'All right, my Lady,' he drawled. 'Better come out, touchstone. She's on to us.'

Shades parted and Dylan appeared. He didn't look too much the worse for wear. He was as angry as she was perhaps but he was alive and not demon touched, thank God.

'Where have you been?' she asked. 'Where's Silver?'

He scowled at the angels. 'Ask them.'

The female angel looked affronted. 'Grigori, such allegations cannot—'

Dad ignored the protestations, fixing his attention instead on Dylan. 'Why do you say that?'

'I think they just wanted her out of this. Like removing a queen from the chessboard. Zadkiel took her. He did something to the Sídheways, tore them or something and she … she jumped in to stop him. To save them.'

All around him, the Sídhe gave gasps of outrage and fear. Brí glowered, her hands knotting to fists at her side.

'What can be gained by that?' she asked in a flat tone. She knew what it could mean, better than Izzy did. She knew that without the Sídheways, the fae were in danger.

Dylan's eyes narrowed. To Izzy's surprise, he glanced at Azazel, who betrayed nothing. And then – she wouldn't have thought it possible – Dylan lied.

'I don't know. You'll have to ask him. But look. What a surprise. He isn't here.'

The angels, demons and Sídhe all began to shout at once but this time it was Brí who silenced them. Furious, she stormed forwards, her gown moving like flames licking the air around her.

'Enough! I am speaking now and you will be silent. I am Brí and you all know who and what I am. Lady Silver is a Matriarch of the Daoine Sídhe. If one of your kind has taken her and holds her against her will, you haven't begun to see chaos.'

Meridian smiled. Izzy couldn't say why she looked that way, why her eyes snagged on those of Holly's daughter. She didn't trust her. Couldn't. Unlike Silver she was Holly's through and through. She'd been there on Montpelier Hill, as tied up in Holly's thwarted plans as Holly herself. What was she even doing here? And why, right now, did she look like she was gloating?

'Of course we haven't,' Meridian said in the sudden silence.

'They care nothing for us. They see us as some kind of subspecies, not even worth talking to. Just another reason why we should band together. At times like this we need the protection of a *strong* leader, one who *isn't* afraid to stand up for us and take her place at the forefront of this battle. Holly will protect us and you all know that.'

'Don't bring her into this,' said Brí. 'We *all know* she's dangerous. You're only here under the promise that you can mediate. If you think to garner her new followers, think again.'

'What is it, Lady Brí?' the Leanán Sídhe sneered, her features hate-filled and all the beguiling beauty drained from her. 'Afraid to lose your precious hounds? Or should I say *more* of them?'

Chaos … Izzy could feel it in the air like ozone, crackling between each party. This was spiralling out of control even faster than she could have predicted. Brí's face flushed with anger and Meridian looked triumphant. Like she knew something they didn't.

'Dad?' Izzy whispered. She needed to warn him. Of what, she didn't know. But she had to tell him that something was terribly wrong.

A rumble like thunder shook the Long Room. Izzy knew it wasn't her this time. It couldn't be. Angry, yes, but not this insanely wild, and nothing like as powerful.

'Izzy?' said Dad, warily and so quietly no one else could hear. The argument in the room fell to silence and they all staggered back, staring at the doors. 'Behind me. Be ready to run.'

'Dad?'

'Get back!'

Another crash followed, rocking them all, silencing everyone. Each face turned towards the end of the room, and fury beat upon the doors. For a moment nothing happened and she thought maybe, just maybe, it was over. That whatever monster was out there had gone.

The doors splintered as they flew open, crashing and falling to kindling.

Holly walked through the debris, Osprey behind her grinning like a wild thing. The Wild Hunt followed, their eyes crazed, their faces filled with bloodlust, like a pack of rabid wolves. Holly raised a hand, holding the Hunt back with her will alone. She glowed, lights dancing beneath her skin, her eyes sparkling like the sun.

'Someone called for me?' she said and smiled her most dangerous smile. Meridian stepped forward, bowing, and all around her the banshees drew hidden weapons, long barbed knives which glinted in the light.

Chaos had arrived.

The dreams were worse than ever. Swirling, bewildering, like running through a Sídheway as it crumbled around him, sights and sounds mixed together like a kaleidoscope. It made him sick, made his head ache, and he couldn't seem to get away.

And then he saw her. Izzy. She blazed with light, far too much light. It wasn't the fire that usually rippled through her, or the light of the dawn that Sorath had filled her with. This was something different, far different. Far too familiar as well.

They stood on an island in a raging storm. Not much there, just rocks and scrappy grass. The scent of blood filled his nostrils, made his mouth water. And Izzy stood over him, illuminated.

His legs gave out beneath him and he hit the rocky ground hard, kneeling before her. She looked down at him, blue eyes blazing, the light beneath her skin shimmering with life, with wonder.

'Mistress,' he said. And he meant it. He meant the word in a way he never had when he said it to Holly. Each time he'd said it for her, it had been ground out of him, forced in order to protect himself, every breath begrudged. But for Izzy ... Oh, for Izzy, it was truth. It was everything. She had been there for him. She'd brought light into his life. She'd shown him kindness, tenderness, love ... and she had killed him. When he had asked her to, begged her for release ... she had killed him.

'We owe allieance to no mistress,' said the voice of the Púca. 'No master either. She must not got to the island. You must not kneel to her. To anyone. Stand up, fool. Don't do this.'

Don't ... that was all anyone said to him. Don't. Even Izzy.

'Don't let it happen to me,' she whispered in his ear. Her mouth didn't move except to smile. But her voice sounded afraid … no, terrified. *'Please Jinx. Don't let this happen.'*

'Where are we?'

'The Thorn Gate. The island. But it doesn't start here. It starts now. Today. Please. Remember.'

She reached out, touched his forehead, and the light exploded in his mind, tearing through him like an inferno. She was in danger, terrible danger.

A shiver ran over Jinx's skin as he woke. He lay in a heap of furs in a small chamber, an alcove, and the curious girl, Jane, was looking down on him with far too much interest.

'I don't think I've ever seen anyone sleep so long through a nightmare. The Briugu said you were exhausted and we shouldn't wake you.'

And yet here she was. Watching. Although, he reflected, as he raked his hand through his long hair, technically she hadn't woken him. The nightmare had done that. She had just watched, which was a whole new level of creepy. As was the manner of her watching – bright eyed, flushed cheeks.

'Jane, wasn't it?'

She curtseyed, bobbing down in a way so alien to him he was sure his mouth dropped open. 'Miss Jane Sherrard,' she said in formal tones. 'My father is Mr Henry Sherrard and he has lands nearby. Perhaps you've heard of him?'

He hadn't of course. And Jinx was willing to wager Mr Henry Sherrard and everyone Jane had known were a hundred years or more in the grave. She'd been taken by these fae but unlike Rothman she didn't appear entirely aware of it.

The thought of Rothman and what had happened to him made Jinx's mood darken.

'The Briugu?' he said, hoping he'd got the right word at least. 'The little tree guy?'

Jane laughed and covered her mouth. 'Yes.'

Briugu was a title rather than a name. He was the one in charge of a household, the one who extended hospitality to a stranger. 'Where is he? I need to talk to him.'

Jane shrugged. 'I'll take you to him if you like. Is it urgent?'

'Yes,' said Jinx and tried to push the nightmare from his mind. Izzy in danger. It was always Izzy in danger. But this time it felt so much more real.

'You're planning to leave us, aren't you? Is it for the Grigori girl?'

Suspicious darkened his mood instantly. 'How did you know about her?'

'I heard the others talking. They said you belong to her. Or that you used to. That she pulls a string and you run to her side. She'll hurt you, Jinx.' She took a step closer, far too close, and Jinx retreated, staring down at her. 'She'll get you killed. Again.'

She had been listening indeed. Listening to everything. Why did fae always assume humans were stupid? Jane was far from it.

'You don't understand.'

'She had you bespelled once, didn't she? Made you her slave. Is that why? Don't go. We'll look after you, take care of you. We'll keep you safe. I'll—'

'She's in danger. I need to help her.' *And I need her.* More than he could heave into words. But he couldn't say it.

'Do you still love her? They said you loved her, but she killed you.'

A wry smile tugged at his lips. He couldn't help himself. 'Twice. But she saved me too. I'm sorry, Jane, but I – '

'Off with you now, Janey my love,' said the Briugu, his wizened form appearing through the door behind them. 'Haw said he found some snowdrops off by the southern pasture. He'll show you where.'

She didn't take her eyes off Jinx, but chewed at her lower lip instead. 'Jinx, you could still stay with us.' With her, she meant. He could see that in her hopeless hopeful eyes. She believed in fairy tales, in love at first sight, in handsome princes. But he was no prince. He couldn't stay.

'I'm sorry, Jane,' he whispered and looked past her at the Briugu, dismissing her. It was kinder, in the long run.

Jane fled, spinning around and running past them as fast as she could.

'Poor Jane,' the Briugu sighed. 'Did you ever do a kindness and wish you'd left well enough alone?'

Jinx thought of the first time he met Izzy, in the alleyway at the gate to Dubh Linn near Silver's Hollow, picking up the broken pieces of her phone from the gutter, walking her out of the fae world and back to her own – yes, he knew that feeling.

'She's right though. I have to go. Izzy's in danger. She needs me.'

'And like a good dog, you must obey.'

He bristled, but he didn't argue. He feared the creature was right. But it didn't matter. Izzy was all that mattered.

'Do you know where she is?'

'Trinity. They're all there. Angels, demons … Aes Sídhe. All of them. But if you leave us now, there is every chance you won't come back. Do you understand? Janey thinks you won't. And she's rarely wrong. And even if you do, she says you'll be lost to us.'

Something in the way he said it sent chills down Jinx's spine. He stared at the Briugu, at the look in his ancient eyes, and his heart began to beat harder than ever, slamming up into the base of his throat. 'Holly's there, isn't she? In Trinity.'

'Oh yes. Where else did you expect her to be? She set this whole thing up. I see things, Jinx by Jasper, aye and feel them too. The Hunt runs with her. If you go there, you'll never be able to resist the pull of it. You know that. Holly knows it. It's the only way she was able to control you in the end. The Hunt. The past. You're a wild thing now, but part of you yearns to be something else. Holly made sure of that. She entwined you with spells, made you think you're worth no more than an animal. She abused you, Jinx, used you, controlled you. She'll make you a slave again. And if she doesn't, that girl will.'

Chapter Eighteen

Death Howl

For a moment, no one moved. Even Izzy's dad just stood there, shocked and open-mouthed. Dylan felt the magic in his body crackle with hatred, with anger, and his mind flew back to the hilltop last Halloween, his body helpless as he knelt at her feet. She'd grabbed his head and bent all his power to her will, using him like a battery, like he didn't matter. She had revelled in it.

And now he saw her anew, this glowing, far more dangerous Holly, with a wild array of creatures at her command. They looked drunk, off their heads, eyes wide, pupils so dilated that they filled the sockets with darkness. Osprey grinned, all his teeth on show, and he leered at those trapped before him. Power, that was the thing. The same magic that had swallowed him whole last night and dumped him in Azazel's clutches. Wild, unstable magic which would destroy them all eventually. If they even lived that long.

Osprey drew his weapons. There were marks on his neck, like those on Jinx's. Weird and intricate tattoos that made Dylan's skin crawl just looking at them. Osprey smiled, mouth wide, swinging his face away from Dylan, and looked straight at Izzy. He lunged forward but stopped suddenly, as if held on an invisible leash.

'An angel first, Osprey,' said Holly. 'They've all been hiding so well there's no picking them off anymore. We just need one. There'll be time for amusing yourself later.'

With that, the angels vanished. Air rushed in to fill the spaces they had occupied a moment earlier, a howling wind, dizzying and desperate.

All but one. Ash remained, tethered to the ground, or to Izzy. Or maybe just too weak to flee like her siblings.

Seized by Meridian's followers, she was dragged forward.

'No!' Izzy shouted, but her father waved her back.

Dylan glanced at Azazel. Ash was related to him as well, surely? But the demon didn't look worried. Maybe demons didn't care about angels, or their own kind. He'd let this happen. Demons didn't care about anyone.

'Let her go,' said David Gregory. 'I won't allow you to do this, Holly.'

'*Allow* me?' She drew a knife, something old and wickedly sharp, polished so many times that its blade was almost paper thin. It was black and shining, like obsidian. '*Allow* me …' The thought seemed to amuse her, and that couldn't be good.

Even Dylan knew that.

'You're forgetting, Lady Holly,' said Azazel. 'The Grigori stand at the centre of the Compact. We are here under a truce. Laws of heaven and hell, foundations of the world, that sort of thing?'

'You're here because I wanted you here.' She smiled, a radiant and beautiful expression, spreading her arms wide and pirouetting around. 'I agreed to no truce. I think you're forgetting something. All of you. The Compact is broken. Shattered. Irreparable. You, Azazel, kidnapped *his* wife, and the Keeper will not let that lie. You've all seen it, felt it, since then, the way they're watching, closing in on us, driving us back. They fear us, humankind. And when they fear something, they're at their most dangerous. You're all too busy fighting each other, trying to get the upper hand. You don't see anything. How else did I bring all of this about? All this and more.' She stopped, facing Izzy's dad, suddenly perfectly still. 'Let me show *you* something David, about what is *allowed*. You're here because I want you here. All those rules don't matter. *Because I don't care anymore.*'

She moved faster than the eye could see, flitting through a motion both graceful and lethal, hurling the knife in a blur of light and obsidian. It flashed for a moment, as it sped through the air, and with a sickening thud buried itself up to the hilt in its target.

David Gregory gasped in shock, doubled over, and fell to his knees.

Two of Holly's bodachs seized him, huge fists closing around his wrists, hauling his hands out wide so she could see what she had done, so they could all see his blood and the shock and pain on his face. The knife hilt jutted from his shoulder. They had manacles on him a moment later.

Izzy screamed, her voice shaking the air, the earth itself. She flung herself towards her father, heedless of the enemies holding him. The Cú Sídhe moved, Brí's followers surrounding her, holding her back. Blythe wrapped her arms around the girl and Izzy kicked and struggled, reaching out for him, trying with words alone to make this untrue.

Fire and lightning wreathed Dylan's hands. The same rage filled him, the anger that came from Silver's imprisonment, trapped in him and desperate for a target.

He lunged forward to attack, but Azazel's hand closed on his wrist, jerking him to a halt. No strength in the world could have broken free.

'Dylan,' said Azazel. 'You want Silver back, don't you? And everything else I can give you? I keep my promises. The offer still holds. You can have the spark. Come with us.'

Go? Run? Silver was everything to him, but the Gregorys were like family. All of them. He couldn't just abandon them. Besides ... Azazel didn't have the spark. He'd said as much. He might know where it was, but it wasn't his to give.

'I'm not leaving them here alone.'

For a moment the demon didn't move. Desire to control Dylan and his magic warred with the need to protect his own skin.

'Come now, or forget it all. They'll drain you dry, touch-stone.'

Dylan didn't budge, and Azazel hissed in frustration. He snatched his hand away as if Dylan's skin burned.

'On your own head then.' The demons didn't hesitate. One moment they were there, and the next the shadows had swallowed them, Holly's power extending no more over them than it did over the angels. Dylan stood alone between Holly and the fae who didn't follow her. His rage knew no bounds. He had lost Silver. He would lose Izzy, not to mention David Gregory, who had been a second father to him.

He advanced and Holly watched him, amused. It should have frightened him, but he didn't know fear anymore. Anger had control. And his magic was a crescendo of white noise inside him.

'*Dylan, no.*' It was Silver's voice. Over the noise of his magic running wild, he heard it and hesitated. '*Please, love, don't. She'll kill you. Worse, she will enslave you. Again.*' For a moment the insane anger faded and all he felt was loss. Emptiness. But then she was gone and the tempest was back, filling him, overpowering him.

He staggered and in that moment someone seized his arms, twisting them behind his back, kicking his knees out from under him. A beaded necklace looped around his neck, choking him.

Meridian laughed, wild and delighted. She released his arms as the strength drained out of him and stroked his head, running her fingers through his hair while all the time tightening the wire around his neck.

'Just what I wanted,' she breathed and kissed his cheek, her lips so cold against his skin. 'To take you from Silver. You and all her power. Don't struggle now. It's already over. You've lost.'

The breathless urgency of combat seized Izzy and the Blade rushed to fill her hand with fire. The Cú Sídhe couldn't keep her back. She wouldn't allow it, not with her dad, Ash and Dylan captured.

Brí stepped forward, her eyes aflame.

'Get away from them, Holly.'

'Or what? Are you finally willing to face me? Over these creatures? Or will you let your pawn there do that? She's part of you, isn't she? Is that why you shield her?' She pointed at Izzy. 'Your daughter. Your heir. And as for David Gregory here ...'

He lifted his head, looking right at Brí, his eyes pleading. Dad had never looked at anyone like that. Izzy knew it. Blythe still held on to her.

'Get Izzy out of here,' David Gregory told Brí, his voice a whisper of pain. 'Get all of them out of here.'

No, he couldn't do this. He couldn't sacrifice himself for them. Not Dad. Not after everything.

'Let me go,' Izzy hissed. 'Please. You have to let me go.' But the Cú Sídhe wasn't listening. She didn't obey Izzy and never had.

Brí shook her head. Izzy's heart stuttered in her chest. She was denying him? Now? But that wasn't true, couldn't be. Brí wasn't even looking at Holly now, just at Dad, and she was denying what he was begging her to do.

'You love him, Brí,' Holly taunted. 'You always have done. Pathetic, if you ask me.'

Osprey laughed and others joined in. A cackling chorus of hatred.

'No one asked you,' Brí murmured, a frown creasing her perfectly smooth skin.

Holly walked towards him, circling him and running her hands over his taut shoulders. She paused at the knife and then shoved it deeper still. Dad gritted his teeth on a groan. 'I'm going to keep him alive, you know? I'm going to bleed him slowly. We're going to the Thorn Gate. Come with us. You know you want to.' She held out a hand to the other Matriarch who stared at it like it was infected.

'Brí,' said Dad, hoarsely. 'Get out of here.'

'David, I can't.'

'You must,' he said.

And Brí erupted in flames. The other fae recoiled, screaming, but Holly moved like a burst of light, her arms spread wide as if to engulf the approaching fire. She lunged forward, throwing all her might against Brí.

Before Izzy knew what was happening, Blythe seized her

bodily and lifted her from the ground, running for the exit at the far end. She screamed in rage, but the Cú Sídhe didn't answer, or let up for a moment.

Osprey was already there. He landed lightly on his feet, that cloak of feathers billowing out behind him and twin swords in his hands. Izzy fell as Blythe skidded to a halt and released her. She rolled as she hit the floor and scrambled up just in time to see the Cú Sídhe leader twist aside, dodging the vicious arc of the swords. She transformed into her hound form, leaving her gown a scrap of material wrapped around her hind quarters.

Izzy glanced over her shoulders to see fae fighting fae, the whole place awash with the light of the fire and the brightness of the sun. The flames licked up the walls and bookshelves, but didn't touch the books, didn't leave scorches behind it. This wasn't natural fire and this was a sacred place. But Holly's light was blinding, too terrible to look at.

Blythe dashed by her, trying her knock her out of the way, as Osprey bore down on them. Instinctively Izzy raised the Blade and it roared from her hand, blocking him. He staggered to a halt, amazed to see her fighting back, and she felt a thrill of triumph. It might not last, but it was the little things.

He hissed something at her in a language she didn't recognise, not anything complimentary, she was sure, and attacked again. She couldn't match the ferocity, barely managed to block the savage blows as he drove her back. Her legs buckled and she couldn't tell where he'd come from next. He was too fast, too strong, everything about him amplified. Suddenly she knew she was in trouble. Deep trouble. She didn't know what she was doing. Not the way he did. She was just lucky he couldn't disarm her.

Unless he ripped her arm off.

He raised the swords, ready to gut her, and she brought the Blade over her in a vain attempt to shield herself.

Blythe went for his throat, claws tearing at his chest and shoulders. For a moment, just a moment, Izzy thought the Cú Sídhe would take him down, and she lunged forward to help, even if she had no idea how to do that. And then, almost in slow motion, one of his swords came up, biting deep into Blythe's torso and bursting out through her back. Blood splattered on Izzy's face, hot and sticky, blinding her. Blythe jerked against the weapon, her body changing back to Aes Sídhe form in a convulsion of agony. She was just a woman, naked and broken, her face a mask of shock as she slid down to the ground. Her eyes turned glassy and unfocused and she gave a rattling sigh.

The death howl of the Cú Sídhe broke out, a harrowing noise ringing through the building and beyond. Grief gripped them all, panic and terror. Blythe was their leader, Blythe beloved of all. They panicked, their ranks breaking, their leader down. And Brí screamed, a sound of such anguish that the windows high overhead shattered. Shards of glass rained down on them as Izzy bent over Blythe's body, tried desperately to help her, to wake her.

But she was gone.

Osprey moved first, grabbing Izzy by the neck. Choking, gasping for air, she couldn't break free.

She saw Blight running towards Brí as Holly's light grew brighter still. He was a silhouette against her, but he didn't stop. He seized his stricken Matriarch and pulled her clear, the pack closing ranks and running. The other fae, those still fighting, fled and in a moment, it was all over.

Osprey dragged Izzy up the length of the library, past bodies and carnage, to where Holly stood with Ash and Dad held captive.

Dad who was bleeding, dying, spilling Grigori blood. The light that was Holly engulfed him, but Izzy could still make out his form, held prisoner, his mouth wide in a silent scream as Holly tormented him. Oh God, Izzy realised, she had Dad. She had all the Grigori blood she needed to bind the other Shining Ones inside anyone she chose. Osprey was already grinning from ear to ear as Izzy tried to get purchase on the ground, tried to find some way to tear herself free. Her feet skidded on the floor, unable to get purchase.

Holly coalesced from the light, visible once more, though her skin still glowed and her eyes were shining like stars. Her golden hair flowed from her scalp like a river of light. And her hand was dripping with blood.

Dad's blood.

'Come here, Isabel Gregory,' said Holly and under the brightness of her stare what else could Izzy do?

Osprey released her and she fell, but instantly stumbled up

from her knees. Her legs moved sluggishly, but without pause, dragging their way forward across the wooden floor. Ash gave a sob, twisting in the grip of the banshee who held her down on her knees. She couldn't escape. Furious with herself for leaving her guardian so weak, there was nothing Izzy could do. Her own body wasn't even obeying her anymore.

'Let her go,' Dad ground out the words. He was so close now she could hear the pain in his voice, but she couldn't respond. 'Don't do this.'

She couldn't help him. All she could do was walk inexorably forward, like a condemned prisoner to the executioner.

'We've been here before, you and I,' said Holly, her voice softer now she had her way. 'You know what to do, Isabel.' Izzy dropped to her knees and Holly reached out a hand, her fingertips stroking Izzy's cheek almost affectionately. The Blade grew still, compliant like a purring cat and Izzy's mind recoiled in horror, but she lifted her face. She felt her lips draw up in a smile. An alien expression on her face. Inside, she was screaming.

Holly looked down on her, wondrous and bewitching. 'Good girl. I never imagined this would be so easy. You're perfect, Isabel Gregory. Look at you. Made for this. Oh, but Sorath was right …'

Izzy drank down the praise, her mind lost in Holly's power, her body compliant and obedient.

'You promised, Holly,' said Osprey, his voice thick with lust, which made her skin crawl.

'Indeed, I did. But in my time, and you would do well to obey me. Bring me the angel.'

Ash was dragged forward and Izzy watched, helplessly. She knew she should be angry, or afraid. She knew she should do something, but it all seemed so distant and far away, and Holly wouldn't do anything wrong. Holly was always right. And nothing else could persuade Izzy differently, not now, when she knelt there drenched in Holly's power.

Holly shushed Ash's protests, her touch as tender with the angel as they were with Izzy. But the power didn't seem to have the same effect. Ash looked terrified. And that wasn't right. She should be happy to be of use, just like Izzy was. She shouldn't be afraid.

Holly placed a finger at the base of the angel's throat. 'Just here. Don't kill her, though. Not yet. There's no fun if it's too quick. And they just smudge. She's such a dark little beauty this one, I want her preserved on the walls of my throne room for eternity. And for that, it has to be slow. Careful. A small cut, Osprey. Just there. An incision.'

He drew a shorter knife and brought it up to Ash's throat.

'Izzy,' Ash gasped. 'Izzy, you have to fight her. Please, Izzy, listen to me.'

Izzy frowned and looked back at Holly, who smiled at her. 'She can barely hear you, let alone understand you. I'm going to make her so much better, little angel. More than a Grigori. She's made for this. Sorath saw to that. A perfect vessel, designed to be filled with power. Look at her, how willingly she submits ...'

'You will pay for this,' Ash blurted out the words. 'For me and for every other angel you've destroyed. Every life you've taken. For every—'

Holly struck her hard across the face, snapping her head to the right and drawing blood from her mouth. Ash spat at her, glared and opened her mouth to continue but that was the moment Osprey chose to cut her.

Just a little cut, a nick, no longer than a fingernail, exactly where Holly had instructed. Ash hissed in pain, in shock, as Holly's hand closed on the wound. And at that touch, Ash's cry of dismay contorted to a piercing scream.

The air around them shook and warped, the pitch increasing in agony. Holly drew out Ash's spark, the part of the divine that lived inside the angel. It shone like moonlight, pale next to Ash's copper skin and Holly's radiance, but so beautiful it captivated Izzy.

'Perfect,' Holly breathed, as she threaded it through her fingers, teasing it out to a shining line. 'So pure and untainted. And so strong. They dismissed you as a mere guardian, didn't they? Fools. Angels get their strength from love, from the strength of those they guide and guard, and you are loved indeed. Not just by Isabel, it seems. By all of them. Oh yes. You're just perfect.'

She reached towards Izzy's throat, the line wrapped around her fingers and Izzy tipped back her head, welcoming her touch.

'No!' Dylan shouted. 'Izzy, no!'

Something jolted through Izzy's body, an instinct, a primal reaction. Her mind whirled, tearing through the spell that suffocated her. She reached out to the shadows that had filled her in Donn's Hollow, the other power she knew was inside her, entwined with the Blade. The darkness to its fire. And she called it down, all the shielding, comforting darkness, called it to her and wrapped herself in it.

The earth shook and night thundered down around them. The spell of Holly's light broken, Izzy threw herself back but Holly's hand closed on her wrist, the spark and the magic of her father's blood searing into her flesh there like a branding iron. The magic enchanting her gone, Izzy screamed and tore herself free.

Something slammed into her from the left, taking her down in a tangle of limbs. Her head struck one of the mahogany shelves and the world turned dizzy and blurred. She hauled herself up to face this new threat, sobbing out her pain and anger.

Hands pulled her to her feet, gentle hands, long fingered and elegant.

'Izzy,' said a voice, an impossible voice. 'Izzy, listen to me. Listen. We have to go.'

She tried to focus. She couldn't just leave. And the voice, oh God that voice – No, she couldn't think that. It had to be a trick. She had to focus. 'My dad, Dylan and Ash – '

'Izzy, please, she's too strong. I can't hold on. The darkness—'

It wasn't possible. He was dead, or a monster, or turned evil. Holly's creature. Holly's thing. But why hadn't he been there like Osprey? Why was he here now?

The air had been stolen from her chest. Shadows surrounded her and ate away at the edges of her vision and his face filled in the rest. Angular and beautiful, stern with fear and determination. The tattoos marking his skin stood out in that familiar stark contrast. And his eyes were golden, instead of grey. His eyes …

But they were still his eyes.

'Trust me,' he said. 'Please, Izzy. Just this once, trust me.'

She wrapped her hand in his and tried to stand. Her other wrist throbbed and ached where Holly had touched her. The darkness around them was fading, and Holly's light grew stronger again.

'I trust you, Jinx,' she whispered. 'Please. Help.'

Her arms wrapped around his neck and as he lifted her, she buried her face in his hair. She felt his body move, transform, flowing beneath her touch until she was on the back of a black horse, her hands tangled in the mane.

She heard Holly's voice, her shouts of rage and promises of vengeance, but the Púca was already galloping down the length of the library, carrying her with him.

Chapter Nineteen

Maelstrom

The crows led him to her. From the moment he left Puck's Castle, they took wing, black birds, filling the sky. Knowing where Holly was now, he took the threadbare Sídheways and they were waiting at the other end. If he hesitated they filled the air with a raucous cacophony and if he took a wrong turn, they dive bombed him until he was back on track. The hound in him panicked, but the Púca knew and understood. Somehow, he knew. Instinct told him, or some other deeply ingrained knowledge – Izzy needed him and the crows were showing him the way.

The Sídheways reminded him of the nightmare. Threadbare wasn't enough of a word for them. He could feel them unravelling as he travelled them, a nauseous gut-twisting sensation that left him lightheaded. Which had to account for the voice.

A voice sang on the edge of his hearing. Too faint to be real.

Too clear to be imaginary.

It sounded like Silver.

Jinx didn't hesitate. He fled, finding the way out into Dublin itself and relative safety. Except nowhere was safe.

Chaos engulfed the area around Trinity. Terrified people poured out of the funnel-like entrance onto Nassau Street, crashing into the roadworks and the traffic, spilling on to the road and up Dawson Street. Inside the campus walls, they tried to find shelter in the university buildings. He didn't pause to question anyone even if he could have – a huge black dog suddenly transforming into a naked tattooed man wasn't going to help matters. Besides, there wasn't time. Izzy was in danger, and he knew what the chief threat had to be. This was all part of Holly's plan – Holly's trap. And clearly Holly didn't care about the mortal world discovering the fae one anymore.

Didn't care, or wanted it to happen.

Sirens blared out across the campus. Gardaí and college security were trying to establish some sort of cordon while at the same time moving a mob to safety.

'What the hell is that?' someone near him screamed, breathless with terror. He turned, expecting an attack, thinking that he had been seen, but they were pointing at the crows, more than he'd ever seen. The birds mobbed the broken windows of the old library building. And they were silent. Completely silent.

Whatever was happening, there was nothing secret about it. Not now. And Holly … Holly seriously didn't care anymore.

Time was running out. No one paid any attention to a stray dog at moments like this, even one as big as Jinx in hound form. And their eyes tended to slip away from him. He moved like a ghost amongst the crowd of refugees and they parted, getting out of his way, as if avoiding stepping on a grave. He took every advantage.

The door stood open and he slipped inside. The little shop beyond it was in chaos, shelves tumbled, trinkets scattered everywhere. There were bodies too, mostly fae, one or two human amongst them. It was worse than he thought. They'd never manage to cover this up. Never.

But right now it didn't matter. Only Izzy mattered and whatever Holly was doing to her.

A terrible howl knocked him from his feet. He shrank back, every nerve quivering with grief and dismay as he felt it tear through him. He whined, trying to flatten his ears to block out the noise but that was impossible, because it wasn't coming from outside. It rang through his brain, through the heart of him, magical and awful. Unable to do anything else, he threw back his head and joined in, howling with an agony which wrenched his voice from him.

Blythe!

He felt her passing like a cold wind through his fur, as a fading perfume, as a phantom touch, as only the Cú Sídhe could. Even though he was Púca now, his heart was still part of that long lost pack. But she was Blythe, the strong and relentless, all the voices he suddenly heard inside his mind cried. She was their leader, their heart, the core of the pack which had taken him in. She couldn't be gone!

But she was. He knew she was. The death howl told him that for sure.

They came down the steps while his mind still reeled with loss, those who could still run carrying those who could not, bundling Brí between them. Jinx saw Blight, saw the surprise on his features as he recognised Jinx.

Get out of here, cousin. All is lost.

Izzy's still in there.

The protest fell on deaf ears.

All is lost, Cú Sídhe. The Grigori, the Touchstone … taken … the angels deserted us and the demons too. Most of the fae fled. Holly is a Shining One, Osprey as well –

'Jinx,' said Brí. Her face was bloodless, her eyes wide with grief. He'd never seen her look anything but calm and cruel. But now – she reached out to touch him and he shied back. 'Jinx … they killed Blythe … my Blythe … They have David and Isabel …'

They had Izzy. He lifted his head as a scent hit him, coppery and sharp. He knew it. Blood. And not just any blood. Grigori blood. He knew that. He had tasted it. The memory made his mouth burn.

Izzy …

'Jinx by Jasper, do what you must.'

Leaping past the retreating fae, he got to the top of the stairs just in time to see Izzy fall to her knees in front of Holly.

The Matriarch's hand was stained with blood and she had an angel's spark between her fingers. He felt the tattoos around his neck turn cold and tighten like a collar. Izzy wasn't fighting or running. She looked up at Holly in worship, in welcome. Just as he once had.

Holly was going to bind her as she had once bound him. She was going to make Izzy into the monster she had almost made of him.

The crows screamed overhead and Holly looked up, startled, a confused frown spreading over her face. There was a moment of balance, of indecision, of pause. And then the birds flung themselves forward, through the shattered windows, a cloud of darkness and whirling feathers.

A moment. He had a single moment. Not for David Gregory, or Ash. Not even for Dylan. But he could get to Izzy in that heartbeat, in that breath and steal her away. He had to. Otherwise there would be three Shining Ones incarnate and the world would be lost. That was what Brí had meant, perhaps foreseen …

He had to trust that this was something she had foreseen.

Do what you must.

In other words *'Save her'*.

He lunged into the maelstrom of black wings and tore Izzy free. They tumbled body over body, even as he transformed back into Aes Sídhe. Grabbing her as gently as he could, he drew her to her feet. She looked woozy and blood trickled down the side of her face. Shit, had she hit her head?

Was she okay?

'Izzy,' he said urgently. 'Izzy, listen to me. We have to go.'

She tried to focus, squinting at him, clearly unable to believe her senses. 'My dad, Dylan and Ash—'

'Izzy, please, she's too strong. I can't hold on. The darkness—'

She almost pulled back, but didn't seem able to look away from him. Or move. Damn it, he needed her to move. Around them the crows were falling, dying. Holly's light was tearing through them one by one.

'Trust me,' he said. 'Please, Izzy. Just this once, trust me.'

It was an impossible request. He knew that. He shouldn't ask it of her but he had to. Just once, he needed her to trust him, and he had no right to ask it of her.

Izzy's fingers tightened on his, squeezed as if trying to see if he was real. The she said the impossible. 'I trust you, Jinx. Please. Help.'

He didn't need her to say it a second time. He nodded and pulled her onto his back as he transformed to the Púca's horse shape. He was already galloping before he had fully trans-formed and Izzy clung to his back, her hands buried in the mane. He could feel her trembling, fighting to stay on, but he couldn't slow. Couldn't hesitate.

Holly shouted his name. She knew him, recognised him. Of course she did. But he was already running and she couldn't catch him. Not now.

The doors at the end of the library stood open and he leaped through, hooves slamming on to the stone staircase as he turned. His hindquarters slammed into the wall and pain speared through him, but he couldn't stop. Thundering down the stairs he prayed Izzy could hold on. He was barely keeping his footing. At the bottom of the stairs he swerved into an exhibition room and crashed through it, sending cases and displays flying. There had to be a way out of here. It was a maze, a labyrinth, and he was hopelessly lost.

Then he saw it. Another door. A way out drenched in light. He burst through it and out into the square behind the building. He made for the open grass of the rugby field, galloping across them regardless of the shouts and cries of alarm. Adrenaline and determination drove him onwards. There was a Sídheway gate near here, he knew that much. He just couldn't remember exactly where. Somewhere on the grounds of this bloody place. There were too many people and it was broad daylight and he was in the form of a fucking horse. He had to get out of here.

And then he saw it, a shimmer of light underneath the arch that led by the Science Gallery. People cowered at the entrance, staring at him with huge, disbelieving eyes. He ran straight at it, leaping through before he could think twice about who might see him and why. An oversized horse running around in broad daylight and vanishing into thin air.

What did it matter now?

Crows came from the windows, so many that they were like

living darkness. Meridian jerked back, her grip on Dylan loosening. Just fractionally, just for a moment, but Dylan was ready. He twisted as she was off balance, and rammed his elbow back blindly. It struck home, her stomach or solar plexus, he didn't know, but somewhere that made her release him. He dived for the floor and crawled to Ash.

Her crumpled form lay unmoving in front of David Gregory's chained body. Dylan looked up. Izzy's dad shook his head even though it clearly took effort to do even that. Blood covered his stomach, soaking through his shirt and dripping down to the ground.

'Get out of here,' he said. 'There isn't time and you can't take us both. Even if I could get these off ...' He yanked the chain forward and gasped, biting back a curse. 'Get going, while you can. We can't afford Holly to have power over you. You're a touchstone, and a powerful one. All of Silver's magic in you, all your music. She's too strong already. Go.' He nodded to the far end of the library.

Damn it, he was right. Izzy would never forgive either of them, but Dylan didn't have a choice. At the heart of that dark tempest, he could just make out Jinx's form. He didn't know how or why, or if it was even real. But it was Jinx.

And this was the only chance any of them would get.

The birds were starting to fall, dying.

'That way, upstairs.' David Gregory nodded to the far end of the library. 'There's a way out. Go to Brí. Quickly, now. Get out of—'

In an eruption of black feathers, a horse burst from the cloud of crows, Izzy clinging to its back. Holly and her followers charged after it and Dylan slung Ash over his shoulder in a vain attempt at a fireman's lift. Lucky for him she was so small she weighed nothing at all.

'Mr Gregory—'

'Now, Dylan! Go!'

He sprinted in the opposite direction, down through the hall. He heard Meridian howling out orders, and then thundering footsteps following him. Not everyone had gone after Izzy. But he knew this place. He studied here. Well not *here* exactly, but he'd done the tour. He knew the university layout, attended classes when he could turn up, when his life wasn't this insane. The spiral staircase would take him up to the next level and at the end, right at the end, there were lifts.

'Ash, can you hear me? How many?' He couldn't look back. Didn't have time.

'Five,' she said, her voice frail but determined. 'Banshee. And her. Holly's daughter.'

Five wasn't bad, was it? Four banshees, creatures who could kill with their voice alone, one of whom had killed his sister while he looked on helplessly, just with her unnatural song. And Meridian who was a psycho, obsessed with getting one over on Silver. Which meant getting him. No. Five was not good.

He grabbed the metal rail of the staircase and flung himself around it and up, almost on all fours at this stage, scrambling up to the next level. As he reached it something locked around his ankle, pulling him back. One of the banshees. She opened her mouth to let out that terrible cry. Ash grabbed a huge tome from a shelf above his head and hurled it down on their pursuers. It smacked right into the leading banshee's face, sending her falling back on the others. Free again he leaped up the last few steps and ran on.

The metal didn't stop them, as he'd hoped it would. They pounded after him.

'Keep going,' Ash told him, her grip loosening. 'Whatever happens – '

'No!' He seized her, hauling her back up and pitching himself forwards so she couldn't let go.

The lifts. He had to make the lifts. He could hear the pursuit again but didn't dare glance back until he flung them both into the tiny metal box and frantically pushed at the buttons. He let Ash go at last and she slid to the floor behind him, but the doors didn't close. He hammered the buttons again. The light flickered, on and off, and around Ash he could see something like shadows of wings, like after-images made of guttering candlelight. They moved, feebly, helplessly, and vanished.

The banshees charged after them. He could see them bearing down, white-faced, vicious, their mouths open and eyes murderous. But as the lead one came within reach of the lift, she shrieked and dropped to her knees, hands in front of her like a shield. The skin on her fingers hissed and burned, the others screeching to a halt around her.

'What are you doing?' Meridian yelled. 'Take them.'

She dived past them, slamming into the lift beside him. For a moment they stood face to face, and he saw the vile grin on her perfect face. Her hands closed on his throat and his head slammed back against the wall.

And Meridian found herself surrounded by metal. Metal which sparked and ran with arcs of electricity, metal which clearly didn't want anything fae near it.

Her face fell, the expression first – a twitch making her eyes look weird, broken – followed by the skin, melting off the bones. Her mouth dropped open in a scream which never emerged. Her grip on his neck slid away, leaving a trail of something like slime behind it, down his chest. Her skin dripped from her hands, her long golden hair coming out in clumps. She fell like a sack of old sticks and clothes at his feet and the lift doors slid silently closed.

The whole contraption jerked as it began its descent. Dylan sucked in a breath, just one which was all he could manage, and fought not to throw up. He ought to look away from the remains of the Aes Sídhe, but he couldn't.

The lift shuddered to a halt and opened to reveal a tall black woman in a charcoal suit, her hair piled on top of her head, an earpiece perched on one ear. She was holding an iron knife which at first glance you might take for a letter opener – just at the first glance – and murder filled her eyes. In her other hand was a small grey rock, entirely smooth except for the hole in the middle.

Behind her stood eight soldiers, all with guns pointed right at him.

'Feck it, Margot,' she said, giving the floor of the lift a look of disgust and ignoring them completely. 'One of the buggers got in. I'm not cleaning that up.'

Dylan gulped in another breath, his gaze flicking between the knife and the guns. How were there soldiers with guns here? He didn't think the Irish army had that many guns. And weren't they meant to be off with the UN or something? 'I didn't— I didn't—'

She shook her head, her face all concern. 'Of course you didn't, love. Come on out of there. It's grand. We need to get you out of the campus. It's too dangerous just now.'

He helped Ash to her feet, carefully keeping her behind him.

'Who are you?' he asked.

'Oh, I just work here. Don't worry about me. Come on, out you come.'

As they stepped out, the weapons followed them, moving fluidly, unerringly. No amateurs these. Dylan had got so used to his life being in peril from magical means that finding himself at the business end of a pile of manmade lethal weapons was unnerving. The woman lifted a hand and Dylan stopped again, trying to hide the fact he was trembling. He hoped it wasn't obvious.

She peered at them each in turn through the hole in the stone. 'Grand. They're human, Margot.'

The stone flickered, like a faulty lightbulb and then went dark again. She shook it, squinted at it and shook it again.

'Hang on.' She looked at them again through it but nothing happened. 'Weird.' She peered at Dylan. 'Did they touch you? Mark you in any way?'

'You know about them?'

'The Sídhe? Of course we know about them.'

'Who are you? The government?'

She actually laughed, a broad and amused laugh which died just as quickly as it started. 'No,' she said. 'Right, well, oddness aside. Margot will evacuate you.'

Whoever Margot was, Dylan didn't know, but at least the soldiers lowered their weapons. He glanced back at Ash, who looked terrified. That scared him more than anything else. If Ash was afraid…

Another woman appeared, dainty and formal, wearing another tailored suit and a narrow pair of glasses. A plastic id badge on a long lanyard hung around her neck and it had her photo on it. And a name. There was a crest of some kind. It looked very official.

'I'll take it from here, Thea,' said Margot. 'Let's get you out of here.'

She led them away from the lifts, Thea and the soldiers, down a flight of stairs and into a tunnel. Water dripped from the ceiling above in a slow, steady rhythm and hit the general area of buckets left at inconsistent intervals. At least Dylan hoped it was water.

'Do you work here?' he asked, curiosity getting the better of him.

'Yes,' said Margot.

'So you're a librarian?'

She smiled, a secretive sort of smile, as if she took pleasure in being obtuse. 'Of sorts.'

'And you know about the Sídhe.'

'Oh, it's our business to know about all sorts of things, Mr O'Neill.'

She knew his name. Dylan stopped, Ash holding on to him even tighter as she limped along beside him. She had heard it too. 'What?' said Margot. 'Do you want to get out of here or not? They're sending the army in, you know. She won't take kindly to it and you did just get her daughter killed. Come on, keep up.'

What else could they do? She had a point. If they attacked Holly, anything could happen. 'They have David Gregory.'

If that meant something to her, Margot didn't react. 'We'll take care of it.' She stopped by the steps. 'Here we are. Head up there, round the corner and you'll see your way out. Don't dawdle. Oh and we'll be in touch. We have rather a lot of questions for you.'

Dylan took one more look at her, at her narrow face and piercing glare, and started up the stairs at a brisk pace, which became a run as soon as it was clear they were away. Ash stumbled after him, trying to keep up. He clung to her grimly. They were outside in moments, and hurrying towards a police cordon and freedom. He heard a sob and glanced back. Ash looked stricken, one hand still pressed to the cut on her neck.

'What is it? Are you all right?'

'They said I was human.' She met his gaze with a horrified expression of her own. 'Those people said I was just human.'

Marked

Music reached into the shadows of her dreams and pulled her out of them. The most beautiful music she had ever heard. It soothed her, made the nightmares fall away. It chased Holly from her head just like magic.

Izzy woke to darkness. She hated that. It made her feel like she was missing something vital. The music faded, gone like her dreams. Her head still ached, as did her arms, and for a moment she didn't know why. But when she moved, it all flooded back. Too many memories, too many horrors, all too fast. She was lying on a pile of furs and she didn't know where she was. But every moment of the events in the Long Library replayed like bursts of fireworks in her mind. She dragged herself upright, listening hard. She could conjure up a flame to see by, but she didn't know if she should. If she did that, she gave herself away to whoever hid in this darkness. She knew they were there, could hear them – every breath, every fluttering heartbeat – so many of them, all terrified. Of her.

And then she heard a voice.

'Izzy?'

She closed her eyes, terrified that it was real, and that it wasn't. His voice. She knew it instantly, it was unmistakable. There was a slight tremble to it, as if it mirrored the shaking in her hands. She curled them into fists to hide it. Creeping forward, she followed the wall with one hand, listening intently.

It *was* him. She knew it. It had to be.

'Izzy,' he said again, more of a sigh this time, perhaps a rebuke. She wasn't sure.

But it was him. Really him.

'Jinx?' she whispered, waiting for the curtain to be pulled back, for the big reveal, for someone to tell her it was all a horrible mistake. And laugh.

Oh, she was just waiting for that mocking laughter.

Torches lit up, running in a line around the chamber, throwing light up onto the bronze ceiling and illuminating everything. She stood in the middle of a Sídhe Hollow. The pile of furs where she had been lying were only a couple of feet behind her in a more private alcove, and were nothing more elaborate than that. Everything here was basic, primal.

The others she had sensed were nowhere to be seen, but she could still sense them. Hiding out of sight, watching her.

But that didn't matter now. She stared at the huge carved chair opposite her, or rather at the young man sitting in it, with a harp in his hands, his long fingers still resting against the strings.

He stared at her with golden eyes that weren't his. Or hadn't been, once upon a time. But everything else was – his mouth, his nose, the stubborn set of his jaw, the long black silken hair, the arrogant arch of his eyebrows. Pale skin and indigo tattoos, like a mixture between Celtic knotwork and something tribal.

'Jinx,' she said again, as if by naming him she could make him real, make this not just another sick dream sent to torment her. Her body wanted to hate him. She could feel that, and it rattled through her, the need to attack the Púca before her. But at the same time, she couldn't move. Wouldn't. She wasn't going to be told, by whatever had programmed her body or her ancestors' bodies, to hate them. It was Jinx. She couldn't hate Jinx.

He rose slowly, setting the harp aside – always the musician, she thought with a pang, so careful of an instrument. Cautiously, he approached her, like someone moving towards a skittish animal that might flee or attack if he made the wrong move.

'What happened to you?' he asked.

'To me?' She couldn't quite grasp the question. She hadn't vanished. But when she thought about it another way, she had. She'd vanished from inside her own head with her memories. 'It doesn't matter.'

'It does to me.' He was almost within reach now. She could throw herself into his arms. She could reach out to him and kiss him.

But she couldn't move. Her body vibrated with need and anger, with suppressed hatred and love.

'How – how did you come back? I killed you. What happened?'

His golden eyes darkened and his face fell. 'Holly. She brought me back, made me her beast again. I did – Izzy – ' He lifted his hands as if he wanted to take hers but didn't dare. 'I did terrible things.'

She swallowed hard on the sudden lump in her throat. 'I know. I saw.'

'Then you know what I am now.'

She frowned, staring at him. He wasn't making sense. 'You're Jinx. You're my Jinx.'

And a Púca? What did that matter? Time was she would have been shocked that he wasn't even human. And now … now …

No one was going to tell her who to hate. No one. Not angels, not her father, not her ancestors and whatever they'd done.

She crossed the last gap between them in a heartbeat, her hands reaching out for him, closing on his shirt and pulling him to her. He answered in equal measure, his hands on her arms, encircling her body, crushing her to him.

It was sudden and brutal but at the same time unbearably necessary. His lips captured her and she moaned, trying to pull him even closer, driving her fingers through his hair. He was warm and vital, all hard lines and muscles, but she fitted against him as if she would never come away from him again.

'Izzy ...' He groaned as he framed her face with his hands, explored the new, short hair and kissed her again. 'What happened to you?'

'I did something stupid trying to find you. So stupid that I lost myself, but I'm better now. Mostly better. Kind of.'

'What happened to your hair?'

She started back, remembering the pain, the shame. She brought her hand up to her short cut self-consciously. 'I ... I cut it.' She bit her lower lip, studying the bemused expression on his face.

A weird sort of smile flickered over his lips, as if he was trying to decide whether to laugh or not, as if sorrow and delight was at odds and he didn't know which to embrace.

'Izzy,' he said again, softly, like a prayer. He held out his hand. She took it more gently this time and he closed his fingers around hers, like she was a precious gift. 'I missed you. Even when I thought I'd never see light again, when I thought I'd lose everything I was, I still missed you more.'

'Jinx, I ...' But what could she say? She had forgotten him? That she hadn't meant to but she'd forgotten him and lost her mind? 'I would have found you sooner, I promise, but I – I didn't ...'

Tears stung her eyes, frustration at the unfairness of it all, at her own foolishness, at all Holly must have put him through in the meantime.

'I was gone, love,' he told her solemnly. 'You couldn't have found me in what Holly made of me. But when I saw you at the Storyteller's Hollow, when she almost had you, I – '

She remembered blood on his face, the fanatical fire in his golden eyes, the horror as he realised who she was, that she was there.

He hung his head. His hair fell forward, veiling his face. 'She made me a monster.'

'No, Jinx ...'

'She made me a reflection of herself, her tool ... A Púca in a hunt is a monster, Izzy. I was lost. I did – I did such things ... I'll never atone for them.'

'She was controlling you.'

He shook his head fretfully and pulled away. 'No. She wasn't. She couldn't. I didn't know it. I thought ... she's always been able to control me so I thought ... I was afraid of her. Terrified of what she'd do. But in the end ... when she tried to use me against you, I couldn't. And I knew she didn't have power over me. Not anymore. That's why Grigori always kill Púca. We can't be controlled. But I'm glad it's you. Just – please – make it quick for me. Like last time. It was ... it was good, that way. Really.'

'I'm not going to kill you. This is nonsense. She has my dad, Jinx. She has my friends. You're all I have. Help me.'

He nodded. 'Anything. You know that. But when it's over ...'

She reached out again, resting her fingertips on his face,

stroking the skin there before sliding it down the taut line of his clenched jaw. His eyes flickered to avoid her gaze and froze. Before she could blink, he grabbed her wrist and turned her arm to expose the skin on the inside.

'Izzy!' The look of horror was almost more than she could bear. The scars, and the fresher cuts ... she'd lost the bandage somewhere. And now he could see every mark, every cut and all the evidence of the past ones. Shame flooded her as she waited for him to chide her or ask her why.

'It's ... it's just ... I couldn't feel anything. Not properly. Or sometimes it was just too much pain – inside, you know? – and the only way to stop that was to ...'

'Oh no,' he said on a whisper and his expression softened with understanding. 'No, I didn't mean ...' He kissed her inner arm, kissed the marks that crisscrossed her skin. 'No. This, love. I meant this.'

And then she saw it.

Encircling her wrist where Holly had grabbed her, a line of intricate tattoos wound through her skin. She stared at them, her hand looking very small in his, the marks looking very sharp and spiny. Her skin itched.

'What ... what are they?'

He pulled at the neck of his t-shirt, exposing the three lines of decoration around his throat. They were the same. She could see it at a glance. Exactly the same.

And those marks had almost made him the vessel of the Shining One that now inhabited Holly, that had meant she had to kill him.

But it had taken Holly three times to get them on him, three sacrifices. An angel, a demon and Izzy's own blood.

And now she had the same three rings of tattoos on her wrist. Three of them all in one go.

'She marked me,' she said, suddenly numb and afraid. More afraid than she could ever remember being. Her legs almost gave out and it was all she could do to hold herself up. Jinx supported her, his grip firm but gentle. 'Jinx? What is she trying to do?'

He didn't answer. But the look he gave her told her that he knew.

And so did she.

Izzy must have slept for some time. She didn't know how long. There was no way of telling in the Hollow at Puck's Castle. She lay in a small chamber without windows, away from the main hall, with only a candle to light it. The bronzed walls and ceiling gave the world a soft glow, warm and soporific. The music that woke her was far off and sad, so sad. She knew it was Jinx playing though. She would recognise his musical style anywhere. Tears stung her eyes. She'd never thought to hear him play again. He brought with him a longing that she didn't hear in Dylan's music. Once he'd said it was all he had, his one freedom. It broke her heart.

The sound of a foot on stone made her start and she turned to see a girl standing in the doorway. She had blonde hair, unbrushed and wild, with some fading flowers threaded through it. Her hands knotted behind her back and she stared at Izzy with wary eyes.

'Isabel Gregory, I assume,' she said, in precise, clipped tones.

'Yes?' She got up carefully. The girl didn't look fae, but she didn't look entirely human either. Or if she was, she'd been living with the fae for a very long time.

'Jane Sherrard,' she replied. Her name, Izzy realised a moment later. She looked about Izzy's age, perhaps a year or two younger. 'He's safe here. You should not have called him to you. He could have stayed safe.'

Jinx? 'I didn't call him. Or at least, I didn't mean to.'

Jane lifted her chin a little, giving Izzy a firm, superior glare. 'He went to your aid. Why does he always go to your aid? What power do you have over him?'

'Me?' This was making her feel distinctly uncomfortable. Izzy rubbed her hands together and felt the Blade kindling under her skin. She didn't want to use it. But that didn't mean she wasn't ready if she had to.

'I see things. In my dreams.' Jane drifted towards her. 'I've seen him for years. I knew he'd come and I waited. I waited so patiently for him.'

'Good for you,' Izzy murmured. Jane had that way of looking at her she didn't like. It made her think of Holly. It was fixed and determined, but not really all there. Away with the fairies … that was the saying, wasn't it?

'And when he came I was so happy. But I've seen you too. I've seen what you'll do.'

'What's that?' Izzy backed up a few steps, but her feet snagged on the furs. Go back further and she'd trip herself up. This didn't feel right. Not at all.

'You'll burn the world. You'll open the gate. You can't go to the island, Isabel Gregory.' The way she said Izzy's full name made her nervous. More than nervous.

'So everyone keeps telling me. Jane? What is this all about?'

Jane's eyes hardened. She lunged forward, swinging a cleaver from behind her back. It flashed towards Izzy's throat and all of her training kicked in. She ducked and rolled. Coming up behind her before Jane had finished the swing, Izzy kicked her in the back of the knees. Jane screamed as she went down, face first into the pile of furs.

Izzy slammed her foot down on Jane's wrist, pinning it and the cleaver to the ground and the Blade flared into life in her hand.

'Who the hell sent you?' she spat as rage flooded her system. She was sick of this. Sick of being attacked, of being in danger, sick of assaults out of nowhere just when she hoped against hope that she might be safe.

'Let me go! Please, let me go!' Jane shrieked at the top of her voice, her screams echoing around the chamber and into the hall beyond.

The fae came running, a maelstrom of them with Jinx at

their heart. Izzy found herself pulled off the girl with ungentle hands, pushed and prodded, overpowered in moments. And Jane stood up, helped by those she had known for years. She sobbed and shook, covering her face with her hands. No sign of the cleaver now.

'She just attacked me,' the girl spluttered in terror. 'I just tried to wake her, and she attacked me.'

'No I didn't, she—'

Thickened air pushed its way into Izzy's mouth, gagging her.

'Let her go!' Jinx yelled, pushing his way through. Before she knew what was happening, Jane pushed herself between them, physically blocking Jinx from reaching her.

'She tried to kill me, Jinx by Jasper. She's crazy.'

Jinx hesitated. Actually hesitated and his eyes met Izzy's, searching hers. And then he frowned. 'Jane? What did you do?'

Uproar followed. Shouts, accusations, arguments. Jinx pushed by Jane and pulled Izzy free. He brushed either side of her mouth and she managed to grab a breath of air.

Another figure bustled in, a little fae who looked to be half tree, and the others all fell silent. He didn't say a word, just walked forward, past the others, and bent over the furs. When he straightened, as much as he could straighten, he was holding the cleaver.

'Oh Janey, my Janey, what's all this?'

Jinx enfolded Izzy in his arms, as much she suspected to stop her going ape on them as to protect her. 'She attacked me,' she said, and was surprised to hear her voice so quiet, so calm. Jinx glared at Jane, who shrank back.

'I had to, don't you see? She has to be stopped. She's full of fire. She'll enslave you again, Jinx. She'll take you away from us. But you could stay here, with us, with me.'

It was the way she said 'with me'. The words broke her.

'Oh ancestors, Jane,' he breathed. 'I couldn't. I never could. I thought you knew that. I love her.'

Loved her? Something hitched in her chest. He loved her?

'You could … you could love me instead,' Jane sobbed. 'I've dreamed of you. For years. So many years. And I couldn't just let her take you. She'll destroy you. She'll destroy everything. She'll make you a slave again.'

She trailed off into incoherent weeping, only held up now by the hands of her companions.

'Briugu,' said Jinx. 'She needs help.'

The little man fixed Jinx with a sorrowful look. 'I'm not sure there's anything more we can do. She's broken our laws of hospitality, Jinx. You know the rest.'

'Cast her out and she'll die. She's mortal. It's been years.'

'She attacked a guest under my roof. I'd have to do the same if it was your girl there, or even you. She knew this. You know this. The law is the law.'

Jane shrieked, trying to pull away from those who held her now. But she had nowhere to go. They startled dragging her forward, towards the tunnels, towards the door. The nearer they got, the louder her screams became. Oh she knew. Once ejected from the Hollow she'd die in the most painful way possible.

'Stop,' Jinx said. His voice rippled with power, magic Izzy recognised from her dreams. The Púca. He said it again, this time louder. 'Stop! You have to listen to me. I'm the Púca. I'll take her punishment. I'll go. Don't kill her. Please, Briugu. I'll do it.'

He shivered, his body tense and barely controlled and Izzy didn't want to let him go for fear he'd do something rash. This was bad enough. He'd just told the world he was the Púca. He'd just claimed as much in the Púca's own Hollow and that had to mean something. She didn't want to think what that might be.

But at least he had somewhere else to go. Like Rothman in Amadán's Hollow, Jane had nowhere. She'd disintegrate the moment she stepped beyond their grounds without protection.

Jane fell silent, staring at him with red-raw eyes, her face white as the ghost she ought to be by now. There was such hope in her, such pain.

'Jinx, no,' she said. 'Don't go.'

He tried to smile and threaded his fingers through Izzy's. 'I have to. Now more than ever.'

Leaving Puck's Castle was harder than Jinx would have

thought. He'd never felt accepted and at home anywhere before, not like that. It had felt like safety, every moment, right up to the end. Jane ran off once released, somewhere into the depths of the Hollow, her sobs echoing after her, haunting him. Izzy stayed close, clearly aware that it was affecting him more than he'd thought.

He'd lost every home he'd ever thought he had – the Cú Sídhe pack, Silver's Hollow and now this place. He'd claimed it, named himself as Púca and that meant something. And now he was rejected again.

It figured. That was the way his life seemed to go.

But at least she was with him, at last. Izzy held his hand as they crossed the threshold and he felt the darkness around it harden against him. He would never be able to go back again.

The nearest Sídheway was a hike in the darkness, out of the fields and down a narrow winding road, but eventually he found it. It didn't want to open for him at first but after a few minutes, and more than a few curses, they were inside.

'Are you okay?' Izzy asked at last.

'I don't know,' he answered, honestly enough. 'But it was the right thing to do.'

There was a long silence. She was thinking, or wanted to say something she didn't quite know how to say. To ask about Jane, he supposed. Damn the girl but she'd implied there was something between them when there was nothing more than her imagination and dreams. Still, he felt Izzy deserved some sort of explanation.

'Nothing passed between Jane and me—' he began, but she put her hand up to his mouth, silencing him.

'I know.' She frowned, staring at his eyes. 'You said you loved me.'

His mind stuttered over that thought. He had, and he'd called her love too. And … and he did. It was a revelation. He'd known it, of course, for so long now. But to find the words to say it out loud and in her hearing … he kept waiting for the sky to fall.

'I did.'

She smiled then, a shaky smile but an honest one. 'That's a promise, you know. And I'll hold you to it, Cú Sídhe.'

'Technically I'm not—' Izzy pulled his mouth down into a kiss before he could finish. From somewhere further off in the ragged Sídheway, filled with glimpses of other roads and different fields, he was half sure he could hear laughter.

But Izzy was still kissing him and he couldn't think anymore.

They were halfway up Killiney Hill when Jinx realised what was wrong. The kissing had addled his mind. That was the problem. It took this long before he could get his common sense back in control. He kept expecting Blythe to appear through the trees, either in hound shape – which would be terrifying enough – or stark naked just for the hell of it. Probably just to see the shock and discomfort on the faces of everyone she encountered as she sashayed through the snow. It was a bright winter's afternoon by the time they got there, sun streaming through the trees like molten honey. And Blythe would never walk through the woods of this hill again in any form.

His throat tightened and he tried to hide it from Izzy. She had told him what had happened, her eyes red-raw and unable to cry anymore. He remembered the terrible bleakness in Brí's face. He would never forget the death howl that had screamed through him.

My Blythe, she had said. *My Blythe.*

While Blight had worn that hard, bitter expression of a soldier who had seen too much and would only feel it later, when he allowed himself to feel again. Or would let it build up until it exploded in some terrible act of violence and desperation.

He had seen it before.

Felt it.

They walked slowly. Izzy had insisted that they come here once she realised there was no one at home.

'It's the only safe space,' she said in a disturbingly logical tone. 'Besides, I need to talk to Brí about ... you know ...'

He did. He knew only too well. The marks on her wrist felt like a living, moving thing. How Holly had gone from leaving one at a time to all three, he didn't know. Because she was now a Shining One perhaps and could work such terrible magic?

Because maybe she carried the seeds of the other Shining Ones, Crom Ceann and Crom Dubh until she could pass them on to Osprey and Izzy. Perhaps she had simply learned of a better way.

He hoped Brí could tell them. More importantly he hoped Brí knew of a way to stop it and get rid of it. Because otherwise he risked losing Izzy when he had only just found her again. And he couldn't face that.

Izzy rubbed her lower arm through the sleeve of her jacket, as if aware he was thinking about it. Or perhaps she couldn't leave it alone. He recalled the scars and healing cuts on her skin.

'Are you okay?'

She nodded. 'It tingles. Like it's under the skin.' She took a deep breath and shuddered. 'I guess I'm lucky she missed my neck. The crows distracted her.'

'I suppose so, speaking of which …' he gestured up ahead with a tilt of his chin. Black birds dotted the stark lines of the leafless trees. They sat in silence, watching the pair of them pass.

'When did that start?'

'After Halloween. After – ' she paused, reluctant to say *'after I killed you'* he guessed. 'After Donn died. They kind of … followed me home.'

'You have his Blade. You have his powers. I suppose that makes you his heir.'

'His something,' she muttered and dropped her chin, push-

ing on up the hill. 'Sometimes they left presents. They never…
they never attacked anyone like that. They aren't fae, are they?'

He shook his head. 'Just birds.'

'Just birds.' She was confused. That was understandable, but
he had never seen her look so lost. Speeding up, he matched
her gait easily. She was exhausted too, but wouldn't admit it.

'Izzy, it isn't your fault.'

'Yes it is, all of it. I was so stupid.'

'There are more people who can lay claim to that than you
alone, you know?'

'Holly has my dad. She's going to torture him and use his
blood for – I don't know what. Something. But she's going
to keep him alive. She used Ash's spark to mark me and if
that hasn't killed her, Holly will. I heard her. And now she
has Dylan, which means she has all of Silver's power at her
disposal as well. None of them would be there if it wasn't for
me. Holly came for me.'

'She came because she wanted revenge. You weren't alone
there, Izzy. She's killed the Storyteller, tried to get Amadán
and broke his Hollow. I was there.'

'Mags told me.'

'Mags? He's … he's dead.'

'Yes. His ghost. Told me, that is. I see ghosts. They won't
leave me alone.'

'Ghosts?'

She smiled thinly, a mirthless expression. 'Yes. Ghosts.
Donn's heir, remember?'

'Oh …' No wonder she was so frantic. Crows, death and ghosts and everything else.

Something squirmed at the back of his memory, something familiar he couldn't quite grasp. But it meant something, didn't it? It had to.

As they walked out of the treeline and past the gorse which stood higher than Jinx did at this point, they both avoided looking at the Wishing steps. Too many bad memories. But Izzy reached out and took his hand, pulling him onwards in case he even thought of hesitating.

Two women walking their dogs stood at the base of the mound upon which the Obelisk stood. They were deep in conversation, apparently unaware that their Labrador-retrievers were following Jinx like devoted groupies. He tried to shoo them away without being seen doing so. It wouldn't have mattered. The women didn't notice.

'They're talking about some kind of attack.'

'Like terrorists?'

'Or a madman.'

'Things like that don't happen here.'

Izzy's shoulders hunched, as she put her head down again and carried on, like someone walking into a gale.

'They do,' she muttered. 'Just no one's ever noticed them. Why do you think that is?'

He didn't answer. He only knew rumours, whispers that the Sídhe didn't dare say any louder. The Keeper. Just a title, not even a name. Never cross the Keeper, that's what they taught fae children from the cradle. He wasn't prepared to dwell on it. Or share it either. If her father hadn't told her that, he wasn't going to share. He'd done enough to piss off David Gregory.

They reached the granite outcrop with rusted metal spikes and rings sunken into the stone, where someone had once tried to lock Brí away. Like trying to close a sliding door on a hurricane. The dogs came to an abrupt halt at the edge of the grass and sat down, wagging their tails uneasily. They gave little whining yelps until their owners finally heard and called them back. If they glared suspiciously at the strange tattooed man and the teenaged girl, they hurried away quickly and vanished downhill.

'Anyone else around?' asked Izzy. Further down the path, at the viewing point looking south towards Shankill, Bray and the Sugarloaf, some people leaned on the metal rails and took selfies. That was it.

'We're ok,' Jinx said. 'If we're quick.'

'We will be.'

They called it *knocking*, but it wasn't really as polite as that. More like demanding, or breaking and entering. Brí must have shown her how, or her father perhaps. And Brí could have blocked it. If she cared to. If she had the wherewithal to do anything after Trinity.

He waited while she closed her eyes. To call it unsettling was an understatement. The Cú Sídhe should have been circling the moment Jinx set foot in their territory, but they had just lost Blythe and who knew how many others. It had to be chaos in there, more because he had seen the grief on Brí's face himself.

They had always been close – the Matriarch and her pack leader. It had never occurred to him what that might mean.

He felt, rather than heard, the knocking, a deep seated, resonant boom-boom-boom which echoed deep inside his stomach. Rock ground against rock and the way into Brí's Hollow opened to them. The last time he had walked this way he had carried Izzy, almost wild under the influence of the fallen angel Sorath. And it had been a trap. He gritted his teeth and promised himself he wouldn't be so naïve this time. He knew what could happen.

But when Izzy stepped forward into the darkness he had no choice but to follow her. Perhaps he never did. The spell binding him to her service – the geis Brí herself had lain on him – was meant to be broken now, but it didn't feel that way. It felt as strong as ever.

'Izzy,' he said, as his instincts warned him of danger. He could smell Cú Sídhe ahead, but this was their primary lair so that was nothing new. And yet still no one challenged them which spoke of chaos and fear, of a pack disorganised. Never a good situation. Or maybe it was something worse. 'Izzy, something is terribly wrong here.'

She didn't reply, but held out her hand. A little flame danced in the air above it, illuminating the corridor, bouncing off the bronze.

'Brí?' she said in a surprisingly calm voice. 'I'm here. Where are you, Mother?'

A figure stepped out of the darkness ahead and Jinx recognised Blight, Blythe's younger brother. He bore scars from the night on the Hellfire Club, all down his face and arm. Osprey's work, no doubt. His nose would never be straight again, but worse than all that was the bleak antipathy in his eyes.

'Jinx by Jasper,' he said. 'My Lady Brí is not prepared to receive you without certain precautions. And surety from you, Lady Isabel.'

Jinx frowned. Blight had always been the one with the jokes and the pleasant demeanour. This Cú Sídhe was something very different.

'What does she want?' he asked carefully.

Blight threw a bag down in front of them. It clanked and Jinx knew what was in it.

'Put them on the Púca. Or else we'll run him into the ground.'

Izzy bent to open the bag, but Jinx didn't dare move, couldn't show any sign of weakness or fear. The pack was enraged, afraid. That they even gave this much of a warning was a blessing he didn't expect.

'You've *got* to be kidding,' said Izzy, her words laced with disgust as she pulled heavy silver manacles from the bag. 'We're here to help and to seek help.'

Blight glanced at her briefly, dismissing her. A mistake, especially when she was angry. Without hesitation she swung the metal chains at him. Blight grabbed them before they could strike him but the flailing end wrapped around his forearm. His skin hissed as it burned in contact with the metal and Jinx bared his teeth in sympathy. He knew that pain, but Blight barely flinched.

There were many kinds of pain. Some worse than others.

'Put them on,' Blight said tightly and threw them right at Jinx.

'No,' Izzy yelled, but Jinx caught them from the air. The metal stung like nettles as he touched it and his hands reddened beneath it. The longer it touched him the worse it would be.

'It's okay, Izzy,' he forced all emotion from his voice. She couldn't know it hurt. 'If this is the only way, then – '

'It's barbaric,' she said. She almost growled and he loved her for it.

'Yes. But they need to feel safe right now.' He held the manacles out to her. 'I'll need your help.'

Muttering curses, she fitted one manacle around each wrist and snapped them closed. They locked themselves, the silver sealing without leaving any sign they could be opened. There wasn't a collar this time, and for that he was grateful. Maybe it was some small sign of hope. Maybe. But the manacles were bad enough.

'I'm sorry,' Izzy whispered and she kissed him. He just nodded, not trusting his voice to the rising tide of pain. Cú Sídhe had problems with all metal, silver most of all. The manacles linked to the silver piercings Holly had given him over the long years in her service, creating a network of agony over his body. He had to focus to put one foot in front of the other, to keep from collapsing. Izzy's fingers threaded with his and he fixed his attention on that and that alone.

'Where is she?' Izzy asked Blight.

The Cú Sídhe gave one glance at Jinx, half disgust and half dismay, and then gestured for them to follow him with a curt nod of his head.

Chapter Twenty-One

Gardens and Graves

The path led down, deep into the hill, twisting and turning until it was impossible to tell which way was back. Not that it mattered. Izzy wasn't coming back out until she had some answers. And Jinx. Yes, she definitely wasn't coming back out without Jinx and given his situation right now – whether he had put himself there willingly or not – that could be a challenge. And speaking of agreeing to put on the chains, her stomach squirmed at the thought of him wearing them. He'd done it for her, to get her here.

It all felt so wrong. Everything felt wrong. Especially the thing on her arm, under her skin, inside her. She'd felt this kind of parasitic thing crawling within her before.

Not again. She was not going to let it happen again.

Brí was probably the only one who knew how to stop it.

Or at least Izzy hoped she did.

The great chamber was dark but for the central fire. Izzy didn't hesitate, walking up to the edge and gazing inside. 'Brí?'

She coalesced out of the fire, but she didn't look as wildly impressive as she had in the past. Tears streaked her face, glistening in her eyes.

'Let me see,' she said and held out her hands. She didn't even need to ask. And she certainly wasn't going to apologise for putting Jinx in chains. Or at least having Izzy do it for her.

'Are you … are you okay?'

'Just let me see.'

There was nothing else Izzy could do but offer her arm to the hands coming out of the fire, that were more than half fire themselves. Brí leaned closer, examining the skin closely but ignoring the scars and fading red lines. She squinted at the tattoos, coming further from her flames as she did so.

'It's the same spell she used on Jinx,' she said at last. 'Luckily it missed your neck.'

'I ducked.'

'Of course you did. If she'd touched you there you would be hers by now. Like he was. Or is.' She glared at Jinx over Izzy's shoulder, but whatever she saw didn't alarm her any further. Izzy had seen him take that captive stance before. She wondered how many times he had used it to save his life. He had it perfected. And yet still his life seemed continually in danger.

'But it hit my wrists,' Izzy said, drawing Brí's attention back to her. 'It was down there and now it's—'

It was halfway up her arm, still itching and squirming under her skin. Somewhere between her wrist and her elbow, it moved slowly, almost imperceptibly. But it still moved.

'I see,' Brí sighed. 'Then it is designed to head for your throat, where it can do the most damage. It will control you later rather than sooner.'

'Can you stop it?'

'Short of amputation?' Brí actually laughed. 'No.'

Oh God, she actually looked like she was considering it.

'You aren't cutting my arms off.'

Brí released her hands with a groan of something like disgust. 'I wasn't intending to. You'd be useless as a Grigori if nothing else and you are all we have now.'

Izzy sucked in a breath as another, more terrible thought occurred to her. 'Is he ... Is Dad ...'

'He's not dead. Not yet. Holly will keep him alive as long as she can. She needs him. But he'll wish he was dead.'

'I should have stayed. I should have helped him.'

'And then you would already be a creature like Holly, but subservient to her like Osprey. You might even be aware enough to know it. Imagine that, and tell me again about self-sacrifice.' She took a moment, letting that sink in. 'Blythe... Blythe died trying to save you. And Holly still wants you. She won't be content to wait, I know that much. She'll come here next, I fear. And I don't think we will be enough to withstand her.'

'But Brí!' Jinx interrupted. She glared at him and Izzy

turned, alarmed to think he'd just overstepped a mark. The same concern reflected in his golden eyes and he swallowed hard, averting his gaze. 'Lady Brí … you're the strongest of the Aes Sídhe. Even the angels defer to you.'

'Do they? Well, it won't matter. The angels are hiding and she needs power. She's looking to open the first gate. And she can't do it alone.'

'The first gate?' asked Izzy. 'To Donn's Hollow? But that's—'

'No. You left that gaping wide open anyway. That was our first Sídheway. We created that when the humans arrived here, when Amergin split the world. But long before that there was another gate, one which closed after us, locked and barred. The Thorn Gate. It leads to heaven, the gate through which we were expelled. And only the combined power of all the Shining Ones could open it. And only then if they have the key.'

'Holly has the power of the three Shining Ones.'

'Only three?' She smiled, a disturbing, knowing smile. 'Then she's miscalculated. There were four, you see? Four seraphim, one to guard each cardinal point, to form a shield around the Creator. But even then, without the key, they could hammer on the opening for a thousand millennia and never get in.'

'And where's the key?' asked Izzy.

'I gave it to Wild, who gave it to Íde. And it broke her mind to pieces.'

'Does she still have it? We could get it from her, keep it from Holly…'

'She wouldn't give it to you. It's all she has left of her lover. She guards it jealously. She's dangerous.'

'All Aes Sídhe are dangerous.'

'Yes. Which means you should listen when we say it about one of our own. Your father would tell you that, wouldn't he? So would your grandmother, and Rachel too. In no uncertain terms.'

Her mum and gran … she hadn't even thought of them since she and Dad had walked into Trinity.

'Where are they?' Izzy asked.

'Your mother and your grandmother have gone to the retreat in Glendalough, I presume, as David instructed. Nothing can touch them there.' Brí's voice shook almost imperceptibly when she said Dad's name. Izzy wondered if anyone else noticed.

'And Clodagh? She's in danger too, isn't she?'

'Your little human friend?' Blight shrugged. 'She came here looking for you. We had to lock her up to stop her running after you. She gets very angry, doesn't she?'

Yes, angry. Clodagh could get angry. And she would. Especially if they'd locked her up. Oh God, she was going to go ballistic. It didn't bear thinking about.

'Let her out. Now.'

And then, Izzy hesitated, realising the awful truth. Then she was going to have to tell Clodagh about Ash.

A pounding from above brought all their heads up. Another knocking? Blight sent two Cú Sídhe off to investigate and moments later Dylan arrived, carrying Ash. Izzy gave a cry, a mix of relief and alarm. He looked bleak, desperate, and Ash could barely walk.

'What happened? How did you get away?'

He nodded towards Jinx, his eyes snagging on the manacles, and he frowned. 'He was quite the diversion. And we were lucky. Very lucky.'

'Dad?' She hardly dared to hope, but the moment she said it she knew from Dylan's expression that her dad was still a prisoner. Her breath hiccoughed as she tried to control it. 'How?'

'We ran. We fought. Meridian's dead.' He said it with relief, and she was struck by how much he had changed. But then, they all had. And Meridian being dead was no bad thing. 'And then … there were soldiers, Izzy. Like for real soldiers. And these women. I think they were librarians or maybe… maybe soldiers too. They said Ash was human. They knew all about the Sídhe, about Holly and this, about us—'

'Ash!' Clodagh ran into the chamber, ignoring everyone else and making straight for the failing angel. 'Ash, what happened?'

Ash looked at her like she was a light in the darkness. 'She took my spark. She took it and marked Izzy. She should have killed me but …'

She would have said more but her strength seemed to fail her. Clodagh tried to catch her as she fell and the two of them went down in a heap, tangled together.

'No!' Clodagh cried out, holding her. 'What's wrong with

her? What's happening?'

'She's dying,' said Brí, too flippantly to be of any use. 'That's what happens to them when they lose their spark. That's their life force. I must say I've never seen one last this long.'

'Holly could make them last for days,' Jinx muttered and Izzy had to resist the urge to hit both of them. Bloody Sídhe. Couldn't they see what Clodagh was seeing? Ash was dying in her arms.

'Yes, but chained up, surrounded by spells. Not running around and – oh ...' Brí stopped, staring at Clodagh's rage-filled face.

Izzy tried to intervene. 'Clodagh, they don't mean it. They don't—'

'Why do you have to have *everything*?' Clodagh snapped. She cradled Ash against her, stroking her dark hair. 'Why does it always revolve around you, Izzy? And whoever gets in the way, well we're all just collateral damage, aren't we?'

'Clodagh, I will never let anything happen to you.'

'Really?' Tears streamed down her face but the words came out as sharp and pointed as knives. 'Like Mari? Like Ash here?' She glanced down then and the rage went out of her. 'Oh God, please, please wake up, Ash. Please don't go.' She kissed the angel's dark lips, her forehead. She rocked her like a child.

And then Brí was there, kneeling in front of her. She reached out and pressed her hand to Ash's forehead.

'Get off her!' Clodagh screamed, but Brí just looked up, right into Clodagh's eyes, and something in her expression made Clodagh's rage fall away again. Something else took its place. Something very much like hope.

Brí whispered something, the words soft and sibilant. It wasn't a language Izzy knew but she saw Jinx straighten and every one of the Sídhe look up with an expression of longing on their faces.

'What is it?' she asked. 'What's she saying?'

'It's the language of angels,' said Jinx. 'I can't ... I can't translate it. But I know it. Oh, ancestors, I know it like my heartbeat.'

Ash stirred and opened her eyes, gazing in wonder at Brí, at the soft light pouring from her.

'I can't make you whole again, little one,' said the Matriarch. 'But I can do this much for the two of you.'

Something trembled beneath them, the ground itself shifting and realigning, or the air around them.

'You can't do that,' Ash said, but there was strength in her voice now which made it clear that Brí already had.

'You'll need to rest. You're only human now. But you'll live. That is what you wanted, isn't it?' Brí looked right at Clodagh who nodded slowly. 'Then look after her. Love her. And don't lose her.'

The grief in her voice was palpable, terrible.

'Matriarch,' said Blight after a moment. He reached out and touched her shoulder and she shuddered, closing her eyes.

'Go, all of you. Find somewhere safe to ride out the storm.'

'There is nowhere, Matriarch,' Jinx told her. 'Nowhere but

here.'

'She'll be coming here. Don't you pay attention to any-thing? They need power. She wants everything. And with you here, with Isabel ... '

'Then how do we stop her?' Izzy asked.

'If Holly gets the key from Íde it is all over. Everything. But Íde won't give it willingly. It's her treasure, all she has left of Wild. I don't think it can be taken by force and she'd never trade for it.'

'I can't come with you,' said Dylan. 'I have to help Silver.'

'What are you planning?' asked Izzy.

'You wouldn't like it, if I told you. Do what you have to, Izzy. That's what I'm going to do.'

The Botanic Gardens in winter bore a different kind of beauty to the rest of the year. As they stepped out of the Síd-heway through an arch into a hedged garden, Jinx couldn't help but shiver, although Izzy didn't appear to notice it.

'Here?' she asked.

'Down that way.' He pointed away towards another arch in the hedge on the far side past the small greenhouse sealed up against the cold and the night. She strode forward, head down, her bright red hair a sharp contrast to her dark cloth-ing and the white world around them. She was holding her arms crossed in front of her chest, as if afraid they might do something independently of her. Or maybe she could feel the squirm under her skin.

'Izzy,' he jogged after her before she could vanish altogether. 'Izzy, wait.'

She glanced back, startled as if she had forgotten he was with her. He put his arm around her. 'You okay?'

Slowly, she nodded. 'You? Are you feeling better now the silver has come off?'

Some of it was off. He was never free of it. Couldn't be. He hadn't really thought about it before but that constant low-level nagging pain was always there. He just had to endure.

'Sure,' he lied and saw a flicker of annoyance in her eyes. She knew when he wasn't telling her everything. He had almost forgotten that. The realisation made him smile. 'It's better, I promise. Just not entirely gone.' He scratched his ear, flicking one of the rings and she winced.

'Sorry,' she said, as easily as that. Those words would choke him. But she wasn't entirely Sídhe, was she? She was Grigori.

The silence went on for a moment too long. He needed to say something to break it, so things would be normal – or as normal as it got for them – and they could carry on.

'I like your hair.' The sentence clunked between them as soon as he said it and a rush of embarrassment flooded him. It sounded so feeble and stupid. She'd cut it off in grief and loss. Because of him. 'I mean, short. It looks good. Not … not that it didn't before. But—'

Izzy lifted a finger to his lips and she smiled, a genuine smile this time.

'Flirting isn't actually your strong point, is it?'

'I don't flirt. I mean, I—'

She kissed him instead and all the words, clumsy as they had been, were gone. Her lips against his pressed close like her body, small and warm against him. But strong. She fitted against him, the missing part of him, so perfect that it felt like it should hurt when she finally moved away.

'I love you,' she whispered.

'And I you. Always.' Truth had never been so easy before. And trust too. He was an open book to her and she could reach in to start ripping out pages if she wanted to. He couldn't stop her. But she wouldn't. He trusted her, where he had never trusted anyone but Silver before. 'Always, Izzy. No matter what.'

Her smile came again, delighted but unsure. For a moment, carefree and then embarrassed. She glanced over her shoulder towards the illuminated round tower in the cemetery beyond the walls and high railings.

'We're being watched,' she said. 'We should go and talk to her. How do we get in there? It's locked up.'

'I can get us in,' he said. But it was Íde's domain. In was easy. He wasn't sure if he could get them both out again.

The gate into the graveyard was locked and the rails rose over his head. Spikes topped them and he knew there would be security cameras too. Not that they bothered the fae, usually. Technology tended to glitch around them and cameras usually failed to pick them up. Further down the ramp, there was a black metal gate set into a grey stone section. And sunken into the stone he saw a keypad.

Jinx smiled to himself and ran his fingers over it. There was a spitting sound from inside and the lock ground open, like something was forcing it. Jinx could open any lock, though he rarely used the ability. Most of the fae could if they concentrated. They hated metal but it seemed like metal hated them as well. With the right amount of force, he could repel it.

They set off again, Jinx using his heightened sight to check ahead. The path was broad and followed the line of the walls, but they could run into security there, so they made their way onto the grass, among the headstones. And there were shadows among the graves, the fluttering of dark birds in the trees above. More crows, he guessed. They followed her everywhere.

She gritted her teeth and, to his surprise, reached for his hand. Her fingers felt so cold, and she shook.

'What's wrong?' he asked.

But Izzy closed her eyes, screwing up her face as if to block something out. She flinched back against him.

'I can hear them.'

A crow called out, just one, a harsh and yet plaintive sound. Something rustled in the darkness. Just an urban fox by the smell. But he knew she didn't mean that. Far off, on the main road, he could hear cars, but nothing else.

'Who?' he asked.

She pointed to the gravestones.

'I can hear them talking. Oh God, I didn't think.' Her legs buckled suddenly but he caught her.

'The graves?'

'The dead. So many of them. The ones with the headstones and the ones without. They're lost or confused. Or angry. Or crying.'

She pulled away again and staggered forward, her hand ripping free of him so she could cover her ears. She half-ran and half-fell into the darkness

'Wait,' Jinx called after her as he followed. 'Izzy, wait!'

He caught up with her kneeling over a grave with a plain stone that pitched over to one side at an angle. Tears made her face gleam in the moonlight.

'She didn't want to marry him, but she didn't have a choice. It was that or the laundries and she wished she had chosen otherwise every time he – oh God, Jinx.'

She forced herself to her feet again before he could help her, but this time he didn't let her go, helping her onwards to another grave where she shivered, her eyes wide.

'He was only my age.'

'Izzy, what is happening?'

'It's Donn's power or part of it.'

'Breathe, love,' he whispered and she forced herself to do so, taking a shuddering, ragged breath which shook her whole body. 'We should go back, try in daylight.'

'We can't. There's no time. Besides, I don't think it'll help and if there are people here they'll think I'm crazy. Come on.'

'Did you know this would happen?'

'I guessed. I didn't think it would be this bad. Get me to the tower. Please.'

No one else said please to him. What else could he do but as she asked? So he did, step by agonising step, while Izzy heard the voices of every ghost there. Finally they reached the wider pathways of the older, more formal part. Here at least it seemed the voices were quieter. She breathed more easily at last and her body began to unwind a little.

Jinx had never come here – what was there here for him? – but he knew enough just from living in the city.

There were more souls laid to rest here than lived today in Dublin. There were mass cholera graves and mausoleums like palaces, the tombs of paupers and heroes. They hurried on through the dark pathways, beneath the dark yews, until Izzy's hand dug into his again.

'Jinx, stop,' she said. 'Please. We have to stop. Wait.'

Dutifully, he drew to a halt. Something moved through the graves up ahead, where they clustered close together, a whirling, dancing figure which seemed to be made of white muslin. The material fluttered around her, trailing after her as she moved with the exaggerated grace that only one of the Sídhe could embody.

She stopped about ten feet from them, studying them both.

'Hello,' he tried, choosing his words with care. 'We seek an audience with the Lady Íde. I'm Lady Silver's emissary.'

Well, he had been. Not that he had seen her since escaping Holly.

The woman laughed and took off again, whirling and dancing through the darkness. Her hands moved like pale birds around her, small wings fluttering.

'Follow her,' said Izzy. 'We can't lose her.'

They ran through the graveyard at night, following the dancer who seemed oblivious to their pursuit. She vanished down the steps to O'Connell's tomb beneath the round tower. The door to that stood open which had to be hopeful, hadn't it? It ought to be locked, the resting place of the man known as the Liberator.

Silence settled over the world as they stepped inside, beneath the beautiful Celtic revival artwork of the ceiling, around the tomb itself, the polished surface carved with a Celtic cross. At the far end of the chamber, there was another door and beyond that the white paint stopped, leaving only granite-finished walls. They almost tripped over the shallow step up as they passed into the space beneath the tower. Jinx felt the ripple of Sídhe magic as they stepped through a gate to Dubh Linn and the tower changed.

Steps unfurled in a spiral above them, step after crystalline step curling around and leading upwards. Light filtered through from above and they began to climb, out of the earth and into the air. The tower above them was made of glass, and the chamber they entered at the top was as beautiful as any Hollow. Jinx tried not to look down. The view was dizzying.

They were already much higher than the tower on the human side, and the night spread out around them, dotted with the little lights of a million souls, sheeries which hovered above the graves of the cemetery. They shouldn't be here, not so many. They should have moved on.

In the middle of the chamber there lay a tomb. At least, he thought it was a tomb. It formed a circle, like a mound, the curb stones placed around the edge etched beautifully with intricate symbols and designs. On top, someone had placed every flower imaginable. Those on the top were fresh and fragrant, but further down, they were rotten, dried out or simply crumbled away.

Izzy gave a sigh of relief to be clear of the graveyard in the human world, but Jinx couldn't relax for a moment. The woman was watching them now, her gaze sharp and unyielding, as piercing as that of Holly or Brí.

They had found Lady Íde.

Chapter Twenty-Two

Forsaken

O n any given night, Temple Bar was thronged with people. On a night in the run up to Christmas you could multiply it by at least ten and still end up counting extras. Ninety percent of them were too drunk to function and Dylan picked his way through the mob out on the narrow cobbled streets like a salmon swimming upstream. He didn't want to be there, but he didn't have a choice anymore. Beside the back entrance to the hotel, the building stood empty. Over the door, the word Dollard was picked out in granite, and the ground level windows had metal rails to keep out everything. In the first floor windows, boards were displayed, each one with a different letter printed on it in red. Perhaps it was graffiti, or perhaps a statement. Or some kind of art installation. They spelled out the word 'Forsaken' and Dylan didn't like the look of it one bit. But he knew what it really meant.

He had just prepared himself to knock on the incongruously modern glass door when another figure ran out of the partying crowds, followed by cat calls and wolf whistles. True to her form, Clodagh turned back to them and made a gesture that would make her parents lock her in a convent until she was twenty-five. They'd even build the convent and import some nuns if they had to.

'What are you doing here?' he snapped.

'Following you!'

'You can't. Go back, Clodagh.'

'Into that? I don't think so. Those people are animals. You'd think they had never heard the word no before. Sad, pervy little creeps.'

He wanted to grab her and shake her. Wanted to yell at her to go home. She was just a kid. She had no business being wrapped up in this. But the look she gave him was acidic and he knew she had learned that one from Mari.

He tried gentleness instead. 'You should be with Ash.'

'Ash is safe and I can't help her. Besides, she told me to come after you. Told me you were doing something suicidal. So here I am.'

'To help me with something suicidal?' He made his voice full of sarcasm and condescension. She shrugged it off.

'To help you get away with it.'

'Ash won't be able to help this time, Clo. You saw her. She won't be flying in to rescue us even if she had the strength. She can't follow us in here. We'll be on our own.'

'Better the two of us than just you. I *am* coming with you, Dylan. You're my friend, one of the best. I owe it to you. Besides, Mari would want me to keep you safe.'

Mari. It always came back to her. Mari and Clodagh had been so close, always together, peas in a pod. So happy in each other's company. He had never noticed a thing, and yet now, when he put it all together ...

'She loved you, Clo,' he said.

She smiled. The pain was still there, the grief. It couldn't be gone so soon. She probably still cried when something reminded her. Maybe that never went away. It certainly didn't for him.

'I know. She told me. And I promised her I'd look after you. Come on, Dylan. Let's do this and get the hell out of here. What is this place anyway?'

He raised his hand and knocked on the door. 'It's funny you should mention hell.'

It swung open into a corridor that could have been any office building in the city. They walked forward, aware that the door closed behind them by itself. It cut off the sounds of the city, isolated them alone in the clinical surroundings. At the end, there was another door, heavy oak, very old, bound with elaborate ironmongery. It couldn't have looked more out of place if it had been deliberate. This one had an iron door knocker. Had they done it on purpose to keep out the fae?

Whatever Dylan was expecting, it wasn't an actual night-club.

Music blared out as the door opened, along with heady scents and smokes that had no business in a place of business these days. Or at least, not in the Dublin he knew. Nor indeed in Dubh Linn. This was somewhere else and he was beginning to regret joking about it.

'Well then, come in if you're coming,' said a voice. And it laughed, a thin and terrible laugh that cut into him like razors. 'He's waiting for you.'

That didn't sound good either. But Clodagh rolled back her shoulders and pushed by him, stepping inside the doorway with one of those saucy wiggles that had every eye looking at her rather than him.

'Super,' she said. 'Lead the way. Come on, Dylan.'

He couldn't stay outside with her in there. She may have promised Marianne she'd look after him but that just meant he couldn't do any less, which was probably exactly what his sister had in mind when she did it.

Heat washed over him, and an aroma that made his head swim. He caught up with Clodagh and pulled her back against him. All around them there were people – or at least he hoped they were people – laughing, dancing, drinking. They called out to them to join in, but quickly lost interest when they didn't, going back to their own entertainments. The surroundings were opulent, all polished, shining, leather bound or lace trimmed, swags of silken curtains and panels which reflected lights from other places. There were people everywhere. So many lost souls. And in the midst he saw shades, flitting from one to the other, darkening their eyes, goading their compatriots on. And demons. There were definitely demons. Their faces shifted ever so slightly, the masks of beauty slipping to reveal something animal, terrible.

They passed through room after room, little chambers lined in velvet and silk, decorated with a thousand patterns, embossed, embroidered, splattered. The light was low and the music loud. He could feel it thundering through him. Music that was deep and desperate, music that pulled at him with every footstep. Each room had another three off it, and the whole place ran on and on like a labyrinth. He couldn't tell which way was back anymore. He couldn't tell which was the way out.

'Hello, my friend,' Azazel's voice boomed out over the crowd and Dylan looked up sharply to see him at the far end of the narrow chamber which they had just entered. The walls were black and crimson, the pattern an elaborate paisley print which Dylan assumed would induce a headache if you looked at it for too long. 'Come to play for us again? We've been looking forward to it.' And then, in a terrible moment, Dylan saw his eyes alight on Clodagh and they glowed from within with a fearsome light. 'And what have you brought for me?'

Oh no. Not this. He wasn't letting Clodagh get involved in this.

'Not her.' He stepped in front of her.

'Really?' Azazel walked forward, the crowd of adoring party goers stepping out of his way, leaving Clodagh and Dylan alone in the centre. Exposed. 'I think you'll find I take whatever I want, especially in here. My stronghold on the earth, and you just waltz in here? That's arrogance, I grant you, but did no one tell you arrogance is a sin? And I feed on sin, boy. I've been smelling sin in you since first we met on that hillside. You're fae touched, and you stink of her power. More than just that, I think. I know what you can do. And would you know it, now you have need of something. So you come to me.'

'Who has Sorath's spark?' Dylan said.

Azazel raised his eyebrows and gestured for the others to be silent. Not that he had to. They were silent, listening intently.

'And?'

'What do you mean, "and"?'

'*And* what do I get?'

That was the question he'd been expecting. And the one he was ready for.

'Me. My music. My soul. That was the agreement, wasn't it?'

'Dylan, no!' Clodagh interrupted but Azazel raised his hand again, a curt gesture. Shades seized her and she gasped in pain, the sound smothered a moment later. Dylan didn't dare look at her. He couldn't show weakness now.

'You don't want her,' he said, moving to block Azazel. 'Not really. She's just a girl. I've got all the power of two Matriarchs flowing inside me. I can make music to drive people insane. You know that. You offered. So here it is. Give me the spark. Let me have a day. And then I'm yours.'

Azazel studied him for a long moment while the crowd surrounding them shuffled their feet and waited impatiently to hear his decision.

Azazel pushed past him and approached Clodagh. As Dylan turned to watch him, he stroked her hair and the shades retreated a little, exposing her face, her huge terrified eyes. As he touched her the pupils shrank to pin pricks and her face paled.

'She's more than any of you realise, this one,' he said. 'Such a mind. And up to such things. Quite the kaleidoscope of desires, needs ... all those sweet, sweet sins.'

'Don't ...' Clodagh whispered.

'Don't what, my darling? Tell him? He already knows. You aren't so opaque as you think. But I can see more. All those grubby dreams of yours. Bold girl. All those things you want but don't really understand. You just can't make up your mind. That's just greedy really.'

She snarled in frustration, in fury. 'It's none of your bloody business. What the hell do you know anyway?'

'Oh, of course,' he said, condescension dripping from his words. 'Gender is fluid and all that. Tell me, did you fancy him or his sister more? Which one was first?'

'Leave her alone,' Dylan said. 'I want an answer.'

'Or what?' Azazel rounded on him. White teeth snapped together right in front of Dylan's face. Two hands closed on his shoulders, pushing him back against the waiting crowd who seized him. Hands pinched and pulled, tightening to painful grips, holding him firm. They sniggered behind his back. Something licked his ear. The more he struggled the worse they were. 'Or what, Dylan O'Neill? What exactly do you think you can do?'

It wasn't a thought. Not really. More like instinct, fear and self-defence. Dylan closed his eyes, threw back his head and let the magic dammed up inside him explode.

It tore through the club like a hurricane, twisted with all the music he hadn't had time to write, all the songs which didn't have lyrics, all the words which couldn't find songs. It was a cacophony of pain and fear, of need and love, of sacrifice and dismay. It wasn't even music anymore. Just noise and pain, just agony. Screams twisted within it, harmonising, shrieks a counterpoint. His heart thundered the rhythm and the hands holding him were torn away. Panic swirled around him, their panic, human and demon, even the shades, everything in that terrible place except for Clodagh and himself. They stampeded, crushing others beneath them, kicking, tripping and trampling to fight their way to safety.

In the middle of it, like the detonation of a nuclear bomb, Dylan felt it all reverberate back upon him, and into him, roaring through him like the water of a tsunami – all that music, the song of the world around him. It hammered into the base of his brain, sending him reeling backwards against the wall. It struck him hard and he slid down to the floor, dazed.

A dark shape loomed over him as he forced his eyes open. The magic tingled at his fingertips, ready to strike again, to defend himself.

'Well, so much for asking them nicely,' said Clodagh. 'What's your encore, Dylan?' Her voice shook but she didn't look hurt. Just scared.

'I'm still working on that.'

She helped him to his feet. The rooms were all empty, tables upturned and glasses scattered everywhere. 'We'd better hurry,' she said. 'They won't stay away for long. Do you even know where this stupid thing is?'

'No but I—' He winced as a sharp pain shot up his back.

'I do,' said another voice. Mistle lurched from the far corner of the room. Dylan knew the voice before he recognised him. The old Sídhe tramp who had been with Sorath on the hill. His unshaven face gave him a ragged look, and his metallic eyes stared too hard at them. He'd lost weight, too much weight to be healthy, as if he'd been starved since Dylan saw him last, starved and tortured. The clothes hung off him, dirty and ragged. And now he looked more like Dylan remembered him. Recognisable.

'Mistle.'

'The same.' He gave a bow. 'Had to hide somewhere, didn't I? Azazel took me in, said I could be useful. And I was. Oh yes, I was. And then … then I wasn't.' To Dylan's horror, tears filled his old eyes, trickled down his lined face. 'I know where she is. She sings to me. You have to get her out of there. He gave her away. How could he have given her away?'

Mistle turned away, staggering as he did. He leaned on the

wall and forced himself forwards.

'Who is he?'

'He's … he was Sídhe. He's the one who tried to give Izzy to Sorath last summer. He started all of this.'

'Are we following him, Dylan? Because from what little I know of last summer, that isn't a good idea.'

'I'm not sure what other choice we have.'

Chapter Twenty-Three

Tower of Glass

Izzy leaned against Jinx, reluctant to let him hold her up but not really having a great deal of choice any more. Her head throbbed with a fierce headache like a migraine on steroids, and all those voices left her wrung out. The new silence was a blessed relief. She had tried not to let on how bad it had been — hundreds of thousands of voices calling to her, telling her secrets, begging her for help, or simply sharing their stories. They should have been gone, should have moved onwards, but something kept them here, tethered.

She closed her eyes tightly and shook her head to try to clear it of the fog and pressure that crushed down on her. When she opened them again, Íde was gazing at her with curious eyes.

Izzy had a fairly good idea what might be keeping the dead here. A Sídhe Matriarch in their midst might do that.

But why?

'Lady Íde,' Jinx said in calm and careful tones. 'My name is Jinx by Jasper and I serve as emissary to Lady Silver, Holly's daughter. This is ...'

But Íde didn't appear to hear him. She was carrying a heap of dying flowers gathered from the graves outside in Dublin, and slowly, methodically, she stripped each bunch of any cellophane or paper wrappers, their string or elastic bands. She laid the little waterlogged cards on the floor where they joined countless others in an elaborate pattern only she could discern. Then she dropped the flowers on to the mouldering heap in the middle of the room. She hummed to herself as she worked, a strange out-of-key tune which seemed to wander where it would.

'Lady Íde?' Jinx tried again.

She turned on him sharply and hissed, her teeth bare. He took a step back, startled into silence, and she nodded, then went back to her work.

'Leave it a moment,' Izzy told him. 'Wait until she's ready.'

Jinx's jaw tightened and they watched the Matriarch in silence. After a moment she realised Jinx wasn't looking at Íde anymore. He was gazing at her, studying her like a textbook he could read and understand.

'Do you need anything?' he asked when he noticed her attention.

She shook her head. The voices were gone now, here in Íde's tower of glass. The lights outside the glass walls were something else – fae things that lingered in graveyards and passed effortlessly between all worlds.

Under her skin, Izzy could feel the Shining One growing, the tattoos twisting and coiling. Her own Grigori mark was so cold it burned, a terrible sign. She thought of Dad, of what Holly could be doing to him right now.

'Jinx? Why did she pick me?'

'I wish I knew,' he replied but she was sure that wasn't the whole truth. Holly hated her, Izzy knew that. Jinx had almost lost himself to the Shining One that now inhabited Holly. Did Holly expect the same thing to happen to her? But Holly was still Holly, wasn't she? She *was*, but she was also something much worse.

Izzy rubbed the back of her neck and the cold turned even worse. She looked up sharply to see that Íde had come back, and was standing right behind Jinx. Before Izzy could say anything the former Matriarch reached out and stroked his hair.

Jinx swivelled around so fast she barely saw him move, his defensive instincts so primed he almost attacked at once. It took all he was to hold back. His self-preservation skills kicked in just in time. He stepped back, bumping in to Izzy but desperate to keep her behind him.

'I thought it was you,' said Íde in a dreamy, sing-song voice. 'But then I said, it couldn't be. He's dead. So many years dead. They had to put you down, you understand? Brí said it had to be done and her young Grigori obeyed. Made sure the old Keeper knew nothing. You'd gone wild. In losing her you lost yourself. You do understand that, don't you?'

'Brí?' His voice shook and he glanced back at Izzy, confused.

Íde thought he was Jasper. Oh God, she was telling him what had happened to his father, what her Dad did at Brí's command.

'Jinx, don't listen to her,' she said. 'Lady Íde, please, this isn't about that. He's not who you think. It was a long time ago and we need your help. We need the key.'

But Íde didn't appear to hear her. Neither did Jinx. All her attention was fixed on Jinx, and all his – sharp and terrible with betrayal – fixed on her.

'Brí and your father? They killed him?'

She nodded reluctantly. 'I only just found out,' she said, as if it was some kind of excuse. How could it be? It didn't help. It didn't change anything.

'Oh poor love,' Íde crooned, trying to touch him again but not quite brave enough. Her hands fluttered around him like birds. 'Poor love, poor Jasper, poor pet. They took Belladonna like they took my Wild. He died at the Council table, poisoned. He wasted away. But I took him back and laid him here. Here forever, lying among the flowers.'

Izzy's stomach twisted in on itself. The flowers covered the corpse of her lover. No wonder it smelled so rank. How long had he been there? Years and years, she knew that.

Jinx was looking at the crazy woman again. 'What happened? Please, my Lady, tell me.'

'And you'll owe me a service?' She cocked her head on one side like a curious cat, a weirdly inhuman gesture.

'Jinx, be careful,' Izzy warned him, or tried to. But he wasn't listening.

'Yes. Okay. Whatever. Tell me what happened.'

'Holly had you, the two of you.' She reached out again, this time stroking his cheek with the back of her fingers. 'And still she couldn't make you break. She did everything – killed you, brought you back over and over again, and made poor Bella watch. It broke the girl's mind in the end. She did it again and again. Quick, slow, however it suited her. And the hound in you faded. Oh but he was loyal. He didn't go. Not until the last time. She realised, you see, love? That you wouldn't change while you had your Bella. So that last time, she killed her first.' Íde laughed – actually laughed in his face. 'Oh, but then you came back, didn't you? Then you changed and she wasn't prepared. She couldn't control you. You went wild and all the wild magic came with you.'

Her hands closed on his and she lunged aside. Dragged with her, Jinx could do nothing but follow. Íde whirled him around in a mad dance, all flying hair and spinning bodies. Jinx stumbled after her, trying to keep up.

'Let him go,' Izzy shouted, trying to catch them. 'Please, stop!'

And Íde stopped, releasing him so that he crashed against the wall and slid down, breathing hard, his eyes frantic. Izzy seized him, dropping to her knees to cradle him, and Íde stood over them both.

'You aren't Jasper. You're the boy.'

'Yes,' he said, his chest still heaving. 'And I need to know.'

'Jasper fled to Brí where he had hidden you,' Íde said in slow, leaden tones. 'He begged to die and the Grigori did it. Púca are hard to kill, harder to tame, impossible to leave roaming free.' She stepped closer, peering down at him intently. At his eyes, Izzy realised. 'You have your father's eyes.'

Izzy's chest tightened. Her dad had killed Jasper. She'd known that and she'd hated him for it. But now … now it was different. He'd done it for Jasper's sake, because Jasper asked. He could have told her that. If he'd only said it … but then, would she have believed him? Would she have listened? And now her dad was Holly's prisoner. She might never see him again. A band like iron tightened around her chest, crushing her breath from her.'

Everyone always said I had my mother's' Jinx replied absently, staring back at her, entranced by this strange creature and her tale.

'Maybe you did, but not anymore. Not since you changed. You're a Púca, like him. A ghost creature, of none of the worlds and all. Holly did this to you, didn't she?' Her hands trailed up his arms, along his neck, far too intimately. Izzy felt him stiffen in alarm, but he didn't pull away and neither did she. She had to keep him safe. 'She marked you, Jinx by Jasper. She would control you where she couldn't control your father. She created the being you have become as sure as your parents created you. She does nothing without reason.'

'We need the key to stop her,' he said. 'Brí sent—'

Íde screamed and flung herself back from them, scrambling to the far side of the room, on the other side of her mound of flowers. She crouched there like an animal.

'You're here with her! You're here to kill me. Just like they said. Oh, they said, they told me, they warned me and I should have listened.'

'Who told you?' Izzy asked. She got up slowly, approaching the woman with caution. Íde just shrank back further.

'Make her stop, Jinx by Jasper. Please! You have to make her stop.'

'We aren't here to hurt you,' Jinx protested as he positioned himself between them again, hands out, trying to stop an attack. 'I'm Silver's emissary. We just need the key Brí gave you. To stop Holly. Izzy won't hurt you.'

'She's a monster!' Íde said. 'A chimera. You don't know what she is!'

'What's a chimera?' he asked.

'A thing made of other things. A thing which cannot be itself.'

'She's a Grigori.'

'Same thing. Oh the same thing.' She curled in on herself weeping. 'I am grief, I am loss. I see it in her as well, the traces.' And then she glared at Izzy from beneath the curve of her arm, her eyes so very bright, like a knife reflecting light. 'Ghosts surround you. You see the dead. Can you hear them?'

Izzy nodded but didn't dare speak. Íde stilled and then uncurled a little, rising in a graceful flow of limbs, her chest still heaving.

'Your dead beloved came back to you, Isabel Gregory. Did you command him from the grave? You are the heir of Donn. Tell me if you can hear him. My Wild, my love. Tell me.'

There was nothing. Not a sound, not a whisper. From the cries and shouts of earlier, of the Dublin side of the cemetery, the tower was frighteningly quiet.

'Izzy,' Jinx said. She knew the tone, the warning way he said only her name. He was trying to circle back towards her, but still trying to keep himself between her and Íde.

Íde turned on him again, and shushed him, her finger shaking wildly against her lips.

But Izzy knew what he meant. Íde knew more about them than she should – Izzy's full name, Jinx's resurrection, what had happened to Donn's power after his death. It suddenly all felt terribly wrong.

'Talk to him,' Íde repeated, each word bitten off at the end.

'I can't. Not if he isn't here.'

'Oh he's here.' And she grabbed Jinx by the scruff of his neck. He gave a cry of pain and alarm. All colour drained from his face as he slammed down onto his knees. He opened his mouth wide and gasped, like he was drowning. She could hear his heart thundering and his face suddenly flushed, his eyes turning glassy with desire. 'I am still a Matriarch, Isabel Gregory. I can kill with a touch. Right now his pulse is so fast, his blood racing, his need so strong his heart could explode if it continues much longer. Do as I say.'

'Let him go!'

'Find Wild. Bring him back. Talk to him. Now!'

Left without a choice, Izzy reached out her mind and felt the Blade fill her. The other fire, the one buried and weak, stirred but she pushed it down as best she could. She couldn't be distracted now. She couldn't show weakness. But she could feel the Shining One inside her latch on to the power of the Blade like a child breastfeeding.

Quick, she told herself. This has got to be quick.

'Wild?' she whispered, aware of the unearthly echo which formed beneath her own voice. Before she had used her power to send spirits on their way, but this time she reached out to draw one back. It felt like dragging her fingers the wrong way through her hair.

The mound of flowers burst into flames, the fire consuming them in moments, a pyre that burnt brightly but briefly. And in that fire she saw a form, a man, young and handsome, holding out his hands to Íde as if pleading with her.

'Wild?' Izzy said again. 'Wild! Talk to me.'

But Wild ignored her, walking forward as the flames licked the floor, ceiling and walls of the glass tower and turned them black. They hung, bright and terrible, around the figure.

'Íde,' he said and the air rippled with his words. 'I need … I thirst …'

'I know, my love. I know. But here they are just as she

promised. The girl to call you back and this beautiful vessel to house you.'

'I need …' he repeated. 'Íde, I thirst …'

He was barely there, just an echo.

Íde lifted Jinx's face towards the spirit. 'Take him. Possess him and we can be together again. Please, my love. Please.'

But Wild didn't move any closer. 'Íde,' he said and frustration twisted her face as he said those same words again. 'I need … I thirst …'

'Your last words,' she said. 'I remember. But here is a new body. Just try it. Please Wild, try!'

Enough, Izzy thought, and something in her surged up, taking back control. Not the Shining One, thank God, but the part of her that did not want to be used again. She reached out, drawing her magic back to her, seizing it. The flames curved around her, cradling her body, and she walked forward to the wan ghost and his desperate lover.

'Enough,' she said out loud and her voice carried a dark undercurrent. 'Let him go. Your lover is dead, Íde, and you hold but a memory here. That's why he just keeps saying the same thing. It's all he'll ever say. You trapped a memory and hundreds of thousands of souls to feed it. There is nothing more of him left. Let them go.'

Íde sobbed and fell forwards in a heap. As Jinx struggled out from under her, he looked up at Izzy and she saw his face change, saw the fear infect it. Fear of her? No, surely not. But fear of what she had become … yes, that was it.

With the flowers burnt away, little tethered Wild's spirit to the earth anymore. Izzy swept one arm out and hot air blew away the cards and notelets, from the newest to the disintegrated ashes of the first. The air blasted through the glass tower and with it went the last echo of Wild.

Íde let out a long, keening wail, a siren of agony and loss. Izzy remembered it – the sound her heart had made when she lost Jinx. The scream went on and on, as the Matriarch tore at her clothes and hair, shredding the fabric she wore, pulling out clumps of her hair.

Jinx got to his feet, came forwards a few feet, almost at a stagger, and he fell to his knees in front of Izzy. He had a wild look of adoration in his face and for a moment she revelled in it, strengthened and thrilled to see it.

But it wasn't love. And her response to it wasn't love either. She'd seen him wear that expression before – for Holly. It was the look of one of the fae kneeing in front of a Shining One, the devotion of an addict.

'Jinx?' she said, and shudders ran through him. Inside her the Shining One lifted its head and lunged up at her. A wall of fire and destruction rushed through her body, and she struggled like a drowning woman.

'Jinx …' she said, thinking if she could hear his voice, if she could connect with him it would be okay.

But it wasn't.

'Mistress,' he said, and gazed up at her in ecstasy.

Chapter Twenty-Four

Spark

The pathway led down. That was the only way to describe it – down and down. The rooms flowed on, less sumptuous the further they got from the entrance. The decorations were older, worn, the lights dimmer. The electricity feeding them browned out and flickered. And finally all furnishings stopped, leaving them following a brick-lined tunnel with water underfoot. But nonetheless, Dylan and Clodagh kept following Mistle. As they walked, Dylan tried to figure out where they were in relation to the city above – somewhere under Dame Street maybe? They couldn't have gone as far as the river or the Castle, not yet, but he wasn't sure which way they were going to begin with. Mistle led the way, muttering to himself, carrying a bobbing light which he'd taken from the last furnished room. Dylan wasn't sure what he was saying. It wasn't English, or at least not a form of

English he could understand. It didn't sound like any modern language Dylan had ever heard.

Beside him, Clodagh hugged herself and pushed on silently, her head down.

'Are you okay?' Dylan asked.

'Just had a demon outing me, so no, not really.'

'Oh ...' And all thoughts of what he could possible say went right out of his mind. 'So ... girls and boys?'

God, it sounded stupid even as the words came out. What sort of thoughtless, invasive question was that?

To his relief, Clodagh laughed. She laughed so loudly that even Mistle stopped his muttering, turned around and stared at her. Her voice echoed back and down the tunnel.

'Yes,' she told him. 'Just people, I guess. To be honest, I'm working it out as I go along.'

'Have you talked to your folks?'

'No, I don't know what they'll do. Or say. Probably tell me it's a phase. They're fond of *phases*.' She couldn't keep the bitterness from her voice.

He reached out a hand to her and she took it, squeezing his palm gently. 'And Ash?'

She smiled and lowered her gaze, her eyelashes casting long shadows on her cheeks. 'Yes. I guess. She's ... she's special. Beautiful and clever. And so brave, Dylan. Kind.'

He shrugged. To be honest he hadn't paid Ash much attention given his relationship with Silver, his music and everything else in his crazy life.

'And she feels the same way?'

'Yes,' Clodagh replied, without a moment's hesitation. The single word shone in the darkness.

'All right then,' said Dylan softly and it was. When Clodagh was so sure, who was he to argue?

'Are you finished?' Mistle snapped. 'Heart to heart all over? Fluffy love all around?' He laughed nastily and then hawked up a throat full of phlegm which he spat into the water. 'Shall we go on?'

Dylan met his gaze with unexpected violence in his glare. The path ahead led further into darkness. They only had Mistle to follow and Dylan knew that wasn't a good position to be in. 'Yes. Where are we anyway?'

But the old Sídhe just muttered to himself, turned around and set off again, his pace brisk and unwavering. The water underfoot was crystal clear and cold, almost ankle deep now.

'I know this place,' said Clodagh, struggling to keep up at his side. 'It's the Poddle, isn't it? We're in the underground river.'

Parts of the stone walls on either side of them formed the foundation stones of the buildings above. Arches held up the brickwork barrel roof over them. They sloshed onwards until the pathway split in two. The route Mistle took narrowed abruptly, becoming painfully claustrophobic. They were heading upstream, towards the Castle. They might even have been under it already. Dylan recalled stories about the underground river of Dublin. It had famously been used to escape from the

Castle, and in an attempted bank robbery. There had been various reports of people appearing out of it or vanishing down manholes. He'd always thought they were slightly cracked. Now he wondered.

Mistle didn't stop beneath the Castle, even though the original portal to the Sídheways, to Donn's Realm, was up there. So he wasn't aiming for that. On and on they went, through the same brick-lined tunnels until suddenly Mistle and his leading light vanished.

Panic swallowed Dylan like the sudden darkness, whole and without a moment's respite. He drew on his magic without thinking, ready for whatever might come at them. It wasn't just dark in the tunnel. There was no natural light at all, not a glow, not a twinkling. The sound of water and their hurried breath surrounded them in total blackness and primal terror surged up to fill it. Mistle had tricked them, got them lost and left them. They were alone, blind, helpless.

And then they heard it, echoing down from above. A voice sang, the voice of an angel. The music drifted, knotting itself around Dylan's consciousness, pulling his attention up, and he saw the gap in the roof overhead, a hole leading up.

And beyond it, the sulphurous glow of streetlamps, and beyond that the stars in the frosty black sky.

A way out. A way up. There was a ladder, of sorts, rungs sunken into the wall over their heads. Dylan lifted Clodagh so she could climb up first and had to jump to grab the lowest rung. Fresh air made his head spin as he climbed, the sudden cold made him shiver, but he kept going until he spilled himself out of the manhole right in front of Saint Patrick's Cathedral.

Traffic rushed by without noticing them. The Cathedral itself stood still and silent, looming over them judgementally.

A group of lads rounded the corner, laughing and singing something unsavoury. They stumbled past the pair of them and one looked back, staring hard, as if trying to bring them into focus.

'Hey,' he said suddenly, bringing the pack to a halt, whirling around dramatically. 'I know you, don't I?'

Oh God, not this. Not now.

'Yeah, I do. I know I do. You're that guy. The one with the song. Aren't you?' And he started singing it, loudly and off key.

Dylan forced a smile. 'Something like that, yeah.'

'Yeah!' the singer whooped in delight and his mates cheered. 'Yeah, you should sign me up.' He started again, jumbling the words up and the others joined in, as if they were serenading Clodagh and Dylan with their wailing.

Clodagh drew herself up to her full height and glared at them. 'Guys, I'm trying to go home with a genuine rock star, do you mind?' That silenced them. Dylan felt his face heat like he was standing in front of a furnace but Clodagh grabbed his arm and towed him away, leaving them behind to cheer him on.

'Your sex are animals, you know that?'

'I'm … I'm sorry?'

'You should be?' asked Clodagh. 'Where did Mistle go?'

Good question, and one to which Dylan had no answer. But now the drunken chorus had gone on their way, he could hear the angel's voice singing again, high and clear. She sang so beautifully that everything in him knew he needed to follow it.

'This way,' he told her and broke into a run, around the corner by the Cathedral entrance and down the narrow, winding road to the point where a gothic style arched iron gate stood locked in a gothic arch of stone. The metal looped and curled in patterns of leaves and flowers, and picked out at the top of the gate were the words 'Marsh's Library'. Beyond, the path turned left and climbed a steep flight of steps. Trees and shrubs filled the space between the high castellated walls and the building beyond. All inaccessible.

Mistle crouched on the ground in front of the gate, rocking back and forth. Dylan knew why. The iron gates kept him out.

'She sings to me,' he said in a broken voice. 'She sings and tells me to rescue her. But the Keeper has her and I cannot go in there.'

They looked up at the front of one of Ireland's oldest and most precious libraries and Dylan cursed to himself. How were they supposed to get in there?

But he could still hear the singing, the voice enchanting and ethereal.

'It's closed. Locked up for the night.'

'There is a way, but I'm not strong enough. Nowhere near

strong enough. I'm old. I'm broken. I can't get in.'

Dylan narrowed his eyes, seeing where this was going at last. 'But I can, I suppose. How?'

'With the Sídheways.'

'They don't go in there. You can't pick and choose – '

Mistle surged to his feet, his eyes wild. 'Oh but you can, if you're strong enough. If you need it enough.' He grabbed Dylan's arm and pulled him forward, down along the wall. Clodagh followed them. As they stopped, Dylan pulled free, glaring at the old fae until he backed off.

'Tell me then. Tell me how.'

'You need to pick one, tear it free and tell it where you want to go. You'll need to hold it open. She'll have to go in.' He leered at Clodagh who took a step back.

'Me?'

'I can't. It's warded against my kind. But you can. You're human. You belong with them.'

'This Keeper, do you mean the Keeper of the Library?'

Mistle laughed. 'No. Far bigger deal than that. The Keeper's everywhere boy. You'll see. And for the last few months any infraction has been dealt with in the worst way. Azazel pissed them off mightily, so much so that Sorath's spark was the Eineclan he had to pay. So you don't want to get caught. Now, you have to do it. You have to be quick.'

It wasn't hard to reach out. He could feel the music of the Sídheways in the air. It trembled on the edge of sound, waiting for him to notice it. It wasn't the discordant noise he'd created in the club, but sweet and elegant. It reminded him of Silver. That's where she was, wasn't it? If he reached for her …

He grasped something, like plucking a cobweb from the air. He pulled it in, reeling it around his hand until he had a firm grip, until he could pull.

The Sídheway tore free and for a moment he felt a brush against his skin, a breath against his ear. Silver called his name, he caught a glimpse of her, like a bright after-image on closed eyelids.

'Don't,' she whispered. 'Dylan, don't do this. Please.'

'I have to. I need you.'

The Sídheway swept her away as he wrenched it under his will and redirected it towards the library.

'Dylan?' said Clodagh, a look of concern filling her eyes. She stood right in front of him and behind her, behind her, the wall melted away, swirling into a maze of dark oak shelves, leather bindings and darkness.

'Quickly,' he said. 'We haven't much time. Where is it?'

Mistle's voice came from directly behind him. 'Down there. At the end. In the cage.'

Cage? What cage? What sort of library had cages? He tried to step forward and the Sídheway lurched up and sideways. He grabbed hold of it again, stilled it.

'I can't go in. Not and hold this thing open.'

'I can,' said Clodagh and before he could stop her, she stepped inside.

'Clodagh, no! Come back here.' Of course she didn't listen.

When did Clodagh ever listen to anyone other than Mari? And maybe Ash. Oh God, this wasn't good. He tried to reach out to Silver again, but all he got back was static. He'd torn this Sídheway free of the others, and there was no connection left. 'Clodagh!' he hissed again, into the darkness. She didn't look back, just a pale form at the far end of a long room, lined with shelves of the darkest stained oak.

'I know where it is,' she said. 'Right down here, there's three alcoves with wire mesh doors. It has to be there. Just give me a second. Hang on. I can see something. There's a light.' She vanished out of sight.

This was madness, worse than madness. This was danger-ous. Besides what they were doing, breaking into a historical building which had to have a state of the art security system with a police station just around the corner. He couldn't see her now. But there was a light, a soft, flickering light like the glow of sunshine through moving leaves. It illuminated the end of the portal, dancing against the dark oak shelves.

A chill spread through him. The song of the Sídheway turned harsh and discordant. He couldn't keep hold of it. But if he let go now, Clodagh would be lost inside the library, left there to explain herself when the alarms went off and the cops arrived. And if she was lucky it would just be the police and not whoever or whatever the Keeper was. The fae seemed terrified of facing them and Dylan didn't want to find out why.

Something rattled up ahead, the door she had spoken of,

he hoped. Then he heard her voice.

'There's a … oh my God, Dylan … the light … like fireflies in a jar, but … It's like … I've never seen anything like it.'

The graffiti angel was what Izzy had seen, the thing that had transferred Sorath's spark to her and had almost allowed the angel to completely possess her. That painting on the wall of a Dublin alley had started all this madness. When Azazel took the spark away it had been in a glass tube. Like a jar.

'Don't touch it, Clodagh,' he shouted, suddenly realising her danger. 'Whatever you do don't touch it!'

But Clodagh didn't answer. There was nothing but that flickering glow. He reached out further, trying to extend the Sídheway so he could get closer to her, so he could reach her. Oh god, what had he done? He stretched too far, he knew it the moment he did it, and the thing slipped out of his control.

'No!' he yelled as it snapped shut, his connection to the library gone in an instant. Staggering back, he almost fell over Mistle and turned on him, grabbing him by the filthy shirt, hauling him from his knees. 'What have you done?'

'Nothing!' And the old fae laughed hysterically. 'Nothing, nothing, nothing!'

Dylan dropped him, ran back to the entrance and seized the gate, rattling it wildly, trying to open it. He turned his magic on it but Sídhe magic didn't work on iron – probably why the library had the bloody gate to begin with. He thought of the women in the library at Trinity, of all they appeared to know. Did they guard this place too? Why the hell weren't they here?

'Clodagh, answer me!' he yelled, no longer caring who heard him or what might happen.

Light burst from the door at the top of the steps, illuminating each branch in the garden and spilling their shadows across the path. It flowed between them like a slow winter sunrise, spreading across the forest floor. She stepped out of the darkness like Clodagh, but so unlike her his heart flinched back, but his body stood frozen.

'Hello again, Dylan,' said the lyrical, terrible voice. She stood at the gate and studied it for a moment, then slid her fingers through the gaps between the bars. They brushed against his and sparks crackled against his skin. He pulled back from her touch. With barely any sign of effort, she wrenched it off the hinges and threw it aside.

Sorath stepped out of the garden and smiled at him.

All the alarms went off at once, everywhere, a cacophony of piercing screams in the night. Dylan only realised after a moment that one of those screams was his own. He was screaming and the angel Sorath reached out and slapped one hand over his mouth to silence him. The other grabbed him by the throat and she flung him after the gate. He hit the wall hard, his head making a fierce crack against the granite wall. Dylan slumped at her feet, half on the gate, half off.

Ignoring him now, she turned to Mistle. 'Get up, dog. We don't have much time. This body won't last. I'll burn through it in a matter of hours.'

'Mistress,' he scrambled to his feet, but kept grovelling. 'What other body will do? The Grigori girl is already grail to another. A Seraphim took her. There was nothing that could be done.'

'It's too late for that anyway.' She stretched out her arms, examined Clodagh's form. 'Things are moving too fast. We must get to the Thorn Gate.'

'But that's locked. Sealed.'

Sorath smiled, a fierce and frightening expression on Clodagh's sweet face.

'Seals can be broken.' She held out her hand to him and Mistle took it, fawning and bowing. 'Someone is bringing a key.'

Chapter Twenty-Five

Compulsion

Izzy blazed with light, not the fire he'd seen in her before, but pure light. Brilliant and chaotic, the flames in her a part of it, but also more, so much more. Her eyes shone and the glow in them filled him with a fierce, insane joy. Jinx couldn't move from his knees, couldn't look away from her. He needed to adore her, worship her, and Izzy – Izzy –

Izzy wouldn't want this. It was wrong. And what he saw wasn't the real her. Izzy never looked so fearful, so concerned. He remembered how she called fire to drive off the Fear, how she had stood there with flames blazing. And Izzy, his beautiful Izzy – even then she had not looked so afraid as she did now.

'Can you hear me?' she said. 'Oh please, Jinx, you need to stop.'

The desire to obey her gripped him again, a mad urge that shook him to the core. But the Púca served no one but themselves, wasn't that what they said? The inner core of him warred with the compulsion that had descended on him.

And it was a compulsion. He was sure of that now.

'I can free him,' said Íde. 'I can release him, but you need to help me. He promised me a debt and this is how I intend to have him pay.'

'No!' said Izzy, her voice low and dangerous. The ground beneath them trembled.

'Do it. Put my Wild inside him. You don't even have to kill him. You have Donn's powers, his Blade, so I know you can do that.'

'But I won't. I won't help you steal his life.'

'Then he'll die with longing. He'll die in agony wanting you.'

Íde's hands seemed to reach inside him and tighten around his heart, squeezing, wringing out an agony of thwarted desire. This was her power, the truth of her name. Íde meant thirst.

'I need,' Wild's ghost had said. *'I thirst.'*

Izzy cried out as she saw the pain fill his face. He couldn't keep it inside. Íde tightened her grip again and Jinx felt his heart strain, stretch as if it would burst.

He'd do anything for Izzy. He had already died for her. Izzy brought him nothing but suffering and pain and yet still he loved her. He would die for her again in an instant. He knew that even without Íde's magic twisting inside him.

Íde's magic, the need and desire, the blind devotion which led men to murder or suicide, to self-destruction in the name of another. Thirst …

'I need. I thirst.'

He lifted his hand and saw her there, saw the truth in the old Matriarch's eyes.

'You killed Wild,' he whispered, barely able to force out the words. 'You killed him yourself.'

Her skin paled, bone white and bloodless and she snarled at him, spit hitting his face. 'You lie.'

'No,' said Izzy, realisation spreading over her face. 'No, he's right.'

'He would have left,' she replied, her voice cold and brittle. 'He planned to go. You don't understand. I couldn't be without him. I wanted to stop him.'

'What did you do?' Izzy asked and her voice sounded almost like her own again. So sad, so broken with sorrow and pity.

'I made him need me and nothing else. I just wanted him to need me, to thirst for me alone. Until he needed nothing else. And would desire nothing else. As you will.'

She smiled down at Jinx, actually smiled, and he saw the madness in her eyes clearly now. Complete madness.

'Íde, please let him go,' Izzy said gently. 'He isn't Wild. He can't be. Wild is gone.'

The smile froze, faded. 'Bring him back, Lady. Please, it is all that I ask.'

'Give her the key,' Jinx said and his breath turned harsh as he looked at Izzy. God, he did need her. She was everything. He ached with need. 'Give her the key and I'll do it.'

'No!' Izzy said and all the gentleness was gone.

But Íde didn't seem to notice. She let him go and sobbed. 'I can't. The key is gone. She promised. She promised.'

'Who?' he asked.

'And what did she promise you?' Izzy asked.

She had moved closer now, almost close enough to touch. He could feel the warmth of her skin, taste her scent. Her hands trembled and her skin glowed as if a spotlight shone on her. So beautiful she stole his breath.

Damn it, Íde's magic was swamping his system. Because that had to be it, didn't it? He wasn't thinking straight.

'What did she promise?' Izzy said again.

'That you would come. That you would do this. What I asked … That you would bring Wild back to me. Why can't you? Why *won't* you?'

'Did you give her the key?' Izzy asked. 'It's okay. Just tell me.'

But Íde didn't answer. Instead, she released Jinx and he fell to the floor with the sudden freedom. His face smacked against the glass, pain pounding through his brain, and the shock of it breaking her spell. His head reeled and his blood felt like ice in his veins. Desire turned to dust. Pulling himself up, he saw Izzy pass him. The light in her was gone now, or maybe he couldn't see it any more. But he could see something else. Shadows clustered around her. They trailed behind her like great black wings.

'Holly lied, Íde,' she said, not unkindly.

Íde screamed – truly screamed this time. It was the empty

howl of all hope gone, the agony as the last scrap of it was torn away by knowledge of the betrayal.

Where she got the knife from, Jinx didn't know. Its iron blade gleamed darkly and he knew it, Izzy's knife, the one she'd taken from the Magpies in the summer. Íde must have snatched it from her at some point. He knew the touch of that blade, the danger it posed. The iron might not hurt Izzy as it would one of the Sídhe, but the knife itself would. It was still a knife, wickedly sharp and held by a madwoman. She drove right at Izzy, her features like an animal, her eyes wild. A burst of energy flared up inside him and he moved, pulling Izzy aside. He raised his forearm, deflecting the blade. Íde staggered back and crashed into the glass wall, knife blade first.

It shouldn't have done anything. But the glass tower was magical and the knife was iron. Or maybe with her insanity her magic was failing. The glass shattered – one second whole and the next composed of a thousand fragments which crumbled away into the night. The little lights outside suddenly surged upwards, as if a skyful of stars fell at once in the wrong direction.

Íde teetered on the edge as they reached her. The nearest one hovered for a moment in front of her and then shot straight through her chest. It burst from her back and flew on, tearing through the ceiling above them, breaking through the glass like a bullet hole.

More followed, more and more. Each one made Íde jerk and left another wound. Each one broke through another part of the tower. And still they came, light after light.

Íde slipped, falling forward into the empty space. The lights followed her as she fell, tearing through her.

Jinx heard the impact far below and Izzy flinched at the sound. The fire behind them dwindled and the lights vanished. A bitter wind blew through the shattered walls. The whole structure groaned.

'What were they?' he asked.

Izzy slipped her arms around him, nestled in against him and he held her, unwilling or unable to let her go. He wasn't sure which. But she was real and here, and he had her. Íde hadn't made him feel something that wasn't real. But it had left him helpless. Again.

'Souls,' she said, her voice trembling now. 'The dead she trapped here. They're gone now. All of them.'

Another ominous rumble shook the tower.

'It's going to come down,' he said. 'Can you run? We have to get out of here.'

She nodded and her hand found his, their fingers tangling. They fled down the stairs and through the gate to Dublin, as shards of glass began to plummet down around them, crashing at their feet. The staircase was falling underneath them, but he pulled her onwards, unwilling to ever let her go again.

'Holly has the key, Jinx,' she said, breathless as they reached the base of the tower. The gate wavered in front of them, shattering like the tower with the death of its maker. They threw themselves through it.

On the other side, O'Connell's tomb seemed strangely quiet, the air cold and too still. There was no light. The gate behind them flickered like a guttering candle and went out. Íde's Hollow was no more.

Izzy pressed her face into his chest and held him against her. She stood there, very still, as if listening to his heartbeat, her eyes closed. Very gently, afraid he might disturb her or worse, make her stop and let him go, he raised a hand to stroke her short red hair.

'I thought I was going to lose you again,' she whispered.

'I'm still here.'

'I could have been like her.'

'No,' he smiled and kissed her crown. What was it about his smile? So rare, so unexpected, that it seemed more beautiful to her than any other. 'No, you couldn't.'

'Holly has the key.'

He frowned. 'I know.'

She sagged against him, letting him take more of her weight. When had she last slept, he wondered. Come to that, when had he? 'Don't let me get lost, Jinx. Please. Don't let this … this thing swallow me up. Promise.'

A promise he wasn't sure he could keep … He was too tired to think but he knew promising anything now was a mistake. Even to Izzy.

'Come,' he told her. 'We have to get to safety.'

She looked up, her eyes lost and hopeless. 'Just take me home.'

Izzy couldn't stop shaking. She did everything she could to hide it but she knew Jinx wasn't fooled. He wasn't an idiot. But she knew the feeling of light and fire had almost overwhelmed her, that the Shining One inside her – Crom Dubh – had been inches away from controlling her completely. And then what? Would she still be conscious of what was happening? Would she be changed until she didn't care?

When it happened again – and it *would* happen again – would she be able to break free again?

She didn't want to think about it. She didn't have any choice. She was so sick and tired of it that she could barely move, but somehow she kept going, following Jinx, trusting him. Because she needed to be able to trust him. Because she needed him to do what needed to be done, if it came down to it.

Just as she had.

She wasn't sure how long they had walked, or what route they had taken. He hadn't spoken the whole time, or at least she didn't think he had. They went by minor Sídheways and through an empty city, along narrow lanes with cobbles underfoot. She wasn't sure if she was in Dublin or Dubh Linn and it didn't really matter anymore. Not really. It was all blurring together, merging, or falling apart depending on which way she looked at it.

Jinx swore and turned left abruptly.

'What is it? What's wrong?'

'The path's twisted. Look.' The way ahead was dark, endless. Izzy shivered, not liking the way it seemed to suck the light away, like a black hole. 'We can't go there.'

She shook her head. That made sense on a visceral level. 'Which way then?'

'Through here.' There was an arch. It looked like something from a church and beyond it she could see stained glass, but when they stepped through, there was some kind of parlour that looked like it had been lifted from the 1950s. It even had pictures of a pope and J.F.K. on the mantelpiece. 'This isn't right.' He turned around, confused. 'This shouldn't be here.' She squeezed his hand tightly.

'Another way?'

She could hear his breath quickening. 'Yes, I … I guess.'

Izzy let him pull her forward, through another door and into a garden, overgrown with weeds. And then onwards, along a laneway which narrowed in nightmarish discomfort. They squeezed through a gap at the end, out onto Dawson Street. But not the Dawson Street of her world, with its road-works and traffic rerouting. The Mansion House looked brand new for one thing. As in the paint was still drying. None of the cafes, shops and restaurants were there.

'What's happening?' she asked.

'It's … it's like they're falling apart. Like Dylan said. Izzy, this isn't good. I don't know the way out.'

'But I do,' said a voice. 'Hurry. You must hurry.'

Silver stepped out of nowhere, lines of light entangling her. She grabbed line after line as they whirled around her, trying to weave them back together. She gritted her teeth and glared at him.

'Jinx, I'm not messing around here. If you want to get out, you need to do as I say.'

'We thought you were lost.'

'I am. I'm trying to hold them together, but I can't do it forever. Now move.'

She held out a hand, letting other strands fly free. They could see the rest now, winnowing through her body, under her skin. Even her hair was tangled with them. Strands of light, but more than that.

'What's happening to you?' Izzy asked as Jinx took her hand in his. Silver curled her fingers around his and tried to smile. It was only then that Izzy saw how much pain she was in. It was killing her.

'I have to stop them unravelling. I have to try.'

'And Dylan's trying to help you?'

'You have to stop him. It's too dangerous. I'll keep going as long as I can, but I don't … I can't … make this last. Here. Out here. You'll be safe.'

'Silver …' Jinx began, but stopped when she fixed her gaze on him.

'Stay alive. Keep her off the island, understand? And Jinx … this isn't yours to fix.' And she shoved both of them hard in the small of the back so they fell stumbling out of the Sídheways.

They crashed against each other and slammed into the door of a toilet cubicle, and Jinx hurriedly pulled open the door. The room beyond was dark, the ceiling so low that he had to bow his head.

'Damn it,' he said. 'Silver?' But the light, and the way into the Sídheways were gone.

'She said they're unravelling,' she said, even though speaking made her head ache. She felt like throwing up, like she was slowly recovering from a three-day migraine. That wasn't all she had said.

Keep her off the island.

And all the time, in the pit of her stomach, she could feel the Shining One, stronger now, preparing. The tattoo at the back of her neck hadn't regained a trace of warmth. The top of her shoulder itched, warning her that the marks Holly had given her had reached that far already.

'Where are we?' she asked, trying to ignore it.

'It's a coffee shop,' he said. It looked more like a bunker. They climbed metal steps from the underground loos and he pressed the door release which let them into the café instead. There was no one there, and all the lights were off. Jinx didn't waste any time. He headed straight for the security system, typing in a rapid series of numbers until there was a single piercing beep.

'Come on,' he said, and flicked the lock on the door open. He turned back when she didn't move. 'What is it?'

She stared at him, not sure how to tell him that her legs didn't seem to be obeying her right now. Or that it felt as if she was falling back inside her own head while something else rose up to take her place. Or that she couldn't tell what was real and what was simply panic at this stage. She felt like something spiralling out of control. How did she explain any of that?

'Izzy?' His hand took hers, as if she had missed a step or two in between. 'We have to go.'

'How do you do that? The security system, I mean.'

He shrugged and gave her one of those cocky smiles that were so rare and so very special. 'Electronics like me.'

'They hate me,' she told him.

'You just need to threaten them a little bit more, you know?'

She smiled, the expression somewhat unexpected, and not entirely welcome on her face. What right did she have to smile when everything was falling apart around her, when Dad was a captive and Dubh Linn was crumbling?

Jinx led her out into the freezing night air. The Christmas lights were out now and the city eerily silent. They stood at the south end of St. Stephen's Green and the next gate was inside it, locked behind iron gates and iron railings. At least she hoped it was. The wind had turned bitterly cold, with the promise of more snow.

'What do we do?' she asked.

'Climb the railings, I guess. Are you up for it?'

They didn't have a choice. 'Okay.' Jinx squeezed her hand

again. He didn't say everything would be all right, or some other pointless platitude, and for that, at least, he was grateful. For him being here, no matter how he might have changed. For all the ways, in spite of everything, that he hadn't changed at all.

The gates in Fusilier's Arch, opposite the top of Grafton Street were out – far too high, and out in the open. But a little along the north edge of the square, where the trees and bushes pressed up against the rails, and the darkness was deep, they could climb over unseen. The problem was, the railings were made of iron. She glanced at Jinx warily, but he just helped her over and then grasped the top. His knuckles turned white and the flicker of pain in his face made her stomach churn. Moments later he was over too.

'Are you okay?' she asked.

'Yes,' he said and that was all he said. No worse than the pain he constantly endured, she guessed, and he wasn't going to go into that. Not Jinx. Stoic to the bone.

The park was worse than the city. The silence smothered them at first, and it seemed darker than anywhere in the city centre should be. But she heard rustling and tiny noises all around them, hidden things, living, breathing things in the dark. She felt eyes watching them pass, the stillness that seemed to go with them which was really watchfulness and fear. So much fear. It tasted like vomit in the back of her throat and her own heart sounded far too loud. The tightness in her chest squeezed painfully on her heart.

Terror in the air. Fear of her and of Jinx rippled all around them.

'Can you feel it?' she asked.

'Yes, just keep walking.'

'What is it?'

'I don't know. Fae, human, maybe a bit of both.'

They crossed the bridge and entered the central Victorian gardens, the formal beds covered in frost, the fountains with their elaborate sculpted bulrushes still and silent. The stars overhead glittered, very bright, and the full moon illuminated the open space. Like a Celtic cross, Izzy realised. The beds and paths made a Celtic cross just like the one on her neck. The one that wouldn't let up with its panicked warnings.

At the far side, near the bust of Countess Markievicz, Izzy saw a figure. It stood very still, silent, arms folded, watching them. She knew that, even though she couldn't see a face. The hood concealed all features and the cloak fell about the body. It was just a shape, made of shadows and darkness. It didn't move as they approached, but continued to watch them. It didn't speak until they were almost level.

'Isabel Gregory.' The voice floated through the night's air. The world seemed to slow, to stop around her, and the figure finally stepped forward, pushing back the hood to reveal a cascade of red hair and pale features, delicately sculpted. Her full red lips drew up in a mirthless smile. Izzy instantly thought of Brí but this was not Brí. There was no gentleness to either of them, but in this woman the sharpness was ingrained, the stark lines of her face far too beautiful. So much so, the beauty became a weapon, lethal. She was older too, far older, and in that age was a profound edge which made her even more fascinating. It went beyond beauty, deep into a source of obsession.

'Who are you?' Jinx asked. He had that tension about him, every nerve on edge, hackles rising, ready to attack.

The woman turned her smile on him, a smile that never reached her dark eyes. She raised a hand, almost lazily, and made a curt gesture of disdain. Jinx stepped back sharply, almost knocking Izzy over.

'You?' he said and she heard real fear in his voice. Even so, he tried to hold his ground, trying to protect her.

'Me,' said the woman. 'Back off, Púca. Or we'll have words. Words you won't enjoy. I will speak with her.'

'You're not allowed. She's Grigori.'

She glared at him, malice infecting her gaze. She didn't like to be crossed, whoever she was.

'We don't *really* know what she is. Not anymore. Don't cross me, boy. I'll decide whether the geis on me holds or not. Isabel Gregory, you and I must talk.'

'Still,' said Izzy, making her voice sound confident and unaffected. 'It's a good question. Who are you?'

'She's the Morrígan,' said Jinx. 'Mistress of war, goddess of destruction, the crone—'

'Oh, seriously,' the Morrígan sighed. 'That's enough.' Jinx stilled, like the world around them, frozen.

'Let him go!'

'I'm not holding him. I'm holding you. We're in a moment, held between seconds. We must talk, you and I. I've been watching you.'

'Well, that doesn't sound creepy at all.'

The Morrígan laughed. 'Oh, I do like you, Grigori. Your kind are always so angry. Not that I get to talk to you very often.'

'And why not?'

'I don't know. A geis. Interference. Divine dictates. Turf war. Bla bla bla.' She shook back her red hair as if dismissing the question. 'But things feel different now, don't they? You feel it.'

'No.'

'Liar. The crows, the power, the passion, and the strength in you. All that power. You're being reforged, girl, becoming that weapon you carry.'

'And what do you have to do with it?'

'You can call me the blacksmith, if you want. But I wouldn't, if I were you.'

Izzy scowled, thinking of all kinds of things she could call her. The Morrígan just watched her with eyes like the crows, smiling as if she knew every thought that passed through Izzy's mind.

'And what do you want with me?'

'It isn't about me, my love. It's about you.'

'You sent the crows.'

'They're drawn to those who are drawn to me. And you

are, aren't you? Drawn to me, that is. Part of me is in there, deep inside you, buried under everything else. Has been right from the beginning … You'll have to choose in the end. You'll choose between the darkness and the light, between total peace and the struggle.'

'War?'

'War is already here, child. You'll know, when the time comes. Reach out to me. I'll be waiting.'

She turned away, pulling up the hood as she did so, and vanished in the darkness. The world lurched forward again.

'Izzy?' Jinx said with a gasp. He grabbed her, shook her, and held her close. 'Are you okay?'

'Yes. I'm fine. Really.'

'What did she do? What did she want?'

'To talk. To make an offer, I think.'

He let his breath out in a long low hiss. 'Be wary. She's .:. she's dangerous.'

'Who isn't?'

'She is not of this world. She picks and chooses how she'll manifest and in whom she'll show herself. She isn't an angel, or Sídhe. She isn't a demon either.'

'What is she then?'

'I told you. A goddess.'

'Jinx, come on. She's another one of you lot. Another – '

'No,' he said firmly. 'She's more. And if she's showing an interest in you, Izzy, you need to be careful. You'll need to be prepared. If she's taking part now, it's almost over. Everything.'

'Why?'

'Because of her. Because she's here. I don't know how or why but I know she's the end of us. Of all of us. And death is coming.'

'Death is everywhere, all around us. It follows us, you and I. Believe me, I know now. Ever since Donn's Hollow … everything changed, Jinx. You were dead and I … I went back. I shouldn't have. But I did. I've been three times. And everything changed. There's only the end now.'

He looked at her like she was mad, or something to be feared. He looked at her like she was a monster. But in his eyes she saw acceptance, defeat, and he lowered his gaze. 'So what do we do?'

'We keep going until we reach it. It's the only way to get Dad back, to stop Holly, if we can. And if not …' She shook her head. 'I don't want to be in Holly's world, Jinx. I don't want to be her creature, her slave.'

'Neither do I,' he whispered. And that was that.

They found the last Sídheway together, mercifully still intact, and stepped through, out into the same night on the hillside beneath the Obelisk, at the foot of the Wishing Stone. It wasn't far from Brí's Hollow, but as they stood there, thick smoke rose around them. The wind, which should have been cold, beat hot against them, rising up from where the gorse bushes crawled down the cliffs to the sea.

And the gorse was on fire.

Everything was on fire.

Chapter Twenty-Six

Into the Fire

lames covered the hillside, and black smoke, thick
and choking, obscured everything. Jinx shifted to his
hound form instinctively, intent only on leading Izzy to safety
somehow. But the fire left him blind, his sense of smell cor-
rupted with the reek of burning wood. The snow didn't limit
the fires. Nothing would stop them. The wind fanned them
and something else. He knew that tang of magic and malice.

'She's here,' said Izzy and he glanced up at her to see her
shining again. Her body shook as she tried to suppress it, tried
to keep control of herself. 'I can feel it, Jinx. She wants me.'

And not just her, but he couldn't say that. She wanted Izzy,
true. And everything else too. She wanted death and destruction. She wanted power.

Other things moved amid the fire. He could feel them, dark
and light, angels and demons. So many. They leaped from tree

to tree, rock to rock. They were fighting, hand to hand, blade to blade. The air charged with power, shaken with aftershocks.

Panic shot through him. The war in heaven had come to earth. They'd destroy everything. He wondered who was out there. Not Azazel and Zadkiel, that was for sure. They were generals, not fighters. It didn't matter to them how many they sent to die.

Izzy and Jinx ducked down behind the Wishing Stair, the fire blazing behind them as it consumed the gorse.

'Which way?' she asked. 'What do we do?'

Screams shattered the night and something crashed to the ground no more than five feet away. An angel flailed its wings on fire, the feathers consumed by the flames. It opened its perfect mouth and screamed again, a noise at a pitch that brought agony to all who heard it.

'We have to help,' Izzy said, starting up, but Jinx growled, knowing what was coming, what was next.

From the ridge above them, a shape jumped. When he landed the ground rocked. Osprey smiled, circling the scrabbling angel, whose hands clawed at the earth in vain. He lifted a sword as long as his own body and brought it down, impaling the winged creature like a butterfly beneath a pin. He stood over it, watching it die, watching its pain and drinking in the final moments of denial and despair. When he yanked out the sword tip, the angel dissolved into ashes and smears of colour on the ground. Osprey looked down on his work and smiled his terrible smile.

Something moved overhead, another winged shadow, and Osprey's head snapped up, following like a cat after prey. He leaped into the air again, and ploughed through the trees to the right after his unfortunate quarry.

Izzy drew in a shaky breath, something Jinx didn't yet feel safe enough to do. He'd seen something else.

A shape flitted through the smoke, silhouetted against the flames, a hound. He knew it at once, knew the shape and what little scent he could still make out. Blight.

The Cú Sídhe ran to them, bowed as only they could, respectful without appearing in any way subservient. Jinx returned the gesture. There wasn't time for it, but he did it nonetheless. It meant they were allies and that was not to be slighted. No chains this time. Everything was different. He didn't know whether to be relieved or terrified.

You need to come with me, Blight said to Jinx. *Now. There's no time. The Hollow will fall but not yet and it is not safe out here.*

What's happening?

What do you think? Holly is happening. She attacked not long after you left. The angels came to stop her, but you can see how effective that was. Then the demons came for them. It's a disaster all over. Now get inside.

Jinx stopped arguing because there was nothing else to do. Izzy gathered up his clothes and followed him, moving slowly, dreamily, which couldn't be a good sign. But at least she was moving. That had to count for something.

The door to the Hollow slammed shut behind them and

Izzy wilted, sliding down the wall. She hugged his clothes against her and her eyes closed, but that didn't stop the light seeping out from beneath her lashes.

He changed back. 'Izzy?'

She just held out his clothes without looking at him. He pulled the jeans on hurriedly, followed by the shirt. Then he slid on the boots as well. Blight, also now in human form, pulled on a pair of loose trousers.

'No time to lose,' he said. 'She wants to see you, Lady Isabel. Then I'm to get you to safety.'

'We're not safe in here?' she asked.

'Not nearly safe enough. The wards won't hold. Not for long.'

They made their way down the dark tunnel, and listened for sounds of pursuit. Izzy seemed to be holding it together for now, but Jinx couldn't help but worry. After all she had been through, with her father a prisoner, and Íde attempting to manipulate them, with the marks on her body and Crom Dubh lurking inside. With the Morrígan watching.

He swallowed hard. She was still watching, he knew that. She was always watching, that was what they said.

You keep Izzy safe, he told her. *You keep her safe and I'll do anything you want.*

But there was no answer.

Brí was waiting, and not just for them. She wore her finest gown, red and gold, and her long hair was unbound. She looked like a queen, cloaked by the flames that rose from the pool behind her. He'd expected armour and weapons, but that wasn't Brí's way. Not really.

'The key, where is it? Do you have it?' she asked, the moment they came into view.

'It's good to see you too,' said Izzy caustically.

'Enough,' Brí growled at her. 'Where is it?'

'She gave it to Holly. The whole thing was a trap.'

Brí sat back in her chair, looked up to the ceiling in despair and sighed. 'And where is Íde now?'

'Um,' Izzy glanced helplessly at Jinx, who didn't know what to do or say. How would Brí take this? They might not have spoken for years but they were both Matriarchs. Holly would celebrate, but Brí? He wasn't so sure anymore. 'She's dead,' said Izzy. 'I didn't mean to. She was trying to get me to put Wild into Jinx's body and it kind of ...'

'I'm sure it did,' Brí replied coolly. 'Well, if she betrayed us to Holly there was nothing else you could do.'

'I didn't kill her because of that.'

'And yet she's dead. Why else do it?'

'I didn't ... I didn't mean to.'

'Íde killed Wild,' Jinx interrupted. 'She didn't mean to either, but she did it. And then she used the spirits of people buried in the cemetery to keep his spirit there. Holly offered her a chance to get him back using Izzy and me. And she took it.'

Brí wrinkled her nose in disgust. 'So Holly has the key. She has the power of a Shining One, or that creature has her, perhaps, and she's taken magic from Donn, the Seanchaí and countless other beings. The powers are moving, powers that never should be disturbed.' This was far from the distraught woman he had seen at the college. She was resigned. And that scared him. 'And what else?' she asked. 'What aren't you telling me? I can smell the lies on you, Púca.'

He glanced at Izzy, knowing she would kill him for telling Brí, but what else could he do? The Matriarch needed to know this.

'The Morrígan manifested. She's watching Izzy.'

Brí pushed herself out of the chair and stalked towards her daughter, never taking her eyes off the girl. Izzy held firm but she looked terrified. Not even she could hide that.

'Where are the tattoos?' Brí asked. 'Show me.'

Izzy pulled down the shoulder of her top. It didn't even have to go very far down. The tattoos Holly had left had risen to her clavicle, just below her neck.

'Turn around,' Brí snapped. 'Let me see the other.'

Izzy did as she was ordered, but he could read humiliation on her features. Brí let out a little hiss of rage. The Celtic cross on the back of Izzy's neck, the one that marked her as Grigori, was full of little fissures. Light spilled out across the indigo, making it look like an old, broken seal. It was crumbling.

'It's almost too late. You need to be able to fight it. You need more strength than you have in you. Even you, Isabel. Listen to me. I need you to step into the fire with me. Be my daughter and take your birthright. Do you understand?'

Izzy turned around to glare at her, hard and determined.

'Okay,' she said at last.

'The Morrígan … she'll offer you only a moment. Sometimes less than that. A single instant, a chance. Hesitate and it's lost. And it might not be when or what you think. She's a goddess, girl.'

'You once told me that you were too.'

'Maybe I did. Maybe I was.'

The fire above Brí's pool flared up as bright as the sun. Too bright to look at without shielding the eyes. Izzy and Brí were no more than dark silhouettes against the brilliance.

Brí reached out her hand, offering it to Izzy. Jinx wanted to tell her to stop, not to go, but it was far too late for that now. Not that she'd listen. Not that he could speak. 'It's time, Isabel Gregory. It has to be now. Will you come?'

Izzy took Brí's hand and Jinx felt himself start forward, his only thought to stop her, to save her, but before he could reach them, she stepped into the wall of flames.

Brí flowed with the flames the same way the Morrígan had with the shadows. They were the same, somehow, Izzy thought. The same but opposite. Completely different and yet, when you got down to it, made of the same stuff. Deep down.

It was curious and though she knew there wasn't time to dwell on it, she couldn't help herself.

'The Morrígan …' she said. Her voice seemed to ripple

with the fire all around. It felt strange, and yet safe. As if she had become whole for the first time.

'It means Great Queen,' said Brí. 'She doesn't even have a name of her own. She doesn't need one.'

'She made me think of you.'

'I'm sure she did. She has that way. We were close, once, but we are not the same. You must take care, Isabel.'

Her voice carried the same strange echoes in these flames that didn't burn. Izzy reached out, joining both her hands with Brí now.

'I will.'

'You have so much you still need to learn. Perhaps I should have been there more for you.'

'I had a mother.'

'You did.' Brí sighed and looked away. 'And a good one. But don't *ever* tell her I said that. She wouldn't know what to do if she didn't loathe me.'

'I need to find Dad.'

'Yes, and I fear you will. Holly is counting on it. She'll use him to get to you, to make you do what she wants. As much as she will use all those close to you. They're your weakness, Isabel. I wish … I wish I could just hide you away. Lock you up to keep you safe. But all there is now is the end. And there is no safe. Not even here. The war is upon us. Angels and demons massacre each other out there. And worse, the humans know.' The desolate smile flickered over her face, illuminated in gold and fire. 'When we first hid, I thought it was madness.

They loved me, my followers, and I needed to protect them. But as the world moved on, I came to understand it. Holly never did. She never changes, you see? Not just physically. Her mind is like stone, fixed and unyielding, obsessed with power. Once she wanted to be the Morrígan incarnate. Now she is something far worse. With the key, with Grigori blood … I'm not certain she can be stopped, save by power. Power upon power. Here.'

She took off the necklace with the amber pendant and placed it around Izzy's neck. Her hands brushed against the Grigori tattoo and it warmed, radiating a peace Izzy hadn't felt in weeks, perhaps months.

The other tattoos, the ones the Shining One had brought with it, seemed to fade for a moment, becoming less real on her skin, less like the thousand pinpricks she felt all the time. But they didn't go entirely. Like a ghost on her skin, they lingered.

The Shining One inside her writhed in anger and thwarted rage. A rush of that anger shot through her unexpectedly and she shook herself free, leaving Brí reaching out to her, her hands wreathed in the flames that were part of her.

Izzy gasped. The necklace felt far heavier than she remembered. In it, she sensed a power, not unlike that of the creature seeking to possess her. Like responded to like and it shook her.

She stared at Brí.

'You're my heir,' said the Matriarch. 'As well as Donn's. You hold the magic of the Storyteller's books and all those lost memories, the power contained in them. You have been a vessel for one of the highest angels.'

'I'm more than just a vessel, Brí.'

'Of course you are. I don't think you can even comprehend how much more.'

'But is it enough?'

'To defeat the Shining Ones?'

'And Holly.'

'I doubt there is much of Holly left now. A liquid assumes the shape of that which holds it, but it doesn't change what it is. Holly never understood that.'

'Brí, this is your touchstone.'

'And I don't need it here. Not now.' She smiled, such a brave, proud smile. 'Now you have to leave.'

'I don't understand. Where are we going?'

'To safety. Far away from here. To your grandmother. Or the Keeper. You cannot stay, don't you understand? If you do, you will succumb to her and everything will fall. She'll take you to the island and everything will fall apart. You have to keep your power from her.'

She leaned forward and kissed Izzy on the forehead in a curiously maternal way. 'All I have, all I am, I pour into you. Live well. Love well. And—'

An explosion tore through the side of the Hollow, ripping away rock and the internal structure, leaving it gaping open to the sky and the sea. A blizzard of snow and ashes swirled around them and Brí's fire went out.

Holly stepped into the chamber, light eddying around her like the aurora borealis. As the Cú Sídhe tried to gather themselves to attack, she swept them back with a wave of her hand and light that blinded them. Stronger than ever, the earth shook beneath her feet.

'Give me the girl.' Her voice echoed with power.

Brí pushed Izzy behind her and for once Izzy didn't care. 'No.'

'There's no one left to aid you. Come, Brí, surely your sense of survival hasn't fled. Bow before me, and all will be forgiven. Better yet, reclaim what was yours and join us. Be all that you once were.'

'I gave that up.'

'Whoever truly gives up what they are? Who can truly change so much? You were a seraph. You split your powers to live here, to be free. Come home to us. I will even raise up your child to our rank. I've already begun that. Listen to me, Brí. Be whole again.'

Brí was a seraph? How was that possible? A thousand questions flew to Izzy's tongue, but there was no time to ask them. She recalled the deference even the most haughty angels had shown her and it suddenly made sense. But why wasn't she imprisoned with the others?

'No,' Brí said again, and this time she flung out her hands. A wall of fire burst into being in the centre of the Hollow, leaving Holly on the far side. 'Isabel,' said Brí hurriedly, strain showing on her face. 'You have to go.'

'But Brí—'

'No time for "buts", Izzy. Go now. I'll hold her off as long as I can.'

And that was when Izzy knew what it meant – the words, the gift, their journey into the fire. Brí wasn't coming with them. She was going to stay behind and she didn't expect to survive. How could she, if Izzy had her touchstone?

'No!' Izzy said again, trying to tear the necklace off her throat, but she couldn't undo the clasp. It seemed to be sealed somehow, Brí's magic no doubt. Brí's stubborn determination and bloody-minded belief that she knew what was best for everyone.

'Jinx! Blight!' the Matriarch shouted as the tension on her face grew worse. She took an abrupt step back and dug in her back foot, trying to hold her ground. 'Get them out of here. That's an order, Cú Sídhe.'

And they would always obey her, Izzy knew that. Even Jinx, who materialised beside her, his hand gentle but firm on her arm. Blight was some distance off with Ash, already making for the remains of the door.

'Now Isabel!' Brí snapped and then, to Izzy's horror, the flames parted and failed. They rolled up across the broken ceiling, leaving dark smears on the bronze. Holly walked through the space where they had been. Jinx grabbed Izzy and lifted her physically from the ground, ignoring her kicking and cursing.

Holly brandished her knife, that god-ugly black-bladed

knife with a viciously sharp point. The shard of obsidian glowed like she did, all forms of light crammed in under her skin reflected in the facets. Brí sagged before her, defeated and broken, with no way to recharge the magic she had spent.

'I'll kill them all, Brí,' said Holly. 'All your precious followers, especially the dogs. I'll make them howl and scream for you. It will be a symphony and it will go on and on until they're all silent. You'll hear the last whimper, every note. You'll feel each and every death howl. And only then will I let you die. Do you hear me?'

Brí lifted her head, proud and defiant. She smiled, her face reflecting the light before her and wonder filled her eyes.

'I hear you.' She shook her head, her long red hair dancing behind her – the same colour as the Morrígan's, the same colour as Izzy's – 'But I choose otherwise.'

She grabbed Holly's wrist with both hands, her bones and tendons standing out like wires, and she pulled Holly into an embrace, impaling herself on the knife. Holly shrieked in rage, catching her body and pulling her off, but it was too late. Brí slumped to the ground, staring blankly at the wreckage of her home.

Izzy screamed, but the fight drained out of her. There was nothing she could do, nothing to be done. Without her struggling against him now, Jinx dragged her to the remains of the tunnel, dodging falling rocks and the fires that sprang up everywhere. He scrambled along the exit and Izzy tried to help, tried to get her feet to the ground, but they wouldn't work, and all she could see was the knife jutting out of Brí's body. Brí with her eyes already glazed like polished stones. Brí. Dead.

He set her down in the open air behind an outcrop of rock. How they'd got there she didn't know. His hands closed on her shoulders with surprising tenderness as he tried to soothe her shaking form.

Shock, she realised. This was shock.

'We have to run, Izzy.' Jinx stared into her face, looking for some kind of response. 'We have to get off the hill, find Blight and Ash. Do you understand?'

'She's dead.'

'Yes, Brí's dead. But we could be too, or worse. Please listen, Izzy. We have to run.'

'Always running, aren't you, Jinx, my boy?' said Osprey, stepping out from between the inferno of the treeline, with a huge sword balanced nonchalantly over his shoulders like a yoke, and the light of a Shining One filling him.

Crom Ceann, said Izzy's mind, and she wondered how she knew that. The knowledge was as sharp as a knife, which made her think of Holly and Brí's death.

She had memories, other memories. Memories which had been sold to the Storyteller. The Shining Ones were three, but once they were four, one for each cardinal point, for each element. But the fourth … the fourth had refused to join in their madness. The fourth had split herself in pieces in order to remain here, with those she loved.

And Brí had loved. So many people.

'Osprey,' Jinx said, with real fear in his voice. He was right to be afraid of the creature before them. Izzy remembered what it could do. What it would do. Fear had kept Jinx alive before now.

Osprey laughed, deep and resonant. 'What I once was is almost burned away now. It's amazing, Jinx, all you turned down, all this power. My nerves are alive to it, my senses too. What a time we could have had, you, me and Holly. Now I guess I'll just have to have it with your little girlfriend here. Can't say I'll mind. She's more my type than you.'

He licked his lips and Izzy's stomach turned with revulsion.

Jinx snarled and threw himself forwards. He transformed as he moved, muscles bunching, teeth elongating as he snarled. He slammed into Osprey's midsection as a great black dog. Osprey went down, but not for long. They rolled across the grass and the paths, Jinx changing again. Jinx kicked, his feet connecting with his foe's chin, and he was up again. He leaped into the air, but Osprey's hand closed on his ankle. He slammed Jinx down on the path, cracking the concrete beneath him. His foot stamped onto his chest, holding him there, and he picked up the sword with a flourish.

'Are we finished?' he asked.

Jinx spat out blood. 'We're never finished.' He was hurt, Izzy realised. Badly hurt.

'Fine. Let's make it quick then. I'll do you that favour.'

He brought the huge sword swinging down.

'No!' Izzy shouted and Osprey pulled the blow, cocking his head to one side, listening to her. 'I'll go with you, I'll go quietly, but only if you let him live.'

'Izzy, don't!' Jinx cried out.

Osprey kicked him in the face. There was a sickening crunch but Jinx's heaving chest kept going. He was still there. Still alive. She needed to keep him that way.

'I'm still listening, Gregory.'

She forced herself to calm down, and drew on the power inside her. The Shining One stirred. It wanted this. That in itself should have been a warning, but one she couldn't allow herself to heed. 'I'll come with you. Let him go. Let him live. I won't fight it.'

'Maybe I like it when they fight,' he sneered. But he held out his hand and she forced herself to take it. His skin was hot and damp, like touching someone feverish and sick. His grip closed around her, painfully tight. 'Come on then. She's waiting.'

'And him?' She glanced down at Jinx's dazed expression, saw the despair in his golden eyes.

'He gets to live knowing that he failed. Good for me.'

And before she could say anything else, Osprey dragged her away. She had no choice but to go. To the island. To the one place everyone said she shouldn't go. The Oracle, Brí, Silver … but she had no choice.

Chapter Twenty-Seven

Heaven's War

'Jinx?' The voice was insistent, determined. And he just wished it would go away. Everything hurt. And he'd lost her. She'd gone with Osprey. 'Jinx, can you hear me?'

Blight. Of course it was Blight. He was probably the only one left.

Jinx opened his eyes to see the Cú Sídhe staring at him. Tears streaked his face, but his eyes burned. Behind him, Ash knelt on the ground praying, the same words over and over again. Apparently to no effect.

He dragged himself up.

'Let me help,' said another voice, one which made every nerve in him stand on end. He jerked back, trying to twist around to face the threat, even though he had no strength left. 'Ach, hush boy. We're all on the same side now whether we like it or not.' Pie knelt down beside him and helped him sit up. 'There now, easy. You'll mend. You just need time. Lucky you're more than just a dog now, eh?'

Amadán leaned into view, smoking a fat cigar. 'Try not to be mean, Pie. He's had an ordeal. If only Brí was here.' At that Blight growled, a deep and threatening sound. 'Ah now, boy. Only saying it as it is. She was always the healer. That was her skill, her shining ability. We'll miss her.'

He continued to push himself up, his arms shaking with the effort. But he could already feel his strength returning. Pie was right. He was no longer Cú Sídhe and the Púca was almost indestructible it seemed. That wasn't to say it didn't hurt. 'We have to find Izzy.'

'Not too much of a chore,' Amadán said. 'Look.'

He pointed towards the sea. Through the smoke and flames, he could see the blackness of the sea, and in that darkness, a light brighter than anything else, a pillar of luminescence, on the island.

'What are they doing down there?' he asked.

'That's where the gate is,' said Ash.

'What gate?'

'The first one. The one that leads back to heaven.'

'And it's forbidden,' said Blight pointedly.

'Do you really think that would stop one of the Shining Ones, let alone *her*?' Amadán replied.

'We have to go there,' said Jinx. 'They have Izzy.'

'She went with them willingly.' Blight paced away, his hands clenched into fists at his side. 'She left us behind, and went with them.'

'She had no choice,' Ash shouted. 'She did it to save him.'

'Children, children,' Amadán said with a sigh. 'Enough fighting. I can take you there. There's a way.'

'It is forbidden,' repeated Blight, biting out each word.

Jinx pushed himself up to standing, his body still aching, his mind never more sure of anything. 'It is. But that doesn't matter now. If Holly opens that gate, we're all done for. Blight, please …'

'Please *what*, Jinx? I've lost my sister, I've lost my Matriarch. Half my pack is dead.'

'But not all of them and they need you now.'

'Yes, they need me.' He growled, his shoulders tightening with rage. But Jinx knew the feeling. How could he not recognise it in another? Frustration, helplessness, and an anger born out of that. But he knew that not to act on that would just make it worse. 'And so do you, don't you? You need the Cú Sídhe, as muscle, as cannon fodder. And you're a Púca. You're Lord of the Wild Hunt. If you demand it, we have no choice but to follow.'

'But I won't demand it, Blight. I'll just ask. We need you, but we'll go anyway, without you if we must. We will always need the Cú Sídhe. And afterwards – if there is an afterwards – we will still need you.'

Blight hung his head. He glanced back up at the hill, where the other Cú Sídhe gathered, and frowned.

'Jinx, do you know what you're asking?'

'Yes. But I need to go and I don't want you dead.'

'You're telling me *not* to come?' He turned on Jinx with a look of affront. 'You can't tell me not to come. We're coming with you and you know it.' He stormed off to check on his pack. Every inch the leader now, for everyone to see.

Jinx shook his head but decided not to argue where he couldn't win. He looked up to find Pie laughing at him. 'What?'

'Stroke of genius that, kiddo. That's how you do it with Cú Sídhe. Tell them they can't do something and they'll run in that direction as hard and as fast as they can.'

'Oh, shut it,' he growled, earning an even wider, more dangerous grin. 'Amadán, can you get us down there?'

'I know the way, the only way mind. There's a secret passage to the island. How do you think they got there?'

'And what's the downside? There has to be one.'

'The downside? They're expecting us? They know how we'll get there? And they'll be waiting? Enough of a downside for you? And there are armies of angels and demons tearing each other apart between them and us, an ocean of a war to wade through before we reach out own battle. If the gate is opening and they realise … anyone could take heaven, boy. And they'll do anything to take it. Anything.'

'Let me talk to them,' said Ash.

'You?' Amadán sneered. 'Why would any of them listen to you, little girl?'

She didn't look like she could stand, let alone confront

Zadkiel and Azazel, but Jinx knew better than to discount the likelihood of Ash failing to do anything Ash set out to do. Even in her current weakened state, he couldn't cross her.

'Is it safe for you?'

'No, but it's less safe for you. Should we encounter them, let me speak. And don't interfere.'

'You're powerless, Ash,' said Jinx. 'You're just human now. Do you think they'll listen to you?' He didn't say that they never seemed to when she was an angel, but he couldn't help but think it.

She glared at him and he instantly regretted it. 'No wonder Clodagh gets so furious with you all. "Just human" indeed.' She stalked off ahead of them, muttering to herself. He didn't know what. Obscenities, probably.

'We should catch up with her,' said Amadán. 'At least she's going in the right direction. Come on, boys.' He ground out the end of his cigar. 'Time is running out.'

Icy cold wind gripped Izzy's body as they stepped out onto the island. She had known this place all her life, had played here, picnicked here on family trips, getting a boat across the narrow but deep sound from Coliemore Harbour. There wasn't much here – a ruined medieval church, a Napoleonic magazine fort and Martello tower, rabbits and feral goats. It sheltered the sound, making the harbour beyond it a perfect landing point. And there was evidence that Ireland's earliest inhabitants had settled here. Every kid in the immediate area did a school project on it at some point. Thorn Island, gave Dalkey its name in both Old Irish and Norse. Human remains and evidence of human habitation had been found from thousands of years ago – pottery shards, beads, shells, bones and skulls. Now Izzy wondered if they had been left as offerings. Or warnings.

She followed Osprey up the slope, unable to do anything else. Now she was here, she had to see it through. She only prayed that she was right, that she was doing the right thing. Because it didn't feel like it. This felt very wrong indeed. The ground beneath her shivered and trembled. On this island, on this sacred space – because it was sacred, she could feel that too – there was no place for the thing lurking inside her. She should not be here and neither should Osprey and Holly. Forbidden. Her every instinct sobbed out the word, tried to warn her, wanted to make her run away.

But she couldn't.

Osprey didn't even look back to make sure she was following him still. He was so arrogant in his way, confident to the point of conceit. He climbed the slope with firm and unwavering footsteps, and left scorched footprints in his wake. Izzy shuddered and climbed as well, trying not to step in the same place. She could feel the Shining One inside her stirring again, drawing strength from the fires in her blood. She pulled her coat tight around her throat and felt Brí's touchstone against her skin. A comfort, she told herself. Her only one.

The ground levelled off and then she saw Holly, standing by the old church, pacing back and forth around a cluster of stones. It almost looked like a stone circle, if you squinted at it and let your imagination do the work. One of them was bigger than the others and there was a bowl-shaped depression carved in it. And lying on that stone …

She broke into a run, not bothering to shout or waste her energy on anything else. She flung herself forward, her hands grabbing the body that was stretched out on the stone.

'Dad? Dad, can you hear me?'

He opened his eyes, exhausted and broken, but when he saw her he tried to smile. Her hands came away from his shirt covered in his blood. There was blood on the stone too. Blood that dripped down into the bowl. Hundreds of cuts covered his body, deep enough to bleed profusely, but not so deep as to kill him. Just to torture and torment, to weaken and slowly drain his life. But he was still alive. She thanked every god and goddess she'd ever heard of that he was still alive. Holly had seen to that.

Grigori blood. That was what she had needed. And Dad had provided it.

He stirred beneath her touch and closed his eyes. Her tattoo was like an icy furnace behind her now and she knew with all her heart that they had never faced anything like this.

'Osprey, secure the path. They'll follow.' Holly walked bare-foot on the snowy ground, and the snow melted after her.

'The boy's broken, Holly,' he said. 'He won't follow. He won't be able to.'

'Do you argue with me?' her voice was icy with precision, each word crystal cut.

An instant too late, Osprey realised his misstep and dropped to one knee. 'No, my Lady.'

'Get up and obey me, or I will make you.'

He looked up at her and Izzy saw fear plain on his face. He didn't move. Didn't dare. Izzy froze too; she didn't know what Holly would do. She might change her mind the moment he stood. Anything could happen. Holly had always been volatile. Now she was completely unstable. 'Please, my Lady, no.'

Good as it was to see the swaggering bastard cowed, it left Izzy feeling empty inside. He looked frozen, every sinew standing out. Slowly, he bowed lower until it was clear the position he took was not willing, but strained and forced. She could see the tension on his face; his hands shook at his side, held there by an invisible force he couldn't fight. His face mashed into the frozen ground, his nose bent painfully to the side, his eye unblinking as the snow filled it. Holly smiled, gleeful as a child, and she glanced at Izzy, as if she wanted approval. As if she needed to see Izzy's reaction. When she saw only dismay there, her smile grew even wider. Better than approval. Suffering.

'What did you think the tattoos are for, girl? I need some way to control you both. When they fully take hold, you'll do anything I want. I'll just think it and you'll obey. Like Osprey here. Isn't that right?'

'Yes, my Lady,' he said, his voice tight and muffled.

Izzy shook her head but couldn't find the word to say out loud. Holly sighed, and just like that boredom replaced delight. She released Osprey with a flick of her fingers and he scrambled to his feet, scowling at them both. That seemed to amuse Holly again.

'Petulant boy,' she said, almost affectionately. 'Now go and guard the path. Neither angel, demon, nor Sídhe is to set foot on this island tonight.'

Turning around, her captives and her servant forgotten, Holly sat herself down on a rock as if it was a throne and stared eastwards, out over the sea to the horizon. 'And now we just wait,' she murmured.

'For what?' Izzy asked, her hands worrying at the knots securing Dad. Not that untying him would help. He'd lost so much blood and taken so much punishment that he wouldn't be able to crawl from here unaided, let alone run or fight his way out. This was up to her. Somehow.

Holly held that knife again. She turned it over and over in her hands. It was old, Izzy realised, older than anything she had ever seen. It was made of stone, obsidian gleaming like petrified blood, tied on to a bone handle with something that looked very much like dried sinew.

'For the sun to rise. The moon is full and it's the longest night, Isabel Gregory. And when it ends, when the sun comes up and shines on the stones here ...'

She turned around abruptly, brandishing the blade, as if that answered any questions Izzy might have had.

'How did you find Íde?' she went on. 'Completely raving or did she at least try to make a modicum of sense to begin with?'

'She … you tricked her.'

'I hoped she'd rid me of a problem. But that wasn't to be. You may not be broken down yet, Gregory, but you will be. Did it destroy Jinx when you chose us over him?'

'I didn't – Osprey was going to kill him.'

'He was going to try. My bloodline don't die so easily. Neither does his father's. Did you ever ask darling daddy about that? Ah – ' Izzy cursed inwardly. She was transparent in front of Holly. 'I see you did. Does Jinx know? That'll make things fun at the wedding, won't it?' She laughed. 'Not that there will be a wedding without a bride, groom, mother *and* father. Dear me, you've lost everything, haven't you?'

Izzy looked away from her, disgusted, back to the coastline, where the hill was still blazing and sirens were screaming, where people were evacuating. She could see cars roaring along the tiny roads and people running, army after army in the field – angel, demon, fae and human. Except not with her eyes. She was seeing with something else. Something other.

'Kicking in, is it?' Holly said. 'You're seeing beyond dimensions, seeing with a seraph's eyes. We can see everything. I watched every step and misstep you made.'

'Why are we here?'

'This is the gate. The first gate. We were exiled here, cast out onto this little rock with nothing. But the one who led us here stayed with us. She broke her power in three in order to do it. But then, Brí always was a fool.'

'Brí was one of the Shining Ones. I know that much. But why do you hate her so much.?'

'The Shining One in me hates her betrayal. And I hate her stupidity, her gullibility and her selflessness. We were just fae, but she had so much power she could have led us back at any time. She refused. She split her powers and took up residence like an exiled queen on her hill, surrounded by her dogs, watching over this.'

'So you killed her.'

'With this,' she brandished the knife again in confirmation. 'The very key she kept safe with her most trusted disciple. But then Wild fell in love and Íde went crazy and it was only a matter of time before I got it. I've worked so hard for this, Isabel Gregory. I'm so very tired. But at last, we're going home. When the sun rises on these stones and I shed Grigori blood with this key, the gate will open.'

'You've been practising on the bloodletting.'

'I get bored easily.'

'Where does the gate go, Holly?'

'Heaven. I'm going to take back my rightful place in heaven … no, that's not fair. *We* – the three of us, you, Osprey and me – *we're* going to take back heaven.' Her eyes burned with the light of a supernova. 'And then we're going to make it all burn.'

She had to be stopped. Izzy knew that now, if it had ever been in doubt. Anything Holly wanted this much couldn't' be good. She knew it more keenly than she had ever known anything. She stood up but felt Dad's hand close on her wrist.

'Don't. It's what she wants – '

'I have to, Dad,' she whispered. 'She has to be stopped.'

'Izzy … please … think. Balance, remember? It's all about balance.'

He slumped back down on the rock again, unconscious.

Balance? There was no balance left. Nowhere in her life. She was spinning out of control without any hope of a fixed point.

She reached inside herself and let the fire of the Blade fill her. She seized the fire in Brí's touchstone and made it her own.

I'll show her what it means to burn, she thought, and advanced on Holly.

Holly who had orchestrated all her pain, who had stolen everything from her.

Flames coiled around her hands, fire filled her mind. She felt the Shining One waking again, uncoiling inside her and starting to feed, to grow. She had to be quick, to cheat the growing light. She drew back her hands, ready to strike.

The ground reached up. Sparse grass tangled around her feet, locking them in position. She stood in the centre of the stone circle and couldn't move. The earth itself held her like concrete. And with it came hunger. She was starving, ravenously hungry. And the fire in her rose to sustain her, and Crom Dubh fed again.

'You never learn,' said Holly with a laugh. She twisted around, the knife still held in her hands. 'Hungry grass, you see? One of those special places, where death and stubbornness meet.'

Holly reached out and Izzy felt the fire in her flare up even higher. She was a bonfire in the night, burning up, the only fuel for the magic and the monster inside her.

'Let me go!'

'Too late for that. And for you.'

Holly came closer, stepping into the circle with her. She reached out and, even as Izzy tried to hit her, or push her away, she twisted, her fingers tight as wire as she captured both wrists. She brought the tip of the knife, so cold, like ice, up to the collar of Izzy's shirt and pushed it back. The tip scoured against her skin, unbearably intimate, but didn't break it, and Izzy sucked in a frightened breath and her skin shrank back from its touch. Other than that, she couldn't move. Holly glowed with delight and Izzy stared at her luminous face. She took her time examining the tattoos.

Suddenly, with a snap like the bolt shutting home on a cell door, the tattoos clamped around Izzy's neck. She gasped, felt all control slip from her fingers like water. The fire still blazed, higher than ever, but it wasn't hers anymore.

'There we are,' said Holly softly, as to a child waking from a nightmare. She released Izzy's hands which fell to her side like stones. Holly's delicate fingers stroked Izzy's hair, and then her cheeks, but the knife point stayed at her neck and that hardly mattered anymore. 'Welcome back,' Holly purred. 'My little dark one.'

Izzy's body dropped gracefully to her knees and she looked up with other eyes, and spoke with another voice.

'Is it time, my Lady?'

'Almost,' said Holly. 'Wait there a while.'

Trapped inside herself, Izzy tried to fight, to struggle, to scream, but she couldn't move, couldn't make a noise at all.

The Shining One called Crom Dubh smiled with her smile, and waited.

The Keeper

He had expected the Gardaí, Special Branch, maybe even the army. He didn't expect the two women.

'Dear me, Mr O'Neill, whatever next?' Thea asked, her wide smile very white in the darkened interrogation room. 'Another incident at another library. Next thing you know you'll be breaking into the Chester Beatty.'

He stared at her, dumbfounded, trying to work out if she was joking. It didn't sound like a joke, not really. The room in the Garda station was so cold his breath misted in front of his face and the handcuffs were cutting into his wrists. He no longer had any idea how long he'd been here. It had been late when they arrested him outside Marsh's. And time had just dragged on since then.

Behind Thea, Margot was tapping something into her phone with a stylus, like a bird pecking at the screen. Thea sat easily in the chair opposite him, and smiled. She gave the guard on duty a pointed look. He looked no older than Dylan and stared at the woman in a kind of terrified awe. Whatever he knew about them, Dylan could tell he didn't want to cross them. And that possibly he wasn't sure why they were even here. But didn't dare ask.

'Uncuff him and off you go then,' Thea told him in a headmistressy tone. He hurried to obey her. The door closed behind him and Dylan rubbed his wrists, trying to encourage the circulation to do its job. He stared at the women the whole time, unwilling to take his eyes off them.

'I said we'd see you again soon,' said Margot. 'But I can't help but feel there's an element of you extracting the Michael here, Mr O'Neill.'

She couldn't just say 'taking the mickey' like anyone else. Oh no, not Margot.

Dylan frowned, waiting.

'Are you going to answer our questions?' asked Thea, her tone a lot more serious than Margot's. There was an edge of threat in her voice he didn't like.

'You haven't asked any yet.' None that he felt like answering anyway. 'Whatever next?' didn't really warrant an answer, did it? He dreaded to think what it might be.

'Where did the angel go?'

'I don't know.'

'Where do you think she went? Don't worry, we'll deal with it.'

He thought of Clodagh and what dealing with it might mean for her. 'You've got to let me out of here.'

'No, we don't. Not really,' said Margot, not looking up from the phone. 'Sighting in Dalkey, Thea. Do we bring him with us?'

'Yes,' he interrupted. 'Yes, you do.'

Thea tilted her head to the side. 'Where's she going?'

What choice did he have? If he wanted to get out of here, he needed to cooperate with them. At least a little. 'She mentioned a Thorn Gate. And a key.'

Margot froze, looking up sharply, and Thea swallowed hard. 'Are you sure?'

'Yes. Listen ... there has to be a way to help Clodagh. She wasn't meant to be involved in any of this.'

'Neither were you, but here we are. And we don't have a lot of time. The war has come to us and we are not unprepared. But if we can stop your friends, we can stop it all. Where is Isabel Gregory?'

'Izzy? Why do you want Izzy?'

'The Keeper's Orders. She's Grigori and her father is missing. So we need that girl right away. Or failing that, someone holding a vast amount of Sídhe magic.' And she glared at him, like she could see inside him.

'I needed the spark to get Silver back,' he admitted. 'To fix the Sídheways. I wasn't going to let them have it but I needed it. For leverage. For the Sídheways ... If they're destroyed the Sídhe are finished. Everyone will know and there'll be no hiding anything. The angels tricked her. She's the only thing holding it all together and if she fails ... '

'They took a Sídhe Matriarch?' said Thea. 'Have they gone insane?'

'Weren't they always a bit insane?' Margot sniped and went back to her phone. 'There's something big happening in Dalkey, on the island. We've alerts springing up all over the place. This really isn't good. We've got to intervene.'

'I have to get Silver and Clodagh back. And help Izzy. Holly has her father. And I can't ... I have to ...'

Panic welled up inside him, blotting out his vision, stopping his breath as if barbed wire was winding itself around him, tighter and tighter.

'Breathe,' said Thea soothingly, but she looked tense, uncomfortably tense. 'The Gregorys are our number one priority. We can help you. Look, Dylan. We aren't the enemy here. And we can help. In so many ways. But you need to tell us everything. Starting with how you're connected to Silver.'

He pursed his lips, trying to think of a way. 'I'm her touchstone.'

'That's impossible.'

'So they keep telling me. But I am. I chose her, and she chose me. And she ...'

'He loves her,' Margot said tersely. 'You can see that, can't you? And the magic is almost spilling out of him so yes, he's telling the truth.' The phone chimed and she looked down at it again. 'Bea?' Doubt filled her voice. Dylan knew the feeling.

'We've a message from the Keeper. She's outside. She wants to see him for herself.'

That didn't sound good. Why was everything going from bad to worse? 'Who's the Keeper?'

'The Boss, of course. Honestly! Come on then.' Thea got up. She even held the door open for him. Before he knew it they were marching down a random corridor of Kevin Street Garda Station.

He'd never felt quite so belligerent before. 'You can't give out because I don't know the ins and outs of your secret bloody society. Who is it? What do you people do?'

Beside him, Margot rolled her eyes. 'Mainly we clean up. Since the magician Amergin first cast the spell that separated the Sídhe from us, we've been charged with keeping things that way. So whenever they come through and tear up the place, whenever the angels and the demons decide in their infinite wisdom to cause a disturbance, we tidy it all up, make it like it never happened. Not the most glamourous job in the world, I grant you. But it has its rewards.'

'What do you think happened after the Fear attacked your Halloween gig?' asked Thea, glancing back over her shoulder.

'They said it was a gas leak.'

'Uh-huh. And who are "they"?'

'You?'

'We put out the story, made sure it made sense if you scratched the surface. We can't change memories, but we can make them make sense.'

'To protect people from the Sídhe?'

'Not exactly.'

Outside the station a black jeep sat with its engine idling. As they approached, a tall, suited man opened the door and another woman stepped out. She wore a suit too, but then she usually did. Her hair was perfect and her smile of relief looked completely genuine, and so familiar.

Rachel Gregory opened her arms to him. 'Thank God they found you,' she said. 'Bea, Margot, we're running out of time. The island. They're both there.'

'*You're* the Keeper?' Dylan asked.

Izzy's mum nodded. 'We're going to get you to safety first.'

'But Clodagh and Silver – '

'You need to focus on *you*, Dylan. Your parents would never forgive me if—'

'Look, I know you think you're here to protect people from the Sídhe but—'

'No, love, we protect the Sídhe. Mankind would tear them apart. David and I have an understanding. He does his job and I do mine. But he's ...' Her voice caught in her throat. 'I have to do both now and I need you to cooperate.'

'Fair enough, but I have a job too. I'm Silver's touchstone and I need to find her. I'm Clodagh's friend and Sorath's taken her. And Izzy ...'

He stopped, unsure how much her mother knew.

'What about Izzy?'

'Holly put the last Shining One in her.'

The confident mask of command slipped just for a moment, but enough. He caught a glimpse of dismay and then despair. Her eyes resonated with pain. She let out a single pent-up breath and then the mask snapped back into place.

'Margot, spread the word. Isabel Gregory must be considered an enemy combatant.'

'You can't!' Dylan exclaimed at the same moment that Thea said, 'But Keeper!'

Rachel silenced them both with a glare. Margot reluctantly began tapping at her phone in silence.

'Bulletin sent, Keeper,' she said mutedly. 'We have clashes between demons and angels widespread across the city, fae on the run in Rathmines. And a massacre in Donnycarney.'

'A massacre of what?' asked Dylan. He really didn't want to know.

'Lower fae from the Market. They were sheltering there when some of Holly's Aes Sídhe found them. We need to get a lid on this fast. Christmas revellers out of control? Or some sort of mass hysteria? Maybe a new hallucinogen on the market?'

Rachel nodded, he wasn't sure to which option. 'See to it. I need to direct our responses. Thea, take him home.'

'With all due respect, Keeper ...' Thea said, and hesitated as if anticipating an argument. 'Can I have a word? We have an opportunity here I don't think we should waste.' The two of them stepped away, taking heatedly but in hushed tones.

Margot bent over her phone, fingers moving furiously.

Dylan stopped listening.

Thea glanced over her shoulder and then looked back at Dylan, her gaze fixed and unyielding. 'So, Dylan, do you want a job?'

'I'm a musician.'

'I know. And a good one. I've heard you play. Everyone knows your name, your voice and your face now. Everyone here in Dublin, probably in Ireland. And beyond, I've no doubt. But that doesn't really come into it. No one is asking you to give up anything, not yet anyway. But I think you have a future with us, maybe part time, maybe more. That's something to be worked out, but being well known to the public isn't a liability. Besides, magic and music go hand in hand, don't you find? Let's call it a work experience day, will we? I have an idea.'

'What sort of "idea"?'

'Trust me,' Thea said, beaming.

'I haven't said yes,' he said, but that didn't seem to matter. 'Can you get me to Dalkey? I can help. I know I can.'

She glanced warily at Mrs Gregory, who just glared at them both. Not a good sign.

'Because "magic"?' she said sarcastically. 'I don't think so.'

'Because I know all of them and we can't let them kill Izzy. Please, Thea.'

Thea frowned. 'Get in the jeep.'

'But—

'Get in the jeep, Dylan.'

There was no arguing with her. Another look from Izzy's mum, a curt nod and he did what he was told. No other choice. He would have to work out some way around this when they finally let him go. Thea got in after him and closed the door.

'Take us to Dalkey,' she said to the driver. Dylan looked at her like she was mad. She raised her eyebrows expertly. 'It's where you live, isn't it? Welcome to the firm.'

Jinx moved as part of a pack, admittedly one made up of the most disparate fae possible, but that didn't seem to matter now. And then there was Ash. She never left his side. Despite her weakened human condition, she was still a warrior, trained and honed. She watched everything with those dark eyes, saw more than he did, he was sure. They were no more than half way down to the rugged coast, walking down the Christmas light decked main street of the little town, when she froze and lifted one hand in a fist. Tendons stuck out on her arm.

'What is it?' Amadán asked.

'Is there a Sídheway near here?'

'Yes, back there, in the lane, but it's—'

'Take cover!' she shouted and dived behind one of the parked cars.

Light burst from the laneway, brilliant and blinding. The rest of them scattered, like startled birds. Jinx managed to stay with the former angel, as did Blight. Brí had tasked him with taking care of her and that was what he seemed intent on doing. They flanked her, the three of them crouched with their backs to the car. For a moment all he heard was their own harsh breath and then … footsteps. Two sets, one delicate and precise, the other shambling. Lights twinkled overhead and on the buildings, but they were drowned out by the light coming from the middle of the road.

'Little Sídhe …' the voice was laughing, mocking, but terribly familiar. 'Little Sídhe, come out and play with me.'

Jinx started to lift his head, unable to believe what he was hearing. Ash grabbed his arm, pulling him back down. She shook her head carefully, but he could see the dismay in her face, the fear and burgeoning grief.

A shout of alarm and rage cut the silence and one of the Cú Sídhe howled in pain. They all heard the crack of bone and the physical impact as a body hit the ground.

'No,' hissed Blight, and he was up before Ash could stop him as well. Jinx followed seconds later.

Clodagh stood in the street, light filling her in soft golden waves. And he knew it wasn't Clodagh, not anymore. The cruel cast of her mouth and the way she looked at him told him that.

'Oh, good,' she said, as if it was anything but. 'I've been looking for you.'

He held his ground, letting her focus on him while Blight got his pack mate clear. The Cú Sídhe was younger than them, a girl with auburn hair and olive skin, and now a leg so badly broken it would take months to heal, even for one of them.

'Sorath,' Jinx said. How? Why? A hundred variations of those basic questions rose at the back of his throat, choking him. 'What do you want?'

'Why, to go home, of course.' She let her hands move like a dancer's, framing Clodagh's body as if she was showing off new clothes. 'I even dressed for the occasion. Do you like it?'

Pie threw himself at her, his knives flashing, his speed unmatchable, but Sorath just slipped to one side, avoiding him. She grabbed his arm at the last second, spinning him around and slamming him into the large shop window. It shattered around him, raining down shards of glass.

'I may have this little girl's pretty body, but you people never learn, do you?' she sneered.

Mistle began to laugh, an awful wheezing sound. Jinx wanted to ram something down his throat just to shut him up. He tried to keep an eye on him too, remembering the feel of the old bastard's hands around his throat.

Pie picked himself up groggily and rounded on her again. This time she grabbed him by the throat and casually knocked his knife aside.

'Really? Is this the best you have? I see you there, Jinx by Jasper. And you, Cú Sídhe. And you …'

Her voice faltered as Ash stepped out of hiding.

'Hello,' she said, her voice very calm and so soft it floated on the air. 'Clodagh, can you hear me?'

Sorath released Pie and took an angry step forward, but stopped just as quickly, confused.

'You aren't an angel. Ashira!' She looked truly horrified. 'What – what happened to you?'

'Holly happened,' said Ash. She approached the fallen angel with care, step by step. Jinx watched, spellbound. He knew he should be circling around, trying to get to a position of vantage, but he had to watch. Needed to. He couldn't help himself. 'Cuileann as she was. But you encountered her before in this realm, during the summer, didn't you?'

'She bound me to the Grigori and tried to kill me.' She smiled, the expression too big on Clodagh's face. 'But we escaped.'

'Because of Silver. Can you see Silver now, Sorath? Do you know where she is? You could see all, once upon a time. Every angel, every fae. Where is she?'

Sorath frowned, confused. 'She's … she's everywhere.'

They stood only a foot or so apart now. Even the air seemed to hold its breath as the two of them met in the middle of the street, one dark, one golden.

'Mistress,' Mistle intoned. 'Beware. This is a trick.' He lunged forward.

Blight grabbed him before he could leap on Ash and Sorath turned slightly, surprised by the sudden move. She looked dazed, spellbound herself.

Ash reached out and touched her arm, so gentle, a warm, human touch.

'Clodagh,' she whispered. 'Can you hear me?'

Sorath's head snapped around to face her again and Jinx saw something else in her eyes, something so very angry.

'Ash?' said a frail version of Clodagh's voice, just for a moment. Then Sorath seized control again. She bared her teeth and tried to pull away, tried to escape, afraid now. Afraid of Ash, as impossible as that seemed.

'Clodagh,' said Ash again, just as softly. 'Clodagh, love, come back.' She leaned forward and kissed her. For a moment it was all force and control. She held Sorath so she couldn't escape. Sorath went rigid, her eyes wide with rage, leaning back.

Slowly, her lips moved, reciprocating the kiss. Her body melted against Ash's. One moment they were watching a conflict, and the next − something altogether different. Ash framed Clodagh's face with her hands, ran fingers through her hair. Clodagh's mouth opened beneath hers, welcoming her kiss, and light burst between them. Jinx had to look away. There was no choice.

Mistle shrieked and sobbed, his ranting ringing off the rooftops, but Blight held him back until at last he sagged and fell on his knees, defeated.

'She was mine. You can't take her. She was mine!' He said it over and over again, until the words didn't even sound like words. And then he said one that did, that Jinx knew. He said it in the same way Jinx had and it was horribly familiar. 'Mistress!'

Ash broke the kiss and stared at him over Clodagh's shoulder, her dark eyes lit from within once more.

'Your Mistress is gone now. There is only me. Never speak of her again.'

Mistle fell to his face, sobbing and wailing, and he scrambled back from her, heading for the lane and the shadows.

'Ash?' Jinx asked warily.

She was still holding Clodagh against her and the girl wore a dazed, wrung-out look. But Ash didn't let her go, and her touch stayed so very gentle.

'I'm still here, Jinx. I promise. Not to worry. Her spark may possess a mortal, but not me. Angels are different, stronger, and those of us who have tested our metal among humans are stronger than the higher choirs could ever imagine. She's safe now, in here, out of harm's way.' She tapped the side of her head. 'I haven't felt this strong in millennia. I can hear them again. The angels, all of them. I can hear them singing. I can join the choir.' She smiled a little drunkenly and then turned all her attention back to Clodagh. 'Are you okay?' she asked, her voice very soft again.

Clodagh's voice came out in a harsh whisper. 'You're all sparkly.'

Ash's smile turned fierce with wonder. 'That was so beyond stupid, love. What were you thinking?'

Clodagh gave her a belligerent look. 'Didn't mean to. But it … it worked out, didn't it?'

'Barely. Clo, she could have killed you, or worse. How could we be together then?'

'I'd find a way,' said Clodagh. She sat down abruptly on the curb, though Ash still held her hands, as if she wasn't actually able to let her go now.

'I don't doubt you. I never will.' She looked up at the others. 'She'll be okay. She just needs to sleep, to recover.'

'No time for that now,' said Amadán. He'd made himself handily invisible during all the excitement, Jinx realised angrily. 'Events are moving faster than we are. We have to reach the island before sunrise.'

'I can manage,' said Clodagh haughtily. 'Let's push on.'

'Too late,' said Pie.

'We're out of time, look!' Ash pointed up the main street, towards the castle. A wall of chaos swept towards them. Dark shadows writhed and coiled, falling one over the other like waves.

'Demons,' said Jinx. 'Quickly, this way.' He darted down a side street and the others followed, past the school and the red brick cottages to the T-junction.

'Here,' Amadán pushed by him, taking the lead. He moved far more quickly than his appearance would suggest. He led them right and then left again, a little shimmy past the same little cottages, one with its side painted an incongruous purple, and out onto another narrow road with a high stone wall on the right.

In that wall, up three uneven steps, there was a blue door. It almost looked like the door of a house, with a door knob and a letterbox.

The Aes Sídhe opened it without hesitation and Jinx saw only a shimmer in the darkness beyond, like a vat of oil sheened with a rainbow. There was no sign of the garden and house on the other side of the wall. This door went elsewhere.

'Through,' Amadán told them and Pie went first, without hesitation.

'I'll hold them back,' said Ash. 'Give you time. Go on, save Izzy.'

'Can you hold them?'

She nodded. 'For a while at least. And then I can talk. You should see me talk my way out of things. Just be careful. There are many rooms in heaven, many types of dimensions to it. The gate on the island leads to the most secret of all, making it a sacred space. The most sacred. That's why it is forbidden. They can't get in, Jinx. No one can go in there. Especially not the Shining Ones.' She glanced at the onslaught of demons pouring down the street. 'Whatever it takes. You stop them there, and I'll stop them here. Understand?'

He nodded grimly and Ash raised her hand. Light sprang up, shielding them, barring the way.

'Come on, Jinx,' said Amadán urgently. 'There's no time and the longer I hold this door open the more chance the demons will get in. We can't wait.'

He looked at Ash in despair, at Clodagh, Blight and the others ready to follow him. He couldn't just leave the angel there alone to face the demons, no matter how important this was, no matter what she said. But Amadán was right.

The longer they held the door open the more chance of the demons getting in.

And then he saw something else, coming the other way on the road up from the harbour. Bright and brilliant, sparkling with wonder. Light glittered off the tips of swords, and rippled from their armour. Faces as hard and implacable as a glacier, relentless and wondrous. Angels. So many angels.

And for once they weren't coming after him.

Ashira smiled, glorious in the light surrounding her, shielding them all.

'My brothers and sisters,' she said, and her voice sounded like music. It resounded with power. 'You're just in time.'

'Ashira?' Zadkiel pushed his way angrily through the ranks in front. 'What has happened? How are you … thus empowered?'

Ashira smiled, radiant. 'I have that which you sought underhandedly. Sorath's spark is part of me now. And I call on our armies to join me in defending the Sídhe and righting a grievous wrong. What do they say?'

'*They?*' Zadkiel almost spat out the word. 'I am in command here. They have no say.'

'They might beg to differ,' she replied calmly and held out her hand. Zadkiel froze, his face a mask of shock and rage as the spear he carried tore itself from his hand and flew to hers. A wind blasted down the narrow road, and the demons stalled their charge. 'I claim the post of General.'

'Ash,' said Jinx. 'What are you doing?'

'Holding the line,' she said and there was no doubt in his mind that she would hold it. 'Go. We have reinforcements. No one will pass here. Now do your part. Protect the Thorn Gate. Save Izzy.'

'I will. I swear it.'

Angels fell on the demons and the light made them all recoil. Jinx didn't dare think about it, even though the others stared in wonder. He had just promised the impossible, but so had Ash and it seemed her promise was already being kept. He could do no less. But he had just agreed to an angel's demand that he protect the gate to the heart of heaven.

And Izzy was there. Worse, Izzy might be one of the ones attacking it.

He stepped through the door, Amadán close behind him, with a hand on his back. Jinx glanced back for Blight and the others, ready to tell them to change where they could, to do whatever it took.

But Amadán slammed the door shut before they could follow.

Chapter Twenty-Nine

The Island

Darkness closed over him on the far side of the narrow Sídheway. It was old, so very old. He could taste the magic in the stale air, like ashes and grit. This path was angel made, rather than the work of the Aes Sídhe. It was strong and fixed, like stone. Not ragged and failing like the others. The last Sídheway, he suspected. The only one left.

'What have you done?' Jinx asked.

'Keep going,' Amadán replied.

'You closed it. You left them behind.'

'I had to. They're safe there. Do you want them dead? We can't have anyone following us here, not even the Cú Sídhe. Can you imagine? Keep moving, boy, or we'll never reach your Isabel in time.'

His Isabel. He didn't even know who that was, or if she was still there to be saved. And Izzy, *his Izzy*, would tear someone a new one for implying that she needed to be saved.

And yet … and yet …

That was what he had to do. No matter what the cost.

A dreadful booming noise rocked the passageway, all around them, echoing back and forth and shaking the ground beneath them. They broke into a run, Pie at the head, Jinx and Amadán following. The problem was, he was pretty sure Amadán was right. He didn't want the Cú Sídhe dead. They were the closest thing to family he had left. His pack, or at least they had been once. The booming went on, rhythmic, relentless. It took a moment to recognise it, the sound distorted by the Sídheway. He could hear the sea, waves crashing on rocks, and the next minute merrow song echoed around him, enchanting, bewitching.

'Don't listen too closely,' Amadán warned. He poked a hesitating Pie in the small of the back. 'They want to eat you not …'

'Lay off,' said Pie, turning sharply, his expression somewhat dazed. 'I heard my brother. He said … he said …'

'You heard what they want you to hear. Anything to drive you back. Fear, need, desire … whatever. Get a move on.'

Jinx stumbled forwards. What he said about fear was probably right. Merrows had almost killed him. Only Izzy had saved him. He needed to get to Izzy before it was too late and that was greater than any want or desire. Greater than any fear but the fear of losing her.

Jinx, Silver's voice whispered in his ear. She sounded weak, desperate. She sounded in pain. It sent a pang through his aching body. Lost in the Sídheways, Silver was almost gone. And still she tried to help him. *Jinx, it's dangerous. It's a trap. Do you understand me?'*

'Of course it's a trap,' he muttered. 'What else could it be? Holly has plans within plans. It's always a trap.'

'Not just her. Get Izzy off the island. Before it's too late.'

And then she was gone. The pathway shuddered again, almost throwing them all off their feet. He glanced back to see that sucking darkness from the direction they had just come, their way back completely obliterated.

Water pooled at his feet and dripped from the ceiling.

'Where are we?'

'Under Dalkey Sound. It's a tunnel, see? As well as a Sídheway. Part here and part there. That's why it's more secret than the others. Because it can't be followed all the way in either Dublin or Dubh Linn.'

'And it's old.'

'Oh yes, very old.'

'It's dying.'

'They're all dying, boy. We need to hurry. Just up there. Run.'

Jinx put his head down and ran after the other two. He had to run because he didn't want to dwell on the thought that plagued him. If the Sídheways were dying, where did that leave Silver? Was she dead too?

The world shivered around them as they reached the end and a blast of air rushed in on them. He could smell the tang of the sea, and something else, dark stones, and fresh water, deep and clear. Wind and smoke. Blood.

His hackles rose.

So much blood.

'Quiet,' said Pie in a low voice, not that anyone had made a sound. He drew the knives he carried and bent down to clamber through the opening. Jinx followed.

The stones around the entrance to the well had been painted white and it led out of the island's steep shore, above sea level. Waves crashed on the rocks beneath them, sending sheets of spray up in the air. But it masked them as well as blinding them. It turned the ground underfoot treacherous. They clambered clear, slipping and sliding as they did so even with Sídhe reflexes, and pulled themselves up the icy slope to spray at the top. Wind howled around them. There was barely any shelter on this island and even less cover. They were exposed.

And Osprey stood over them, waiting, sword at the ready.

'I was hoping it would be you,' he said, glaring down at Jinx. 'Don't you ever learn? Or isn't one beating a day enough?'

'It's a new day,' said Jinx and he surged up, his body ready to change, to flow into a more lethal shape. Pie stepped in beside him, knives ready, still angry from Sorath's treatment, itching for a fight.

'You too? Didn't he tell you how he got your brother killed?' Osprey circled to match them, keeping them on either side but in view.

'Mags?' Pie glanced at Jinx suspiciously. 'What happened to Mags?'

'Him,' Jinx replied firmly and Osprey swooped in on them, the sword flashing moonlight and death. Jinx ducked, knocking Pie aside as he did so. Much as he loathed the Magpies he didn't need another death on his conscience.

Jinx gave in to the need to attack and slipped into hound form, snarling as he leaped for Osprey's throat, but the Shining One moved faster than even he could follow. The fist that knocked him aside felt like iron. Even with Pie, Jinx knew he didn't stand a chance and Pie had stopped moving. Osprey loomed over them.

'Explain it again, like?' asked Pie.

'Your brother tried to stop me taking him. And so he died. Actually, once I gutted him, he bled out. Jinx here just ran.'

There was no way to make it sound any better. Pie scraped the knives together, frowning as he thought. It took an interminable time.

'You got my brother killed, Jinxy boy? By him?'

Osprey brought a foot down on Jinx's chest, hard. Right on the solar plexus, driving all remaining air from his body, leaving him gasping like a fish. 'He told me to run.'

'Right so,' said Pie. More to himself than anyone else. He started to turn away and Osprey laughed.

And then Pie jumped right at him, throwing himself back through the air. The knives dug deep, biting into the chinks in the armour, and into the skin beneath it. Blades ground against bone.

Osprey howled a cry of rage as well as pain, the shock of the unexpected attack. They whirled around, Jinx forgotten. He rolled out from under their feet and for a moment he could only stare as they crashed down onto the ground, Pie on top or he would have been crushed. Osprey had him by the face, digging fingers into his flesh, trying to get to his eyes. Pie bit him, sinking teeth into his hand, and Osprey kicked and bucked, trying to roll again.

One of the knives lay on the grass and Jinx grabbed it. His fingers curled around the bone handle, and he lifted the iron blade, like the one Izzy carried. Its twin. She'd got hers from the Magpies. It had killed him twice. Two Magpies, two knives.

'Jinx!' Pie yelled. 'For fuck's sake, Jinx.'

He stopped thinking. Osprey was down and needed finishing. He'd only get one chance. Throwing himself across the grass he fell on him, all his weight driving the knife into his hated enemy's throat. Every beating, every kick, every snide word, every blow, every put-down, every grand and petty cruelty went behind that knife, all the weight of pain in his miserable life. He'd been a child when Osprey had first taken his place in the systematic abuse and ever since – ever since – with Holly's blessing and his own delight, he'd continued to wield threat and intimidation like whips.

Light burst from the wound as he pulled out the knife. Blood came with it, so much blood. Osprey stared up at him, eyes bulging, and tried to speak, but the blood bubbled from the gaping hole in his neck. Again, Jinx brought the knife down, and again. He lost himself in the action, repeated and repeated, until, exhausted and shaking, the strength went out of him and he realised Osprey had long since stopped twitching. His eyes stared blankly at the night's sky. His head was almost severed.

Blood splatter blinded Jinx and he tried to wipe his face clear, but just succeeded in smearing more blood on himself. It got in his eyes, clogged his hair. His hand still gripped the bone handle of the knife so hard his whole arm hurt. But he couldn't seem to let go. Like his fingers had spasmed and locked.

'Take the weapons,' said Pie softly. His voice sounded curiously calm. Almost peaceful, and far more gentle than Jinx had ever heard him be.

'Weapons?' he asked, his voice thick with emotions he couldn't yet identify, let alone name.

'Mine. And his. As many as you can.' Pie swallowed hard and made a compulsive gulping sound. His face was even paler than usual and his mouth looked slack. 'Don't need them now.'

He held himself too stiffly, as if he didn't dare move. But he glanced down and Jinx's gaze followed his, confirming his worst suspicions. Osprey had got in a killing blow of his own. Pie's abdomen gaped open and not all the blood covering them belonged to the Shining One.

'Pie ...' He didn't know what to say. There was nothing he

could do. No words of comfort. 'Where's Amadán?'

Pie laughed, a horrific, hacking, gargling sound. 'The Old Man can't do shit about this, you dope. I'm dead. The noggin hasn't caught up with that yet is all. Go and find yer wan. She needs you. Never saw anyone get herself into so much trouble, except maybe you. You're a match made in heaven. If heaven bothered with that kind of guff.'

'I can't just go and – '

'You can and you will. I'm not on my own anyway.'

He looked up and a shadow crossed his face. A magpie circled down. It landed on his shoulder, watching Jinx with beady eyes while Pie just kept staring at the moon.

And Jinx realised he was already dead.

Amadán was nowhere to be seen. Jinx struggled to his feet and helped lie Pie down so he wouldn't just fall, smoothing his eyes closed. The magpie hopped around the body, but didn't interfere. He picked up the other knife, but left the sword. He didn't want anything of Osprey's. What would he do with it anyway? The bloody thing was almost as tall as he was. He tried to say something, but there were no words. Commend his soul to heaven? Even if Pie had a soul, he doubted heaven wanted it. The magpie just stood there, watching him.

'I'll make his death mean something,' he said and felt a shiver in the air. As if he had just made some kind of deal he didn't want to think about too deeply. Death surrounded him. War was here.

He turned towards the little ruined church and saw the

ground just in front of it blazing with unnatural light.

Holly gave a growl, something deep and guttural, torn out of the heart of her.

'Osprey,' she said, under her breath. It wasn't a lament, more like a curse. 'Your dog killed him.'

Izzy thought about that, distant and unconcerned. Abstract thoughts that didn't quite seem to be hers. Her dog. Jinx was here then. Of course he was here. She recalled the way his eyes shone as he knelt before her in Íde's tower, golden like the dawn. He'd called her his mistress. Of course he followed her here.

But that felt wrong. Inside her own mind, she struggled against the weight of non-feelings crushing her down. She had been here before, up on that very hill with the gorse smoking and black, covered in ash and destroyed by fire. Sorath had taken control of her and would have won too if it hadn't been for Jinx. She was a grail, made to hold such power, but she had taken back control then. When she tried now, it wouldn't work. She wasn't strong enough and the Shining One had sent its evil barbs through every part of her, the consummate parasite.

'Izzy?' His voice rang out over the gale. She saw him struggle up the hill, through the wind, trying to reach her. She watched, dispassionately, studying him, but she didn't move.

Why should she? He was coming here anyway.

'Will we strike him down together?' asked Holly. Her arm snaked around Izzy's shoulders, pulling her close, and she laid her head on Izzy's shoulder. She felt like a flame. They watched, two predators watching the prey coming towards them, into the killing field. She could taste his blood on her lips, or imagined that she could. She longed for it, hungered, and that was almost the same thing, wasn't it?

And then she saw the boats. Out in the sea, tiny boats came towards the island, moving from wave to wave, leaping from the crests and taking flight in the madness of the storm. Black figures crowded on them.

'Someone's coming,' she told Holly.

'The storm will hold them back. It's old magic, the oldest. We used it to keep the Milesians from us. Humans. Stupid, glorified apes. Nine waves and no closer. And they don't have an Amergin among them, not this time. No one alive can wield magic like that bastard magician could. But all men die. As they'll find out soon enough.'

'Amergin? I remember Amergin.' And she did. Or at least she thought she did. His eyes, bright with magic and human, a bard, a lawmaker, and yes, as Holly said, a magician. 'He tricked the Daoine Sídhe. He split the world into two, made Dublin and Dubh Linn. And he died.'

'They all do. Will we start with that one? Your one.'

'My one?'

Holly pointed at Jinx. 'Well, he was mine first. My monster.

My dog. And he could be again. He can belong to both of us. Oh the things we can do to make him howl. He took Crom Ceann from us when he killed Osprey, Isabel. Oh, it doesn't matter. Not really. I can still open the gate come the dawn. And to be honest, he was an irritant. I probably would have killed him myself. But now we have Jinx. He screams so well. Sometimes he sobs, when he's broken. And it's quite something to see. And to do. To break him. Do you want to?'

Izzy watched him coming closer, watched him struggle onwards. But she had seen him broken, hadn't she? She had seen him on his knees. She had seen him die. She had seen him wild with madness, crippled with grief. She knew him inside and out.

'He's mine,' she said.

'Yours? I made you. I made him too.'

She considered that. Calm, even though deep inside she wanted to scream. 'Yes. But he is mine. And always will be. I … I took him from you.'

Lightning burst from the heavens and hit the stones, illuminating the island for a moment. Jinx fell hard, crashing into the ground. He was almost here now, almost at the stones in which Holly and Izzy stood watching.

Holly raised the knife. 'You did not take him from me, impudent child.'

Inside her own body, Izzy felt the darkness rising again, a total contrast to the light of the Shining One possessing her. Fire blazed through her, fire in her blood, Brí's blood, and

Brí's power in the necklace, and the Blade. But behind it, after the fire, she saw the darkness.

Brí had made her, not Holly. Brí, who had split her power into pieces and scattered them so as not to be like the other Shining Ones. In Izzy. In the pendant. In the knife.

Izzy's hand shot up and she grabbed the knife, the key. Obsidian cut into her hand but she held on, the grip slick with her blood. Grigori blood.

She embraced the darkness, the passion, and the destruction all around her, and in her the three elements that had been Brí joined together. She turned, fluid and strong, grabbing Holly by the neck and forcing her to her knees. She went slowly, shock making her face like a plaster mask, a death mask. 'What … what are you?'

The night filled her, the storm raging around her, and black wings flocked across the raging water, black birds which alighted on the stones and the ground, oblivious to the storm. Izzy smiled and the darkness inside her rose up in a wave, smothering Crom Dubh which was a pale shadow in comparison. She was all things, all those shattered components. She was Brí, and Brí's daughter, and the knife itself. The key. All these things combined. And more. What Brí was long ago.

The power in Holly hung tantalising just before her, a blazing fire, a light that glistened and moved and shimmered. It was life and it was power because power was life. And life needed power. It was death because all Holly did was kill. And it was strength. It flowed with passion, with need, and it raged with a wildness that could not be contained in that form.

So she reached for it, releasing it, and drew it in to herself, welcoming it home.

'Surely you remember me,' she said. 'You made me, after all.' And she knew what she was at least, what she was always meant to be. From the first. No wonder she could never have been whole as just Isabel Gregory, no wonder she was never going to be acceptable as a Grigori. No wonder the angels had never cared for her. Because she wasn't human and never had been. She was so full of power that she was overflowing with it. She had been bred, her ancestry controlled by Sorath and Azazel, by Brí, until her body could contain any amount of magical energy, far more than anyone else.

Because she was a goddess.

The light of morning crept over the horizon.

Chapter Thirty

Morrigan

The boats waited at the tiny harbour, high powered ribs manned by soldiers dressed in black. Dylan saw them from the window of the jeep, the steep slip a hive of activity even in the darkness. Thea opened the door.

'Come on then,' she said to Dylan, but he hesitated as he stepped out, staring across the short distance to the island, no more than three hundred metres from the mainland. The ruined church was the most visible thing from here, lit by an incandescent blaze, with the silhouette of the Martello Tower falling into shadow on the far end. For a moment he thought the light had to be a bonfire and he wondered who would do that? Who would light a fire there, tonight, in the small hours of the morning? And then he realised it wasn't a fire. It was a figure.

The wind buffeted him as he followed Thea down to the

boats. Some of them were already setting out, tearing through the stormy sea where no one in their right mind would go. The ribs leaped from wave to wave, the roar of their engines drowned out by the tempest that threatened to swallow them all.

Thea shoved a perilously slim life vest over his head and strapped on her own.

'Get in.'

'We're going over there?'

'It's the only way.'

He swallowed hard. He had always hated the sea. Boats made him sick and the thought of being out there even covering so short a distance made his insides somersault with anxiety.

But Thea was already in the boat, holding out her hand to him and he couldn't do anything else now. He climbed in beside her, and the boat bucked and pitched beneath him like a theme park ride.

This was madness. Reckless. Terrifying. But Izzy was over there. If he didn't go his best friends was lost. Hell, everything was lost.

Ahead of them, the first boat neared the island, rounding the edge of the treacherous rocks to make for the little inlet with the jetty, when something hit it and hit it hard. Or rather it hit something. It suddenly upturned, as if it had run full speed into a brick wall.

Bodies flew everywhere, swallowed by the sea. They came up, just for a moment, black shapes in the black water. Pale, claw-like hands rose out of the waves, grabbing the screaming men and pulling them under the surface.

'Merrows!' Thea yelled into the radio. 'I repeat, we have merrows in the water. And something else. What did they hit?'

The radio crackled and he couldn't hear the replies. Dylan clung to the wooden plank-like seat for dear life, his fingernails digging into the surface.

Izzy had told him about the merrows and he thought he could hear them now, even above the storm. Because they were singing. Shrieking in triumph, laughing but above all, they were singing as they killed.

Another boat neared the island, slower this time. It came to a halt, the waves lifting it almost vertically.

'It's a barrier of some kind. Relay that to Margot. I need intel. We can't get closer.'

'Any idea what's causing it, ma'am?' asked one of the soldiers.

'At a guess, them.' She pointed at the two figures engulfed in light standing before the church.

Dylan stared at the water, at the way it surged and broke. And he listened to the merrows' song. It was hypnotic, the combination.

'*Nine waves,*' said a voice in the back of his mind which sounded suspiciously like Silver. '*The Milesians came to the land but were driven back. They could come no closer than nine waves. Until Amergin the bard arrived. He sang the spell away. Can you still sing for me, Dylan?*'

Sing? He only felt like vomiting but he knew she was right. He knew what he had to do.

'Thea,' he said, surprised at how calm he sounded. 'Take us closer.'

'Are you crazy? Until we know what we're dealing with – '

'But I do know. It's the nine waves spell, from the story? The Book of Invasions. Amergin's song.'

They were almost within reach of the island regardless. Almost at the nine waves mark where the barrier had been raised. Dylan felt the boat lurch and rock precariously. He just wanted to huddle in the bottom of it but that wouldn't do for now.

No, that wouldn't do at all. Zadkiel and his followers had told him to act as a representative of his kind – to be the human voice. They'd wanted a puppet, true, a figure to make up the numbers and do as he was told, that was certain, but they'd named him as such. Annointed him, Silver would say. So right now in spite of storms and magic and merrows, he needed to be that representative. As Amergin had been, long before history began.

And Amergin was a bard.

They weren't so different really.

Dylan crawled to the bow of the boat and put out his hand until he could feel the barrier. Even with the churning sea and his unsteady footing on the edge of the rib, he held firm, reaching for the point where the air thickened and made his skin prickle with pins and needles.

He sent out a thought – *Let me in. Accept me. I belong here.*

It rippled through the air, strong, but not yet strong enough.

Opening his mouth he began to sing. It was a love song, one he had written for Silver. He closed his eyes, sure that no one could hear him over the noise of the sea and the storm. He sang his longing, the pain of separation, his need to find her. He sang the same thoughts.

Let me in. Accept me. I belong here.

He sang of pain and loss. And somewhere – somewhere far away and at the same time so unbearably close – she sang with him, her voice in harmony, her notes clear and high entwined with his.

Merrows broke the surface all around him, their long hair streaming in the waves, their mouths hanging open in shock, revealing row upon row of sharp teeth, dead eyes staring up at him. He didn't dare stop. If he stopped singing, if he failed, then like Orpheus amid the Maenads, they'd tear him apart.

'Ready,' said Thea, her voice a low warning. 'Stand ready.' She vibrated with tension.

And still Dylan sang. His voice rose over wind and wave until abruptly they calmed. The barrier melted before him, but he didn't dare stop. Not yet. The rib edged forward, up to the manmade jetty, and Dylan reached out for the shore. He moved faster and with more surety than he would have believed he possessed. Silver's magic roared within him as he set foot on the island.

The storm stopped. All at once, as if it had never been.

Voice hoarse, body aching, Dylan collapsed on the concrete jetty.

He was sure he sensed Silver's smile.

Was she real? Was she a ghost? And if she was haunting him, that meant she had to be dead. But she couldn't be. She just couldn't. Not after all this, not when they'd finally found some kind of equal standing.

He dreamed she would be here, on the island waiting for him. But he knew the moment he touched land, she wasn't.

'Fan out.' Bea's voice rang out. 'Surround those stones. Take them alive if you can, but you have your orders. Team one, team two, report in.' Black-booted feet pounded by him. She pulled him up and moved him off the path.

'You did good, kid. Now don't get in our way.'

'Don't hurt her.'

She grimaced. 'Can't promise anything now. Sorry. Stay down.'

He saw them all running through the darkness, and he had to follow. He couldn't let them hurt Izzy, no matter what. And he had to find Silver. She'd be wherever the danger was. Eventually. He knew she'd come. And the danger was all focused squarely on the stone circle and Izzy.

The light in the centre flared, brighter than the sun, and suddenly went out. The fire that leaped up in its place was red and fierce.

He saw the soldiers hesitate and stop, their black-clad forms clear in silhouette. Crows flocked around them, and they were almost like crows themselves, standing there, transfixed.

One by one, they went down on their knees and never made a sound.

Jinx had just stumbled over the line of stones when dawn broke, slow and insidious, and then all at once, a line of brilliant light across the suddenly still sea. The storm fell to silence, and Izzy's blood fell from the obsidian knife to the ground.

Holly screamed, piercing and desperate, terrified, and she wasn't perfect, flawless Holly any more. She wasn't a radiant Shining One insane with power, or an implacable Matriarch made of cruelty and capriciousness. She folded up like crumbled paper, aged and wretched as she fell. Powerless. Completely powerless.

Whereas Izzy …

Izzy burned. She was made of fire, her red hair, her gilded skin, the brilliant blue of her eyes. The tattoos around her neck flared to incandescence and evaporated, leaving only the Grigori mark. She shone like the heart of the sun, meeting the dawn. She raised her hands to her face, examined them, flexing each finger. And she smiled.

It wasn't her smile. But it wasn't Crom Dubh either. It was something altogether different. She smiled at him and stretched out her hand. His heart leaped and he reached out to her, ready to take her hand even if it burned him away

424

completely. But before he could, Izzy stopped, jolting back. Briars burst from the ground, with thorns as black and sharp as old teeth. They twisted around her, enveloping her arms and legs, binding her in place.

'Jinx?' she said, her voice a thin, wavering sound. Not like her voice at all. He had to help her. This was some final trick of Holly's. Her eyes went dark.

Something hard and unyielding struck Jinx across the back, sending him forward on to his face. He only just missed the nearest boulder. The air left his lungs and when he tried to get up, sudden pain sent him down again. Broken rib, he guessed, his mind oddly detached.

A foot in an expensive shoe kicked the knife clear of his grasping hand.

'Stay down, boy,' said the Amadán. 'It's easier all round.'

'You brought him,' Holly cried out, her voice twisted with age. 'Finally. Help me. Look at what she's done.'

'Oh, I see. Look at our girl indeed.'

Izzy. He meant Izzy. Jinx could hardly look at anything else.

'Amadán,' he gasped, trying to get his breath and failing. 'What are you doing?'

'Fulfilling my promise, Jinx by Jasper. I said I'd get us back home and I will. If it kills us all. Well …' he walked towards Holly who was trying to struggle to her feet, wretched and broken. 'It'll kill some of you faster than others.' He stopped, looking down at her in disgust. Then he swung back to Jinx. 'It will kill you, of course. We needed a creature of pure chaos to make it work. You and David Gregory. Chaos and Order.'

Jinx looked up, helpless at Izzy's still form. The thorns pressed against her skin, ready to draw blood again the moment she moved. She stood like a glowing statue, her eyes completely black and painfully alien.

He understood now, too well. Far too well. They'd needed a Púca as a source of chaos and the Grigori as a source of order so they had used the one thing that meant the world to them both – Izzy. And they had tried to make her one of them – a Shining One.

Except, he realised, Amadán wasn't a Shining One. He was still just Aes Sídhe.

'Why not change yourself?' he asked, tearing his eyes off her because he could hardly bear to look anymore.

'Change and become like that?' His gaze flicked contemptuously to Holly. 'Or like Osprey was? They're insane with power. Your girl is holding up well, I grant you, but it won't be long. I don't like to lose control, Jinx. Never have. So no, I won't accept the honour.'

Jinx squirmed. Pie's knife lay out of reach in the snow. If he edged around slowly, he might be able to get to it. If he took his time and didn't alert the Amadán to –

The sword blade came up against his throat. Osprey's sword. Amadán had taken it.

'Do you need blood, Holly? Would it help? Or can I just take his head off and be done with it?'

Holly laughed, crazy laughter, that made him want to crawl

away and hide. But there was nowhere left to hide, not on this island.

'The head it is then,' said Amadán and drew back the blade.

'No,' said Izzy, drawing both their attention back to her.

Feathered wings swept around her, black as the night, iridescent with a sheen like oil. They formed a cloak and the fire turned inwards, making her at once terrible and untouchable. Not a girl any more.

A woman.

A goddess.

The crows flocked to her. From over the sea, hundreds of crows and, as if she had summoned them, he saw black-clad soldiers running from the shore. They reached the hill leading to the stones, running up from the jetty, but as they saw her shock spread over each face. He watched it transform them, recognition and then … peace?

They fell to their knees, dumbstruck by wonder.

For a moment he thought they were an illusion, but then he saw their weapons, all state of the art, but useless in hands which could never bear to use them against her.

Jinx rolled sideways, away from the rocks and halfway down the slope again. He found himself looking up at the endless sky and the shining blade descending to kill him.

'No!' Izzy yelled again. She flung one arm out towards him, tearing through the thorns and leaving scarlet gashes down her arm. Her blood splattered on the ground beneath her.

Two shapes dropped out of the darkness, black and white,

furious and vengeful. They dived at Amadán with beaks and claws, with beating wings. Their voices screeched raucously. The old Aes Sídhe swiped at them, the sword wild now but far too big to have any effect. And then he fell.

Jinx grabbed the knife and came up, ready to finish the job. Up again far too quickly, Amadán whirled around and he stabbed.

And missed.

Amadán grabbed the knife, twisting it out of his hand and slamming his wrist against a rock, leaving his whole arm numb.

'You were always more trouble than you were worth,' he spat and lifted the sword again, ready to impale him.

'No,' said Izzy one more time. This time her voice came to them faint and cold, but it vibrated with power beyond power. 'He's mine.' Amadán froze, his eyes going wide in shock. She held him somehow, frozen in the full force of her will.

Jinx turned his attention back to her, felt the same wonder surge through him. When you came down to it, whatever he was, he was a soldier too.

'Mistress,' he whispered and found himself on his knees.

The wind fell to silence, the air unnaturally still, and she turned her face to look at him. His voice carried too loud now. He wished he hadn't spoken.

Her eyes were still so blue.

'Jinx … what is happening to me?'

He couldn't answer, couldn't find his voice. She was a wonder, but she had always been that to him. A goddess. How did you tell someone that?

'Open the gate, Isabel Gregory,' said Amadán, his voice thin and stretched, forced out. 'Open it and all your questions will be answered.'

Still she hesitated, staring at Jinx. 'Come with me,' she said. It wasn't a request, he knew that. It was a command. His body trembled as he tried to fight it, but he couldn't. He couldn't hold anything back. Not from her, not now. This was what everyone had warned them of. Izzy must not go to the island. Jinx must not call her Mistress. But it was too late.

'Of course,' said Amadán. 'Delighted to, if you'd just – '

'Not you,' she said, with a new vicious chill in her tone. 'You stay.' The rocks tore themselves up from the earth and slammed into him, knocking him over and pinning him down. 'I have my warriors. They'll come. Jinx will lead them.'

She held out her hand to him and Jinx moved in spite of himself, his body wanting nothing else. He was Púca. He had been born for this, for the chaos only she could bring.

But he couldn't. He had to stop her.

It was what Izzy had asked him to do. The only thing she had asked of him.

'Please!' he said, but he was too late. She knew him better than he knew himself.

His body changed, sliding into the hound form with which he was so familiar. The wild will of the Púca seized him and he lost himself in the darkness. In her darkness. Moving swiftly, without hesitation now, he went to her side.

The being that had been Isabel Gregory opened the gate.

Chapter Thirty-One

The Thorn Gate

The world around Izzy shimmered and swam. She gazed out through a heat haze, admiring the way everything made sense now. The darkness inside her that she had always known swept up and over her and she felt comforted, safe in a cocoon. The Thorn Gate swung open wide and the dawn filled it. The sun opened the path and the path opened in the sun. It was a small step to make.

So why was she hesitating? Why were her feet refusing to move? Thorns still held her, still tore through her skin and made her blood flow and fall to the hungry earth. Blood on the stones and the soil, blood in the risen sun, opening the gate. It was a magic as old as time.

The Blade filled her hand, a sword ready for battle, and her heart thundered in her chest. This was her chance, to end it for once and for all, to take her war to the heart of the angels'

431

stronghold. And Jinx was beside her. With Jinx at her side she could do anything.

He'd understand. Eventually he would understand. But she couldn't let them all run her life any more. Her dad, the angels, the demons … and the Sídhe. Not even Jinx. She needed to be her own person, her own self.

With that fixed in her mind, she stepped forwards into the light and it swallowed her up, wild and dangerous, a maelstrom that swirled around her. At first it was too bright to see, but after a moment, with the power of the Morrígan at her command, she felt her eyes adjust. The path to the heart of heaven lay ahead, like a mist over the sunrise, light layered upon light, ephemeral but clear to her now.

And on that path a figure stood, blocking her way.

She frowned, lifting the Blade, letting its fierce song fill her mind. Jinx growled, protecting her.

But the figure didn't move. Not an inch.

Silver appeared to be made of mist and shadows. She looked so weak, almost broken, the edges of her torn and ragged. Her smile flickered on her face like ancient cinefilm, but after a moment she seemed to become more solid, fixed.

'Hello, Izzy,' she said.

'What are you doing here?'

'Waiting. For whoever came through that gate. It's the source of the Sídheways, the place they came from, you see? The last place, now they've gone.'

The Blade turned brighter in Izzy's hand. Anger raced

through her. How dare she be here in the way?

'Let me through, Silver.'

'For what? For what possible reason, Izzy?'

War, she wanted to say. A war to end all wars. She would put a stop to the angels and their incursions on this plane. She would destroy them all and seal the gate forever –

'This isn't what you want, Izzy,' said Silver, her voice strangely gentle.

Jinx lunged forward at her, his teeth bared. He would protect her, even against Silver. He'd make sure nothing hurt her. He was devoted. Wild and violent, the Púca in hound form was enormous, a killer ... But Silver didn't even flinch. It took a moment for Izzy to realise why. Jinx would never hurt Silver, not willingly. He was all bluster. And Silver knew it.

'You promised not to let that happen to him again,' she said. Her voice was still music, although now in a minor key.

'Let what happen?'

'He never wanted to be a slave. Not to Holly. Not even to you. And he loved you, Izzy. I've never known someone love another the way he loved you. Don't enslave him again, Izzy. Don't become like Holly.'

'I'm nothing like Holly,' she said. 'You're more like her than I am. You're her daughter.'

'And you are Brí's. Otherwise none of this could ever have happened. But the power is volatile, Izzy. It's changing you. And him. Don't you see? Look at him.'

Jinx slowly changed back to his Aes Sídhe form, crouched

at her feet. She'd seen him like that before Holly, cowed and beaten. Bowed in complete submission. A slave.

And now he was hers.

'No!' she shouted and charged towards Silver, the Blade of Donn tearing through the air. Death came with her, and she was death, death and war.

'Izzy!' Dylan shouted, his voice coming from the darkness behind her. 'Izzy, stop!'

She whirled around to see him standing in the gateway.

'You can't be here.'

'Neither can you. Izzy, please, think. Just for a moment. Take a moment and think. This isn't you.'

'I have to. I have to stop them.'

'Who's *them*? You stopped Holly. You beat her. The angels will withdraw. The demons can be contained. This is what Holly wanted, Izzy. What the Shining Ones wanted. You can't.'

'Dylan, I ...'

The words choked in her throat and she staggered back.

'You're my friend, Izzy. You always have been. And you would never do this. I know you.'

Her friend. Yes, he was, had always been. And look at all it had cost him. No one had changed as much as Dylan.

Except perhaps her.

What was she doing?

The Blade turned to mere flames and faded back into her. She sagged and looked back towards the light ahead.

It was beautiful. So beautiful it brought tears to her eyes.

'I can't go back,' she whispered to no one in particular. 'Not now.' The light called to her, drew her forwards. She pushed by them, climbing to the light, ready to throw everything away just to reach it, just to get a glimpse.

'Izzy,' Silver's hand closed on her shoulder and the fires all burned down, a soft warm glow. The light that threatened to overwhelm her shrank to be a flame. 'Izzy, look back, away from the light. What do you see?'

In the darkness behind them, she saw Jinx. He was looking up at her, still on his knees, but with an expression of such despair. Heartbroken, she saw him say her name.

But she couldn't hear him. He was in the shadows now, the light drawing her away. But she could hear a rhythmic beat, a heart, his heart beating for her.

'Jinx,' she whispered, and tore herself free, running back to him. As she reached him, the crows took flight, out into the night. Her feet thundered as she hit the hard ground of the island and a wave of icy air stole her breath.

He caught her in his arms and pulled her to him. 'Is it you? Tell me it's just you.'

'It's me. I'm sorry, Jinx. So sorry. I didn't mean – I never – '

'I know.' He kissed her. A light and delicate kiss, his hands so strong and determined on her back and yet so gentle. 'I know. But this … *this* is you.'

The light faded, the gate closing now she'd left. And Silver was still on the other side.

'Wait!' Dylan yelled. 'Silver.'

He ran towards her, but Silver held up her hands. 'I can't, Dylan. The Sídheways are gone. It took all I was to hold on this long. They left me here. I've nowhere else to go. I'm bound here.'

'You can't leave.'

'You're free, my love. Free and safe from me. My magic won't destroy you now.'

'But it won't anyway. Silver, if you go … if you leave … That will.'

She hesitated, reluctant and unsure, then lifted her head a little, looking beyond them.

'Amadán wanted war,' said Izzy. 'He wanted to take back heaven.'

Silver smiled. 'He wanted to go home. Like a child. So did Holly, when you get to the bottom of it. It's what all of us want.'

And that was what she was doing, going home. Tears stung Izzy's eyes. No one going home should look that reluctant to leave.

'But you don't belong there,' said Dylan softly. 'You belong here. This is your home. You're needed here.'

'Yes, you are,' said a voice, a voice from the stones and the shadows. She stepped out of the darkness by the stone where Izzy's father lay, as if she had grown out of his blood. 'But someone must pass the threshold, now the Thorn Gate is open.'

The Morrígan swept forwards, her feather cloak sweeping

across the grass. She stopped beside the rocks holding Amadán and with a flick of her hand sent them flying away. He righted himself, attempting to brush off his clothing.

'My Lady,' he said with a bow, instantly adjusting to a new power before him, immediately looking for a way to manipulate it.

She looked him up and down, and her face showed only loathing. 'You wanted me called and used the girl to do it. Were you too afraid to do it yourself? To make me part of yourself?'

'I couldn't do such a thing,' he replied. So arrogant, so bloody full of himself. 'I was an angel of the highest order.' Like Zadkiel, Izzy realised. He had once been like Zadkiel and that had never really changed. He'd just learned to mask it better, to fit in with a world he despised.

'And do you know what I am?' asked the Morrígan. She held out her hand to Izzy and there could be no doubt of what she wanted. Before Izzy even knew what she was doing, she handed the goddess the obsidian knife. The Morrígan closed her hands around the hilt and it was as if a great weight had lifted from Izzy's shoulders.

'No,' he replied.

'I didn't think so,' she said and slit his throat. He swayed before her for a moment, shock making his eyes wide and desperate, and he gasped for air, but it wouldn't come. The light in his eyes flared and then faded. He came apart like scraps of paper. The Morrígan watched them float away on the breeze. 'Well then, Isabel Gregory, you don't want to be me, I believe.'

'Not … really.'

'With all due respect? And words to that effect?'

'Morrígan, don't tease,' Silver admonished gently and to their surprise, the goddess smiled at her. Silver blushed and bowed her head.

'Very well then. Bless me, daughter,' she said to Izzy. 'Give me what is mine, and I'll be on my way.'

'Bless you?'

She shook her head and brushed Izzy's face with her hand, a tender, maternal gesture born of somewhere and someone else. 'That'll do. She was right about you, your mother. And this is an unholy mess. Silver, you'll need to clean it up.'

'Me? But I – ' She glanced back at the gate and only then seemed to notice she was no longer inside it but standing on the island.

'You're needed here. Besides, you will have help. The Keeper has been recruiting, isn't that right Dylan?'

'The Keeper?' Silver took a step back and stared at him. 'She has?'

'She's on her way. She might want to do some more work with her soldiers though.' The Morrígan smiled as she looked down on their kneeling forms. 'I'll keep an eye on them too, keep them blessed. But for now, I release them.' She held out a hand and one by one they fell gently to the ground, asleep.

'But the Keeper and the Sídhe – '

'Will need to work more closely together. It's worked for the Grigori, after all. Maybe she seeks to train a successor.'

'What about the Sídheways?'

'What about them? You have an Amergin by your side, Silver. You don't have to do everything by yourself. Don't you understand that yet? Look.'

Dylan seized Silver's hand before she could argue again. Light spilled out of their joined fingers, threads of light which knotted together and spun a glowing net in the air. It sank into the earth beneath them and into the sky over head. It flowed out over the sea to the mainland and when the light faded, the earth hummed with new life. Dylan still held Silver's hand and this time Izzy knew he would not let her go. She felt the same way about Jinx.

'So, the things that are mine …' said the Morrígan, turning her gaze on Izzy again.

Izzy took off the necklace and handed it to her. She pressed it against her chest and it flared, fading into her. Light upon light pulsed through her, waves of energy, and suddenly it wasn't the Morrígan alone standing there. It was Brí too. And something else, something far greater.

'Time to go,' she said and her voice swam around them, music and all the sounds of nature. Light from the sun flowed like honey over her form, and it was almost like there were three different women standing there, each one more enchanting than the last. Layer upon layer of light and wonder. 'Be good. To each other. To yourselves. Oh, and Izzy, a parting gift if you will. For my grail. Use it wisely.'

She stepped into the gate and the light swallowed her whole. For a moment it wavered there, and then it was gone, swallowed up by the sun.

The bright winter sunlight of the shortest day touched Izzy's face and she felt the tears on her face for the first time. But it was her face, her feelings, her tears. Everything else was gone.

'Izzy?' Mum shouted and Izzy turned to see her running up from the jetty, through the dazed and confused soldiers who were just coming back to their senses. And then she screamed. 'David!'

He was still lying there, pale as a corpse, covered in blood, on the cold hollowed-out stone. His eyes were closed and for a moment Izzy thought he was gone, that she'd been too late. Her heart jarred inside her and she was back in that hospital room, after the crash last summer, when he lay on life support, when she'd—

A gift for my grail.

Light swirled in the base of her throat, tingled at the end of her fingertips. It wasn't death this time, or the Blade. That was all gone. But it was something magical and she remembered it from the summer as well.

'I need water. Quickly. I need something to give him to drink.'

She ran towards her father, and Jinx pelted off in the other direction, hound in his speed, and his determination. He was back a moment later, cupping spring water in his hands. It flowed through his fingers, almost all of it. But not quite all.

'Here, it's from the well.'

She held out her own cupped hand. Half a handful, that was about all the water there was left, but she took it, cold and icy on her skin, and poured that last glimmer of power into it. She grabbed her dad's jaw and tipped it into his mouth.

'Please,' she whispered. 'Please, please, please …'

She looked up into her mum's desperate eyes and saw her pleas echoed there.

He gasped for breath and sat up so suddenly it sent her back on her heels. She would have fallen if Jinx hadn't caught her.

But Mum seized him, holding him close and sobbing his name. When the soldiers came, to everyone's surprise, she ordered them away. Even more surprising, they obeyed without hesitation. They called her ma'am.

'We're going home,' she told him. 'It's going to be okay. We're going home.'

Dad tried to smile. He wasn't dead, but he wasn't fully healed either. 'Yes, Keeper,' he whispered.

In the whirl of everything that followed, Izzy let herself be ordered around. It felt good, almost normal for once. The most normal things had been in so long that she didn't want to upset things by doing anything except go along with it.

Her arms still bore the marks and scars, but the need to cause them, to feel pain, had faded somewhat. She could press an ice cube to her skin instead and that seemed to help. It gave her a measure of control. Day by day, she settled into the grooves of her old life.

And the next thing she knew it was Christmas Day.

They'd gone all out, Mum and Dad. It was the most Christmassy Christmas she had ever seen. The lights probably threatened the National Grid. The house groaned with all the extra food. It was corny and embarrassing and totally over the top and she didn't care at all. Ash and Clodagh came by with gifts, and Dylan and Silver made an appearance too, taking time off from settling fae in the new Dubh Linn they had created. But Jinx hadn't appeared.

With a flick of her fingers, little flames danced in the palm of her hand. They weren't powerful, or anything like the power she had wielded, but traces remained of Brí's legacy, of Donn's power. Echoes of the other Aes Sídhe in her blood now, part of her.

Silver had spoken of the dangers facing them all, of the need to rebuild, of her explorations of the new Sídheways. For the first time, Izzy felt part of the conversation. Mum had been frighteningly insightful. Izzy didn't know she could feel that proud of anyone.

'And Jinx?' Izzy asked Silver as she and Dylan made ready to leave. 'Where is he? What's happened to him?'

Silver smiled, or at least she tried to. 'He's a Púca. They tend to be wild. But your guardian angel sent a directive that he's to be left to his own devices, that no creature is to be targeted for their nature alone. Although I wonder if there's more than a little of Brí behind that. She always did have a soft spot for Jinx. Even made whole again as the Morrígan, I doubt that has changed. I'm surprised Ashira didn't tell you this.'

Izzy thought back to the last time she'd seen Clodagh and Ash, and directives from higher angels had been the last thing on their minds. Dancing, laughter, and pizza had been more important. But then, here in Dublin, Ash was still masquerading as a normal girl. Her adoptive parents didn't have a clue.

'If you see him …' Izzy said, but even as she said it, she knew Silver didn't expect to see him. Perhaps not ever.

'Wild fae don't tend to come home, Izzy,' she said. 'King of the Wanderers, that's what he is now. And he can't go back to Puck's Hollow from what you told me. So I don't know where he will go. I wish I did.' She tried that smile again. It didn't work any better this time. 'I would take him home in a heartbeat. He's still my nephew. He always will be.'

It was dark by the time they finished dinner. Izzy left her parents together in front of the TV, and went outside. She just couldn't settle, not tonight. Call it instinct, call it magic. It didn't really matter. She knew.

He was waiting for her in the garden, a black and blue striped hound, far bigger than any natural dog would be. When she closed the door, he slipped into a more human form.

Izzy smiled at him. 'I was wondering where you were.'

'I had to get away for a while. I wandered the Sídheways. They're beautiful.'

'Well, they would be. They came from Brí.'

He grinned. It was unexpected, that expression. Reckless and more than a little wild. It suited him.

'I saw Silver,' she said. 'She wants you to go home.'

'The Market? I could I guess. She asked me to.'

'You saw her?'

'She left messages. Everywhere. She's persistent.'

Izzy smiled. He was still a master of understatement, even if he didn't realise it.

'Here.' She held out the little backpack she had waiting for him. Because if she'd learned anything, it was to trust her instincts.

'What is it?'

'Present. Clothes and something to put them in. Maybe you could keep it on your back. You know, for emergencies. Like this.'

'Funny. Can you give me a moment?' he asked, and pulled on his new clothes.

'I have something for you too,' he said and she turned around, smiling to see him removing something from around his neck. It shimmered in the light from the kitchen.

'What is it?'

'Have a look.'

He pressed something cold and hard into her hands. She

lifted it to the light and saw a little silver pendant in the shape of a salmon. She stared at it, unable to believe he'd thought of it.

'I just thought … I mean, I remembered …'

She flung her arms around his neck, holding him close, and kissed him. She took her time, exploring him, revelling in every movement, every soft groan and sigh. This time, Jinx kissed back with an equal fervour once the surprise faded. It was, she decided, a wonder. 'I missed you.'

'You needed time.'

'No I didn't. After all that, who needs more wasted time? You're an idiot. Don't do it again.'

He smiled. Such a carefree, joyful smile. 'Yes, my love.' He kissed her again, this time indulging himself. 'Never doing it again. Promise.'

'What happened to Holly?' she asked, pulling back at last.

His face darkened, the golden eyes turning grave. 'Silver has imprisoned her, but I doubt there's any need. She has no power anymore, and her mind is shattered. Whatever you did to her … well, she's no threat anymore. She's nothing.'

'Nothing?'

'Broken. And she's nothing to the Sídhe now. She was prepared to kill us all, or let the angels do it for her. No one will follow her now.'

'But she …'

'She's never getting out. She is bound in chains of iron in the Market, behind bars, and she will never escape. No one will help her. She has lost everything.'

'I thought the Sídhe would want her dead.'

'Many do. But it would make her a martyr of sorts. Whereas now … she's a crazy old fae with not a scrap of power left in her. Like I said, she's nothing.'

'I hope Silver is right.'

'She usually is.' He blushed. 'She told me to come here. To see you. And to see your father.'

'My father?'

'Both your parents really. But … I need to ask him about Jasper.'

She nodded and led him to the door, holding his hand. 'Don't let him bully you,' she said gravely.

He looked worried, all of a sudden. It was one thing to say he wanted to confront her dad. It was another to actually do it. 'Okay.'

'And don't let him bluff either.' She opened the door. 'And don't lie to him because he smells lies.' She pulled him inside after her. 'And don't forget Mum. She's … um … she's more than she looks.'

Jinx swallowed hard and nodded. But he didn't hesitate to follow her.

Out of the darkness and into the light of home.

Words & Phrases

Aes Sídhe: (Ay Shee) The highest caste of the Sídhe, most angelic in appearance, the ruling class.

Amadán: (Am-a-dawn) meaning Fool, also known as the Old Man and the Trickster. Member of the Council.

Amergin: (Am-er-jin) Chief bard of the Milesians. The first Keeper.

Aíocht don deoraí: (Ay-ocht dun Jor-ay) Hospitality for a stranger.

Bodach: (Bud-ach) Giant. A lower caste of the Sídhe.

Brí: (Bree) meaning Strength. Member of the Council.

Briugu: (Brih-uh-goo) A title, rather than a name, for a host, one who always offers hospitality to strangers. Strict rules govern their households.

Coire féile: (Core Fay-la) literally a cauldron of generosity, denoting the cauldron of a briugu from which all were welcome to eat. Sanctuary.

Crom Ceann: (Krom Ken) One of the Shining Ones.

Crom Cruach: (Krom Cru-ak) One of the Shining Ones.

Crom Dubh: (Krom Dove) One of the Shining Ones.

Cuileann: (Cul-een) meaning Holly. Holly's original, angelic name.

Cú Sídhe: (Coo Shee) Shapeshifting Sídhe who sometimes take the form of a large hound. A lower caste of the Sídhe.

Donn: (Don) Lord of the Dead. Member of the Council.

Dubh Linn: (Dove Linn) The black pool, original name for Dublin.

Einechlan: (I-ne-chlan) Honour price.

Eochaid: (Yeo-hey) King of the Fear or Fir Bolg.

Geis: (Gaish) A taboo or prophecy, like a vow or a spell, which dictates the fate of a member of the Aes Sídhe.

Íde: (Ee-da) meaning Thirst. Member of the Council.

Leanán Sídhe: (Lee-ann-awn Shee) Fairy lover, the muse, Sídhe who feed from the magical lifeforce of others, but can inspire unbridled creativity in return.

Míl Espáine: (Meel Es-pan) meaning Soldier from Spain. An early Grigori who entered into legend as the father of the Milesians, the group mentioned in the 11th-century *Lebor Gabála Érenn*, the Book of Invasions, as the last to arrive in Ireland.

Morrígan: (Marr-egan) the Great Queen, Goddess of war, battle and fate.

Nemed: (Nem-ed) Sanctuary, sacred place.

Oigidecht: (Ee-ji-deck) Hospitality.

Púca: (Pooka) Shapechanging supernatural creature, king of the wandering fae, those not affiliated with any of the Hollows. He often takes the shape of a wild black horse, but can take human form as well, though retaining animal features such as horse's ears and hooves. He can be helpful, or extremely dangerous.

Sídhe: (Shee) Irish supernatural race.

Seanchaí: (Shan-a-key) Storyteller. Member of the Council.

Suibhne Sídhe: (Shiv-na Shee) Sídhe with birdlike attributes. A lower caste of the Sídhe.

Tearmann: (Ter-man) Sanctuary, refuge.

Touchstone: the source of a Sídhe leader's power.

Tuatha dé Dannan: (Too-atha Day Dan-ann) The People of the Goddess Danu, or The People of God, the Irish faeries.